ISOLATION

ISOLATION
Dwayne Morrow Mystery #5

Darin Miller

Copyright © 2023 Darin Miller.

All rights reserved. No part of this publication may be reproduced, distributed, or transmitted in any form or by any means, including photocopying, recording, or other electronic or mechanical methods, without the prior written permission of the publisher, except in the case of brief quotations embodied in critical reviews and certain other noncommercial uses permitted by copyright law.

ISBN: 979-8-9867566-2-2 (Paperback)

Library of Congress Control Number: 2023906731

Any references to historical events, real people, or real places are used fictitiously. Names, characters, and places are products of the author's imagination.

Front cover photography by Darin Miller.
Front cover shot on location at Sexton Manor, Sherborne Rd, Minford, OH

Printed by Kindle Direct Publishing, in Columbus, OH, USA.

First printing edition 2023.

www.darin-miller.com

For Mom and Dad

Not a day goes by…

Table of Contents

Chapter One 1
Chapter Two 13
Chapter Three 26
Chapter Four 39
Chapter Five 53
Chapter Six 66
Chapter Seven 79
Chapter Eight 93
Chapter Nine 105
Chapter Ten 118
Chapter Eleven 131
Chapter Twelve 144
Chapter Thirteen 156
Chapter Fourteen 169
Chapter Fifteen 181
Chapter Sixteen 194
Chapter Seventeen 206
Chapter Eighteen 219
Chapter Nineteen 233
Chapter Twenty 246
Chapter Twenty-One 259
Chapter Twenty-Two 272
Chapter Twenty-Three 286
Chapter Twenty-Four 299
Chapter Twenty-Five 312
Chapter Twenty-Six 325
Chapter Twenty-Seven 338
Epilogue 350

CHAPTER ONE

I spent most evenings on my front porch, moving slowly back and forth on my glider, watching day trade places with night.

I couldn't admit it, but I was struggling. Everything I knew had been turned inside out, and even though I was finally home, I couldn't just pick up where I left off. The world had stopped making sense, and the urge to sleep was almost overwhelming.

My name is Dwayne Morrow, and I don't know what the hell I am anymore. Once upon a time, I was in a comfortable little rut, operating a one-man PC support service out of my two-story farmhouse in Grove City, Ohio. Never much for organized education—or organized religion, for that matter—I gained my skills courtesy of YouTube and good old-fashioned trial-and-error. Hardware upgrades, software installation and network configuration—those are my specialties. I have built a small but steady client base that keeps the bills paid and the lights on, but the work is redundant and ultimately unfulfilling.

Nearly a year ago, I had a Major Life Event. MLE, for short. I was nudged out of my comfortable rut by the temptation contained within an invitation to my high school reunion. As my primary social circle had constricted to include just me and my black cat, Dexter, I thought it might be time to check in with some of the old classmates and see what life had tossed their way. Before I even made it back to my hometown of Lymont, I learned my best friend, Ryan McGregor, had been murdered, and the suspect remained at large. His mother, Sarah, had been like a second mom to me, and there was no way I could refuse her request for me to ask around, to see if any of our old mutual acquaintances might have some information that would help. Before I knew it, I was in so far over my head I could barely stay afloat. It was terrifying and exhilarating in equal measure, and in the process of finding the truth behind that horrible event, I began an entirely unexpected new relationship with Ryan's estranged widow, Melanie. She and their daughter, Jasmine, have since moved to Columbus so Melanie could pursue better employment opportunities and college courses, and who was I to argue? Long distance relationships are hard.

I also experienced the first hint of discontent in my own career trajectory and decided I might be better suited for private investigation. I had renewed an acquaintance with an old schoolmate, Doug Boggs, who ran his own PI agency in Lymont and convinced him to open a satellite office off West Broad in Columbus so I might work as an apprentice, logging field hours with Boggs Investigations as I worked toward my own license. In its original version, my plan had me taking cases in Columbus while Doug and his overbearing mother, Loretta, who also served as his office manager, remained in the southern part of the state. None of that had gone exactly to plan, and both were underfoot far more often than I liked. But they had me over a barrel. Even after stumbling through and solving two more fairly high-profile cases, I needed them as much as they needed me.

Then I had to go and have another Major Life Event—*er,* MLE.

These things never ask permission, they just barge right in, upending everything around you. My brother, Matt, got married, and I lost my sister, Gina, in a matter of days. The particulars are fully detailed elsewhere, but the aftermath has left me in an unfamiliar and uncomfortable state.

I'm not entirely sure I can trust my own memory, and that has destabilized me in a way I'd never imagined. And it's not like I can talk about it with anyone. If my memory is sound, I grudgingly made a promise that I wouldn't discuss it, not even with Melanie, and ain't that some shit? Trying to grow a relationship under the constant shadow of a lie isn't where I want to be. And if my memory *isn't* sound, then I'm probably bound for an institution, anyway.

ISOLATION

I glanced over my shoulder as a persistent thumping sounded against my front window, punctuated by the occasional screech of claws on glass. Dexter stared at me from inside, his head cocked, unaccustomed to being anything other than my constant companion when I was home. I had never spent so much time in sight yet out of reach. Seeing that he had my attention, he paused long enough to issue a silent peep before resuming his two-handed assault on the glass. I rapped a knuckle at face level, startling him and prompting a hiss before he jumped from the sill and back into the living room.

Whoops.

I had attracted unwanted attention. I heard footsteps approaching the front entrance from within, and soon the screen door opened. Brady Garrett poked his head out, dangling two beers in front of him.

"Hey," he said with a grin. "Want some company?"

He didn't wait for an answer as he closed the screen door behind him and joined me on the glider. I took the beer he offered and nodded, thinking this whole evening had been a bad idea, but Melanie wouldn't budge. Brady is a reporter with the *Columbus Dispatch* who has inserted himself into a couple of my escapades, the last of which nearly cost him his life. Initially, I couldn't stand his smarmy disposition and relentless determination, but I have to admit, he's been a valuable resource, and maybe he isn't such a bad guy after all.

I decided to steer the conversation before he attempted to take the reins.

"So, it's Donna, is it?" I asked.

"Dusty," he corrected.

"Sorry," I grinned. "I was close. That was fast work. How'd you manage that?"

He ran a hand through his dark curly locks. "She's a nurse at my rehab facility. Worked with me three times a day, and I dunno—" He shrugged. "I guess she's just into me."

I nodded as laughter spilled out from inside the house. Whatever Melanie and Dusty were discussing was amusing to both parties, but I wasn't curious enough to investigate. I took a long pull from my beer, preferring liquor, but I was less picky about my alcohol these days.

"Thanks for inviting us over," he said.

"All the credit goes to Melanie. Where are the kids? They're suspiciously quiet." Brady had brought along his son, Billy, and his friend, Scott Nichols, to keep Jasmine occupied while we adults had our little dinner party.

"They're holed up in your office playing Xbox. I told them if they got bored, they could mess around with any of the shit on your desk. You wouldn't mind."

"You're an asshole, you know that?" I wasn't *really* concerned. All three of those kids had better manners than Brady.

"Yeah, well, it's good to see you, too, buddy. I mean, you look like shit, but it's good to see you."

We floated into uncomfortable silence, sipping our beers, and just as Brady started to open his mouth, I thought of another distraction to pursue. "How's your recovery coming along? Are you back at work yet?"

"Soon," he said. "I'm taking a couple more weeks' disability just because I can. My benefits are good, and so are my savings. I pretty much feel back to normal, though."

"Good, good," I nodded, adding, "I'm glad."

As if to reinforce how genuine my feeling actually was.

And back into uncomfortable silence.

Now, I wanted a cigarette. I quit smoking years before, but alcohol seemed to trigger that weakness in me. I didn't have any cigarettes, and no one else in the house smoked, so I was shit out of luck.

"How 'bout them Bengals?" I said, aiming for the inane.

"The season is still a few weeks away," he said. He finished his beer and sat forward, placing the empty bottle on the porch before clasping his hands together between his knees. "You know, if you ever—"

"I don't."

"But you might—"

"I wouldn't."

"You never know—"

"I'm positive."

"Hey!" Brady sat back, throwing his hands up in surrender. "Can I even finish a thought, here?"

I sighed, closing my eyes tightly and rolling my head from side to side, trying to loosen the knots that seemed to have taken residence in my neck.

"You know how sorry I am about your sister," he said. "But you can't just keep going like this. You need to talk to someone."

I threw my head back and laughed. "And that someone should be *you?* That's rich, Brady. Next thing I know, every single thought I shared would be all over tomorrow's *Dispatch*. I mean, you have no *idea* what this is like—"

My words caught in my throat, and I mentally kicked myself as I watched his expression drop. Brady's entire life had been punctuated by grievous loss, every bit as cutting as my own, if not more so. He lost his wife in an automobile accident, his parents in a plane crash and a recent girlfriend to a psychopathic killer. What in the hell was *wrong* with me? He shook his head, rising from the glider while I stared, slack jawed and gobsmacked at my own callousness.

"Oh, God, Brady," I said, getting to my feet. "I'm so sorry, man. That was a horrible thing to—"

He held up a finger, stopping me. "I didn't deserve that," he said quietly. "But I'll let it go, because believe it or not, I *do* understand. And while I don't particularly want to do it right this moment, I *am* here when you're ready to talk."

I nodded, rightfully feeling like a fool.

"I'm going to collect the kids and my date, thank Melanie for a wonderful evening and get out from underfoot," he muttered, picking up his empty bottle before going back inside. Under his breath, he muttered, "Dickhead."

Dexter stared at me from the window. There was no mistaking his expression. He was extremely disappointed in me, too.

*****

"I've got Jasmine settled upstairs," said Melanie, sliding in beside me on the glider and tucking herself underneath my arm. Four more empty bottles of beer had collected near my feet. "I thought I might take her to a movie tomorrow afternoon. There's a new Pixar playing. Wanna come?"

I stared at the stars visible in the distance from beneath the porch roof and shrugged. "I don't know," I said. "Maybe."

She nodded, taking my hand in hers. "Might be a nice distraction, but you know—whatever you want to do. Just wanted you to know you're welcome."

"Mmm-hmm."

"Brady took out of here kinda fast, didn't he? Did something happen between the two of you?"

I smiled wistfully. "I need to work on my manners."

"Ah," she said. "I'm sure it will be fine. Brady's a good guy. He thinks a lot of you."

"I know. I just wish he'd use a whole lot less words. It's—triggering."

"What did you think of Dusty?" she asked, and when I glanced, her eyes were floating toward the heavens, and she looked like she'd just smelled something revolting.

I laughed. "I can't say I paid that much attention, but apparently you have some thoughts on the matter."

"I don't understand why Brady doesn't just go back with Nina," she said, referring to Nina Crockett, our FBI friend. She and Brady had dated briefly when we were all pursuing—and being pursued by—a serial killer. "He keeps going for these fake blondes with fake tits and minimal brain cells. It's so high school."

"I thought she was a nurse."

"A nurse's *aide,*" she informed me. "A custodian of bedpans. A changer of linens and trash liners."

"That isn't what a nurse's aide does."

She scoffed. "I can't believe they'd trust her with much more. She thought a uvula was a type of birth control, and I won't even tell you how we got onto *that* topic."

I tightened my arm around Melanie and kissed the top of her head. I didn't know how much slack she was willing to cut me or for how long, but I appreciated her patience and understanding more than she could possibly know.

"You wanna watch a movie?" she asked, looking up at me.

I shrugged and shook my head. "I think I'll sit out here for a bit longer—if you don't mind. I'm just trying to—"

She placed two fingers against my lips. "Say no more. It's a little after ten. I'll go up and fall asleep to some TV in our room. But you better spend a little time with that cat of yours. He's starting to take out his displeasure with you on me, and he never liked me that well to begin with."

She leaned in and kissed me softly before standing.

"I love you," I said. She winked, blew me another kiss, and went inside. A moment later, the living room light winked out.

Our room.

It warmed my heart that she thought of it as such. We didn't live together, although we may as well for all the time she had spent fawning over me lately. She was doing everything she could to prop me up until I could figure a way out of this funk. I honestly don't know if I would have had the patience.

I didn't deserve her.

I caught the sound of an engine in the distance, drawing nearer, which was a little odd for the hour. Orin Way is a narrow, gravel lane that runs straight as an arrow east to west, and I have no neighbors within visible range on either side of my property. A large part of the appeal to my farmhouse was the relative solitude while still remaining within easy driving distance to Columbus. I watched a pinprick of headlights pierce the eastern horizon, propelled by an engine that would soon need a new muffler.

It sounded vaguely familiar.

The oddly shaped silhouette slowed as it neared the mouth of my driveway, its appearance activating a motion-detect security light mounted at the apex of the roof of the old barn across from my drive. I recognized the Pontiac Aztek immediately and groaned.

Doug Boggs.

Shit.

His driver's door shrieked in protest as he opened it and hopped down. It positively screamed when he slammed it shut. I made a mental note to get him some WD-40 for Christmas. His expression was unreadable at that distance, but he held a camouflage hat in his hands, and I took that as a good sign. I squinted at the passenger side and saw no trace of his mother, Loretta. That was *definitely* a good sign. He was short, stout, and I couldn't believe I had missed the parallel to a teapot in all these years. The buttons of his red-checkered flannel shirt strained to contain his barrel shape; his neck alone had the top button on life support. He chewed on a soggy, unlit cigar as he bridged the distance between us, rotating his hat through thick fingers.

"It's a little late, don't you think, Dougie?" I called as he ambled up the wooden stairs to my porch. "Maybe you could have called?"

He paused on the top step, sighing as the security light winked out behind him. For a moment, we were both plunged into darkness. "I've been *trying* to call," he said. "For *weeks.*"

"Is the phone proving a little too challenging? It's not that hard. You just enter the number and press the green button. You could have your mommy add me to your contacts, and you wouldn't even have to remember the number." I gasped. "These newer phones? You can even *talk* to the Google. Ask it to call me for you!"

It's entirely possible that alcohol makes me mean, but there's absolutely no doubt that Doug Boggs does.

A light flicked on upstairs, casting an oblong rectangular glow over my front yard from above. I heard a window slide open, and Melanie called out, "Is everything all right down there? I thought I heard voices."

"Yes," I said. "It's just Doug."

"*At this time of night?*" She wasn't amused. "Douglas Boggs, I told you I'd have Dwayne call you just as soon as he possibly could."

I covered my grin while Doug squirmed uncomfortably. She had been running interference for me!

"It's okay," I said. "He won't stay long."

"N-n-no, ma'am," he stammered, and it was everything I could do to keep from bursting out laughing.

After a brief silence, Melanie replied, "See that you don't."

The window banged shut, and the light winked out.

"Talk about mommies," Doug grumbled, before resuming the nervous rotation of his cap. "Look, um—I, uh—first, I want to tell you how sorry me and Ma are for you and yours. It's just an awful thing. I wanted to say something at the—um, you know—um, service, but I ain't good with words and you had all those people around you. I didn't want to butt in."

I stared at him for a moment and nodded.

"Well, see—I've been trying to call you, but I either get the answering machine or your lady won't patch me through. I didn't have no choice but to come out here and see you face to face." He was rotating that cap so fast I expected it to suddenly break loose and fly across the yard.

"What's this about, Doug?" I asked.

"I already told you I ain't good with words, so don't get mad when I ask this," he hedged.

I nodded, unconsciously clenching my hands together. Lord only knew what would come next, but I would be damned if the next few chapters of my life revolved around my exploits in prison. "Go on," I said.

"I need to know when you're coming back to work," he said, each word running into the next. "I mean, I need to know *if* you're coming back to work."

I cocked my head and stared at him, counting to ten. Then twenty.

I took a deep breath, leaned back in my glider, and exhaled slowly. It wasn't an unreasonable question. I had been equally negligent in tending to my consulting business. My savings were dwindling and soon enough, utilities were going to start winking off, one by one.

"I don't know," I finally said. "Soon. I think."

Doug sighed and began pacing the length of my porch. "I'm gonna need a little more than that."

"What do you want from me, Doug? I'm doing the best I can."

He stopped pacing and looked down at me. "I know. I hate like hell to be standing here putting you on the spot like this. But we're circling the drain, here."

"What do you mean?"

He resumed his pacing. "I only opened the office on West Broad to help you get your hours in, you know? Help you get your PI license. Did you change your mind? Did you decide this isn't what you want to do after all?"

"No," I said. "That isn't it. It's just that with everything that's happened, I'm—I'm—"

He stopped pacing and held up a hand. "I get it. I really do. But the truth is, I can't keep this office open if you aren't a part of it. I can't afford to pay another associate, and let's face it, Ma is an awesome office manager, but not so good in the field."

I had my doubts about both, but I kept my mouth shut.

"My bread-and-butter is in Lymont, and if we can't figure out a way to make this work, I'll have to close the West Broad office next month," he said. "And that won't benefit either of us. Remember, you're on the lease as a responsible party, too."

I bit my tongue and started counting again. Ten. Twenty. Thirty. Forty...

I had stupidly signed a contract indebting myself to Boggs Investigations in a way I had never imagined. Doug must have sensed my escalating rage because he was quick to continue.

"But that isn't all I'm here to talk about," he said, attempting a smile but looking as though he may have shat himself a wee tiny bit. "I've got a real opportunity to share with you while you make up your mind what you want to do."

I weighed my options. Throw him off the porch or let him wade in a little deeper? I chose the latter.

"What?"

Doug relaxed, seemingly pleased he had overcome this latest obstacle. "Boggs Investigations has been offered an all-expenses paid pass for six—next weekend—*Labor Day weekend!*—to partake in a trial run of a new mystery adventure on Marble Toe Island!"

I stared at him vacantly, uncomprehending.

"*Marble Toe Island!*" he repeated, clapping his hat back onto his head. "In Lake Erie!"

I shook my head, still not sure where he was going with this.

"It's a team building exercise!" he enthused. "It's exactly what we need!"

I groaned. "Are you *kidding* me?"

"Not at all! I mean, look," he said, and the pacing continued. "Let's face it, you and Ma need a whole lot of work. You and me—well, you have a little problem with authority. I think it's exactly what we need to figure out if this whole arrangement is even worth it."

I chewed the inside of my jaw. I had counted to nearly two hundred and thought I might be able to speak without devolving into violence. "You, me, and—" I shuddered. "Your mother. That's three of six. Who else?"

Doug paused, spreading his arms wide. "Entirely up to you."

I raised an eyebrow. "Really?"

"Absolutely!"

I sighed. "I don't know, Doug. How soon do you need to know?"

He clapped his hands and headed for the porch stairs. "No rush! No rush at all!" He turned as he reached the bottom of the stairs and the security light winked on again, casting him in silhouette. "Just let me know by end of day tomorrow, okay? Or our tickets will go to the next in line, and I'll have to close our Columbus branch."

I stared at him devoid of expression. I let my middle finger do all the talking.

CHAPTER TWO

I was wrenched from sleep around two the following afternoon by the persistent jangling of my landline. After six rings, my machine answered the call downstairs.

That's it, I decided to myself. *That thing's gotta go.* I made a mental note to switch to strictly cellular first thing Monday morning. Possibly afternoon. Probably afternoon.

I turned over, pulling the pillow over my head, and trying to find my way back into a dream I was having. In the dream, I was racing toward something, running—almost *flying*—with a sense of urgency that was tangible. I didn't know where I was going or what I was looking for, but I knew it was vital that I not let it slip away.

I felt the pinpricks of tiny claws poking the base of my neck, just beneath the pillow. I cast it aside and rolled over, coming face-to-face with the mighty Dexter, who peeped a tiny greeting before rubbing his nose against mine. He ran the length of his body across my face before settling in beside me, pleased with himself. A gentle rumbling began deep within his coiled frame. I tried to keep as much airborne fur out of my eyes and mouth as possible while giving him the stink eye. Whatever urgency the dream held was long gone.

Melanie had prodded me gently around noon to see if I was going to accompany her and Jasmine to the movie, and I don't think it was a surprise to anyone when I passed. They were grabbing lunch beforehand, then catching an early matinee and might tack on some shopping before heading back. The mere thought of doing all that exhausted me. She kissed my forehead before letting me drift back into sleep.

Now that I was mostly awake, I snagged my cell phone from my nightstand and noted I had already missed three calls from Doug Boggs. I had heard none of them as I had fallen into the habit of muting my cell while I slept. Was this his idea of giving me until the end of day to decide? I wouldn't be returning the call until late evening, just to even the score for the previous night. It wouldn't kill him to wait, and I still hadn't decided if I was actually even considering his proposal. Just for grins, I opened the Huntington app on my phone and logged in to catch a glimpse of my current financial status. *Yikes!* That did the trick—I was awake now.

I spent a few moments scritching the area behind Dexter's ears, listening as the intensity of his purr approached that of a power tool. I felt I owed it to him after my latest inattentiveness. It also delayed any further decision-making on my part, which was just fine with me. I would just lie there, petting my cat until Melanie got back, hopefully with food.

Apparently, I ground in place for just a moment too long, as Dexter abruptly nipped at the back of my hand and hissed, jumping down from the bed, and exiting stage left. I shifted positions and suddenly realized my bladder was well into the red zone, stretched almost beyond capacity.

I sighed. Time to get up.

*****

The front door flew open, banging against the wall as Jasmine tore through the living room bound for the stairs and clutching several plastic bags.

"How was the movie?" I called after her from the kitchen as she pounded up the stairs. I was washing the few breakfast dishes they had used while I slept the morning away.

"Good," she called back over her shoulder. "Mom cried."

"*Jasmine!*" Melanie called breathlessly after her, struggling to coax her key from the lock without dropping the bags in her own hands. "Take it easy on the door! No need to bulldoze every single place you go!"

I tossed the dishtowel I was using over my shoulder and leaned against the doorframe between the kitchen and living room. "Cried, huh?"

She finally got her key free but left the door open to allow extra light through the screen door. She shook her head casually. "I wouldn't exactly call it *crying*—"

"Yeah?" I crossed the room and helped her unburden herself. Once her arms were free, I scooped her into mine. "What exactly *would* you call it?"

She stood on her tiptoes and kissed the tip of my nose. "Oh, you know how these Pixar movies are. They always work out in the end, but not before running you through the emotional wringer along the way. I daresay you would have had a lump in your throat, too."

"Glad I passed, then," I said, giving her backside a playful swat with the dishtowel. "I've had enough lumps in my throat for the time being. What was Jasmine in such an all-fired hurry for?"

"New Xbox game," said Melanie, beginning to sift through her own bags, examining her purchases. "She can't wait to get it loaded and play online with Billy and Scott. You'll be paying for that one. It's her price for taking care of your cat while you were out of town."

"Fair enough, I suppose."

Melanie stopped and turned, her face squirreling up. "You seem a little more—yourself," she noted cautiously.

I shrugged. "I'm out of booze."

She placed her hands on her hips, looking mildly exasperated.

"I'm kidding," I said. "Mostly."

She smiled. "It's good to see you doing something productive."

"I'm trying."

She nodded, turning back to her purchases. "Is it normal for a girl Jasmine's age to spend so much time with the guys playing video games?"

"Define normal," I said, heading back to the sink to finish drying the last of the dishes.

"I wasn't even allowed to *talk* to boys when I was her age," she said, laying a few newly purchased acquisitions on display across the back of the sofa. They were undoubtedly rounding out her wardrobe for her new job, with the possible exception of the last item, a red lace negligee that was cut both low and high in all the right places. I whistled, dropping my towel on the counter before moving toward her.

Melanie scooped the negligee up and stuffed it back into a bag behind her back. "You weren't supposed to see that," she said, blowing a loose strand of hair back from her forehead.

"A little late for *that*," I said, grinning and reaching behind her. "Let's get a closer look—"

She swatted my hand. "Dwayne Morrow. You know I can't stay over tonight. I have to work tomorrow, and Jasmine has school."

I sighed, pulling her to me and nibbling on her neck. "Fine."

She pulled back and handed me a paper bag. "I brought you a couple of Tony's Coneys."

"*Aha!*" I said, seizing the bag and letting her flop to the couch. I pried the bag open and took a deep breath, smiling broadly.

Melanie laughed. "I see where your priorities lie. So, should I be worried about Jasmine?"

I backtracked to the kitchen to retrieve a Pepsi from the fridge. "I don't think so. We know both of the boys she's battling online, so it's not like they're strangers. Are her grades holding up?"

"She hasn't been in school long enough to know," she said. "I think so. I see her do homework. I just don't want all of her social interaction to be virtual. It isn't healthy. I worry that she isn't making friends in her classes."

"Give her some time," I said. "You worry too much."

"Maybe," she said, but she didn't sound convinced. "So, what was all that with Doug last night?"

"He's really pressuring me to come back to work. Said he's going to have to close the West Broad location if I don't."

"That little asshole—" she began.

I waved her off as I returned to the living room and plopped down on the sofa opposite the one where she had displayed her outfits. "I mean, *yes*, he's an asshole, but I get where he's coming from. He doesn't have the manpower to keep both offices going, and I can't fault him for that. While our arrangement might not be exactly as I imagined, there wouldn't be an arrangement at all if I hadn't pushed for one. He wants a decision by tonight, but he's already been leaving messages—"

As if on cue, the landline began jangling again in the hallway.

"For heaven's sake," said Melanie, dropping the blouse she was folding onto the couch and pivoting toward the phone. "He's not going to like getting hold of *me*." She snatched the cordless from its base. "Hello?" she asked sharply.

I turned to watch her over the back of the sofa and saw her stance relax.

"Oh, hi," she said. She listened for a moment, and her hand flew up to her mouth.

"What?" I asked, getting to my feet, and instantly filling with dread. Lately, it had been my go-to state of mind.

She turned her back to me, holding a finger up as she continued to listen, slowly beginning to nod. "Give us about a half hour. We'll be there."

I was behind her as she replaced the handset on its charger. "*What?!*"

Melanie couldn't contain her smile as she turned around. "That was your brother," she said. "He and Sheila are at Riverside having your little niece or nephew."

*****

I couldn't remember the last time I'd been to the hospital for something good.

Jasmine had been a real trooper about cutting her game short with the guys. She was more excited about the new arrival than I would have expected her to be. We opted to take separate cars since I was liable to be there much longer than Melanie could; she and Jasmine had work and school in the morning, respectively. Melanie tailgated me the entire way, so close I could practically see the individual hairs of her eyelashes. This normally would have driven me crazy, but I was afloat in a sea of new emotions, and I barely noticed.

I texted Matt once we were in the waiting area, and after a few moments, he joined us, beaming from ear to ear.

"Matt Morrow," I said.

"Dwayne Morrow," he replied, and we looped through our names twice more as was our odd yet customary greeting. By the third pass, we were circling each other, going in for a bear hug at the end. Melanie leaned in and kissed him on the cheek, patting his arm.

"I cannot believe this!" I said. "I mean, we all knew it was gonna happen, but it's like—now! Do Mom and Dad know?"

Matt nodded, unable to lose the goofy grin. "They're on their way, but I only just called them right before I called you, so it will still be a little while before they get here."

"How is Sheila?" asked Melanie, putting an arm around her daughter.

"Scared. Happy. Mostly scared," said Matt. "All her friends have warned her how long labor can last with your first child, so she doesn't know what to expect."

"I was in labor with this little turd for almost forty-eight hours," said Melanie, giving Jasmine a squeeze.

"We've been here for six," said Matt. "We didn't call right away because she's already had Braxton Hicks twice, and we wanted to make sure it's the real thing. It's the real thing." His laughter was a tiny bit delirious. "I should get back in there. I'll keep you posted."

"Give Sheila our love," I called after him.

"And don't mention the forty-eight hours!" Melanie advised as he disappeared down the hallway. She looked back at me with a smile. She placed her hand against the side of my face. "Uncle Dwayne."

"Aunt Melanie."

She gasped, and her mouth dropped open. "Are you asking me to marry you?"

I stammered and stuttered—a deer caught squarely in headlights.

She patted my cheek and giggled. "You goon. You're such an easy target."

*****

"Well, hell-*ooo*, little lady."

I turned around at the sound of my father's voice and saw him extending a friendly hand toward Jasmine. "Good evening, Mr. Morrow," she said, smiling and giving it a shake. He looked up at me and winked.

Mom blew right past them and grabbed me in a fierce hug. "I can't believe I'm finally going to be a *granny!*"

I stepped back, looking at her curiously. "Granny? I never in a million years would have guessed you'd go for that."

She put her hands on her hips and looked at me defiantly. "And just what's wrong with 'Granny?'"

I shrugged. "I don't know. I just always saw you as more of a 'Mimsy' or 'Mimi' or 'Gran-Gran.' It seems a little *Beverly Hillbillies.*"

She playfully smacked my arm, finally noticing Melanie who had shrunk into a corner. "Well, hello, Melanie! It's lovely to see you."

Melanie stepped forward and awkwardly hugged my mother. She has the most ridiculous notion that my mom doesn't like her, and I can't seem to change her mind. "Likewise."

Mom turned her attention to Jasmine, stooping down and exchanging pleasantries while I shot a bewildered look at Melanie. She just shrugged and continued to look uncomfortable.

"Melanie, would you mind texting Matt and letting him know the folks are here?" I asked.

"Of course," she said, looking grateful for something to do. She excused herself from the room while Dad continued to occupy Jasmine with one fanciful tale after the other. I'd never fully realized how very good he was with children.

"So," said Mom, fixing her attention firmly on me.

"So," I returned, crossing my arms, and dreading what might come next. I had mostly been successful in avoiding the topic of my sister and desperately wanted to keep it that way. The look on my mother's face suggested I might have little say in the matter.

"Are you doing—okay?" she asked, her hazel eyes probing beneath a cap of silvery-gray curls. I had never noticed they were the same color as Gina's.

I took a shuddery breath and exhaled slowly. "I'm trying. How about you and Dad?"

She swallowed hard and nodded. "It's nice to have such a distraction," she said, indicating the room. "I can only imagine how excited Gina would have been."

Shit. Here we go.

"I know, Mom, um—I don't really think I can—oh, look, Mom! It's Matt!"

Matt and Melanie rounded the corner into the room, and I couldn't have been a greater fan of their timing. I was instantly forgotten as Mom and Dad closed in on him, hugging and congratulating him on the impending arrival. Melanie crossed over to me and put an arm around my waist, giving me a quick squeeze.

"Hey, listen everyone," said Matt, holding up his hands. "The doctor says it's gonna be quite a while before anything really happens. He suggested we all grab a bite to eat down at the cafeteria while we still have a chance. Sheila's been given something for the contractions, and she's kind of in and out right now. Last time she was in, she insisted we go. What do you say?"

A general murmur of agreement made the rounds, and we were soon following my brother to the elevator.

*****

The ladies staked out a table large enough for the six of us, while we menfolk carted the cafeteria trays laden with chicken nuggets, salads, burgers and soft drinks. The price was more than a little exorbitant, and Dad wouldn't hear of anyone paying for it but him. I distributed the orders as animated conversation burbled all around me.

"Will Sheila's parents be here soon?" Mom asked Matt.

"They're flying up tomorrow. Couldn't book a flight any sooner," he replied. Sheila's parents were retirees who had given up on Ohio's unpredictable weather years before.

"Oh, good," Mom said, beaming.

"*Jo!*" Dad chided as Matt's eyes widened. "That's not very kind."

Mom shrugged. "They will never know I said a thing, Todd. But here amongst *my* family, I couldn't be more pleased to get a little time with our grandchild first."

"There's no guarantee of that," I reminded. "She could be in labor for hours and hours yet."

"Heaven forbid," sighed Matt, taking a bite of his cheeseburger.

"And you don't know the sex?" asked Melanie. Matt shook his head, his mouth full. "I'm surprised. I wanted to know right away so I would know how to plan."

"Well," said Matt, swallowing and wiping his mouth. "It isn't that we didn't *want* to know, it's just that baby is—I don't know how else to put it—camera shy. Sheila's doctor couldn't tell from any of the sonograms."

"Have you picked out names?" asked Melanie.

Matt smiled coyly. "We have a few in contention."

My father cleared his throat. "If it's a boy, I've always been partial to Todd with three Ds."

"That's dumb, Dad," I laughed, and his exaggerated look of wounded betrayal soon had us all in stitches.

"Um, Uncle Matt?" Jasmine had eased out of her seat beside her mother and now tugged at Matt's shirtsleeve, her eyes wide.

Matt looked down at her with a grin. "Yes, little Miss?"

Jasmine pointed to the ceiling where a page was sounding through the building. "I think that's for you."

Our laughter died away as we listened for the page to be repeated.

"Would Matthew Morrow please report to second floor maternity right away? That's Matthew Morrow."

We looked at each other uneasily before pushing our chairs back and abandoning our barely touched dinner.

Something was wrong.

*****

I could barely keep up with Matt as we left the others behind, racing to the elevators without waiting for them to catch up. The fear in Matt's eyes was evident, and my throat was home to a large knot that refused to loosen.

As soon as we arrived in maternity, a nurse took Matt by the arm and led him back to Sheila's room, whispering urgently. Try as I may, I couldn't pick up even the slightest word.

This was so unfair.

To say that Sheila's pregnancy had not been without its complications would be the understatement of the century. She had been stabbed multiple times by a serial killer a few months prior, a direct result of my proximity to that particular case. Mother and baby had survived the incident, but it was very touch and go for a while. Matt had only recently let go of the blame he held for me, only when what happened to Gina—happened. This family had been through so much grief. The baby simply *had* to be all right.

Mom, Dad, Melanie and Jasmine hustled into the waiting area, and Mom was nearly hysterical. She grabbed my shoulders and looked up to me with tearstained eyes. "What's *happening?*"

I shook my head. "I don't know anything. They took Matt straight back."

"Oh, my *God!*" she cried, folding into Dad's arms before falling apart. Judging from his own ashen complexion, Dad was barely holding it together himself.

Melanie stood back, holding tight to Jasmine, whose own tears flowed freely. I felt utterly defeated, and the concern on Melanie's face told me exactly how I must have looked. I stepped outside of the waiting room, unwilling to lose it in front of everyone, but unable to keep my shit together for much longer. I blinked back tears and took deep, steadying breaths until I felt I could control myself.

Just as I started back, Melanie poked her head out into the hall. "There's a nurse here to give us some information. C'mon."

Darin Miller

*****

We sat quietly in a semi-circle in the far corner of the room, waiting for news. A few other families waited for news of their own, but none with the obvious distress we shared, and they all kept a respectful distance.

As Sheila's contractions had begun to accelerate, the doctors noticed an alarming rise in the baby's heart rate which coincided with them. It was determined an emergency C-section was the best option for both baby and mother. Matt had gone into the delivery room over an hour ago, and now we waited. The silence was complete, save for the occasional snuffle from my mother, and it was excruciating. I watched the second hand on the wall clock sweep around for what seemed like the millionth time. It was almost nine o'clock. I glanced across Melanie, whose head rested on my shoulder, toward Jasmine, who was practically asleep.

"You and Jaz should go ahead and go home," I whispered to Melanie. "You've both got an early day tomorrow."

Melanie's head jerked up. "I don't want to leave you here alone."

I kissed her forehead. "I'm not alone. Mom and Dad are right here. I'll call you just as soon as I know something."

She looked uncertain. "Are you sure? I don't mind—"

"I'm positive. I mean, look at Jasmine. She'd die of embarrassment if she found out she was snoring out loud."

Melanie grinned and cupped my face in her hands. "Call me the very minute—"

Matt stepped through the doorway, clad in a paper gown and cap, a mask pushed down below his chin. Swaddled in his arms was the most perfectly tiny human being I had ever laid eyes on. We all struggled to our feet, gasping and straining for a view. Mom's tears had morphed into pure joy as she took in the miracle that was her first grandchild.

"Mom and baby are fine," said Matt, his voice a little shaky. "And may I present to you our daughter, Abigail Regina Morrow."

Abigail Regina.

My smile was bittersweet. Gina would have most certainly approved.

*****

I walked Melanie and Jasmine back to their car and saw them off, thoroughly wrung out by the emotional rollercoaster we had only just experienced. What remained was a warm, fuzzy feeling that kept a smile on my face as I slowly strolled back toward the hospital.

Almost as an afterthought, I pulled my phone out of my pocket and knew immediately I had missed calls and messages from the way it vibrated in my hand on contact. I had forgotten to turn the ringer volume back up from when Doug had been persistently trying to ruin my sleep.

Thirteen texts and nine missed calls, all from Doug.

I didn't even have a chance to scroll through the texts before my screen lit up, an unflattering picture of the man himself glaring back at me.

"Hey, Doug," I said.

"I *told* you I needed your answer by end of day." He was already off and running. "Now if this is truly how you feel—"

"It's fine, Doug," I said.

Silence.

"What?"

"You can count me in for the mystery weekend. I'm pretty sure Melanie will be game, but I'll have to check and see if Brady and his lady friend can come. I'll let you know tomorrow." I disconnected before he had a chance to reply.

I smiled contently. This brand-new life had inspired me to turn over a whole new page.

CHAPTER THREE

A-1 Fertilizers closed up shop early on Friday to give its employees a head start on the holiday weekend, cutting Melanie loose at noon, so we only had to wait for the kids to finish their school days before loading up and heading north. The mystery weekend didn't officially start until Saturday, but Doug had secured "early bird" passes that would allow us to spend Friday night there as an additional perk.

We had only been on the road for an hour, but it easily felt like three.

We traveled in a three-car convoy. I took the lead with Melanie in the passenger seat and Brady and his airhead girlfriend, Dusty, in the back. She had been chattering nonstop nonsense ever since we had pulled out of my driveway. Brady continually cooed sweet nothings and nibbled at her neck while repeatedly trotting out the phoniest laugh I'd ever heard. He was clearly under the influence of the little man below the belt, and Melanie looked like she might be sick at any moment. I wasn't far behind.

Directly behind us and a little too close to my rear bumper for comfort was Doug Boggs in his ugly, rusting Pontiac Aztec with his dour-faced mother, Loretta, planted in the front seat beside him. Today, her color scheme appeared to be classic Lifesavers Five Flavors. Her yoga pants were bright orange while her sleeveless top and hair were matching lemon. Her eyeshadow was pineapple, and her lips were cherry red. Wisps of bright lime green highlights crept from her temples into the rest of her lemon hair, which was swept up in a mini beehive. Every time I looked in the rearview, her expression was the same, eyebrows knitted together angrily while her mouth worked overtime, keeping her fleshy neck pulsating in time. Doug looked appropriately miserable, his eyes fixed on the road ahead.

Bringing up the rear, Nola and Wendell Caudill had Jasmine, Brady's son Billy, and their temporary ward, Scott, in their minivan. They were bound for a prepaid weekend getaway at Cedar Point, courtesy of me and Brady. It was the very least we could do for them since they had agreed to watch the children while we participated in this "team building" exercise. I was growing quite fond of the Caudills and hoped we weren't taking too much advantage of them. If we were, they showed no visible signs.

My parents had jumped at the opportunity to take care of Dexter for me. They had been staying at my house ever since little Abbie was born, and it gave them all the excuse they needed to stay just a little bit longer. They couldn't get enough of their new little granddaughter; I just hoped Mom was playing nice with Sheila's parents, who were also in town through the weekend. It hadn't taken long at all to figure out Jo Morrow was an alpha granny.

"So, I really don't get it," said Dusty. I glanced in the rearview mirror to find her pouting and examining her ridiculously elongated artificial fingernails. "I mean, what exactly is it we're doing this weekend? Is it like a haunted house?"

Melanie sighed quietly, and I could tell she was clenching her teeth from the way the muscles in her jaw flexed. We had been over this before. Twice.

"No, baby," cooed Brady. "It's just a big ole silly game. Someone will pretend to get murdered, and it's up to us to figure out whodunit." He resumed nibbling the base of her neck.

"And people pay money to do this?" She giggled and playfully slapped at Brady's hand, which was trying its darnedest to sneak underneath her skintight blouse. "It seems kind of dumb."

Melanie laughed from the back of her throat, and I could nearly read her mind. The pot calling the kettle black, the blind leading the blind—insert appropriate analogy here.

"Hey, Brady," I warned. "Don't make me be the hall monitor. Let's keep our hands above 'see' level."

"I don't mind," squeaked Dusty.

"Oh, but we do," said Melanie, shaking her head and shielding her eyes.

"So, will one of us get killed?" asked Dusty, her eyes comically wide. "I don't think I'd like it if I was dead."

"Would you stop worrying your pretty little head?" Brady took her chin in his hand and directed her gaze toward him. "It's all in good fun. No one's going to get hurt. First thing in the morning, we'll have an orientation with the people who are hosting the event. They'll lay everything out all nice and simple. But tonight? Tonight belongs to us. And I, for one, plan to make the most of it." He went for her neck again, eliciting yet another squeal.

"Oh, my *God!* Am I gonna have to get a water bottle to spray you two down?" I shook my head. "I want to see daylight between you—starting right now."

Brady laughed, scooting a little to the left. "Jeez, Dwayne. I didn't realize you were such a prude."

I narrowed my eyes. "And I didn't realize you two were a traveling porno. Time and place, people—time and place."

"*Ooo! Ooo!*" Dusty straightened in her seat and began waggling a finger toward the passenger side. "I see a Sheetz! Mama needs to make winkles and get a Mean Bean!"

Melanie sighed, less quietly this time around. "*Again?* We just stopped for 'winkles' a half hour ago."

Dusty's big eyes turned to Brady for support. He shrugged. "When you've gotta go, you've gotta go."

"Well, maybe she wouldn't 'gotta go' quite so often if she'd cut back on the Mean Beans," I muttered. "I'm just sayin'." Nevertheless, I activated my right turn signal giving the rest of our convoy ample notice of our impending pit stop.

I eased into the crowded lot and around the bank of gasoline pumps, finding a parking spot along the side of the red-brick building. Sheetz was really hopping. Doug opted for the other side of the building while the Caudills found a spot several down from our own. I had barely put my SUV into park before Dusty was out the door, Brady hot on her heels like a love-starved schoolboy. They disappeared around the corner, and I sat back, closing my eyes.

"This was a mistake," I said.

"Oh, now, it will be *fine*," said Melanie, patting my arm. "Once we're not in such close proximity, anyway. I'm just happy you're getting out of the house. I've been worried about you."

I turned toward her and smiled. "Baby steps. I can't keep dwelling on things I can't change."

"But you know you can talk to me about anything," she said, taking my hand. "I may not have a lot of answers, but I'm a great listener."

"The best." I squeezed her hand. "We should check in on the others."

We got out of the SUV just as Doug Boggs rounded the corner. He was flushed, huffing and puffing his way toward us. He ran a hand through the dark stubble on his head and wiped his sweaty palm on his jeans.

"Sorry about this," I began. "Brady's girlfriend—"

Doug waved my words off. "Not a problem. I was about to call you to ask you to stop. Ma had the Taco Bell for lunch, and it ain't sittin' well. For either of us. She needed the bathroom, and I needed some fresh air, if ya catch my drift. Hey, listen, I just wanted to tell you again how glad I am that you decided to go. I really think this team building exercise will be good for us."

"It certainly can't hurt," I said. "If we're going to be able to work together, we have to establish better communication. You know? *Two-way* communication."

"Of course, of course," said Doug, retrieving a well-chewed cigar from his front shirt pocket and stuffing it into the corner of his mouth. He didn't light the smelly thing, just rolled it around and scattered tobacco across his lips. "And also, of course, we have to understand that—as in any organization—there is a chain of command. Everything must follow that chain of command."

I chewed my bottom lip and nodded slowly. "All right. But we must *also* understand that keeping an open mind is essential to any business's *growth*. For example, I should be able to recommend a potential client without feeling you've already decided against them—you know, before I've even had a chance to explain the merits."

Doug nodded, continuing to chew at the end of his cigar. "Agreed, agreed. But we must *also* understand that if senior management decides *against* taking a case, that's it. No more behind-the-back bullshit." By now, he practically had loose tobacco crawling up his nostril.

At some point, I had begun to grind my teeth. Just another typical business conversation, careening toward the deadlock we always found ourselves in. Doug was power mad and having the final say was absolutely everything to him, and heaven help me, I had a mind prone to independent thinking. I had to constantly remind myself that working with Doug counted towards the experience I needed to obtain my own private investigator license, because the balance of pros versus cons in this arrangement was razor thin. I focused on my breathing to keep my blood pressure in check.

Melanie sidled up beside me and wrapped an arm around my waist. "Boys," she said. "Might I make a suggestion? How about a moratorium on shop talk for this weekend? Unless, of course, the host of this event asks you anything specific that might help you learn how to work together better. I mean, that's the whole point of this exercise, right? Team building. You should start on that whole 'open mind' thing by seeing what they have to teach. It might give you an entirely different perspective."

"I think that's a fantastic idea," I said, letting my breath out in a long whoosh.

"Well, yeah—sure, I can do that," said Doug, plucking the cigar from his mouth and returning it to his pocket.

"Can I ask you for one little, tiny other favor, Doug?" asked Melanie sweetly, and I had no idea where she was going with this.

"Sure," said Doug. "I mean, if I can."

"We thought it might be nice to shake things up a bit. Would you mind if Brady and Dusty rode with you from here? I know you don't know Brady very well, but it would be a good opportunity to get a little better acquainted before we start working as a team."

Doug was a little flustered, but no match for the wide-eyed gaze Melanie had locked onto him. "That's probably a good idea," he said. "Sure."

"Great! Thank you, Doug. Why don't you go intercept them while we check in on the kids?" She was all smiles while I struggled to keep from grinning too broadly. "And—well, you've got a little something-something—" She indicated the area of his face where the cigar's tobacco had crept in an ever-widening circle.

Doug turned and scurried to the entrance, brushing at his face the whole while. Melanie turned to me with a satisfied grin.

"Have I ever told you how much I love you?" I asked.

"You just keep right on doing that," she said. "Now, come on. We really *should* make sure the Caudills and the kids don't need or want anything while we're here. Although I'll bet you this is the first of several stops before we actually get there. The only thing smaller than Dusty's brain is her bladder."

*****

We rode in blessed silence for a while, heading toward Bucyrus after shifting to State Route 98 near Waldo. I was singing softly to classic rock playing on the radio while Melanie was completely immersed in her laptop, pecking away at the keyboard.

"Whatcha working on?" I asked when Sirius played a song whose lyrics eluded me. "School?"

"No," she said distractedly. She had recently enrolled in several classes at Columbus State. "No homework hanging over my head this weekend." She paused and reread what she'd written, deleting the entire paragraph before scowling at the screen.

"Looks serious."

She shot me some side eye and angled the screen away from me. "You should be watching the road, not my screen."

The cruise control was set, the road was straight and other than our own little convoy trailing behind, there were no other cars nearby. I leaned over and tried to take another peek.

Melanie closed the laptop lid and slapped my arm. "Would you stop it?"

I grinned. "What's the big deal?"

"It's personal."

I returned my attention to the road ahead and scowled. The next classic tune began, but I didn't know its lyrics either. Melanie had lifted the lid on her laptop, continuing to keep it angled away from me as she tentatively began to type again. I could sense her eyes policing the boundaries.

"So, when you say *personal*, do you mean—"

"*Dwayne*. It's pretty self-explanatory."

My scowl deepened. "I share everything with you."

Even as I recognized the petulance in my own voice, Melanie threw her head back and laughed. "Yeah, right."

"I *do!*" I insisted. "What exactly do you think I've been holding back?"

She looked at me dubiously. "You shouldn't ask questions you don't want answered."

My mouth opened and then snapped shut. I could persist, but I knew what she meant. We still hadn't discussed everything that happened in West

Virginia. I couldn't. I had made a promise. It didn't make me any less curious about what she was working on.

I was relieved when the next song was one I knew. Soon enough, I was going to California with an *aa-ee-aching* in my heart, and Melanie had resumed typing with her laptop screen averted. We passed the next several miles somewhat uncomfortably until Melanie sighed and closed her laptop.

"Listen, Dwayne, I'm sorry," said Melanie. "I'm not trying to rush you into talking about what happened with Gina, honestly. I'll be here if and when that time comes. But there are some things I need to keep to myself, too, and this is just one of them. I really hope to share it with you someday, but not yet. I promise you it's nothing bad." She smiled at me crookedly, and I had a sudden thought.

"You're writing a children's story!" I snapped my fingers, remembering the writing workshop she had attended the previous spring with her college professor while I was busy trying to avoid a serial killer. "Of course!"

Melanie sighed and dropped her head. "Okay, yes. I'm writing. But that's all I'm saying. I'm still figuring out if I can even do this. But I would no more let you read what I've got so far as I would feed you raw ingredients for a recipe. I want the finished product to be good, and it's still evolving. And I don't want you asking me about how it's going, either. No external pressure. I'm already hard enough on myself."

I reached over and squeezed her hand. "I'm so proud of you."

"Shuddup," she muttered, and I saw color creeping into her cheeks.

My phone rang through its Bluetooth connection to my Hyundai. Doug Boggs's name and number appeared on the screen in the center console.

"Twenty dollars says Dusty has to pee again," said Melanie.

"Uh-unh," I said. "No deal. Total no-brainer."

Melanie giggled. "Your words, not mine."

I pressed the button on my steering wheel to answer the call. "Hey, Doug."

"Hey, man. Can I talk to Ma? She left her phone in my car."

Melanie and I looked at each other blankly.

"Not sure why you're asking *me*," I finally said.

"Very funny, Dwayne," said Doug. "Can you hear me, Ma? *Ma?*"

"She's not here, Doug," I said. "I mean, why would she be?"

I could hear Dusty's high-pitched squeak in the background followed by something unintelligible from Brady.

"Hang on just a minute," said Doug crossly, putting his phone aside so he could focus his attention on his other passengers. Doug's vehicle and flip phone far predated Bluetooth technology, and hands-free communication wasn't even an option for him. We heard a trio of voices rising and falling, and suddenly Dusty was bawling, Brady doing his very best to soothe her.

Doug picked the phone back up. "We have to go back."

"*What?*" I groaned. This was rapidly becoming the longest two-and-a-half-hour drive ever.

"Ma had to, uh, drop some pollywogs off in the pond—if you catch my drift. I thought it would be a good idea if she rode the rest of the way with you and your lady, and Dusty was *supposed* to let you know."

A fresh wave of anguish erupted in the background. I heard Brady say, "She told you she was sorry, Doug. Don't be a dick."

I was exasperated. "Why would you *ever* think it was a good idea for your mother to ride with *me?* She *hates* me!" I wasn't fond of her either but felt no need to elaborate. It was pretty generally understood.

"What do you mean?" Doug's voice was jumping octaves. "Melanie said it would be a good idea to get to know each other a little better before we started working together as a team. I thought it would be smart if you and Ma could find some common ground before we got there. This was really all *her* idea."

Melanie dropped her face into her hands.

"*Shit*," I muttered, massaging my forehead. We had been traveling for at least a half-hour since pulling out of Sheetz's parking lot. "Okay, okay—

doesn't really matter who did what. Let's get this motorcade turned around. We're losing valuable time. Mel, can you call the Caudills and give them a heads up?"

Melanie nodded, tucking her laptop away and retrieving her phone from her purse.

"Oh, man," muttered Doug. "She's gonna be *pissed.*"

I signaled left and slowed, preparing to initiate a chain of awkward, illegal U-turns and hoping they would go unnoticed by anyone affiliated with law enforcement. "One more thing, Doug," I said.

"Yeah?"

"She's riding with you."

I disconnected before he could object.

*****

"Is that woman *always* so unpleasant?" snuffled Dusty, working to repair the damage her eyeliner had sustained once her tears had dried. We had resumed custody of her and Brady after Doug had collected a white-hot Loretta Boggs back at Sheetz in Delaware. A little distance seemed prudent lest our mystery weekend take an entirely unintended turn.

"You have no idea," I said. "But, I mean, it isn't exactly like you left her stranded on the side of the road. Oh, wait—"

"Knock it off, Dwayne," said Brady, pulling Dusty into the crook of his arm. "She didn't do it on purpose."

We had parted ways with the Caudills and the kids in Sandusky, leaving them to their weekend of overpriced food and amusement rides and were headed to Catawba Island where we would park our vehicles and catch a ferry to Marble Toe Island. I had never been to any of the Great Lake islands but had always hoped to one day visit Put-in-Bay. Lots of day drinking and zipping about on golf carts—it frankly sounded like a lot of fun. Marble Toe Island was privately owned, and to be honest, I had never even heard of it. I was curious to see what it would be like.

"You can probably take solace in the likelihood that she's used up all her fury on her son," I said, glancing in my rearview mirror and grinning at Doug's pained expression. Loretta's painted eyebrows were practically stitched together beneath her furrowed forehead, and her flapping mouth didn't let up for an instant. "He's certainly used to it by now."

Melanie stiffened as Dusty suddenly leaned forward and grabbed a section of her ponytail. "Hey, Mels, where do you get your hair done? I really like this color."

"Thanks," said Melanie, easing forward to carefully extract her hair from Dusty's grasp. "My sister, Cheryl, does it for me whenever I'm back home."

"*Mmmm*. It almost looks natural. It would probably turn out better if you went to a professional."

Melanie stiffened visibly in her seat. "My sister has been a professional beautician for over ten years."

Mercifully, the soothing voice of GPS chose that moment to cut through the mounting tension, announcing an upcoming right turn in a half-mile. I squinted, straining over the dashboard to spot a road sign, but all I saw were expanses of trees and tall grass, whipping lazily past us. We had already passed all the signage for Miller's Ferry, so I assumed we must be departing from a different dock, but there had been no additional signage indicating as much. Traffic had lightened considerably, so I was able to reduce my speed as the remaining distance before the turn ticked down on the screen. I still didn't see a road.

"Take the next right," the female GPS voice intoned blandly.

"There," said Melanie, pointing. "Do you see the reflector?"

I came to a complete stop. Sure, I saw the reflector, but I didn't see a road, only an extremely narrow set of muddy tracks that trailed back before disappearing into woods crowding in from either side.

"Turn right," GPS insisted.

ISOLATION

I looked at Melanie and shrugged, eased off the highway and into the uneven tracks, gently pushing forward. I looked in my rearview to see Doug had also made the turn, and Loretta's mouth had finally stopped flapping. Its corners had disappeared into her jowls, deepening into an ugly grimace as she surveyed our surroundings with unmistakable disdain. I wasn't sure I disagreed with her on this one. It felt like we were leaving civilization completely behind, and Lord only knew what waited for us on the other side.

We bumped and jostled along the narrow path for the better part of a half mile before the trees abruptly parted, and we emerged on a sandy beach. An area designated for parking, cordoned off by railroad ties and posts connected by thick, weatherworn rope, lay to our left and straight ahead was a small wooden dock that stuck out like a tongue over the deepening waters of Lake Erie. Tethered to the dock at the far end beside a downward leading ladder was a wide, flat pontoon boat. An elderly man with frizzy, receding white hair peeking out from underneath a captain's hat stood in the center of the boat, watching our slow progress from behind a pair of sunglasses. He wore an unbuttoned Hawaiian shirt that allowed his considerable sunbaked paunch to distend over his khaki shorts. If I wasn't mistaken, there was quite a collection of empty beer cans at his feet. We pulled into the parking area and began piling out of our vehicles.

"Y'all here for Marble Toe?" he bellowed.

I nodded as I unloaded mine and Melanie's bags from the Hyundai's boot end. I figured Brady could handle his and Dusty's if he could ever extract himself from the nape of her neck.

"Yer late," the old man groused, climbing the ladder to the dock but showing no inclination whatsoever to help with the luggage. "You was supposed to be here an hour ago. Nearly left, I did. *C'mon! C'mon!* I got better things to do than just stand around here waiting."

I took a quick glance at Doug, who was struggling to unload his lone army duffel amidst his mother's three-piece bright pink hard-shell luggage collection. Loretta observed from his side, still rankling from her earlier abandonment, and refusing to make eye contact with any of us. I had envisioned proper transportation to and from the island, much like the ferry that serviced Put-in-Bay. I wasn't sure this party barge was of sufficient size to handle all of us and Loretta's luggage, too.

What kind of Mickey Mouse mystery weekend had we signed up for?

CHAPTER FOUR

"The name's Cap'n Jack," growled the old man, standing aside as we loaded our bags down onto the boat. He made no effort whatsoever to assist, and I half-expected him to follow up with *'Argh, me mateys!'* I caught the unmistakable scent of startled skunk and realized beer wasn't the only thing keeping the captain's eyes glossy this afternoon.

"Well, hello, there, Mr.—er, Captain Jack," said Dusty, dipping into a sort of curtsy while offering a dainty hand to the old geezer. He just stared at it while she continued, her ample bosoms defying gravity at his eye level. "I'm Dusty. This is my guy, Brady. These are Brady's friends—"

"Don't bother with all the names," barked the Captain, waving her away and kicking his pile of empty beer cans toward a plastic tarp at the rear of the boat that likely covered more of the same. "No sense in trying to remember 'em. Probably won't see you folks ever again 'cept for maybe the trip back unless God grants me mercy and strikes me dead in my sleep." He laughed until he wheezed, apparently having tickled his own pickle. The rest of us looked expectantly toward Doug, as if he might take the lead since this whole thing was his idea, but he was too busy trying to untangle a knot in his shoelaces to notice.

"Everybody cop a squat," Captain Jack ordered, indicating the bench seating that ringed the boat's wide, flat interior. "I might have a life jacket or two somewhere on here, but let's all just stay on board so's I don't have to find 'em, alrighty then?" He dropped into a well-worn seat behind the boat's controls and fired up the noisy engine, sending a plume of blue-gray exhaust into the air while we hurried to secure seating.

Doug guided his mother starboard where they could sit close to the captain. It was apparent he was intrigued by the mechanics of the process and was trying to absorb everything he could by osmosis. By the end of our journey, he would no doubt be an armchair expert at piloting a pontoon. Loretta clung tightly to his arm, afraid of losing her balance and looking a little green around the gills. Dusty dragged Brady toward the bow, and I could nearly see her trying to force a reenactment from *The Titanic*. Melanie and I exchanged a dubious look before settling along the port side. With a lurch, the pontoon headed out.

It was nearly six o'clock, and the September sun was drifting toward the western horizon in a nearly cloudless sky. We still had a couple of hours of daylight left, but at the pace we chugged along, I wasn't sure we would make our destination by dark. Vessels of varying sizes and models passed in the distance, carrying passengers excited to enjoy summer's last big Labor Day weekend hoorah. By comparison, our little group was downright sullen.

"So, what's the history of this Marble Toe Island?" I called to the captain above the roar of the engine.

Jack turned toward me, squinting against the sun. "This ain't no guided tour," he said, cracking open another beer. "I just haul you to and fro. If there's questions, they'll have to keep until morning." He returned his sour gaze to the waters ahead.

"How many others are there?" asked Melanie.

"How the hell should I know?" he asked without looking back. "Two, twelve, twenty—I got no fucking idea. I think it *all* sounds like a bunch of horseshit, but you know—whatever."

Melanie leaned in toward me. "Should he be drinking?"

"Nope," I said, counting the number of empty cans near the captain's feet. I could only pray they weren't all from today.

ISOLATION

We slowly passed between Kelleys Island and South Bass Island, home to Put-in-Bay. Both were popular vacation destinations for tourists, and I would've gladly traded places with any of them at this point. I couldn't imagine what kind of company would hire a man like Captain Jack to be the face greeting its customers. I had bought into Doug's plan sight unseen, and I was having serious buyer's remorse. I could only attribute it to a fog of delirium prompted by the birth of my niece. Why else would I have agreed to this without a little independent investigation?

I was beginning to wonder if our final destination was Canada when I spotted a small land mass straight ahead of us. Thick woods covered most of what I could see, and I couldn't help but notice its uncanny resemblance to *Gilligan's Island*. Captain Jack guided the boat to the right, and as we slowly closed the gap, a weatherworn boathouse emerged on the sandy shore. The bow of a small speedboat was barely visible through its main entrance which was flanked on either side by a deep set of floating docks that formed a slip, bobbing almost imperceptibly in the lake's calm water. A pair of matching golf carts were parked underneath a metal canopy to the right of the boathouse, and beyond the shallow beach, a thin dirt path ascended a well-tended grassy knoll, rising about ten feet and suggesting civilization somewhere ahead. This suggestion was reinforced by an overhead power line running from the nearby woods to a light pole at the edge of the dock on the right.

"Everyone keep yer asses planted," said the captain as we approached the opening between the two floating docks. "This can get a little bumpy."

He wasn't kidding. He misjudged the angle, striking the side of the pontoon on the dock just below where Melanie and I sat, which in turn caused the boat to skitter to the right, striking the other side. Thank goodness he had slowed to a crawl, or he would have likely damaged the boat, the docks or both. It was, however, the end of Loretta's tenuous grip on the contents of her stomach. With a horrific horking sound, she leaned over the rail and deposited her lunch and all of her travel snacks into the Great Lake below.

Captain Jack regarded Loretta with unmasked disdain as he began mooring the boat to a nearby dock piling. "All right," he announced. "Everyone out. I'll be hard pressed to get back before dark, and I got a life of my own. C'mon."

"But what do we do from here?" asked Melanie, already hurrying to get her bag to the other side of the boat. "Doug, do you have instructions?"

Doug looked up from where he was tending to his mother. Her complexion had gone from green to clammy cottage cheese, and a sheen of perspiration had broken across her brow. "I thought someone would be here to meet us."

"C'mon, c'mon," said the captain, scowling. "I ain't got time for this."

I boosted Melanie up onto the dock and handed her our bags before debarking myself. Dusty and Brady repeated our maneuver, and the captain was already fiddling with the rope that kept us tethered to the dock. Doug handed me his and Loretta's bags, and he began angling his mother toward the edge. It took me and Brady pulling on her arms and Doug pushing from behind to lift her off the boat, and everything we had to keep her upright on her wobbly legs. She was beginning to go green again.

"Are you gonna make it?" I asked Loretta as she pulled her arms free from me and Brady.

"Just give me some air," she said, breathing deeply, and I gladly backed away. She looked like she could hurl again at any moment.

Tipping etiquette would normally dictate a gratuity for our pilot, but I don't think any of us were really feeling it at this point, and frankly, neither was Captain Jack. He had already unmoored his vessel and guided it back out into the open water. Once clear of the docks and without a single look back, he throttled the engine, emitting a last noxious blue-gray cloud before heading toward the mainland.

ISOLATION

*****

"These golf carts look relatively new," said Brady, examining the pair under the canopy. In the driver's seat of the one on the right, a 9 x 12 manila clasp envelope lay with Doug's name written in block letters on the outside. He picked it up and handed it to Doug.

"Well, that's something, I guess," said Melanie, looking around dubiously. "I hope we're not supposed to stay in this boathouse."

"Naw," said Doug, opening the envelope. "Supposed to be real fancy accommodations."

"Do you think there's sharks?" asked Dusty, studiously scanning the lake surface. "I hope not. I hate sharks. I thought I saw fins a little while ago."

"No, baby," said Brady, wrapping himself protectively around her. "The Great Lakes are freshwater. Sharks can only survive in saltwater."

"Well, except bull sharks," said Melanie, barely able to suppress a grin.

"*Oooo!*" squealed Dusty, squirming in Brady's embrace. "I *knew* I saw fins!"

"*Very* unlikely," soothed Brady, tossing a dirty look in Melanie's direction. "The water's too cold for bull sharks, especially at this time of year."

"I've got three housekeys here," said Doug, handing one to Brady and one to me. "And there's a note inside." He cleared his throat and began reading in a stop-and-start monotone that gave me a wild flashback to junior high English. "*Hello and welcome, Mr. Boggs and Friends. Please feel free to use the golf carts to transport yourselves to the manor, keys are in the switches. Just follow the shoreline up and around the bend, and you'll see where to turn in. There are ten guest bedrooms on the second floor of approximately equal size. Please choose whichever you like. The only room that is off limits is the master bedroom which belongs to the owner, and it's been locked. While there is no cell service here, we offer complimentary satellite broadband, and you will find a network password on each of the desks in the guest quarters. Once you enable your phones for wi-fi calling, you'll be able to use them as* normal. *The fireplaces in the guest suites are strictly for show, so please do not use them. Their flues have been sealed for some time, and any attempt at lighting a cozy fire will only result in smoke backing up into your rooms. My apologies for any inconvenience. The kitchen has been stocked with hot dogs, burger patties, fresh veggies and potato salad—please help yourselves. There is a gas grill on the patio and games in the shed to keep yourselves occupied. I will arrive with our other guests and support staff around eight, but we'll officially kick things off at ten, with a breakfast get-together in the dining hall. I look forward to meeting you all! Sincerely, Anyssa Williams.'"*

"Dining hall," repeated Melanie. "Sounds—fancy."

I grabbed our bags and loaded them into the back of one of the golf carts and seated myself behind the wheel. Melanie slid into the passenger seat while Brady loaded his and Dusty's luggage. Ever the gentleman, he then held Dusty's hand while gently boosting her onto the rear bench seat behind Melanie. She fluttered her eyelashes appreciatively, and he raced around the rear of the cart to slide in behind me. Loretta was already in the passenger seat of the other cart, fumbling for the controls that might allow her girth to be accommodated with a little less proximity to the dashboard. Doug's cheeks were bright red as he huffed and puffed, boosting Loretta's bright pink luggage into the back, and I couldn't help but wonder again exactly how much this woman had packed for a three-night stay.

Once we were all loaded, I started the engine and took the lead, pulling out from underneath the canopy, with Doug following closely behind. As the note instructed, I followed the shoreline as it veered left, gradually rising away from the small beach and bridging the gap between it and the well-maintained lawn above. As we wrapped further left, Melanie suddenly gasped, Brady whistled, and Dusty cooed. I braked to see what they were all staring at.

Nestled deep in the woods to our left was an enormous manor house. The steeply pitched roof suggested at least three interior elevations with wide, black shuttered windows promising ample natural lighting from just about anywhere within. Private balconies extended both to the front and the sides of the house, assuring that no guest room was less desirable than any other. A deep veranda ran the entire width of the front of the house under a roof supported by a series of fluted pillars painted bright white and matching the trim around the windows in the slate gray siding. I spotted the shed set off to the left and near the woods, a miniature replica of the manor itself. The aforementioned gas grill sat on a cozy brick patio along the western side of the house. Along the eastern side was another small metal canopy, presumably under which to park the golf carts on this end of the path.

"I don't think fancy even begins to cover it," I muttered, creeping forward to where the sandy path transitioned into a cobblestone drive. It led to a circular brick slab in the center of the front lawn, the middle of which was inhabited by a low fountain featuring a mossy, concrete cherub that burbled crystal clear water from the pout in its upturned face. I eased to a stop near the front steps, and Doug lurched to a halt beside me before we both quieted our engines. Our entire party stared in stunned silence at the sprawling house before us.

"Holy shit," Doug finally said. "I had a feeling this would be good, but I had no *idea.*"

It was almost second nature—not to mention incredibly easy—to find fault with Doug's typical plans and schemes that I remained at a loss for words. We collected our respective bags from the rear of the carts and gathered on the porch in front of a windowless mahogany door that would have served equally well as the entrance to a castle. I used the key that Doug handed me to disengage the deadbolt and depressed the thumb lever above its cast iron handle.

The door swung inward into a high-ceilinged foyer that elicited another round of audible, appreciative gasps. One by one, we passed through with our luggage and collected beneath a wide chrome and crystal chandelier that promised to dazzle once illuminated. Straight ahead was a staircase straight out of *Gone with the Wind*, rising midway to the second floor before branching off in opposite directions to feed the corridors on each side of the manor. Pristine marble flooring straddled the staircase, forming wide corridors in both directions. The interior walls featured rich, mahogany paneling stretching from floor to molded chair rail, above which gold and green damask wallpaper reached the intricate crown molding near the ceiling. To our immediate left was a handsome parlor, its pocket doors opened wide to display a Victorian era grouping of sofa, stiff-backed chairs, and low coffee table atop an ornately patterned Persian rug. In the area nearest the front of the house, a grand piano stood ready for entertaining, its top board held open by its prop. Dark emerald velvet curtains with gold rope ties covered the windows, casting the room in deep shadow. My eyes followed the corridor beyond the parlor to its neighboring room behind a closed set of double doors and beyond, where it opened into what looked like might be the kitchen. The corridor to the right of the stairs housed a series of closed doors spaced at regular intervals. Soon enough, we would investigate what was behind each, but for now, we gathered at the bottom of the grand staircase like a bunch of slack-jawed fools.

With a gleam in her eye, Melanie was the first to break the silence. "First one up gets choice of rooms!"

She launched herself up the staircase pivoting left at the landing before continuing on. With a high-pitched squeak, Dusty trotted up the stairs after her, followed closely by Loretta, grunting with each and every step. Doug, Brady and I were left behind with the luggage, our opinions unsolicited and clearly irrelevant.

"*Women*," grumbled Doug, beginning the first of several trips hauling luggage up after his mother.

Brady and I exchanged a private grin. Like *Doug* had any idea about women. We then grabbed our luggage and followed our ladies like the subservient pups we were.

*****

ISOLATION

Anyssa's note told no lies.

Each of the guest quarters was equally luxurious with en suite bathrooms and comparable square footage. While some views may have been deemed more desirable than others, I guess it was really a matter of personal preference. Melanie selected a room toward the front of the house that afforded a spectacular view of Lake Erie while Dusty chose a room for her and Brady several doors down, its lake view partially obscured by thick woods which leant a greater sense of privacy. Loretta and Doug selected neighboring rooms on the opposite side of the house, and for once, everyone seemed completely satisfied.

The spacious kitchen ran the entire width of the back of the house. It had been fairly recently renovated, with a large center island featuring a six-burner cooktop and indoor grill underneath an industrial-grade hooded vent complete with an Ansul Fire Suppression System. A wide, two-door refrigerator and double-decker oven were mounted within the inside interior wall separated by capacious pantries fully stocked with dry goods. A two-basin sink with detachable faucet was centered beneath a double-paned casement window as the centerpiece of the counter running the length of the rear wall. An industrial dishwasher was to the right of the sink, and cabinets lined the wall flanking the window, providing ample storage for dinnerware and cookware.

Melanie began slicing tomatoes and onions while Dusty tried her hand at hacking a head of lettuce, using a cleaver in a way that suggested her familiarity with kitchens was limited to what she had seen on television. Brady and I wandered out through a set of double French doors in the rear left corner, stepping down onto a flagstone patio that was home to an outdoor table large enough to accommodate twelve. The sun had quite nearly set by this point, and there was nothing obvious to provide shelter from the elements, should the need arise. After a little nosing around, Brady found a switch that activated a retractable segment of roofing that slid out and over the entire patio. We decided to leave the space open while we fired up the gas grill and placed a row of burgers and dogs across the cast iron grate.

Doug headed to the shed at the rear of the property, and soon enough, he was dragging a set of Ohio State cornhole boards out onto the level grassy lawn between the patio and the edge of the woods. He placed them parallel to the patio, counting out twenty-seven steps between the interior edges of each; it was a fair approximation. It wasn't like this was regulation play. He headed back to retrieve the beanbags as Loretta came through the double doors toting buns, a plate of cheese and assorted condiments tucked into her armpits. I was glad to see she had calmed down after the fiasco at Sheetz. Her ability to hold a grudge is damn near legendary, which could have made this the longest three-day weekend in the entire history of time.

"Grill food up!" Brady called out as I used a spatula to arrange the burgers from rare to well done on a large serving plate Melanie had brought out along with disposable plates and utensils. Dusty followed with a large tub of deli potato salad. We had our choice between soft drinks, wine coolers or beer, and seated ourselves at the table after making our selections. Doug, Melanie and I chose one side of the table while Brady and Dusty cozied up across from us. Naturally, Loretta took position at the head of the table where she could keep tabs on everybody's business. She cleared her throat loudly, silencing our various conversations.

We stared at her expectantly while Doug's head automatically dropped to his chest. Melanie clued in quickly, squeezing my hand and lowering her own head. Brady swallowed the bite of burger he had already taken and dabbed at the corners of his mouth before looking down guiltily.

Dusty looked up from the hot dog to which she was applying a thin line of mustard with an inordinate amount of concentration. "What?" she peeped.

Loretta sighed. "At *my* table, we say grace before we eat," she said haughtily, her hands clasped firmly before her.

Dusty's eyes widened. "This is *your* table? I had no idea—"

"No, no," said Brady, scooping Dusty's hand up into his own and kissing her knuckles. "It's just a figure a speech, kitten. It's a religious thing."

"Oh," said Dusty, nodding. "Okay. But I don't do religious things."

"Clearly," muttered Loretta, passing judgment with a significant arch of her eyebrow. "Just keep your mouth shut and humor me, will you?"

Dusty started to reply but mercifully, Brady quieted her with a quick shake of his curly head.

"Thank you, dear Lord, for the bounty of sustenance we have before us and please bless the hands that prepared it. May this weekend be one of learning and mutual respect from which a bond of brotherhood is formed. *Ahhh*-men." Loretta signed off with a quick nod of her head, which I spied out of the corner of my eye. While it says absolutely nothing about my religious convictions one way or the other, I could never resist the urge to peek during prayer to see who else was doing the same.

"That was lovely, Loretta," said Melanie.

Loretta gave another curt nod before double-fisting a loaded burger. "Now, let's eat!"

*****

The sun had fully set before the end of our feast, but Brady found the switches for the outdoor lighting on his first trip back to the kitchen for more beer. A trio of halogen lights was mounted along the side of the house with equivalents across the lawn, perched high on poles that were nearly invisible against the wooded backdrop. The combined effect was almost like stadium lighting, casting aside all shadows in our direct proximity yet enhancing the gloom beyond its periphery. If it weren't for the full moon riding high in the sky and reflected in the waters below, the portion of Lake Erie visible from the side lawn would have disappeared entirely.

Darin Miller

I stuck to Pepsi while Brady and Doug went for more beer. I wasn't exactly counting, but Brady had consumed enough that his eyes were beginning to twinkle. Melanie and Dusty opted for wine coolers while Loretta seemed perfectly content with a mug of tepid water from the tap. We divvied up along our natural fault lines to form teams for cornhole. Doug and Loretta challenged Brady and a less-than-enthusiastic Dusty to the first round, while Melanie and I pulled up chairs from the table to spectate, waiting to take on the winners of the first round. Once nicknamed "Dead-Eye Dwayne," I had proven time and again to have unerring aim, and no one argued with giving us advanced placement in the championship round.

The rules of the game were fairly simple. Each team was given four bean bags of a like color to denote the team—one set was scarlet, the other gray—naturally. Each team would be represented by a member from each standing beside the cornhole boards at opposing ends of the field. Players on one end of the field would take turns throwing bean bags at the board on the opposite side, hoping to either sink the bag through its hole or at least place the bag somewhere on the board's surface. Sinking a bag was worth three points and placing a bag was worth one. It was also fair play to knock an opposing player's bags off the board, thus reducing their score. Once one side had exhausted their supply of bean bags, the score was tallied for that round and the players on the other side collected the bean bags and did the same in the opposite direction. The winner would be the first team to reach twenty-one points.

Loretta, who shared a side with Brady, proved herself surprisingly adept at the game, sinking several bean bags directly through the hole while also demonstrating quite the knack for knocking Brady's bags off the board and noticeably getting under his skin in the process. This was even more amazing as she gave the bag absolutely no lift whatsoever, only firing them across the way in a nearly straight line. Doug played well enough, but his delivery was pure comic gold—protruding tongue stuck through pursed lips and punctuated by an audible grunt on every single throw. I'd be lying if I said I didn't manage to capture a candid shot or two on my cell phone—good for a laugh whenever needed. Dusty grew bored quickly once she proved incapable of getting the bean bags any farther than halfway to the opposite side. Soon, she was whining and her motivation flatlined entirely.

"How much *longer* does this go on?" she moaned. "I'm getting eaten alive by mosquitoes." She made a spectacle of slapping at her own bare shoulder. Melanie looked at me and rolled her eyes. She was always first to notice when mosquitoes were present as they seemed especially drawn to her. They certainly weren't bothering her now.

"*Woo hoo!*" Loretta exclaimed, throwing her fists in the air. She had just sunk the second of two bags through the hole in the board, pushing her team's tally to twenty-three. "For you losers, it ends right now." She cackled and performed a rather unsightly jig. So much for good sportsmanship.

I pulled Melanie to her feet. "Let's get this over with."

"If we must," she sighed.

"That's right," sneered Loretta, full of herself now, and on the offense. "Let's just see if ole 'Dead Eye Dwayne' can keep *this* champion from filling her hole first!"

"Oh, my Lord—" Melanie dropped her face into her hands while I burst out laughing. Loretta was completely lost. She had no idea what she had just said. I joined Doug at the end of the field while Melanie met up with Loretta on the other.

The game was fairly evenly paced, and as the rounds passed and the score progressed at a snail's pace, Loretta's penchant for smack talk intensified. Doug had placed two bags near the hole in the board, and if I couldn't knock at least one off without knocking it through the hole, they were going to win, and I just couldn't have that.

Just as I was focusing on my aim, Loretta said, "So, I guess that Todd and Jo Morrow are just too good to teach their children to say grace before meals?"

I launched the bean bag and hit her directly in the pelican-like waddle of her neck, knocking her backward onto her not-so-insubstantial backside.

"You did that *on purpose!*" she shrieked, pointing at me with her entire face mottling.

"I thought I saw a mosquito—" I barely managed before doubling over with laughter. Despite her best effort to remain stoic, Melanie had caught the visual and was laughing herself into tears while hiding behind me.

Our escalating situation evaporated immediately when Dusty abruptly shattered the night with an ear-splitting shriek.

CHAPTER FIVE

"There's someone *down there!*" Dusty cried, tucked against Brady's side and pointing a shaky finger toward the house.

"Down where, baby?" Brady asked, kissing her forehead as we gathered closer. I kept Melanie between me and a still-fuming Loretta—my survivalist instinct had been triggered.

"There," said Dusty in a shaky voice. She pointed toward the nearest two-pane window embedded in the manor's foundation, presumably looking into its basement.

I leaned in, but there was nothing to see. "What am I looking for, here?"

"It was a face," said Dusty. "A pale white face. I saw its *eyes!* They were looking right at me!" She shuddered and hid her face against Brady's chest.

"It was probably just a reflection of the full moon," I said. "I mean look." I pointed to its position in the night sky, a near straight line over Brady's shoulder.

"It was *not* the moon! It was a face!" Dusty was adamant. She looked up at Brady and cooed, "You believe me, don't you, baby?"

Brady sighed, shooting us all a pointed look. "Of course, I do, kitten. C'mon, folks. Time to make sure our perimeter hasn't been breached."

We exchanged glances and followed Brady as he led us back into the house. Whether any of us were buying it or not, our previously ebullient mood was supplanted with a sense of creeping dread that even the bright kitchen lights couldn't dispel. The manor was enormous, and we had only investigated a very small portion of it. We thought we were supposed to be the only ones on the premises tonight, but who could be completely certain? The house was suddenly alive with phantom noise—the electric thrum of appliances, the random creak of floorboards settling, the vague buzz from the overhead fluorescent lighting. Almost unconsciously, we each armed ourselves with a kitchen implement for protection before proceeding. Most chose knives. I grabbed a meat tenderizer. Loretta went old school with a cast iron skillet.

"Anyone know where the stairs to the basement are?" asked Brady.

After a round of mumbling affirmed the negative, we were left to sample the various doors in the kitchen. None of them led where we desired, although I discovered a veritable liquor store behind one. We expanded our scope out into the hallway, and Melanie signaled victory as she opened a door in the interior wall running below the rail of the grand staircase.

"Found it," she said, reaching in and searching along the inside wall for a light switch. I heard the distinct sound of the switch being flipped repeatedly, but the deep gloom that lay beyond the doorway persisted. "You have got to be *kidding* me!"

Brady fumbled with his phone and turned its flashlight on. "Here, let me, Mel," he said, easing by her and stepping through the door. Dusty was directly behind him, holding onto his free hand as if her very life depended on it. Melanie looked at me expectantly.

"What?" I asked.

"Are we just gonna stand here and wait?" she asked, adding, "Big hero?"

I rankled. "What was I supposed to do? Push him out of the way? It's his goofy girlfriend who's seeing things. Why *shouldn't* he go first?"

"Oh, for heaven's sake, I was just *teasing*," she said. "Don't get your panties in a twist." She followed Dusty through the door and into the fading light cast by Brady's phone.

"Now, wait just a minute!" I called after her. "I'm certainly not afraid to go down there." I hurried along before the light fully diminished, Doug and Loretta close behind.

I heard more clicking before Brady said, "Lights are out down here, too."

"Hello?" I called out loudly as we reached the bottom of the wooden slat stairs. "Anyone down here?"

Nothing, save for the soft hiss of natural gas maintaining the temperature in the double hot water tanks across the room and against the exterior wall. The rough concrete floor of the basement appeared to be dry, yet a certain dankness hung in the air, suggesting that wasn't always the case. Bright moonlight spilled through the narrow windows positioned at regular intervals along the foundation, and Brady shone his light toward the one Dusty had undoubtedly pointed to from outside. Metal shelving units were on either side of it, holding partially used cans of paint, turpentine, and other painting supplies. Discarded pieces of furniture and mismatched boxes collected dust in various orderly piles along both the exterior wall and underneath the stairs we had just descended, a clear wide path separating the two. Midway along, the path wrapped left into the cavernous space below the other side of the house.

The hairs on the back of my neck prickled. As bright as Brady's phone was, it couldn't dispel all the gloom. There were too many places where anyone could hide, and I had a perversely paranoid sense of being watched.

"Hello?" I called again with a lot less bravado.

A can of turpentine leapt from the metal shelving unit and landed with a metallic clang on the concrete floor, followed immediately by a distinctly feline shape who leapt down and scampered off, having successfully elicited a handful of high-octave shrieks from the lot of us while executing a classic jump-scare with perfect precision.

The laughter that spilled from my mouth sounded unhinged even in my own ears. "It was a cat," I said. "Just a cat."

"No," insisted Dusty. "I don't think so. I would recognize a cat. This was a person, a scary looking person—"

"Kitten," said Brady soothingly, tucking her against his side. "It was just your eyes playing tricks on you. You've been telling me all evening how spooky you think this place is—"

"Well, it *is!*" she said, pulling away. "I mean, who owns a place like this and just leaves it empty? I feel like someone has been watching us off and on the whole evening—hasn't anyone else picked up on that?"

The rest of us looked at each other, slowly shaking our heads to indicate we hadn't.

"And how weird is it that *all* of the lights are out down here?" she challenged.

"I don't know what to tell you," I said. "But this *is* a mystery weekend. Who knows how much of this could be groundwork for when the weekend actually begins tomorrow?"

Brady nodded, succeeding in pulling Dusty back against his side. "Dwayne's right, kitten. I think your imagination is playing tricks on you."

"But—" she pouted, glancing around the darkened basement as uncertainty began to creep back in. She looked up at Brady. "Can we just go to our room, baby? I don't want to be down here anymore."

"Of course, kitten," he said, immediately steering her back toward the stairs. The rest of us trailed behind, unwilling to fall too far outside the ring of LED light cast by Brady's phone.

"I'm going to go on up to our room," said Melanie as we emerged in the hallway on the main floor. "I want to touch base with Jasmine and the Caudills before it gets any later."

"Sure," I said. "Give the kiddo my love. Doug, Loretta and I can handle cleaning up the patio."

"*Oo-o-oh* no," said Loretta, shaking her head. "It's past time for my nightly beauty regimen. You boys can surely handle the cleanup without *my* help." She didn't wait for a response before heading for the stairs.

I started to make a quip about how time travel would be required for a beauty routine to have any impact on Loretta, but I reminded myself we were here to learn how to work as a team. It wouldn't kill me to let it go—although it *would* sting a bit. We headed back out to the patio.

I began gathering leftover burgers, hot dogs and condiments, transporting them to the kitchen where I covered them with plastic wrap before stowing them in the refrigerator. Doug dismantled the cornhole setup and returned the boards and bags to the shed at the rear of the property. He then attacked the grill with a wire brush while I carried a garbage bag around collecting used plates, plastic utensils and empty cans.

I glanced at my watch, and it was nearly ten o'clock. "I suppose we should call it an evening," I said. "The big fun starts tomorrow."

Doug nodded, inserting his nub of cigar into the corner of his mouth before lighting it and taking an aromatic puff. "I'll be right behind you. Can't smoke this inside. And Dwayne?"

"Yeah?"

"I really am glad you're giving this a shot. I think we could really make our mark in Columbus if we can work past your attitude."

My mouth fell open. "*My* attitude? I cannot *possibly* have heard you correctly. I—"

Doug waved my words away. "All right, all right. I didn't mean it like it came out. I admit, I need to work on my verbal skills, too. What I'm trying to say is I'm glad you're back on board. Now, get some rest, and let's hit the ground running tomorrow."

*****

I could hear water running from the shower in the bathroom as I entered our guest quarters. Melanie had placed her soft-sided travel bag on the left side of the king-size bed, its top unzipped and open from where she had retrieved a change of clothes and various toiletries. My bag lay where I had left it on the floor beside my side of the bed.

"Did you get hold of Jasmine?" I called out.

"*What?*" she yelled from behind the bathroom door.

"*Jasmine! Your daughter!*"

"*They're fine! After they checked in, they grabbed a bite to eat before the kids hit the water park.*" We had booked them a suite at the Great Wolf Lodge in Sandusky. With its indoor water attractions, it was practically its own self-contained amusement park.

"*What about Billy?*" Brady's son had spina bifida and was confined to a wheelchair. His activities were a lot more restricted. "*I hope Jaz and Scott aren't leaving him behind.*"

"*Of course not,*" she called. "*They know better than that. Can we talk after I get out of the shower? I'm getting shampoo in my mouth.*"

"*Sure, sure.*"

I kicked my shoes off and sat on the corner of the bed, absorbing our space. Melanie had effectively commandeered the small writing desk beneath the window at the front of the house, her laptop screen open and lines of text running partway down a Word document.

Hmmm.

I *knew* better from Melanie's reaction to my peeking while in the car, but curiosity is a mighty powerful seducer, and let's face it, I'm weak. I stood, inching closer to the desk, ready to pivot away if I heard the falling water in the shower cease. As I neared the straight-backed antique desk chair, words began to swim into focus.

> Daryl had an awkward charm that was hard to quantify. My late husband had practically gushed over his intellect, but I couldn't really see it. I genuinely wanted to know him better because I thought it might fill in some of the gaping holes of backstory Mac had never been willing to share, but conversation was difficult. I found myself spilling about my own difficult upbringing and

immediately felt more vulnerable than I had ever intended. I was supposed to be gathering information, not providing it. The urge to excuse myself for a restroom break only to make a mad dash through the nearest exit was almost overwhelming.

I frowned and leaned forward, making a mental note of the current page number. I then used a series of keystrokes to jump to the top of the document.

My Latest Mistake
(Lessons in Love)
by
Melanie McGregor

I had just returned the cursor to its previous position in the document when I sensed rather than heard her behind me, a damp warmth from the heat of the shower radiating against my back and shoulder.

"What do you think you're doing?" Melanie asked quietly, and I stiffened. I had been so distracted with what I was reading I hadn't heard her turn off the water. She reached around me and gently closed the lid of her laptop.

I turned to face her, not sure what to say. I was stunned, a feeling of betrayal overwhelming me. I hadn't read much, but it didn't take a rocket scientist to figure out who the people in her story actually were. She stood expressionless in a complimentary white terrycloth bathrobe, her hair piled high atop her head in a matching bath towel, dripping on the ornate rug beneath our feet. I felt heat rising in my cheeks as guilt and anger fought for control of my mouth.

"What the fuck is *this?*" I spat, indicating the laptop. Outrage had swallowed my guilt whole. "This isn't a children's book."

Melanie didn't even flinch. Her cool stare remained fixed on my face as she slowly folded her arms across her chest. "No, it's not. I don't believe I ever said it was," she said evenly. "I also believe I told you I wasn't ready for you to read it yet."

"*My Latest Mistake?!* Is that what I am?"

Melanie sighed and at last looked away, dropping her forehead into her palm. "You might not want me to answer that at this particular moment," she said, and now she was *pissed*. I could tell from the set of her jawline and the unmistakable fire in her eyes. I was rendered speechless, although my mouth kept opening and closing ineffectually.

"Tell you what," she finally said, walking to the side of the bed where my travel bag rested on the floor. She stooped down and snagged it by its handles, carrying it to the door. "I think we better just stop right here before one of us says something we might regret." She opened the door and pitched my bag out into the darkened corridor.

"Are you *kidding* me?" I was astounded. Exactly how was *I* the bad guy here? I crossed the room to retrieve my bag.

"Not even slightly," she said, pushing me out into the hall. "There are plenty of other guest rooms. Find one. I don't want to look at you right now."

"*Melanie!*"

"Nope," she said, slamming the door in my face. I stared at the door as the sound echoed down the corridor.

Dammit!

The last thing I needed was to have to explain myself to anyone else in our group. I chose the neighboring guest room and threw my bag on its empty bed, visible in the light from the full moon spilling in through the window. I closed the door behind me and climbed, fully dressed, on top of the mattress, stretching out and staring at the ceiling.

I felt like I had stepped on a land mine and blown up my entire life.

ISOLATION

*****

I tossed and turned for what seemed an eternity, but when I finally consulted my cell phone, it was barely after midnight. The house was quiet, save for the occasional creaking pipe or settling floor joist. I sat upright on the edge of the bed, staring off into the distance and feeling completely sorry for myself.

My mind wandered off to the liquor pantry I had discovered earlier in the kitchen.

I mulled it over for all of five seconds before feeling around in the darkness for my tennis shoes only to remember I had kicked them off in what was now Melanie's room.

Dammit!

I took a deep breath. Fine. I didn't need shoes. I just needed a tipple of whiskey. Just enough to make sleep possible. Certainly, no more than that. I didn't want to be hungover in the morning, for sure.

I eased out of my room and waited for my eyes to adjust to the darkened corridor, pulling the door closed silently behind me. Enough moonlight spilled into the hallway courtesy of a large window installed above the massive front entrance, meant to showcase the magnificence of the chandelier when lit but only casting lengthening shadows now. I descended the grand staircase, passing through the landing at its midpoint and sliding a hand along its rightmost mahogany rail, admiring the workmanship that had gone into its construction.

Once in the kitchen, I turned on the single bulb above the sink and crossed to where the liquor lived. Surprised to find my normal Canadian Mist amongst the selections, I retrieved the bottle and rummaged through cabinets until I found a shallow glass. I filled it with ice from the freezer and retrieved a Pepsi from the fridge as a chaser. I filled the glass about halfway with whiskey before wondering how much of its volume was being occupied by ice. I shrugged and filled it the rest of the way. I then tucked the bottle underneath my arm. Maybe I *did* have a problem. Well, it was a problem to solve another day.

My face still felt hot from my earlier exchange with Melanie, so I decided to take my contraband and ease myself out to the patio and sit at the table. I left the spotlights off to mask my presence should anyone else wander into the kitchen. The cool night air was refreshing, a light breeze blowing in from Lake Erie, its shimmering surface partially obscured by the woods surrounding the property.

I tossed back a bigger shot than anticipated and nearly choked while fumbling to open my can of Pepsi. I sat back and pressed the cold can to my forehead and wondered what had gone wrong. Based on what I had read, *everything*. But it didn't make sense. Why would Melanie have relocated with Jasmine to Columbus if her feelings for me hadn't been at least partially genuine? Self-doubt is a bed of quicksand, and soon enough, I was up to my neck, unable to find a way to pull myself out. I felt the last of the whiskey in my glass slide down my throat as cubes of ice clinked against my teeth.

Well, *huh*...

Apparently, the ice *was* displacing much of the volume of the glass. I felt a slight warmth from the liquor, but my head was clear. I allowed myself a second serving, capping the Canadian Mist and setting it on the ground beside me—as if that would stop me should I elect for more. But I was fairly resolute that I needed to behave myself and this should be sufficient.

I slid my socks off, allowing my bare feet direct contact with the cool surface of the patio. The moon reflecting from Lake Erie's surface as water lapped at the shore was practically hypnotic, and I tossed my second drink back before deciding to walk down to the boathouse. I set my glass aside and headed across the grassy plateau to where the cart path transected the lawn. The grass was like a dewy velvet carpet, soft against my skin, and soon my feet were damp. Uneven tendrils of fog had rolled in from the lake's surface, diminishing the effect of gas vapor lights which dotted the perimeter of the sandy beach. The boathouse itself was nestled in a thick bank of mist, a setting worthy of a horror movie, and I fleetingly wondered what Dusty would see if she were here now. I was drawn to it, the soft sand sifting through my toes as I stepped off the lawn and bridged the distance.

I stepped out onto the nearest of the two floating wooden docks and sat at its end, dangling my feet into the cool water below. I leaned back, propping myself up on my arms and took the crisp, clean air deep into my lungs. When that didn't help, I laid flat against the wooden slats of the dock, staring at the full moon and a legion of stars overhead.

A sudden image of Jasmine sprang to mind, her pug little nose centered between freckled cheeks, her fiery red hair just beginning to recover from a tantrum-induced bout of self-sabotage. I thought about all the progress we had made since we were more or less forced into each other's orbits. I knew less than nothing about children and the way their little minds worked. She had lost her father who, while well-intentioned, was frequently less than honest with both Jasmine and her mother before eventually getting himself killed. We had worked through most if not all of our trust issues, and I had quickly learned that although she was barely a teen, Jasmine was smart, funny and resourceful. I don't know why I never considered those traits a possibility in someone so young, but these things couldn't be attributed to age alone, and it was a point completely underscored once I met the utter vapor lock that was Dusty. I had become very protective of Jasmine, and we could sometimes connect on a level that was strictly off-limits to her mother—I mean, who other than Doug Boggs shares *everything* with their mother?

Who was I kidding? I had come to love her as if she were my own, and now it looked like we would be saying goodbye.

A hard lump formed in my throat, and I pressed away hot tears collecting in the corners of my eyes. I was *not* going to cry about this. I didn't give two shits how society felt about men who cried, I simply hated the process. It didn't feel like release, just loss of control, and it only made me angrier and more disappointed in myself. I didn't have a clue what I'd done wrong, but I'd surely done something.

I sat upright and pulled my feet from the water. I glanced at my cell phone and was surprised to note it was almost one-thirty in the morning. I stood and brushed myself off before beginning the short jaunt back to the manor.

The fog had thickened while I was on the dock, and it was difficult to see much of anything even fifteen feet ahead of me, although the muted glow from the lampposts provided ghostly guidance where the shore met the property line. As I crossed the path used by the golf carts, my bare foot finally buckled as my arch found the jagged edge of a rock embedded in the dirt. I muttered a few choice obscenities, pulling my foot up to see if I had broken skin. Confirming this wasn't the case, I rubbed my foot before tenderly placing it back on the ground and standing erect.

I froze in my tracks.

A hooded figure stood stock still underneath the phosphorescent glow of the lamppost furthest down the sandy beach. It seemed to be facing my general direction.

A quick proximity check informed me I was about as close to the left side of the manor's massive, covered porch as it was from the right. From what I could tell, the front door remained closed, and all interior lights were still dark.

"Brady?" I called, squinting to no avail. The figure was too large and foreboding to be anyone else—in fact, it seemed a little larger than Brady, as well. I was beginning to feel uneasy.

Silence, save for the chirp of crickets and the lake lazily lapping at the shoreline.

I took a couple of quick steps toward the house, and the figure immediately matched my moves, advancing toward the house from its direction. As I stopped, it did, too.

"C'mon, Brady," I tried again. "This isn't funny."

ISOLATION

I took another step, and watched as the figure deliberately kept pace, freezing in place when I did. It turned slightly, cocking its head as if challenging me to make my next move. The chirp of crickets and lake sounds were now keeping time to the beat of my heart, which was thudding heavily in my chest. I licked my lips and attempted to calculate the distance between each of us and the house. Even a fool could see it was practically a draw. I allowed my eyes to wander to the thing's feet, and even on a fog-shrouded night, I could see the reflection of moonlight against rubber on wading boots that stretched practically to its knees. I looked down at my own bare feet.

Fuck.

I took a deep breath and launched myself toward the house, keenly aware of the menacing figure barreling toward me from the opposite direction.

CHAPTER SIX

I was nearing the porch when two things occurred to me, the most obvious of which was we were bound to arrive at the front door at practically the same instant. The second was I hadn't come outside by way of the main entrance, and it would likely be locked up tight. I went to one knee as I course-corrected, my bare foot sliding forward on the dewy lawn, before regaining my balance and veering toward the darkened patio. Why in the hell had I thought sitting out here in the dark was a good idea?

As soon as I rounded the corner, I lost sight of my assailant, spiking my adrenaline, and providing a much-needed boost. I could have run across a field of razor blades, and my bare feet would've been none the wiser. I couldn't, however, keep myself from flying forward when I tripped over the bottle of Canadian Mist I had left near the patio chair. I went down hard on the semi-circular stone steps that led up and into the kitchen. I gathered myself quickly, sure I would be assaulted at any moment. I pulled myself to my feet by the handle of the storm door, opening it and twisting the knob of the entry door behind it.

It was locked.

Fu-u-u-ck!

I hadn't locked it myself—I was sure of it. I began pounding on the door like a madman, firing off names like a roll call—I think I even threw Dexter into the mix. I nervously glanced toward the front of the house, and there it was. The hooded figure stood at the edge of the patio, its arms splayed as if ready for a gunfight, its head once again slightly cocked, regarding me curiously.

I renewed my efforts, leaning my full weight against the door while pounding on it. My voice was working in a range where no words lived, only sounds of white-hot terror. I was just about to make my peace with God when the door suddenly opened, and I tumbled through.

"Dwayne?" It was Brady, clad in sleep pants and a dark blue robe he wore uncinched over his shirtless torso. He carried what smelled like hot chocolate in a steaming mug, a cannister of whipped cream waiting on the counter. "What the hell, man?"

I scrambled the rest of the way into the kitchen and slammed the door shut, locking it behind me. My eyes darted in every direction as I struggled to breathe normally. "There's someone out there," I gasped, suddenly aware of warm blood flowing down my leg from where I had lacerated my knee on the steps outside.

"What's all the commotion?" I looked up and saw Melanie framed in the open doorway. She was wearing one of my old shirts, and her tousled blonde hair suggested she had been rousted from sleep. "Dwayne—?"

Brady flipped a series of switches beside the door frame, and the exterior lighting sprang to life, casting away shadows that had shrouded the patio and side yard. He reached for the lock, and I grabbed his hand, stopping him. "I'm not kidding," I said. "There's someone out there. Someone—*big*."

Brady looked side to side through the nine-pane glass. "I don't *see* anyone."

"I'm telling you, it was right there." I peered over his shoulder, seeing nothing but a well-lit lawn.

"What was right where?" Doug entered the kitchen, also clad in a dark blue robe that must be standard issue for guests. He also left it uncinched to reveal an off-white, ribbed and stained A-shirt, stretched to its limit over his rounded belly, although unlike Brady, cinching it simply wouldn't have been an option. Below that, he wore a pair of boxer shorts adorned with repeating images of Cupid armed and in flight. He spotted the blood which was now drying on my leg. "What happened to you?"

"Dwayne thinks he saw someone outside," said Brady, and the note of skepticism in his voice wasn't lost on me. Melanie stepped forward and looked over Brady's other shoulder. I could pinpoint the exact second she spotted the bottle of Canadian Mist I had knocked further underneath the table on my mad flight to safety. She shot me a disgusted look, and any concern she might have had completely evaporated. She crossed her arms in front of herself and stepped away from the door.

"I don't *think* I saw someone, I *know* did," I insisted. "It chased me."

The corners of Brady's mouth curled upward. "*It?* Now we have an *it?*"

He reached for the lock again, and once more, I stopped him. "You're not going out there unarmed, are you?" I asked, a fresh wave of panic coursing through me.

"Was *it* armed?" asked Brady.

"Well, no—but it was *big*. And I mean really big. Looked like it could tear you apart with its bare hands."

Brady's smile widened as he tapped his chin and deliberated. "Was it a— *hmm*, I don't know—was it a *Sasquatch?*"

"Fuck off, Brady," I groused as Melanie burst out laughing. "We gave more credence to your dipshit girlfriend's phantom kitten in the basement. At least we went prepared for something worse. All I'm saying is we should do the same here."

"Agreed," barked Doug, pulling a butcher knife from the block on the counter. Again, I grabbed the trusty meat tenderizer, not really sure why bludgeoning seemed more appropriate than filleting. It felt like Brady was mocking me when he chose a serrated bread knife.

"I'll wait here, if you heroes don't mind," said Melanie, leaning against the center island. "You boys will need someone to *not* call 911 once you

ISOLATION

find this has all been the whiskey-soaked delusion of a man who can't tell fact from fantasy."

Wounded, I looked toward her, but she was studying the high ceiling, unwilling to even glance my way.

This time, I didn't prevent Brady from twisting the lock and opening the door. He crept down the steps to the patio in an exaggerated tippy-toe, bread knife held high but upside down, and it took everything I had to keep from using the meat tenderizer on the back of his head. Instead, I pushed him forward, making room for me and Doug to join him.

There was no sign of the hooded figure.

The bright exterior lighting made short work of inspecting the side grounds, and I even peered around the corner of the manor toward the main entrance and the lamppost under which I had first seen it. There was nothing to see.

"Are we done here?" called Brady, scooping up the toppled bottle of whiskey I had left underneath the outdoor table. "I was in the middle of a little something-something when you interrupted."

"*Fine*," I groused, defeated. I knew I hadn't imagined it, but there was no way I would be convincing anyone anytime soon. I grabbed the bottle of whiskey from Brady as well as the shallow glass I had left on the tabletop, and the three of us stepped back up into the kitchen where Melanie waited. She was finally looking in my direction, but only to share her disdain for what I carried in my hands. I rinsed the glass out in the sink and returned the whiskey to the pantry where I had found it.

"Where's Loretta?" Melanie asked Doug. "I'm surprised she slept through all this lunacy. Lord knows, *I* couldn't."

"CPAP," he said gruffly. "She's got the apnea. Can't hear a thing over top of it."

"*Bra-a-a-a-dy*," called Dusty from somewhere near the top of the stairs.

"Yes, kitten?" he cooed in reply, sliding the bread knife back into the block and retrieving his mug of hot chocolate and the can of whipped cream from the counter.

"Can't you find the whipped cream?" she called, her voice affecting a babyish lilt. "Your dirty little Dusty knows just how to put the cherry on top."

Melanie rolled her eyes and pivoted toward the stairs. "You two are so gross. I'm going back to bed."

Doug stood with his mouth hanging open, his cheeks burning a deep crimson red. He was clearly unaccustomed to such overt titillation, and I was loath to imagine the fantasies it might be currently inspiring. He shuffled out of the kitchen awkwardly, his hands shoved deep into the pockets of his robe.

Brady grinned at me and winked, taking a quick shot of whipped cream from the can. "I've got it right here, boo. I'm on my way," he called, sauntering out into the corridor and up the stairs, leaving me behind to ensure the main floor was locked up tight.

*****

Morning came mighty early.

I was surprised I found sleep at all, but I did, still fully dressed and curled up on top of the thick mattress in the guest room next to the one I should have been in. I glanced through squinted eyes at my cell phone, its alarm gently announcing the nine o'clock hour. Bright sunlight spilled through the double doors leading out to my own personal veranda, and I detected the faint but enticing aroma of coffee wafting up from the main floor.

I slid out of bed, crossing the room, and stepped out onto the terrace, which overlooked the patio and side yard below. Melanie, always an earlier bird than me, was already up and seated at one end of the table, a steaming cup of coffee beside her laptop upon which she was busily pecking away. I could only imagine the new source material I had inspired from the previous night's adventure. I backed into my room and closed the doors gently, not particularly wishing to be seen.

I almost felt human after brushing my teeth and standing beneath a cascade of water turned just as warm as I could tolerate. I had neglected to properly tend to the two-inch gash below my right knee before turning in, and dried, crusty blood flecked away and disappeared amidst sudsy water down the drain at my feet in the spacious standing shower stall. I opted for khaki carpenter shorts and an OSU t-shirt that made my chest look more impressive than it was before remembering once again that my shoes were still in Melanie's room. I deliberated a few moments before deciding she would never know if I slipped in to retrieve them. I needn't have worried; I nearly tripped over where she had left them just outside my door. I slipped them on and proceeded downstairs.

Once on the main floor, I caught the unmistakable smell of bacon comingling with the allure of coffee, and I was practically salivating. My eyes followed the delectable aromas to the end of the corridor where I spotted two uniformed women working in tandem to prepare what promised to be a sumptuous breakfast feast.

A set of pocket doors along the same long wall as the formal living room but nearest the kitchen had been opened, revealing a glimpse into the grand dining hall. I spotted Doug standing just inside the door, deep in conversation with an equally height-challenged, balding, middle-aged man I didn't recognize. I followed the smattering of voices and polite laughter drifting my way from down the corridor and stood at the entrance, awestruck at the opulence of the space.

Twin miniatures of the chandelier from the foyer were suspended above each end of a rich, mahogany table fully capable of seating twenty, although only eleven places were set—five on each side, and one at the end furthest from the kitchen. The walls were a continuation of what we had seen in the formal parlor. An enormous fireplace featuring an ornately handcrafted mantel and molding was centered along the side wall, its soot-stained inner hearth cold and dark behind a grate. Dark portraits of unsmiling people, presumably long dead, lined the walls in place of windows, looking down on us as if passing judgment. The overall effect was weirdly claustrophobic, despite the enormity of the room.

It was apparent our other guests had arrived. Near the head of the table, Brady and Dusty were engaged in light-hearted banter with another young couple of our own approximate age. The man was lanky and lean, leaning into the conversation earnestly, his sandy brown hair swept across his forehead and barely extending over the collar of his pale peach polo shirt. The woman standing beside him wore a sleeveless, one-piece dress that accentuated her tanned and toned arms and muscular legs. It was easy to picture her on a tennis court, firing off a scorching serve. The platinum of her shoulder-length hair was an achievement of the sun, and when she laughed, her freckled nose crinkled up over a dazzling smile.

Loretta looked completely miserable seated at the table beside a woman only slightly younger than herself. The woman had piles of frosted auburn hair pinned in curls to the top of her head, and clearly shared a similar fondness for bold, primary colors in her choice of cosmetics. A voluminous paisley cotton blouse struggled to contain her pendulous bosoms but hung just low enough to obscure the camel toe undoubtedly visible in ill-fitting beige yoga pants. She was dominating whatever conversation they were having with exaggerated hand gestures, punctuating it with startlingly loud guffaws that sent Loretta's eyes to the heavens with each ungainly burst. I almost felt sorry for her.

Melanie brushed past me, her laptop underneath her arm just as the grandfather clock in the outer corridor signaled ten o'clock. Without a single glance in my direction, she joined Brady and his party, and I watched rather than heard polite introductions being made.

Another set of pocket doors leading directly into the kitchen slid open along the back wall, and one of the two women I had seen preparing food rolled a cart laden with shiny silver serving platters into the room. She was followed by an elegant young woman wearing a fitted gray pinstriped pantsuit. Her doe-like brown eyes swept the room, taking inventory and nodding at each of us in turn. She needed no cosmetics; her ebony skin was flawless, her hair short and natural. She carried a messenger bag over her shoulder and set it on the floor as she positioned herself behind the captain's chair at the end of the table farthest from us. She leaned forward, retrieving a flute of water and a fork. She clanked the fork against the side of the glass, smiling warmly while looking around the room expectantly.

"If you will all take your seats, please," she said. "We have a marvelous breakfast ready to serve, and an exciting weekend to get underway!" Her smile widened as she clapped enthusiastically, and soon, everyone else joined in the applause. "Let me introduce myself briefly while Maria unloads her goodies onto the table. My name is Anyssa Williams. Welcome to my home!"

More applause while Anyssa beamed at us and Maria unloaded her cart, expertly weaving between guests to evenly spread our bounty before us. I struggled with self-control as a platter of crispy bacon was positioned dangerously within my grasp.

"*Your* home?" asked Melanie. She had chosen a seat across the table and beside Dusty, literally as far away from me as physically possible. "Your note indicated the master bedroom was off limits because it belonged to the owner. So, the owner is—"

"Me," nodded Anyssa. "The manor has been in my family for generations, but it only became mine fairly recently. It still doesn't seem real."

"It's gorgeous—well, at least what I've seen of it," said Melanie.

"Thank you so much! I'm so excited to have you all here," she said. "Please, help yourselves to breakfast. While you are filling your plates, why don't we start with introductions—we can start with you, Miss." Melanie raised her eyebrows, placing a hand on her chest, and Anyssa nodded.

"Sure, since your kind words have already made you my favorite—just your name and a brief little something about yourself."

Melanie cleared her throat. "Melanie McGregor. I'm a single mom—widowed. I'm originally from Lymont but recently moved to Columbus with my eleven-year-old daughter, Jasmine. I'm here as a guest of—" Her eyes flicked to me as she hesitated. "—Doug Boggs Investigations."

"So nice to meet you, Ms. McGregor." Anyssa nodded to Dusty.

"I'm Dusty Rhodes. I'm also from Columbus where I work at Mount Carmel St. Ann's as a nursing assistant. I'm here with this cutie pie, so ladies—keep your hands off!" She draped an arm around Brady's shoulders and emitted a playful peep, but everyone knew she was completely serious.

Anyssa chuckled. "Dusty Rhodes—that's a clever name! I'm guessing you don't spell your last name R-O-A-D-S?"

Dusty looked lost. "I don't get it."

"Never mind," said Anyssa with a quick shake of her head. "Welcome aboard, Ms. Rhodes! Now how about Mr. Cutie Pie?" She winked at Brady, and he lit up like a Christmas tree.

"Brady Garrett, at your service, ma'am," he said, prompting daggers from the eyes of his current plaything.

Anyssa leaned forward against the back of the captain's chair and put a finger to her chin. "Why does your name sound familiar to me?"

"I work for the *Columbus Dispatch* on the crime beat. You might have read my coverage of the serial killer last spring."

"Oh!" Anyssa's eyes widened. "I *did*, but that's not what I'm remembering. You were seriously injured investigating a more recent case."

Brady's chest puffed out as he scowled and nodded. "It's what I do."

I rolled my eyes. As if getting shot repeatedly was a 'special skill.'

"Well, we're glad you're with us this weekend, Mr. Garrett—"

"Please—just call me Brady."

I was losing my appetite almost as quickly as Dusty was losing patience. She slumped back in her chair in a huff while Brady kept Anyssa firmly in his sights.

"All right—Brady. Wow, I never expected we'd have a local celebrity," said Anyssa, fanning herself ever so slightly. She moved on to Loretta, who had just reseated herself after snagging a trio of sausage links from the middle of the table.

"Loretta Boggs, Office Manager, Boggs Investigations," she said briskly, with a nod that set her waddle in motion. She nudged Doug who had taken the seat vacated by her earlier companion in conversation. "This here is my boy, Doug."

Doug looked up, his mouth crammed full of omelet and nodded.

"*Douglas Lee Boggs!*" Loretta barked, appalled. "We haven't even said grace yet!"

"I'm sorry, Ma," he said, chewing diligently. "I didn't want it to get cold."

Anyssa laughed, clasping her hands together. "Well, we wouldn't want *that*, would we? It's perfectly all right, Mrs. Boggs. It's rather cruel of me to have Maria place this feast within arm's reach and then hold you hostage with introductions, yes? How about I say grace so you may eat while we continue?" She scanned the table, and seeing no objections, bowed her head. "Heavenly Father, please bless this food and the hands that prepared it. May this weekend be the beginning of many more to come, with existing friendships strengthened and new friendships formed. Amen."

A ripple of '*Amens*' swept across the table in response.

"Okay!" said Anyssa, her bright eyes twinkling. "Other side of the table—let's start in the back. Go!"

"Rob Jenkins," said the sandy-haired man, sweeping his bangs back across his forehead. "First-year medical student at Case Western in Cleveland."

"Nice to meet you, Mr. Jenkins," Anyssa said with a smile.

"And I'm Kit," the freckled blonde said with a brief wave. "Kit Scarberry, liberal arts freshman at Oberlin. I'm also Rob's fiancée. Rob and I have known each other since about the third grade. We went to school together in Chillicothe, and I've got the pictures to prove it."

"How adorable!" said Anyssa. "Welcome, Ms. Scarberry!"

Next was Loretta's new friend. She took a sip of water and adjusted the curls atop her head, causing her collection of gaudy bracelets to jangle up her arm toward her elbow. "Sandra Poole, but everyone just calls me Sandy. I work part-time as a receptionist for a mortgage company in Reynoldsburg, Residential Mortgage. Maybe you've heard of it? No? Well, of course not. Why would you? It's just a little locally-owned outfit with an office on Brice Road and another—"

"Jesus, Sandy!" interrupted the short, stocky man seated beside her and next to me. "You wanna tell 'em your bra size, too?" He reached over and scooped one of her enormous breasts into his palm and gave it a quick squeeze while everyone at the table looked away uncomfortably.

Sandy blushed and giggled, brushing his hand away but not before emitting a brief snort. "Le-*roy!* Please excuse my husband, everybody. He can be such a rascal!"

Leroy—the man, the myth, the legend—leaned back in his chair with a self-satisfied smirk on his face. "I just calls 'em as I sees 'em, Dollface. Hiya, people, I'm Leroy James Poole, and I'm a financial advisor, self-employed. Normally, I couldn't give two shits about some hoity-toity mystery play-pretend, but Sandy's all revved up seeing as she won our tickets on WNCI, and hey—I'm for anything that's free, right?" His laughter was guttural and vulgar, and I tried to discreetly inch my chair away from him before I caught some of the random spittle escaping his lips.

Even Anyssa's smile had dimmed by degrees. "Well, all right then. Mr. and Mrs. Poole—I hope you enjoy your weekend." She turned to me, more than ready to move on.

"Dwayne Morrow," I said, casually dragging a fork though the sausage gravy and biscuits on my plate. "I'm also here with Boggs Investigations. Apparently, we're trying to learn how to play nicely together." I looped a finger from me to Doug to Loretta and back.

"Dwayne Morrow," Anyssa repeated, connecting inevitable dots now that she had placed who Brady was. "Of course! You worked with Brady on those previous cases!"

"Well, not exactly," I said. "I was already working them, and Brady sort of attached himself like a fungus to me. Every time I turned around, there he was."

Brady threw his head back and laughed. "Now, *Dwayne*. You know how much you rely on my assistance," he said, shaking his head and grinning at Anyssa to indicate I was being less than forthright. I could hardly believe his brazen attempts at flirting with our host while his girlfriend fumed only one chair away. Dusty was by no means bright, but even *she* couldn't miss what Brady was putting out.

"I think you're overestimating yourself, Garrett," I said.

"And I think you're trying to hog the spotlight," he countered. "Without me, you probably would've never solved those other cases."

It was my turn to laugh. "How does nearly getting yourself killed translate to helping me solve a case?" I challenged.

"Well," said Brady, scrambling for a witty reply. "Maybe not in *that* particular instance, but how about last night, huh? How about that?"

"Last night?" Anyssa's curiosity was piqued. "What happened last night?"

"It was nothing," I said, telegraphing a visual cease-and-desist to Brady. "Probably."

"What do you mean, 'probably?'" she persisted.

I sighed, pinching the bridge of my nose. "I was out past my bedtime—"

"*Drunk*," interjected Melanie.

"I was *not* drunk," I said defensively, sending a dirty look that was met with cool nonchalance. "I just—I thought I saw something, that's all."

Anyssa took her seat, leaning in and giving me her full attention. "What did you think you saw?"

I shook my head. "I'm sure it was nothing. Just a trick of the moonlight."

"Tell me."

I laughed sheepishly, making a mental note to make Brady pay for embarrassing me like this. "It was like this big, ominous—I don't know—sort of *hulking* figure. It looked like it was wearing some sort of hooded shirt."

The smile fell completely away from Anyssa's face as she gasped, her hand flying to her mouth and bumping the glass of water beside her plate, spilling its contents down the middle of the banquet table.

Maria appeared in a flash with a dish towel, sopping up the water before it could travel too far.

"What?" I asked, sitting up straight. "What was it?"

Anyssa recovered quickly, her smile returning as she ran a hand through her short hair. She sat back as Maria poured her another glass of water from the pitcher on the table. She returned her attention to me, her brown, almond-shaped eyes twinkling. "As you work in private investigation, I'm guessing you've done a little research into the history of Marble Toe Island, yes?"

I stared at her vacantly, feeling a bit like a student who had forgotten to complete his assignment. "Um, no. Was I supposed to?"

She sighed then chuckled, shaking her head. "Wow. I don't know what to say, then. As many times as I've been here, *I've* never seen it."

It was my turn to persist. "Seen what?"

She shrugged. "It would seem you've met our ghost."

CHAPTER SEVEN

Murmurs erupted around the table, while I examined Anyssa's face for any sign of playful deception. I'd already caught enough shit from my own companions; I wasn't about to take the bait so easily.

"So, you're telling me there's a *ghost?*" I asked incredulously.

"I can only tell you the legend," she said, standing to move once more behind the captain's chair and use it like a podium. Voices trailed off, and she had everyone's attention once again. "As I've said, I've never seen it myself. But your description certainly fits. That's why I assumed you already knew the history of the island. Is *anyone* familiar with the legend? No? Well, then. I was prepared to share the history of the property with you but was undecided on whether I should mention our ghost, but I guess that decision has been made for me. Let me start at the beginning.

"In the mid-1800s, my great-great-great-great-grandfather, Leland, was the youngest son of six children born into the powerful and wealthy Williams family in Lexington, Kentucky. His father died when he was very young—a hunting accident that is its own mystery for another place and time. He was raised by his mother, Amelia, with the assistance of his brothers, sisters, aunts and uncles. The family was well-represented in legislative bodies throughout the state, but most of the family fortune was derived from their stake in the slave markets—and a secret stash of gold buried on the Williams property. The Williams' men never fully trusted in traditional banking. You see, Lexington, along with Louisville, was considered one of the premier slave trade centers of Kentucky, and vast amounts of money changed hands every single day."

Loretta thrust her hand in the air, looking utterly constipated. "But I don't understand. How could your family have made its money selling slaves? I mean, you're—*black*." She whispered this last word as if it were a secret.

Anyssa smiled and pointed to Loretta. "In fact, I am! Very good, Mrs. Boggs! Leland Williams and his immediate family were white as the driven snow, settlers who could be traced back to the original colonists in America. And this is where our story *really* begins.

"On a warm, summer evening in the 1850s, Leland was helping process the latest import of human cattle, herding them into holding pens where they could be cataloged and priced for auction over the weekend. He was struck speechless when he cast eyes upon a young woman struggling to hold her composure amidst the chaos. Make no mistake, this process of 'inventorying' was brutal. They understood what was being done to them, and some fought and were beaten into submission or to death, although that was never the goal. A dead slave held no value. Others cried in terror as they were separated from their loved ones, never to see them again. But this young woman—her name was Mary—she was different. She spoke very little, but there was no denying the fierce intelligence in her eyes. She attempted to fade into the background, absorbing her circumstance and looking for some way—any way—out of it. For Leland, it was love at first sight."

Anyssa paused and smiled.

"And sometimes the way out is the way in," she continued. "Leland's family owned a handful of slaves themselves. They didn't need many, as they weren't working the land like many of their neighbors. Just enough to run the kitchen and perform other household duties, such as laundry, cooking, cleaning and childcare. Leland had never chosen any of the household servants; it was a task left to his eldest brother, Julian. But he wasn't about to let this dark-skinned beauty out of his grasp. He arranged to bring her home with him that evening rather than chance her being sold before he could return in the morning. He brought her in through the servants' entrance and took her directly to his room, where he insisted she sleep in his bed while he stood watch from a chair across the room. He had never seen a woman so beautiful.

"They were awakened in the morning by his mother, Amelia, screaming from the doorway in horror at what she'd found when checking in on her youngest and most favorite son. Leland tried to calm her, imploring his mother to allow him to keep Mary, much like a boy might beg to keep a pet. All the commotion brought Leland's brother, Julian, running. From the doorway, he saw his younger brother on his knees, pleading pathetically with their mother's hands clasped in his own, Amelia's face twisted in anger and revulsion. Julian's eyes drifted to Mary, perched against the headboard of the bed with its comforter pulled up tight beneath her chin. Naturally, he was smitten, too."

Anyssa paused to take a sip of water. The room was still, save for dueling clinks and slurps courtesy of Doug and Leroy. They continued to eat with purpose, as if the title to my grandmother's 'Clean Plate Club' was at stake. In near-perfect synchronicity, Loretta slapped Doug's arm while Sandy urged Leroy's fork to the table. The rest of us remained totally rapt.

"Against her better judgment," Anyssa continued, "Amelia allowed Mary to stay, although under the watchful eye of Julian. Leland was to have no contact with her whatsoever, which naturally broke his heart, and for the first time in his entire life, it eventually inspired defiance. But not before Julian had done as he so often did with the servant girls he found most attractive. Not even a fortnight passed before he forced himself on her in the back of the horse stables. Mary fought with everything she had, but it only infuriated Julian, who proceeded to beat her within an inch of her life.

And as she lay there, swollen and bleeding, he persisted in violating her while she screamed and cried helplessly."

"My God," said Melanie, a hand fluttering to her mouth as her eyes widened with horror.

Anyssa nodded. "Yes. Julian's wife, Diana, was fully aware of what went on, but she turned a blind eye, focusing instead on raising their children and preserving her own social status. In fact, it wasn't even uncommon. These weren't *women*—they were *property*."

"Outrageous," said Rob, sitting back in his chair.

"Yes, well, Leland most certainly agreed with your assessment, Mr. Jenkins," said Anyssa. "When he saw what his brother had done to Mary, he was furious. He confronted Julian at the marketplace, threatening him if he ever laid a hand on Mary again. Julian's response was predictably violent. He was a large man, hulking and formidable. He assured Leland he would do as he damn well pleased with Mary, but not before breaking Leland's nose in a public beating that set tongues wagging in the community. Humiliated and desperate, Leland again begged Amelia to allow him to care for Mary, and while I believe her love for her favorite son may have given her a moment of uncertainty, ultimately, she couldn't shake her disdain at the thought of her son's infatuation with someone who, to her, was little more than an animal. She *did* have strong words for Julian for his treatment of his youngest brother, but Julian remained unrepentant. He believed it was his right to assert dominance, acting as man of the house ever since his father's unfortunate—accident. In fact, he was *so* enraged that Leland had essentially gone 'running to Mama,' he decided to make his point crystal clear.

"Waiting just long enough for Mary to heal and be returned to her normal duties, Julian cornered her once again in the horse stables. He had her trapped among bales of hay, already loosening his belt and making his intentions clear when Leland walked in behind him. What Julian didn't realize was his youngest brother had been watching him, too, and this time, he came prepared.

"Julian turned at the sound of the first gunshot, feeling the searing pain in his shoulder blade but unable to reconcile the obvious. He opened his mouth to demand an explanation just as Leland pulled the trigger again, shooting his brother in the face and dropping him like a stone."

Dusty gasped, starting visibly while the rest of us absorbed the inevitable outcome of the brothers' short feud. Nobody had any delusions it could ever end well.

"Leland took Mary and ran," said Anyssa, sitting back in her chair. "What choice did he have?"

"Surely, the police would see there were extenuating circumstances," said Kit, nudging her plate aside, her appetite gone.

Anyssa scoffed. "This was *murder!* And all over a piece of *property!* No, there would be no mercy—no leniency for Leland. He left his mother behind to deal with the stain of controversy besmirching the family name and bereft at losing not just one, but two sons, neither of whom could she give a proper goodbye. Julian's face had been ruined by the bullet that took his life; his funeral was closed casket. Leland disappeared into the night, taking Mary north across the Ohio River, and settling for a while under assumed names in the woods of Indiana. He kept Mary safe, and he kept her to himself, unwilling to take another chance their growing love might be hampered again by ignorance and prejudice. She was thirsty for knowledge, so he brought her whatever books he could lay his hands on, reading to her until she eventually learned to read and write herself. By summer, she was pregnant with their first child, and for a time, they were very happy.

"But happiness is short-lived when you're on the run. By winter, whispers of Leland's whereabouts began to trickle back to interested parties in Lexington, and soon, a band of vigilantes was dispatched to locate the fugitive and return him to answer for his crime. But Leland had made a valuable connection in his time in Indiana, befriending a man who was sympathetic to his situation, even if Leland didn't realize it at the time.

"Joshua Appleby ran the local general store and was Leland's point of contact for trading goods and services. He was also actively involved with the Underground Railroad, helping escaped slaves reach safety in Canada. Joshua completely understood how fractious the issue of slavery was becoming, and as such, kept his own strong feelings to himself. He was a more effective ally hiding in plain sight. But as proprietor of the only trading post in the small village, he knew about the men as soon as they arrived in town in search of Leland and his stolen bride. He also learned the truth about the young man he had grown to admire and respect in the short time he had known him.

"It only took a bit of misdirection to send these men on a wild goose chase, giving Joshua a chance to warn Leland, providing him and his pregnant wife with basic supplies before sending them to a trustworthy contact with the Underground Railroad in the next county. They headed northeast through Ohio toward the Wilson Bruce Evans House in Oberlin. From there, they would catch a transport ship across Lake Erie to Niagara Falls, eventually crossing into Canada. The journey was difficult, to say the least. Bitter cold and frequent snowfall slowed progress, not to mention by then, Mary was heavily pregnant.

"On the final leg of that journey, as they crossed Lake Erie toward Buffalo, a fierce blizzard descended upon the ship shortly after it had set sail at dusk. With near zero visibility, the ship's captain sought a safe haven in which to ride the storm out. What he found was this," said Anyssa, smiling and indicating everything around her. "Marble Toe Island. Uninhabited and undeveloped, it provided a place to drop anchor until the storm eventually passed. Leland, Mary, and several others who were traveling with them were initially quite relieved. That is, until Mary went into labor.

"Her labor lasted a full forty-eight hours, far longer than the raging storm, which petered out by morning. Fortunately, one of their fellow passengers had acted as midwife on more than one occasion for her former master, and she stayed by Mary's side as the ship's captain made the risky decision to remain docked. He was concerned about the ice forming across the Great Lake's surface and understood the perils of traveling in such conditions. Mary eventually gave birth to a healthy baby boy, my great-great-great-grandfather, Abraham. He was named after a young up-and-coming Congressman from Illinois of whom you've probably heard."

"Abraham Lincoln," I said softly.

"That's right," confirmed Anyssa. "They remained docked for almost two weeks, their food supply running dangerously low before they were able to resume their journey. But they reached their destination without further incident and spent the next several years building a modest life together in a small Canadian village near Niagara. They had three more children! Another boy and two girls. It was only just before the American Civil War that their fortunes would once again change.

"Back in Lexington, the Williams family wasn't faring so well. Amelia, having lost her favorite son as well as the one upon whom she relied to run the family business, slipped into a deep depression, relying on alcohol to ease her constant sorrow. The remaining siblings, two men and two women, had never expressed any interest in the family business and were completely ill-equipped to manage it. They squandered both opportunities and resources until the family was nearly destitute, although none of them were privy to the secret stash of gold their late father had hidden on the property. It was something Amelia had only shared with Julian, as the new man of the house, and Leland, because as her favorite, she shared nearly everything with him. As rumblings of war threatened the family's very livelihood, Amelia became increasingly untethered, swept away in a sea of dementia. She couldn't remember the names of the faces surrounding her but asked frequently about Julian and Leland, unable to recall why her two boys were no longer at her disposal. On a lonely winter night, much like the one on which her grandson whom she would never meet was born, she wandered out to the horse stables, a bottle of Kentucky's finest bourbon clutched against her chest. She was found the next morning, blue lips frozen in a silent scream and wide sightless eyes, empty whiskey bottle by her side."

We sat in collective silence, moved by a tragedy so personal to our host. Eventually, I broke the silence, asking, "But how does that explain all this?" I indicated the luxurious accommodations surrounding us.

Melanie gasped. "The *gold!*"

Anyssa's smile widened, and she clapped her hands. "You are all *very* good! I see why you work so well together!"

I tried to catch Melanie's eyes across the table, but she quickly looked away.

"Leland remained in contact with Joshua Appleby long after he and Mary had made their great escape," Anyssa resumed. "And Joshua's contacts were many. When he learned of Amelia's fate, he felt it only right to pass the news along to his friend. Even the most contentious of relationships needed closure, even if it's only one-sided. And Leland did, in fact, grieve. He grieved for the mother he had known, a kind but sheltered woman who knew only what she had been taught. He firmly believed she would have had the capacity to eventually accept Mary had she been given the opportunity, but Julian had ruined all of that for everyone. His loathing for his brother only intensified, but it was a full month before he recalled the secret shared by only him and his deceased mother and brother. And it wasn't just the allure of personal wealth that motivated Leland. He intended to repay the kindness that had granted freedom to himself and his beloved Mary. After several weeks of intense planning, he set back out to the States, accompanied by Joshua and a few of his trusted comrades. Word of the attack on Fort Sumter in Charleston, South Carolina, had spread, and the men hid under cover of chaos and uncertainty, traveling back to Lexington and the once-grand property formerly owned by the Williamses. Leland knew exactly where to take them, a wooded section at the farthest edge of the vast property. Under the light of a full moon, the men exhumed as much treasure as they could possibly carry, heading north before the sun rose in the eastern sky. They traveled without incident, returning home but not before Leland shared his bounty with those who helped him retrieve it. There was plenty to share. With what remained, he purchased this island and built the place we now inhabit, a port in a storm for anyone seeking shelter. He and Mary lived the rest of their days here, long after the war ended. In fact, they are buried in a small cemetery near the middle of the island."

"So, what about the ghost?" asked Kit.

Anyssa seated herself once more in the captain's chair. "Ah, yes. The ghost. As you may recall, I told you Mary was very intelligent. Her thirst for secular knowledge was quite consuming, but she was also very spiritual. She believed those who had passed without some sense of closure were capable of manifesting in one form or another in our realm. A fleeting shadow on the wall, an inexplicable orb of light in a photograph, a sudden icy chill permeating the room—all examples of typical manifestations. Unsettling, yes, but ultimately innocent. Some whose lives ended unexpectedly and as a result of extreme violence seemed capable of presenting with a more tangible malevolence. Mary believed Julian was one such spirit.

"Throughout the years, she claimed to have seen Julian on multiple occasions and in a variety of places, but always on this island. The first time was shortly after construction of the manor house had been completed. She was carrying linens to the second floor when she had the sudden sensation of being watched. She looked up and spotted his hooded form waiting for her at the top of the stairs. It startled her so badly, she dropped the bed sheets and tumbled down the stairs, fracturing her arm. Leland came running at the sound of her scream, but by the time he arrived, the apparition had disappeared."

"Whatever I saw last night was wearing some sort of hood," I interjected.

"So, you said," Anyssa nodded. "And that's consistent with all of the other sightings throughout the years. It is believed he wore a hood to cover his ruined face—to look upon it could drive a person mad."

"You would think he would want to show himself and spread hysteria," said Melanie.

"I think it may have been a matter of simple vanity," said Anyssa. "Julian was a ruggedly handsome man, and he used it to his full advantage. It likely pained him to see what had become of his own face—if he was even capable of seeing his own reflection. I don't know how these things work. But Mary had no doubt it was Julian based on his build, his stance. She had become intimately familiar with his demeanor during her short time in his charge."

"Did Leland ever see him?" asked Kit.

"Oh, yes," said Anyssa. "Several times, and his sudden appearance always seemed planned for maximum effect, an effort to invoke chaos or cause harm, although Mary's broken arm was the most damage he actually managed to achieve. Sightings weren't limited to Leland and Mary. Several of their children, grandchildren and guests reported contact throughout the years. But once Leland and Mary had passed, the sightings became increasingly less frequent and more something told around a late-night campfire. In fact, Mr. Morrow, your sighting is the first I've heard in—I can't even remember how long."

This wasn't particularly a distinction I wished to claim. I'm up for a good ghost story as much as the next guy, but nobody here had seen what I saw. Whatever it was certainly *seemed* substantial, and there was no mistaking its threatening intentions as it attempted to cut me off at the pass. I was acutely aware of the stinging lacerations under my right knee. I found it hard to believe they were the result of some spectral menace.

"So, you're telling me this isn't part of our mystery weekend," I stated more than asked.

"Not at all!" exclaimed Anyssa. "As I told you earlier, I had always planned to share the history of this place and how it eventually came to be mine, but I was honestly leaning *against* sharing its paranormal reputation. I didn't want to take away from the experience we have planned for you. In fact, I'm a little perturbed at Julian's timing." Her laughter was a bit uneasy.

"I don't like this," whined Dusty, tucking herself tightly against Brady. "I wasn't sure how I felt about this whole thing to begin with, but now—"

"*Shhh,*" Brady soothed while sending a not-so-discreet wink to Anyssa. "I won't let anything happen to you."

"Do you promise?"

"Of course, kitten."

"And obviously, no one is being forced to stay," added Anyssa. "Participation is entirely voluntary. If you'd prefer to return to the mainland, our transport will be heading back around two o'clock. While I'd rather everyone remain, I should point out it will be the last opportunity to leave the island until the boat returns Monday morning." I couldn't tell if her smile was for Dusty or Brady; our host seemed to be falling victim to Brady's inexplicable charm.

"I'll stay," said Dusty, putting an arm protectively around her date. Apparently, she sensed a threat in the air, as well.

"Good," nodded Anyssa, standing and clasping her hands together. She looked at the mostly untouched plates around the table. "Now, look what I've done. I've kept you from your breakfasts, and I'm sure your food has grown cold. Maria? Would you clear the plates and ask Constance to bring some fresh ones? Thank you so much. Please—let's try this again, and I'll keep quiet, I promise. The food on the covered serving trays should still be quite warm but do let me or Maria know if that isn't the case. Once you're finished, we'll discuss the specifics of our mystery weekend and how your complete cooperation is essential if our experience is to be successful."

Quiet conversation crept around the table as Maria and Constance cleared and reset the place settings. Melanie engaged in conversation across the way with Rob and Kit, while Brady continued to soothe his agitated plaything. Dusty seemed less sure of her commitment to stay than she was only moments before. Doug was loading yet another plate with scrambled eggs and sausage gravy while Loretta reminded him he had eaten practically everything on his first go-around and should leave some for the rest of us. Directly beside me, Leroy was soundly dismantling his wife's bright-eyed excitement about the resident ghost, assuring her only an idiot could believe such foolishness, much less feel threatened by it. To whom he was referring wasn't lost on me, and it took a considerable amount of self-restraint to keep from sticking him with a fork. With no one nearby I wished to engage in conversation, I felt completely orphaned. Melanie was deliberately avoiding my gaze, and her cold shoulder was starting to make me belligerent. After all, *I* should be the one who was upset. I certainly hadn't called *her* a big mistake. I dragged my fork around my plate, forcing myself to eat although I really wasn't feeling it.

After Maria and Constance had once again cleared the table, pouring coffee for anyone interested, Anyssa clinked her fork against her water glass, quieting the room.

"As I may have briefly mentioned, this spectacular house and beautiful island upon which it stands have now been passed down to me. I spent most of my teenage summers here as the guest of my Aunt Mavis and Uncle Simon, its previous owners. They never had any children of their own and always treated me as if I was their own daughter. Most of the family fortune belonged to my aunt and uncle, my father having fallen out with my grandfather over, of all things, his choice for a bride. My mother is white, and *yes*—I see the hypocrisy. But race relations are nothing in this country if not needlessly complicated. Uncle Simon offered to split the inheritance with my father, but Dad was a proud man and wanted no part of it. There were no hard feelings between the two brothers, however, and our families were always close.

"A little over five years ago, Aunt Mavis was diagnosed with an aggressive form of cancer, and shortly after that, Uncle Simon began to exhibit signs of dementia. So much of their money went toward care and medical expenses. Aunt Mavis passed away last fall and Uncle Simon this past spring. While I am extremely honored they saw fit to bequeath all of this to me, as you might imagine, maintaining it all is rather costly. I've consulted several financial advisors, all of whom assure me my best option is to sell the house and its land. I would likely never have to work again, but I simply cannot stand the thought of losing this piece of family history, and that is precisely why we are here.

"This is a trial run for a new type of mystery weekend. Most events like ours are restricted to just a few hours. Ours will be held every other weekend, running Saturday through Monday at a cost of $2,500 per guest—we're still fine-tuning the details. This weekend we aim to learn what works and what doesn't, and that is why we have invited you all here, free of charge and as my guests. The only thing that I must absolutely insist upon is complete and total cooperation from each of you if this is to work."

Anyssa pulled a stack of stapled papers from her messenger bag and a handful of pens. She handed me half and Doug the other half. "If you would be so kind as to take a packet and pass the rest down," she said.

"What are these?" I asked, doing as she requested.

She shrugged. "There's a release and indemnity agreement as well as non-disclosure agreement for each of you to sign. It's just a formality, really. But anyone who refuses to sign either document will be traveling back to the mainland with our ferryman."

Her eyes scanned the room as we began to flip through the pages, a wave of disgruntled murmurs spreading as we struggled to comprehend the legalese upon which our stay was contingent.

For the first time, the warm smile dropped from Anyssa's face. "Sorry—there will be no exceptions."

CHAPTER EIGHT

As the discontented grumbling gained volume, Rob and Kit signed without question. Melanie reached out to prevent their forms from sliding back to Anyssa at the head of the table.

"What are you doing?" she asked them. "You couldn't have possibly read these already."

"We didn't come all this way just to turn around and go home," said Rob, wresting the papers free and sending them on their way. "What's the big deal?"

Dusty was now officially in tears, clinging to Brady's arm. "If I sign these, does it mean I agree to be killed?"

Exasperated, Melanie turned toward Dusty, her eyes wide. She gestured toward the other woman. "Exactly *how* are you a nurse, can someone please explain that to me?!"

"A nursing *aide*," corrected Dusty, defensively. "And it wasn't easy."

"Now, *that* I believe," said Melanie.

"C'mon, Mel, knock it off," said Brady, but even he was having difficulty keeping a straight face. He tucked Dusty against his chest and sent an apologetic look toward our host, who nodded appreciatively.

Beside me, Sandy was also on the verge of tears, prevented from signing her documents by her husband, who was currently ranting about how outrageous this whole thing was. "Bait and switch! *Bait and switch!* That's all this is. Get us all the way out here and change up the rules."

"I'm not sure you understand what bait and switch means—" I began, shielding myself as best as I could from the frequent spittle flying from Leroy's flapping yapper.

"Did I ask your opinion?" he snapped at me. "Why—I oughta *sue!*"

"I think that's exactly what she's trying to prevent," I added, defiantly determined to opine away.

"I don't give a good goddamn what you think!" He puffed his chest out like he was preparing to square off against me, pushing Sandy right over the edge. She erupted into sobs, begging Leroy to calm down.

I rolled my eyes and shifted my attention across the table. Doug had neglected to surrender his plate and continued to shovel food into his mouth with vigor, completely oblivious to the chaos erupting around him. Loretta had her tortoiseshell horn-rimmed glasses perched on the tip of her nose, lips moving as she followed her finger along the text in the documents. She didn't seem particularly outraged.

Suddenly, the room was startled into silence by an ear-splitting whistle as Brady moved to Anyssa's side and placed a finger and a thumb in the corners of his mouth and let 'er rip. Our host hugged herself tightly, clearly upset and caught off guard by the group's negative reaction.

"People, people, *people!* What is *wrong* with you?" Brady demanded, handing his own signed documents to Anyssa. "After inviting us into her lovely home and providing such a wonderfully *fun* opportunity—and just look at this breakfast! We should at least give Ms. Williams a chance to speak, don't you think?"

The loud complaints subsided into disgruntled murmurs. Brady had successfully managed to take the temperature of the room down a few degrees. Anyssa laid a hand on Brady's arm, her gratitude apparent. She took a deep breath, regaining her composure and chuckling lightly.

ISOLATION

"*Whew!* As I mentioned just moments ago, we're here to learn what works and what doesn't. I think I've just figured out the first thing that *doesn't*. I should have sent this paperwork to you prior to your arrival on the island so you would have had a chance to look it over at your leisure. I honestly didn't mean for you to feel ambushed—it really never occurred to me. The release is essentially the same as what you'd find at any theme park when riding the rides. It says you will not hold us responsible for damages beyond our control or acts of God. The second is to protect the concept of our mystery weekends and calling it a 'non-disclosure agreement' is really a misnomer. I *absolutely* want you to talk about your weekend! Spread the word far and wide! Word of mouth could do a great deal to ensure the success of this place! What I *don't* want is for specifics of the mystery to be divulged, especially to someone working undercover for a rival company. It might seem overly cautious, but industrial espionage is a real thing, even in this line of work. We currently have a fairly limited number of scenarios, so we will be reusing the successful ones while retiring and replacing ones we feel don't perform as well. And truthfully, I can no more prevent you from oversharing than I can stop someone from spoiling a good movie when exiting a theater. I just hope you will understand what I'm trying to do here and act in good faith." She held her hands out, palms up, in supplication.

"There's nothing complicated about the wording at all," said Loretta, shaking her head as she finished the last of the documents. "I don't have a problem signing off." She followed up by doing exactly that.

It was good enough for Doug, too, who had finally pushed his plate away after what I could only guess was four servings. He took the pen from his mother and signed his own paperwork.

"Please, by all means, take your time," said Anyssa. "I am *not* trying to rush you. But I must have them signed before the ferry heads back to the mainland at two. If I'm selective about compliance, I open myself up to another whole area of liability."

I was already signing mine. As much I doubted Loretta's capabilities in oh-so-many areas, her ability to construct and interpret contract language was pretty much proven. In fact, it was her fancy footwork that had me currently tethered to a financial stake in Boggs Investigations' ability to survive in the Columbus market. You might think this alone would cause me to pore over the documents in great detail, but I sensed no deception in Anyssa's words. I preferred to believe that except for a select few exceptions, I was a pretty good judge of character.

"So, what do you say, Dusty?" asked Brady, still at Anyssa's side.

Dusty sniffed and pouted, shifting from side-to-side. She pointed toward Melanie. "I'll sign if *she* signs."

Melanie flinched. "*Me?* Why *me?*"

"I trust you," Dusty said simply.

After some exasperated floundering, Melanie grabbed the pen. "*Fine. For shit's sake!*" She handed the pen to Dusty after sending her signed paperwork down the table with unnecessary flourish. With intense concentration, Dusty did the same.

That only left Leroy and Sandy, and the set of Leroy's jaw assured everyone he wasn't ready to play nice quite yet.

Realizing as much, Anyssa nodded her head. "All right, then. Let's see—it's almost eleven-thirty now. Let's reconvene here at one o'clock to go over the particulars about our mystery." She turned her attention to Leroy and Sandy. "Please, take your time and go over the papers, but you'll need to make your decision by then. Fair enough?"

The scowl on Leroy's face suggested nothing was ever fair enough, but he simply grunted. He marched out into the hallway with the documents clutched in his fist, Sandy clinging to his other arm and pleading the whole while. I could only imagine dinner at the Poole house—*yikes!*

Rob and Kit followed, smartly opting for the opposite direction once out in the hall.

Anyssa took Brady's hand, smiling at him. "Thank you so much for calming things down, Brady. I certainly didn't anticipate a reaction like that."

Brady caressed her fingers with an 'aww-shucks' grin, and I sensed rather than saw the burning embers of jealousy setting Dusty on fire. She grabbed Melanie by the hand. "Come on, girlfriend. Let the boys figure this shit out without us. Let's discuss strategy."

"Wait—*what?*"

It was all Melanie had time for before she was practically dragged from the room.

Anyssa dropped her face into her hands, hugging herself and laughing. "Oh, wow," she said. "I think someone is in a little trouble."

"Oh, it's nothing," Brady assured her, although I was fairly confident she was completely correct. He looked at me. "I guess it's you and me, man. Just like old times."

I sighed and shook my head.

Awesome.

*****

We stepped out onto the patio into a bright, cloudless day. The sun was high in a brilliant blue sky, the temperature still suitable for short sleeves despite a slight breeze drifting in across the lake's surface. The cool air and open space were refreshing after a lengthy breakfast in a windowless room which had turned both volatile and claustrophobic.

I didn't see any sign of our fellow guests as Brady and I retraced my steps across the lawn and down toward the boathouse. The memory of being chased seemed ridiculous in the light of day, but whatever it was, it hadn't been a dream.

"Looks like you've got a little thing for our host," I observed, stepping out onto the wooden dock.

He grinned like a goon. "I think she might have a little thing for me, too. Did you see the way she was looking at me?"

"*Everyone* saw the way you were looking at each other," I said. "Including your date. What's the deal, man? Don't get me wrong, you've already had more patience with Dusty than I could have ever managed, but don't you think you're kinda rubbing her nose in it?"

"Hey, I didn't expect Anyssa to be such a smokin' hot babe," he said. "I thought I held back pretty well."

I laughed and shook my head. Brady's lack of self-awareness was astonishing at times.

We had reached the edge of the slip within which this morning's ferry was anchored. It was a significant upgrade from the pontoon we had arrived in the previous day, freshly painted with sparkling chrome rails and fixtures. I didn't see any sign of its skipper but assumed it had to be someone other than our cantankerous Captain Jack. There was nary a crushed beer can in sight. We kicked our shoes off and sat at the edge of the dock, dangling our feet into the cool lake water.

"So, what did you do that's got Melanie so pissed off?" he asked, squinting against the sun. "I mean, I've seen her mad at you before, but—"

"I don't want to talk about it," I said, chewing on my bottom lip, yet replaying the events of the previous evening in my mind. Each time I did, I only felt more justified in my response. I looked up and realized Brady was still studying me.

"You look like you lost your best friend," he said, matter-of-factly. "Come on. You can talk to me. It might help."

I sighed. I supposed it couldn't hurt. "I really don't know what happened," I said, staring out over the open water. "I thought things were going pretty well, but I guess I was wrong. I think she's done with me."

"Well, that's kind of *sudden*, don't you think? I mean, just last week, you were hosting a dinner party together. Her kid has a room at your house.

You finish each other's sentences so often I can barely follow you, and it's gross."

I shrugged. "I don't know, Brady." I looked at him. "She called me her latest mistake."

"Wow," he said, leaning back and propping himself up on his palms. "That's harsh."

I nodded earnestly, pointing at what he'd said. Harsh, indeed!

"She actually *said* that? 'Latest mistake?'"

"Well—not exactly *said*. She had written it down."

Brady's eyebrows knitted together in confusion. "Wait a minute, let me get this straight—is this some new thing your therapist has recommended? Passing notes instead of arguing verbally?"

I scowled at him. "No part of us is in therapy. Not me, not she, not *we*—"

"Then help me out here," said Brady. "You were talking to each other in the car, so this clearly happened after we got to the island. It's not like she had time or the means to send you a 'Dear Dwayne' letter—oh God. She didn't send it in a *text*, did she? I *hate* it when girls use technology—"

"And actual *words*."

"—against me." He shot me a dirty look. "Rude. Now, *explain*, please."

I pulled my feet out of the water and stood, pacing the dock. "I'm sure you've heard Melanie mention her interest in writing."

"Yeah," said Brady. "Children's stories, I think. She mentioned something in passing about submitting one to some contest."

I placed my pace on pause, scowl deepening. Melanie hadn't mentioned anything to *me* about entering a contest. I hated it when Brady knew more about my own girlfriend than I did—or ex-girlfriend—or *whatever* she was now.

"Well, she's been working on something new, and it's sure not a children's story." I shuddered as the recollection lit me on fire all over again. I was suddenly flying air quotes and using a tone abrasive even to my own ears. "*'My Latest Mistake, Morons Who've Fucked Me Over'*—or some such shit. I don't know if it's supposed be semi-autobiographical or some sort of survival guide, but there's a Daryl in there and a Mac, too, and it doesn't take very much to realize she's talking about me and her late husband, Ryan. She described me as—dumb."

"*Well—*"

"Shut up, Brady!" Tinges of red nibbled at the corners of my vision, and I valiantly resisted the urge to shove him into the lake. "It was—hurtful."

Brady pulled his own feet from the water and pivoted toward me, sitting lotus style while rubbing the bridge of his nose. "This still isn't making much sense," he said. "So, knowing we had the entire three-day weekend ahead of us, Melanie decided *now* was a good time to spring this, this—whatever this story is on you?"

"Well, not *exactly*," I hedged.

Brady stared at me expectantly.

"She was working on her laptop in the car with the screen sort of turned away," I said. "She got a little testy when I tried to sneak a peek. Said she didn't want me to read it until she was ready."

"Uh-huh," Brady nodded. "Go on."

"She was in the shower when I went up to our room last night, and her laptop was open on the desk. I didn't *set out* to look—but it was right there."

"You couldn't have possibly read very much if she was in the next room."

"Well, no, but enough—and then she was standing behind me, all pissed off. *I* should be the one pissed off! You should've *seen* what she wrote in that—"

"Sentence?"

"Paragraph," I defiantly corrected, hands on hips.

Brady dropped his head into his hands, laughter slowly building. "Oh, my Lord, Morrow. You really *are* a moron. Is Melanie like your very first girlfriend—*ever?*"

"I went with Angie Turner my freshman and sophomore years, and I had dates for both of my proms," I said, loathing how defensive I sounded. "Okay, Marcia Burton was my mom's friend's daughter, but I dated Marcy Clevenger almost my entire senior year."

"And when you say, 'dated,' do you mean—?" I don't have words to describe the lewd pantomime he launched into, but I'm sure my face reflected my revulsion.

"We were just *kids*, Brady," I said. "We grabbed pizza and a movie on weekends, talked a bunch on the phone, sang together at Bible school—"

"*Bible school?* I didn't think you cared much for organized religion."

"I was invited by Marcy's parents, and—" I shook my head, cutting myself off. "What *difference* does it make?"

"That isn't a real relationship," said Brady. "That's barely puppy love. Do you know how many girls I'd been with by the time senior prom rolled around?"

"I'm guessing just a few more than the number of times you had to be seen in the free clinic—am I close? I mean, excuse me, but I never looked at my journey to adulthood as a race to chlamydia."

Brady grinned, waggling a finger at me. "Good one!"

"And talking to you is supposed to be *helpful?*" I turned, grabbing my shoes and heading toward the sandy beach. "Fuck you, Garrett. I'm sorry I even tried."

"Wait!" said Brady, springing to his feet and catching me by the arm. "Look—my point is, I've learned something from every single one of my relationships, and most times, it's something *I've* done wrong. With Mel, you're so caught up feeling sorry for yourself that you're missing the entire point!"

"And what might that point be?" I turned around to face him, still debating the merits of pushing him into the lake.

Brady threw his arms up in exasperation. "You invaded her privacy! She clearly didn't want you to look, and yet you did!"

"But how does that excuse what she's written? I mean, it *certainly* wasn't the children's story I expected."

"Did she ever once *say* it was a children's story?" challenged Brady, crossing his arms in front of his chest.

I thought back to my earlier conversation with Melanie in the car. "Well—*no,* but—"

"But nothing! How about you tell me something she actually *did* say?"

I scowled and took a deep breath, trying to recall the conversation in its entirety and not just the selective version that savagely wounded my pride. "She said she didn't want me to read it until it was finished, and—"

My breath caught in my throat, and I squeezed my eyes shut as her words came back to me.

"And?" urged Brady.

"She promised it wasn't anything bad." The words came out quietly and in a rush as the tips of my cheeks began to burn.

"Admittedly, I haven't known Melanie quite as long as you have, but I've never known her to lie," he continued. "In fact, at times she can be painfully direct. Do you think she's lying now?"

I shook my head. "But why would she *write* that?"

"You have no *idea* what she's writing," he said, slipping his feet back into his shoes. "I'm guessing she isn't exactly sure, either, and that's why she isn't ready to show it to you."

I wanted to believe him, but I couldn't completely shake my doubts, and it must have shown clearly on my face.

"Listen," he continued. "I'm a writer, too. I do it for a living. Sure, Pulitzer Prize-worthy journalism is a lot different than whatever it is Mel is doing—"

I groaned at his abundance of narcissism.

"—but I don't care what kind of writer you are, no one wants to have their work seen before it's ready. You might be surprised to learn I've taken a crack at fiction before, sat in on a workshop or two. That shit ain't easy.

Original ideas are hard enough to come up with let alone flesh out. The workshops teach you to write what you know. It supposedly helps you connect emotionally with your readers."

"Yeah? Did that work for you?" I asked.

"Hell if I know," he grinned. "I never could make it past the 'original idea' stage. Everything I came up with was basically lifted from something I'd seen on TV. But fiction just ain't my thing. Let's assume Mel's using elements of her own life as a framework for this story she's trying to tell. She's already asked you to back off once politely. But here you come again, great big dumbass that you are, sticking your nose back into her unfinished story—a story that even *she* might not know the ending—and by God, one paragraph in, you've got it all figured out! And I may be going out on a limb I have no business being on, but after everything Mel has done for you since you got back from West Virginia, the way you're acting is just stupid and hugely disrespectful."

My jaw muscles clenched and unclenched as I struggled for words, but nothing came. I could feel the hot shame intensifying in my cheeks as I recognized the truth in Brady's words.

"*Shit,*" I finally managed.

Brady nodded, clapping me on the shoulder. "That's right, my friend, and you have stepped squarely in the middle of it. The question is, what are you going to do about it?"

I had no fucking idea! While I didn't want to admit it, Brady was pretty accurate in his assessment of my romantic past. The few real relationship issues I'd ever navigated had been with Melanie, and they usually involved her slapping me in the face to make me see the error of my ways. This was different; she had never turned me away before. It felt like the ball was completely in her court, and any wrong move on my part would only make things worse. I could only shake my head.

"Let me give you a hint," said Brady. "*Apologize*. Unequivocally. No ifs, ands or buts. Any attempt to justify yourself will only make it worse."

I nodded slowly, dropping my shoes back onto the deck and slipping my feet into them. "Thanks, Brady."

He put an arm around my shoulders as we headed back toward the manor. "Glad I could help."

"And while we're being all analytical, can I make a suggestion to you?" I asked.

"Sure. What's that?"

"Watch how you're acting around Anyssa," I said. "I get the attraction, I do, but you brought Dusty here as your guest. I'm not even gonna pretend that I like her all that much, and I'm sure your 'relationship'—" The air quotes flew from my fingers entirely involuntarily. "—will run its course soon enough, but she doesn't deserve this sort of humiliation."

"Fair enough," he nodded. "I will do my very best."

I looked at him doubtfully.

"*Okay!*" he laughed. "I'll do better than my best. Now, let's get back up to the house and find out how this whole mystery thing works. Hey! If we get back before Mel and Dusty, I might have a chance to slip Anyssa my number, you think?"

He waggled his eyebrows and broke into a run. I couldn't help but grin.

CHAPTER NINE

Anyssa stood behind the captain's chair once more, smiling warmly at us as we settled back into our seats around the table. "Please help yourselves to coffee. Maria brewed a fresh pot and brought some delicious pastries," she said, indicating a sideboard along the long wall behind Doug and Loretta.

I was surprised to see Sandy and Leroy already seated at the table as Brady and I entered the room. Apparently, Sandy had successfully convinced her husband to sign off on the documents, although his expression suggested it was under extreme duress. Sandy was all smiles, though, bright-eyed and flushed, ready to begin our game.

Melanie's pained expression was impossible to miss as she remained hostage to her new best friend. Dusty had scooted her chair closer, putting herself practically into Melanie's lap. Apparently, she had cast aside her fear of being legally murdered so she might rescue Melanie from the obvious missteps she made on the daily regarding her skincare. She breathlessly spouted beauty regimens, most of which included inventive use of exotic fruits and/or animal secretions. Melanie's face suggested murder wasn't off the table quite yet, be it legal or otherwise. I tried to catch her eye, but she was too busy attempting to extricate herself and reattach Brady to his date to even look my way.

Doug dabbed at the glob of jelly that had oozed from the backside of his doughnut and onto his flannel shirt with a dampened kitchen towel. It only made things worse. Loretta snatched the towel away and started going to town, much to Doug's embarrassment. I had never appreciated my own mother more.

"I'm pleased to inform you that Leroy and Sandy have elected to stay," Anyssa said with a smile, and an inexplicable smattering of applause passed across the table. "So, without further ado, let's get started. What we have planned for you is a living, breathing *Choose Your Own Adventure*. Did anyone read those books when you were young?"

A glance around the table found five of us nodding—me, Brady, Melanie, Rob and Kit—with the rest either shaking their heads, or in the cases of Doug and Leroy, looking like they had never read anything voluntarily in their entire lives.

"I loved those books!" enthused Melanie. "You could read them over and over, and depending on your choices, arrive at any number of outcomes."

"That's right!" said Anyssa. "And that is how things will work this weekend. My team has prepared a very flexible script—think of it more as an outline. Soon, there will be a crime, and it will be up to you to find and decipher the clues, providing a resolution by noon on Monday. You can work independently or in groups, that's entirely up to you. Clues could be scattered all over the island, so I encourage you to explore it fully."

She held up two perfectly manicured fingers in a V.

"That being said, there are two places which will remain off limits during your stay. The first is the master bedroom; of this, you are already aware. The second is a section of island at the far end of the path that skirts the property. It is roped off and marked 'No Trespassing.' You couldn't possibly miss it. It leads to another, smaller dock on the far side of the island. This is where you go when you die."

She smiled slyly as Dusty gasped audibly, the color draining from her face. It seemed our host rather enjoyed the ability to make Brady's date uncomfortable.

"Relax, Ms. Rhodes," said Anyssa. "No one is any real danger. However, as choices are made, consequences will be realized, and it is imperative for the success of the game that everyone here fully commits to following the rules. If a member of my team approaches you with one of these," She held up a tarot card—naturally, it was Death. "You must accompany them immediately. They will whisk you away under cover, and you will spend the remainder of the weekend—or until the mystery is solved—off premises. And while our dwelling for the deceased *is* much smaller, it is still quite luxurious, I assure you. Any questions so far?"

Anyssa scanned the group as we looked at each other, and I put my hand in the air. "Where does the island get its power?" I asked.

Anyssa smiled. "Very good question, Mr. Morrow! The island has electricity courtesy of a power generator housed in the shed behind the patio. We are very fortunate to have a natural gas well here on the island, and the generator has been modified to use it as a source for fuel. We also have a fresh water well on premises, so in that regard, we are pretty self-sufficient. Anybody else?"

Loretta raised her hand. "What if we have a real emergency? You know, like someone gets sick or something?"

Anyssa nodded. "Of course. In the welcome packets I left in your guest quarters, there is an emergency phone number you may use if needed. It goes directly to a member of my team, and we have someone covering the line 24/7. We can have emergency medical assistance dispatched from Cleveland, if necessary. Please remember that we have no actual cellular service out here on the island. You will want to use the wi-fi password included in the packet for our guest network with your phones. You must then enable wi-fi calling for your phones to make and receive calls and texts. If anyone is unsure about how to do that, please come see me."

"Didn't I see another boat out in the boathouse?" I asked.

"Yes," said Anyssa. "It's just a small watercraft that belonged to my uncle, and I wouldn't recommend taking it out, but if it gives you peace of mind knowing it's there—" She looked knowingly at Dusty, whose only response was to snuggle closer to Brady. It was all so very high school. "Any other questions?"

We looked around the table at each other, but no one spoke up.

"Good," said Anyssa. "Would anyone like to hazard a guess as to what our mystery is about?" Her eyes twinkled as they passed over it."

"The gold?" ventured Melanie.

Anyssa laughed and clapped her hands. "You *are* good, Ms. McGregor!"

Melanie grinned sheepishly while I was completely stunned. I had absolutely no idea and judging from the expressions on my fellow guests' faces, they didn't either. It wasn't the first time it occurred to me Melanie might be in the wrong line of work.

"That's right!" said Anyssa enthusiastically. "Think of it as a treasure hunt. But you're not the only ones looking for it."

"We're not?" asked Sandy, her hand fluttering to her throat.

"Heavens, no! The Williams gold is every bit as legendary as the ghost of Julian Williams. Folks have been trying to find it for years. It's up to you to locate and secure the gold before anyone else."

Leroy raised a finger. "Is this here *real* gold?"

Anyssa cocked her head and smiled. "What do *you* think, Mr. Poole?"

His look was unreadable, so she moved on.

"Simply go about your business and let our mystery unfold around you. You are on your own schedule. There is no set dinner time, and there will be no catered dinners or room service. Prior to catching a ride back with our ferryman to the mainland, Maria and Constance have prepared a few dishes that will be at your disposal in the refrigerator, all of which can be easily reheated in the microwave. Any other items you find in the freezer or pantry are up for grabs. All I ask is that you throw your waste in the trash receptacles and rinse and stack your dishes on the counter by the sink."

Conversation percolated around the table as we all stood and Anyssa gathered her papers into her messenger bag. "That's a pretty nice boat you have docked out there," I said to her, indicating the general direction of the boathouse.

She smiled. "It's a relatively new acquisition. Jeremy keeps it running smoothly and shining like a diamond."

I chuckled. "A definite upgrade from your other transportation."

Anyssa paused midway through zipping her bag. "Excuse me?"

"Don't get me wrong, I'm not really complaining," I said, waving her concern away. "It certainly did the job, and I realize you were providing early access for us, but—"

She looked at me, clearly confused.

"—you should probably know that I'm pretty sure Captain Jack was at least a little inebriated out there," I said. "I would hate to see all your hard work get sidelined with a liability like—"

"Captain *who?*"

"Captain Jack. You know—" I grinned uncertainly and called out to my own merry band of travelers. "Hey guys! I was just telling Ms. Williams she should probably have a word with Captain Jack about his professionalism."

Loretta shuddered. "Disgusting."

"I thought he was *cute* for an old goat," offered Dusty. "And I'd never been on a pontoon before."

Anyssa's eyebrows knitted even tighter, "A *pontoon?*"

And that's precisely when a shrill scream echoed down the hallway.

Everyone froze, our previous thread of conversation entirely forgotten as a slow smile spread across our host's face. She cupped an elegantly manicured hand to her ear and said, "I think our mystery has begun."

*****

We stood in a semi-circle around Maria, who lay prone at the bottom of the stairs. She was still wearing the same uniform and apron in which she had served us our breakfast, but her eyes were closed, and her tongue lolled slightly out of her mouth.

"Oh, my," gasped Anyssa, steepling her hands over her mouth and nose.

"She's not dead," said Dusty, staring down at the woman.

"I *thought* I saw her eyes fluttering," added Sandy, loudly snapping a piece of gum she had in her mouth.

"Oh, I think she's dead, all right," said Anyssa. "Take note of what you see."

We leaned in for a closer look.

"What's that?" Melanie pointed to her neck.

"Looks like some sort of ligature marks," I noted.

"*Ligature marks*," mimicked Leroy, twirling a finger in the air. "*Whoop-dee-doo!* Scooby-Doo has arrived!"

I was beginning to actively dislike this man.

"And look," said Brady, leaning down to inspect her apron. "Her pocket's torn."

Loretta was busily taking notes on a memo pad while Doug chewed his unlit cigar at her side, trying to look engaged but only managing hopelessly befuddled.

"She's not dead," insisted Dusty, prodding Maria in the stomach with the toe of her espadrille. "I see her breathing."

One of Maria's eyes fluttered open, and she swatted Dusty's foot away before she went lifeless again. Anyssa cleared her throat. "Let's keep from touching the victim, all right?"

"But—" Dusty protested as Brady eased her away from our corpse, but not before Maria sealed the deal with a sneeze. Dusty pointed an accusatory finger. "*A-ha!*"

Anyssa clamped a hand to her forehead. "Well, alrighty, then! I guess we've discovered *another* thing that doesn't quite work."

Maria's eye slowly opened again, seeking out her employer.

Anyssa shook her head and forced a laugh. "It's okay, Maria. You did your best. It's not like you're an actress. You may get up now."

Maria looked unsure, her tongue still lolling out.

"It's okay," reassured Anyssa, offering her hand. Reluctantly, Maria took hold and pulled herself upright. Retracting her dangling tongue was her last move before brushing herself off and bowing apologetically to her boss. She scampered down the hallway and disappeared into the kitchen.

Leroy howled with laughter while Rob and Kit looked utterly perplexed. Dusty wore her vindication like a badge of honor, smiling victoriously at Anyssa.

"Is that it?" she squeaked. "Did I solve the mystery?"

"I don't think so, kitten," said Brady, shooting another apologetic look to Anyssa.

"Ain't *nobody* gonna pay $2,500 for this kind of shit," said Leroy, his belly practically gelatinous from guffawing. His complexion had deepened into a worrisome shade of red.

Sandy smacked his arm. "Stop it, Leroy James Poole! You're embarrassing Ms. Williams!"

"No, no, it's all right," said Anyssa, massaging the bridge of her nose as she managed another smile. "I knew there would be a learning curve, and here we are. I assure you, there will be no more staged corpses for you to find during your investigation. This was only a starting point. For all intents and purposes, Maria is dead. Some of you have made note of physical evidence on the body. Now, it's up to you to decide what to do next. It's nearly two, and I need to join the others at the boathouse. I will see you all again Monday morning. Good luck and have fun!"

With one last dazzling smile, she headed down the hall toward the kitchen, leaving us to mill about at the foot of the grand staircase.

"So—" began Kit. "What do we do next?"

"This is such a load of shit," said Leroy, prompting Sandy to smack his arm again. "*What?!?*"

"If you're going to be like this the entire weekend, Leroy James, you can just stay in our room. You're ruining everything," huffed Sandy.

Loretta continued to furiously scribble into her notepad while Doug shifted the soggy stump of his cigar from one corner of his mouth to the other. Brady and Dusty were in their own world, resuming their nauseating game of kissy-face; I wondered if there might be a spray bottle in the kitchen I could use to put a damper on their endless passion. It worked for my cat's occasional deviant behavior, and I longed to give it a shot with these two horndogs.

Melanie looked at me expectantly. "So, Mr. Big Shot Detective. What *do* we do next?"

"Well, okay," I said, taking the lead since nobody else would. I began pacing around the foyer. "We know that someone killed Maria—"

"Huh-unh," interrupted Dusty, pointing. "She just went out through the kitchen."

I scowled at her. "Work with me here, Dusty. Ms. Williams said we were to consider her murder the starting point of our mystery. So—"

"But—" Dusty's face couldn't have been any more blank.

I silenced her by holding up a finger, and not the one I wanted to use. Brady stood beside her grinning like a fool while enjoying the spectacle of my mounting frustration. I took a deep, calming breath.

"We're going to use our imaginations here, all right?" I asked, surveying the group, but landing on Dusty. "Maria has been killed and her body has been taken away by the authorities. Before she was removed, I noted ligature marks on her neck, and Brady noticed that the front pocket on her apron had been ripped. Did anyone notice anything else?"

"But—" Dusty's mouth would *not* stay shut!

"Anyone *other* than Ms. Rhodes?" I leveled a glare, and if looks could kill, Dusty would have been our second victim.

"One foot was resting on the bottom step," offered Kit. "Kinda like she had fallen down the stairs, maybe?"

"Good!" I said, moving toward the foot of the stairs and looking up. "So, if we were to assume she fell down the stairs after being attacked, that would mean—"

"The killer's still upstairs!" exclaimed Melanie, knocking me over and leading the stampede up to the midpoint landing. Loretta brought up the rear, grunting with each step. Once there, they split, with Melanie, Brady, Rob and Kit thundering up the stairs to the left while Doug, Loretta, Leroy and Sandy went right.

A shadow fell over where I lay at the bottom of the staircase, and I looked up. Dusty lingered, shifting from foot to foot while fussing with her hands. She shrugged and smiled.

"If the killer's up there, I'd really rather stay here with you," she said. "If that's all right."

I took a deep breath and forced a smile, getting to my feet. "Sure. Why not?"

*****

Dusty and I rejoined the others in the kitchen. Doug and his team had discovered a second, decidedly less grand set of narrow stairs at the end of their branch of the second-story hallway, leading back down to the part of the kitchen nearest the laundry room. This was clearly a corridor intended for the house staff so they might carry fresh linens, food or anything else up to guests, while remaining largely out of sight. Dirty half-footprints on the upstairs carpet suggested our "killer" had taken this as an escape route.

Dusty had clamped back onto Brady's arm. "Are you telling me the killer passed through here while Dwayne and I were just down the hall?"

"Looks that way," said Melanie. Dusty squeaked and buried her face in Brady's armpit.

"She *does* realize this is all just a game, doesn't she?" Kit leaned in, whispering to Melanie.

"I suspect she still believes in Santa Claus," Melanie returned, and they giggled conspiratorially.

The door to the patio was ajar, and we drifted in that direction, Dusty offering Brady up as a shield. I stepped outside and glanced around. One by one, the others joined me, and we soon reached a consensus. There was nothing to see.

"Well, huh," said Sandy, her multiple bracelets jangling from her elbows to her wrists as she planted her hands on hips. "Where do you suppose the killer went?"

"Fucking waste of time," grumbled Leroy as he slumped into a chair at the patio table. "Don't know why I ever let you talk me into this."

Exasperated, Sandy turned on him. "Because it was my *turn*, you asshole! We're *always* doing what *you* want to do! I swear to God, if I have to sit through one more *football* game, one more *basketball* game—Lord help me, one more afternoon of televised *bowling*—"

Leroy leapt to his feet, waggling a finger in his wife's face. "A man's entitled to relax on his time off! I work hard all week long! I should have *some* say in what we do."

"I work every bit as hard as you do, Leroy James," she said, waggling a finger right back. "And I should have some say in what we do, too, but do I ever get it? *No-o-o-o!* If I'm not getting dragged out hunting or fishing or camping, I'm putting up with that spoiled bitch daughter of yours and her nasty little brats tearing my house apart and breaking all of my knick-knacks—not to *mention* the way they torture my sweet little Baboo."

She turned to us like we were the jury.

"Baboo is the sweetest little Chihuahua you can even imagine, and these—these—these *hellions* just pinch and squeeze and poke and prod until she's lost all control of her bowels and bladder, and who do you think has to clean that up? *Me."* She placed a hand on her chest and rolled her eyes towards the heavens.

"Don't you be picking on Tammy," Leroy roared. I could only assume Tammy was his daughter. "She's had a rough go of it ever since Eddie left her. And those kids never act up when *I'm* around—"

"Un-*true!*" she interjected. "You just never pay any attention! You're too busy watching your sports, drinking your beer, entertaining your buddies—"

"And talk about throwing stones at a glass sheep—" Yeah, I had no idea either. "At least *my* daughter ain't working some titty bar on Trabue Road bringing God-only-knows *what* home with her. Nice lessons she's teaching *her* girls."

Sandy reared back like she was ready to slap Leroy, and I didn't care for the way he was clenching and unclenching his fist. I pushed my way in between them and braced for potential assault from either side.

"*Whoa! Whoa!*" I shouted, holding a hand in front of each of their faces. "Everybody needs to take a deep breath and take it down a notch or—ten. I don't want to have to use that emergency phone number to call for help with a domestic violence situation."

Sandy turned away, embarrassed, while Leroy looked as though he'd just as soon go ahead and throttle me. His complexion had deepened to crimson, and I could practically see his heartbeat in the vein throbbing at his temple. I held his glare until he finally turned away. It was the only way I knew to deal with hotheads like him, even if it occasionally cost me a punch in the nose. Everyone else remained frozen in place, watching from a safe distance. If I wasn't mistaken, Melanie gave me the slightest nod, as if in approval.

"If you all want to hash this out, do it on your own time," I said, backing away from them as they slowly separated. "The rest of us are here to solve a murder, not referee your shitshow. Can you rein it in?"

"I'm sorry," Sandy said sullenly, looking at her feet.

Leroy still looked like he wanted to kill his wife and me, in no particular order. He slumped back into the chair at the patio table and burned holes through me with his eyes.

"Surely, nobody thought we'd find the killer out here in the side yard, fifteen minutes after the first body was found, right?" I asked, looking at the group. "This would be the shortest mystery weekend ever."

"So, what should we do?" asked Rob, his arm around Kit.

"First, we should *relax*," I said. "Let's enjoy the weekend. The weather's nice. Maybe it would be a good time to explore the island."

Heads slowly began to nod in agreement.

I started to ask if this was something we should undertake as a group, but the question died in my mouth. If a murderer were on the loose in a real-world situation, safety in numbers would likely dictate the protocol, but quite frankly, I was sick of a handful of these people already. If I could figure out a way to convince Melanie to go explore the island with me, I might just be able to find the words to apologize for being such an idiot earlier.

"My stomach hurts," said Dusty, clutching her midsection. "I don't think I'm up for some big trek to nowhere."

"Yeah," agreed Leroy. "I think I'm going to spend the afternoon seeing what I can find on the boob tube in our room." He cast a dismissive glance at his wife. "You do whatever you want to do."

"Well, Rob and I think that sounds like a great idea!" enthused Kit.

"Tremendous, then," said Doug. "You lead the way, and me and Ma will follow."

The look that passed between Rob and Kit was comically transparent. Melanie interjected, "Um, Doug? I think they want a little alone time."

It took surprisingly long for Doug to get the gist, but the second he did, his complexion flushed from shoulders to the top of his head.

"I think I'm gonna sit this one out, too, Dougie," said Loretta. "I didn't really bring the right shoes to go traipsing around the island, and I'm still having a little of that same trouble with my lower half as yesterday." As if on cue, her digestive tract gurgled audibly.

I turned to Melanie just as she clamped onto Brady's arm.

"C'mon, Garrett," she said. "Let's see what there is to see."

"But—" I began, watching her steer him to the edge of the patio.

"Hey, guys!" Sandy called out, waving an arm, and sending her bracelets into a frenzy. "Can I tag along?"

"Sure! The more, the merrier," said Melanie. "Let's see where the beach leads."

"But—" I held up an unseen hand as Sandy practically skipped over to them, and they headed toward the narrow strip of sand at the foot of the grassy knoll.

I looked around. Leroy and Dusty had already gone inside, and Loretta was heading for the door. That only left me and Doug.

"So, whaddaya say, Morrow? Wanna take in the sights?"

I sighed and considered my options. I really didn't want to be under the same roof as Leroy and Loretta, and I wasn't a good enough swimmer to make it back to the mainland.

"Fine," I grumbled.

CHAPTER TEN

Doug wanted to check out the boathouse, which was fine with me. I had already been down there with Brady, but it would give the others a head start so we wouldn't be right on their heels. There wasn't an easy option to go the other direction from the beach; thick woods sprang up directly beside the boathouse, and I wasn't sufficiently schooled in identifying the variety of poison oaks, sumacs and ivies that undoubtedly lurked all throughout. I wasn't about to go wandering through them in my khaki shorts.

"So, what do you think so far?" Doug asked, still gnawing on the disgusting, soggy nub of his cigar. We stepped out onto the floating dock and into shade provided by the boathouse. The sun was high in the midday sky, and it had grown quite warm for this time of year.

I shrugged. "It's okay, I guess. Not really sure how it's teaching us to work as a team, though. I mean, we couldn't have splintered off into separate groups fast enough back there." I was doing my best not to be too disappointed Melanie wasn't ready to speak with me yet, but it was difficult.

"It's still early going," said Doug, peering in through one of the boathouse windows. "Nice work with the Pooles, by the way."

I looked at him, surprised. I wasn't accustomed to positive reinforcement from my generally gruff and contradictory boss. "Yeah?"

He gave a short nod. "I really thought we were gonna have a situation there. I have a feeling that Leroy is going to be a real troublemaker. He's got a temper on him and is unpredictable. Dangerous combination. It's probably a good idea to keep an eye out."

I nodded, feeling a little light-headed. Were we actually agreeing on a common approach to something?

A door to the boathouse was underneath the metal awning covering the empty pad where our golf carts had been parked. Doug tested the knob and, discovering the door unlocked, stepped inside. I followed.

He let out a long, slow whistle as he eyed the small speedboat bobbing gently in the shallow water. "She's a real beaut."

I didn't know shit from Shinola about boats, but it was nice enough. With two bucket seats in front and a narrow bench seat just behind, it could accommodate four passengers comfortably, five in a pinch. A small, shiny new motor was mounted to the rear of the craft. Doug eased himself into the cabin, sitting behind the wheel on the captain's side. The wonder on his face as he pretend-steered made him look like an exuberant kid on a carnival ride.

"We should take her out," he said, his eyes gleaming.

I remained on dry land, scowling down at him. "Anyssa said we shouldn't."

He waved my concerns away. "Oh, they're long gone. She'll never know. Come on!"

"Do you even know how to operate one of these things?"

In response, he started the engine. "I've always wanted to do this. This is *sweet!* Get in!"

"I don't know—"

"Oh, for heaven's sake, Morrow, don't be such a fucking wuss," he challenged. "Make up your damned mind. I'm going with or without you."

"Fine," I grumbled, walking around the back of the boathouse to approach what I considered the "passenger side" of the boat. I nearly lost my balance as the shift in the boat's load caused it to lean first one way then the other. I dropped into the bucket seat clumsily and reached for the safety harness, fastening myself in.

Doug reached behind himself and pulled the rope loose tethering us to the dock. He fiddled with the controls, and soon we were easing forward, out of the boathouse and onto Lake Erie. He was surprisingly adept at navigation, and I began to feel anxiety loosening its grip as I took a deep breath of fresh air.

"I didn't realize you were into boating," I said, leaning back and feeling the warmth of the sun on my face.

"We don't really talk about that sort of thing, do we?"

I frowned. I guess we didn't really talk about much of anything. Ours was more a relationship where we jockeyed for position. He enjoyed power and the control that came with it. I enjoyed free will and democracy. It didn't leave a lot of room for idle chit-chat.

"Look at that over there!" He pointed excitedly ahead where I spotted a disturbance in the water. "If I'm not mistaken, that's an Asian carp. Look at that thing leap!"

"And that's a good thing?" I asked, shielding my eyes from the sun, and taking another glance.

"They're considered an invasive species," he said, finally sticking his soggy cigar stump into his front pocket. "Basically, they're not native to the Great Lakes, so they're impacting the ecosystem. Time will tell if that's good or bad."

We sailed along for a moment in silence.

"This is something I used to do with my dad," said Doug. "Makes me feel close to him."

My frown deepened. I guess I always *knew* Doug had a father—don't we all? It was just easier to imagine Loretta lining the walls of a cave with her egg sac before depositing her progeny on the dusty floor to inevitably claw its way to freedom.

"He liked to fish?" I asked.

"No, not really. He just liked to be out on the water." He smiled. "I think he enjoyed taking a little break from Ma sometimes. They couldn't have been more different. I liked to tag along. Watched him like a hawk, but he never let me steer."

I tried to picture the man with all my might but came up empty. I was unsure if I had ever laid eyes on him.

"What was he like?" I asked.

Doug shrugged. "He was quiet. Read a lot. Seemed to really enjoy that old, hard-boiled detective stuff, like what Ray Chandler and Dashiell Hammett wrote." He pronounced it *Dash-ull*. "We had a basement full of those old books."

"Is that where you got the idea for Boggs Investigations?"

The suggestion seemed to surprise Doug. "Never really thought about it. Maybe. He was just so tired all the time. He was a pharmacist at the Walmarts in New Boston with a pretty regular schedule, but by the time he got home, all he wanted to do was eat dinner, read for a bit, then hit the sack. He had a buddy that owned a boat he kept docked down near the floodgate in Portsmouth. He let Dad borrow it from time to time on weekends. It gave him an excuse to dodge Ma and all her loony church friends, and thank God he took me with him. It was—I don't know—sort of our time."

I nodded. "With my dad, it was bowling. To this day, he still bowls in leagues on Tuesdays and Thursdays. My brother, Matt, and I spent a whole lot of evenings at Sunset Lanes when we were growing up. Dad is pretty good, too. He's done the Hoinke Classic a bunch of times, and occasionally his team brings back trophies. I always loved to bowl, and he was determined to make me a better bowler. Still is, actually. I've only beaten him maybe twice in all the times that we've bowled together. It got us out of the house when Mom was watching the Reds or the Bengals."

"Your mom's a sports fan, huh?"

"Not as much now as she was then," I said, before adding, "Thank God. Back then, you didn't want to be in the house if either team lost. Her mood for the entire day tanked."

"*Really?*" Doug laughed. "Your family always kinda reminded me of the Brady Bunch—well, without all them extra step-kids. It's hard to imagine your mom even being mad."

I smiled, thinking back. It really *had* been a while since Mom had so thoroughly obsessed over her Ohio sports teams. It triggered one of the only real arguments I can ever remember between the parents. Gina, Matt and I had retreated to Gina's room to weather the storm as their voices continued to grow louder. Dad had eventually given Mom an ultimatum: Either learn to deal with the occasional losses or stop following the games altogether. Ultimatums don't usually go over very well with most folks, but somehow, that one achieved its intended purpose.

Doug continued to stare straight ahead while easing the boat to the left. "I was only thirteen when Dad had his heart attack. It sucks growing up without your dad, you know? You're lucky you still have yours."

I was—there was no doubt about that.

"I'm sorry, man," I said. "I guess I just didn't realize."

He shrugged. "It was a long time ago. And you know, Ma really ain't so bad. She's got her quirks, but she means well."

It was my turn to laugh. "I'm pretty sure she doesn't mean well with me."

"Well, you provoke her. And you're always antagonizing me. She's just being protective."

I considered his point and decided it was valid. My mom had some choice words of her own about Doug and Loretta when I told her how they had tricked me into assuming a share of the financial responsibility for our satellite office on West Broad. Of course, every story has two sides; sure, they could have been more forthcoming with the contents of the contract, but I should have been more diligent in reviewing it before signing. Mom completely overlooked my own culpability. I was her youngest—her baby, as she so often told people, and much to my embarrassment. Jo Morrow might be a petite, curly-headed little lady who barely measured five feet when standing tall, but she was a ten-foot mama bear when someone crossed her children, especially me.

"Enough of this touch-feely horseshit," said Doug. "Let's see what this thing can do."

With that, he pushed the throttle forward, and the boat shot straight ahead, skipping across the lake's surface. I finally was able to relax as it became apparent this wasn't Doug's first attempt at navigating a boat. We were several hundred yards away from the island, circling around to a portion we hadn't previously seen during our initial approach. Refreshing mist stirred by the boat's forward motion cooled my face, and I loosened the belt around my waist so I could look around more easily. Glancing behind us, I spotted a couple of inflatable life preservers and a first-aid kit on the floorboard, and a nondescript black plastic hard-sided case on the bench seat. Never one to suffer a shortage of curiosity, I reached behind me and snagged the case by its handle, pulling it into my lap. I slid the handle lock back and was soon holding a very nice pair of field binoculars. I lifted them to my eyes, and the diminishing island leapt into soft focus. With a slight adjustment to the lenses, it was almost as if I was onshore.

"See anything cool?" Doug asked, cutting back on the throttle.

"Woods, woods and *more* woods," I said. "Wait a minute—I think I'm picking up a path."

"Yeah? Let me see," said Doug, cutting the engine altogether and reaching for the binoculars.

I swatted his hand away. "Hold on—I think I see something. Yep, it's them all right."

"*Who?*" Doug made another attempt to grab the binoculars, but I angled away from him.

"Melanie, Brady and Sandy," I said, releasing my safety harness and standing to get a better look. Melanie was chatting animatedly while Brady nodded, and Sandy was focused on the uneven terrain below her feet. "They're walking through the woods over there. I don't think they've noticed us." I pointed in the general direction.

"Well, let me *see*," insisted Doug, snagging the binoculars' neck strap and tugging.

"*Fine*."

I started to hand him the binoculars, but just as I began to lower them from my eyes, something crossed my field of vision. I yanked the binoculars free from Doug's grasp. "Hang on a sec."

"*What?!*"

I lifted them back to my eyes. "Give me just a second, will you? I thought I saw something else."

I picked up our fellow sleuths readily enough, Sandy now adding to the conversation with animated hand gestures, and Brady and Melanie listened attentively—to what I could only imagine. It was like watching a silent movie with no subtitles, and I never could read lips. I scanned to their left and to their right. Nothing. I expanded my scope, scanning deeper into the woods behind them.

I froze, my breath catching in my throat.

A hooded figure much like the one I had seen the previous evening was traversing a parallel path, and he was *moving*. By my best estimation, his path would intercept the one our friends traveled in several hundred yards.

"*Shit*," I muttered, just as Doug succeeded in wresting the binoculars from my grasp.

"Let me *see*," he said, standing and lifting them up to his eyes.

"We've gotta get over there, *right now*, Doug," I said, grabbing his arm. "That—that *thing* from last night is out there on another trail."

Doug lifted the binoculars away from his eyes and looked at me doubtfully. "That *thing?* Are you referring to the great ghost of Marble Toe?"

"I'm not kidding, Doug," I said, reaching for the binoculars again. "This thing was really scary, and I don't think it was up to anything good—will you give those back to me?"

Doug pushed my hand away. "I'd like to get a look at this *big scary thing.*" There was no mistaking the sarcasm in his tone. He lifted the spyglasses to his eyes and began scanning the wooded shoreline.

I made a grab for the binoculars, but Doug swatted my hand sharply. "*Shit*, Doug! Give them back!" I demanded.

"Okay, I see Melanie, Brady and that other gal," he said, continuing to scan. "But I don't see anyone else."

Panic was welling, and I could feel the steady buzz of adrenaline coursing through my veins as I helplessly stood by, unable to see anything without the aid of the binoculars. I lunged for the strap again and succeeded in pulling the binoculars away from Doug's face.

"For God's sake, Dwayne," snapped Doug. "Let *go!*"

He yanked, and the binoculars were suddenly airborne, sailing out over the water and far away from us. They dropped into the lake with a *ploink!*

We looked at each other, our mouths agape.

"You're paying for that," we said in almost complete unison.

"The hell I am!" roared Doug. "If you had given me just a *minute* to look—"

"We don't have time for this!" I interrupted. I strained to get a glimpse of our friends, but we were too far out. I was beginning to feel nauseous. "Their paths are going to cross, and Melanie won't even see it coming. You have to get us in there."

Doug looked at me incredulously. "Are you kidding me? Even if this thing you saw *is* real, it's gotta be part of the script, right? You're freaking out over nothing!"

I thought back to the previous evening and the menacing way the hooded figure behaved. There was nothing playful about it. It mimicked every move I made, and its intention certainly didn't feel benign. I needed to warn them, and I needed to warn them now!

"Take the boat in," I said. "Do it."

"There's no dock over there!" objected Doug. "I got no idea the depth of the lakebed or what we might run into. Bad enough you lost those binoculars. I won't let you fuck the boat up, too!"

"Fine," I said, trying to push him out of the captain's chair. "I'll do it."

"Stop it, Dwayne! You don't even know how to operate this thing!" he said, pushing back. We were causing the boat to rock as we continued to struggle, and it was impossible to stand my ground when the ground kept moving.

"Then *you* do it!" I practically screamed, raking my hands through my hair. "We can't just *sit* here!"

Doug sighed, claiming the captain's chair by settling back into it. "I'll tell you what. Let's take the boat back to the dock and grab a golf cart. We can catch up to them on land."

I could feel the veins in my temples throbbing. Why couldn't he understand the urgency? This could be a matter of life or death! Anyssa had been genuinely surprised to hear about my encounter with this hooded specter, and I didn't believe for a minute what I was seeing was part of some script.

"You do that," I said, fishing my cell phone and car keys out of my pocket. I handed them to Doug.

Doug looked at me, perplexed. "What's this?"

"It's for safekeeping," I said, and launched myself over the side of the boat.

*****

ISOLATION

Here's the thing:

I was literally making this shit up as I went along, driven entirely by panic and fear for Melanie's safety. Okay, I might have been a little bit worried about Brady, too, but let's keep that between us, okay? It probably sounds awful, but I didn't give much thought to Sandy; we had only just met, and she wasn't the priority.

The lake water was colder than I would have ever imagined for late summer, but once I was fully submerged, there was no turning back. I began kicking my legs and using my arms to propel myself toward the island. The problem was, I was never a really good swimmer. I had taken classes at the YMCA when I was young, but I never mastered the simple act of floating, much less achieving a breaststroke or anything more functional than a doggy paddle. With my face buried in the water, I relied on the strength of my legs to carry me forward, and while it was somewhat effective, I had to remind myself to breathe. Coming up for air broke what little rhythm I had, and I would occasionally inhale a mouthful of muddy water, breathing in before I was actually above sea level. I could hear my heart beating loudly in my ears as I tried to maintain focus.

I may have had the foresight to leave my phone and keys with Doug for safekeeping, but it had never occurred to me how incredibly heavy my khaki shorts and lightweight t-shirt would become once completely waterlogged. I hadn't thought to step out of my shoes, either, and I surrendered them to the bottom of the lake in very short order. I felt like I was trying to swim through marshmallow, my strength ebbing with every forward stroke.

I paused, treading water. My vision was blurry from the water in my eyes, and my lungs burned as I pulled sweet oxygen into them. I might have bridged half the distance, it was difficult to be certain, but I was sure I saw the silhouettes of my friends scrambling down to the water's edge through the thick woods. I tried to call out to them but was only rewarded with a mouthful of lake water. I gagged then spat it out, taking as deep a breath as I dared before plodding forward.

A field of stars had invaded the periphery of my vision, and my arms felt heavier than ever. For the first time, it occurred to me that I might have bitten off more than I could chew. As far as I had come, as much effort as I had put into this, the island was still so very far away, and I wasn't sure I could make it.

I paused again, treading water and breathing in deeply—raggedly.

I looked behind me, but the boat was nowhere to be seen. Doug had apparently sped away just as soon as I hit the water. I turned toward the island, but my vision was getting so damned blurry. Where I thought I had seen Melanie and Brady, I now saw nothing. The afternoon sun shone above in a cloudless blue sky, and as I looked up, it doubled before tripling, and I knew I was in serious trouble.

I made a half-hearted attempt to resume my path, but the field of stars was growing with black dots interpolating. I kept pulling lake water into my mouth and choking, and my arms felt completely detached from my body. My sense of urgency hadn't diminished one bit, but I could no longer make my limbs obey my direction. I was so disappointed in myself. I was drifting away, and I was failing Melanie!

The black dots connected, coalescing into a black hole that swallowed the field of stars as if they were nothing. I closed my eyes, helpless against the gravity that pulled me down into Lake Erie's murky depths.

*****

I was choking, endless water gushing from my mouth.

I squinted against the brilliant sunlight, my eyes still stinging from the lake water. Blurry figures hovered over me, but my ears were full of water, and their words were distant and muffled. I became aware of the jagged bed of uneven rock upon which I lay, water sloshing up and over my feet. I tried to move but only succeeded in abrading my bare legs.

A quick succession of slaps landed on my cheek, and Brady's face leapt into focus, his dark curly hair wet and dripping down onto my face.

"*Dwayne!*" He sounded a million miles away, but he had a firm grip on my chin, forcing me to look up at him. "Speak to me, buddy."

Melanie leaned in from the other side, concern evident on her face. "What *happened*, Dwayne? What were you doing in the lake? You nearly drowned! If it hadn't been for Brady—"

I tried to speak but somehow only found more water to expel. My vision was beginning to clear, and my ears depressurized with a pop. With a sudden start, I remembered where I was and why I was there.

I had lost all sense of time, and the hooded figure could be anywhere!

I struggled to rise up on my elbows, adrenaline roaring back like a tsunami. I pushed Brady aside, turning to frantically scan the woods behind us.

Melanie leapt to her feet, backing away from me. "What *is* it, Dwayne? You're really starting to freak me out!"

"Did you see it?" My voice was foreign in my own ears, strained to its limits after expelling what felt like gallons of Lake Erie. "*Did you see it?!*"

"See *what*, Dwayne?" asked Brady, giving me space as I pushed myself to my bare feet on the rocky shore.

"The thing from last night! The hooded thing I saw last night!" I was completely hysterical, wild-eyed and looking in all directions.

"You've got to be kidding me," said Melanie, shaking her head and turning away. "Not that again."

"I'm not making this up!" I shouted. "Me and Doug—we took the boat out, and I saw it through the binoculars! It was coming towards you all! It was—"

The words stuck in my throat as I suddenly realized what should have been obvious.

"Where's Sandy?" I asked.

Brady and Melanie exchanged perplexed glances.

"She's up on the trail," said Melanie. "She was afraid she'd twist an ankle down here."

"We told her to stay put," added Brady. "What's the big—"

An ear-splitting scream reverberated throughout the woods, stopping Brady mid-sentence. It certainly sounded like Sandy.

CHAPTER ELEVEN

We only hesitated for a second before scrambling through the foliage.

I followed Brady and Melanie, partly because they knew where they were going, but also because I was still really sapped from what had apparently been a near-death experience for me. My arms and legs felt rubbery and unreliable as I struggled to keep up. At least Sandy's scream had accomplished what I had been unable to. Brady and Melanie were finally taking the threat seriously.

I was gasping for my breath when we finally emerged onto the path I had only previously seen through the amplified lenses of the binoculars. I knelt forward, supporting myself with both hands over my knees, inhaling deeply to prevent the field of stars trying valiantly to regroup in my line of vision. Melanie and Brady separated, scouring the area.

"Sandy?" called Melanie, uncertainly.

"*Sandy!*" Brady thundered. Is it petty that I felt a pang of vindication at the urgency I detected in his voice?

As my breathing leveled out, I stood, examining the area around me. I caught a flash of color in the foliage to my left. Closer examination revealed it to be the left half of a pair of pale green Skecher tennis shoes.

"Hey, guys?" I said, holding up my find.

Melanie gasped. "That's her shoe!" she said, taking it from me.

Brady shrugged, continuing to search farther along the path. "If you say so. I can't say I ever looked at her feet."

I stooped, examining the area more closely. "Look at this," I noted, pointing at the ground. "There's a whole cluster of footprints here, and—oh, shit."

"What?" Melanie knelt beside me to see what stopped me cold.

"Is that blood?" A trail of dark droplets soaked into the ground near where I had discovered the shoe. "I think that's blood."

Melanie leaned in, then looked around before smacking my arm. "That's just *you!*"

"*What?*" I was genuinely perplexed, hopping around in an awkward semi-circle until I realized my waterlogged shirt and shorts were steadily dripping onto the ground around me. It wasn't blood at all, only water from the lake.

"I don't see her anywhere," said Brady, rejoining us. "I don't see *anyone* else. I see the footprints you're talking about, but they only extend a little way beyond where you're standing. The dirt on the path is packed too hard over here. It's not like we can follow them. My guess is Sandy is the weekend's next victim."

"How can you be so casual about it?" I demanded, completely exasperated. My blood pressure felt high enough to blow my head right off my shoulders.

"And why are you acting like such a lunatic?" countered Melanie, throwing hands into the air. "You *are* aware this is a mystery weekend, aren't you? I mean, that was how you explained it to me when you invited me. I swear, you're beginning to sound like Dusty."

"Now, hold it right there," I said, leveling a finger at her. "That's completely uncalled for. You would totally understand me if you had *seen* this thing!"

"Like how Dusty saw a face in the basement window?" asked Brady, barely able to suppress his grin.

My mouth snapped shut. I was never going to be able to justify my certainty about this hooded figure when facts and logic could so effectively dismantle my every argument. I closed my eyes, pinching the bridge of my nose before taking another deep breath, willing myself to relax.

"Even Anyssa was surprised when I mentioned the hooded figure," I said, keeping my voice even and calm. "Didn't you see her reaction? It wasn't part of her script."

"How can you be so sure of that?" challenged Melanie. "I mean, you just said it yourself. This whole *thing* is scripted. Anyssa's entire narrative was a well-rehearsed performance. For all we know, Anyssa Williams isn't even that woman's real name. She could be a professional actor hired to play the part. Didn't you notice how stilted her language was? I mean, who talks like that?"

"What's wrong with the way she spoke?" asked Brady. "I thought it was kinda sexy."

Melanie rolled her eyes. "After conversation with Dusty, I'm guessing you'd find a See-and-Say sexy."

He frowned. "That's low."

"You didn't see the way this—*person* was hauling ass to cut you all off," I interrupted, trying to bring us back on point. "I can't imagine it was just to show someone a tarot card and escort them to the back half of the island."

Melanie laughed. "Really? It doesn't seem like such a stretch to me, considering how wild your imagination seems to be lately."

Ouch.

I knew she wasn't just referring to our current circumstance and wondered when I'd ever get a chance to apologize properly for my earlier transgression. I didn't like being the bad guy.

Our debate was sidelined by the faint hum of an approaching motor in the distance.

"What's that?" asked Melanie, turning toward the sound.

"Probably Doug," I said. "He was afraid of damaging the boat if he brought it too close to shore, so he was going back for a golf cart."

"Why were you guys in the boat? I thought Anyssa said it was off limits," said Melanie.

"She didn't say it was off limits." It came out overly defensive, considering it wasn't even my idea. "She said she didn't *recommend* it, but Doug insisted."

"Surely, he won't try and drive the cart along this path," said Brady. "He'll never make it. The ground's too uneven. It's not like it's an all-terrain vehicle."

As if on cue, the motor abruptly cut off and a stream of obscenities sailed through the air. Brady and Melanie hurried toward the sound while I hobbled along, my bare, tender feet unaccustomed to the flooring Mother Earth installed. We followed the path as it wound back through the woods, rising and falling before rising once more.

After cresting the first mound, I was literally left in the dirt as my so-called friends raced ahead. I assumed they found Doug when his colorful exclamations died away, a fact confirmed once I crested the second mound. All three of my companions stood in a semi-circle, studying the teetering chassis of the golf cart, its right front passenger end angled down into a culvert. It had dropped so far below the path that the left rear tire wasn't even touching the ground. Doug's face was a deep shade of crimson, and by the time I caught up with them, he was already well into his version of events with Brady, arms flailing in every direction.

I pointed at the wreckage, eyebrows raised and mouth hanging open, no question necessary.

Brady sighed, shaking his head. "He ran out of road. I think the axle is busted. This thing isn't going anywhere."

A strange, hysterical laugh slipped through my lips. First the binoculars and now this. I really hoped Anyssa had good insurance on this place, or this trial run may well be her last.

*****

I was pretty sure blisters were forming on the bottoms of my feet by the time we made it back to the manor. Doug's avalanche of excuses had dried up pretty quickly once he realized he wasn't getting any sympathy, and they were all irritated with me because I couldn't keep up with their pace. Brady was still irked by Melanie's inability to hold her tongue regarding his date, so we traveled beneath an albatross of silence. It was preferable to anything that might slip from our lips in our currently agitated states. I almost wept with relief when I stepped onto the soft, velvety lawn of the front grounds.

Melanie was the first to break the silence. "What time is it?"

Brady checked his cell phone. "Almost four-thirty."

"So, who's going to tell Leroy about Sandy?" she asked.

"We should tell him as a team," I said. "We need to start acting like a team. Isn't that what we're here for?"

"Absolutely," said Doug, nodding earnestly. At some point, he had rediscovered the nasty cigar nub in his pocket and was once again spreading bits of loose tobacco far and wide across his mouth and chin.

"Well, then," I continued. "As the leader of Boggs Investigations, and the man who invited us all here, I would think that you should take the lead for your team, Doug."

Brady nodded. "It makes the most sense."

"Wait just a minute," protested Doug. "I didn't actually *see* anything myself. Why should I—"

"Why *wouldn't* you?" I interrupted. "That's how we do things back at the office. I make all my reports directly to you, and you are the face of Boggs Investigations to the clients. In fact, you have ordered me *not* to have direct communication with clients on more than one occasion. I'm really only following your own rules."

"But Leroy isn't a client!" he objected.

Melanie tsk-tsked. "You're just splitting hairs, Doug. Besides, we'll be right there to back you up. You'll do just great."

I smiled. At least *this* was fun!

The enormous front door flew open just as we reached the top of the porch stairs, Loretta filling the lower third of its frame.

The fun was over.

"Where in the *world* have you all been?" she demanded, hands on her hips. Her left eye was twitching beneath a thick layer of neon blue eyeshadow.

"We told you we were exploring the island," I said, still dripping slightly onto the wooden slats of the porch. "You were welcome to come along." It was a safe thing to say after the fact.

"I didn't think you'd be all *day*," she said, futzing with her hands and looking over her shoulder back into the house.

"What's wrong, Ma?" Doug asked. He took the cigar from the corner of his mouth and started to put it back in his pocket, but Melanie snagged it, and sent it flying to the furthest corner of the yard. "*Hey!*"

"Let it go, Dougie," said Loretta, stepping out onto the porch while continuing to nervously glance over her shoulder. "Of all the bad habits you've picked up from that Morrow boy over the years, that cigar is the worst."

I blinked. "*What?!* I've never smoked a cigar in my—wait a minute. Did you say, 'all the bad habits?' What bad habits?!"

Doug placed a hand on his mother's arm. "What's going on, Ma? Did something happen while we were gone?"

Loretta chanced another glance over her shoulder. "Yes. No." She sighed and shrugged. "I don't know. Why is Dwayne all wet—and where are his shoes?"

"Long story," I said. "What happened?"

"I went up to my room to stretch out for a bit. I had *Matlock* on the TV—it was that really good one where Billy got kidnapped instead of Leanne—"

"*Ma,*" Doug coaxed her back on topic.

"I started hearing these strange noises," she said, shivering visibly. "It was sort of—a scratching noise. And footsteps. At first, I thought it was Leroy, or that dingbat Brady brought—"

"Excuse me?" It was Brady's turn to play for the defense.

"—but every time I checked the hallway, there was no one out there. It wasn't constant, but every time I thought it stopped, I'd hear it again. The acoustics in that room are weird. I could swear it was all around me. Even in the walls."

We exchanged perplexed glances. Loretta wasn't exactly known for her imagination.

"Maybe it was Rob and Kit. Have you seen them?" I asked.

Loretta shook her head. "Not since they left earlier. And it wasn't voices I heard. Just—sounds."

"Why don't you go check it out, Doug?" I suggested, squirming in my soggy clothes. "I smell like the lake. I need to grab a shower and get into some dry clothes."

"I wouldn't mind grabbing a shower, too," said Melanie, discreetly testing the air near her pits. "I managed to work up a sweat out there."

"I should probably check in on Dusty," Brady added. "If Loretta thinks she's hearing noises, Lord only knows what Dusty has talked herself into believing."

"I didn't imagine it!" protested Loretta as she stepped aside to let us enter. "Those noises were just as real as—hold on. Wasn't that loud woman with all the costume jewelry with you?"

Melanie nodded, heading for the stairs. "Sandy. We're pretty sure she's dead."

Loretta's hand flew to her mouth. "*What?*"

Brady shook his head, patting Loretta's shoulder as he passed. "Not *dead* dead. Dead like Maria was this morning. Your Dougie gets to break it to her husband. Should be interesting." He trotted up the stairs behind Melanie.

I was still torn regarding how innocuous Sandy's disappearance had actually been, but I was absolutely certain I didn't want to partake in the revelation to Leroy, at least not right then. My damp garments clung to my skin, and I was beginning to itch. I hobbled toward the stairs on the sides of my aching feet.

"Now, just hang on, here," Doug objected. "Where is everybody going? You said you had my back."

"And we do, Doug," I said. "Just stay clear of Leroy until we get back. Give us maybe a half-hour? That should give you time to check out what your mom heard."

Loretta snorted. "It almost sounds like you believe me."

I flashed upon the hooded figure from the previous evening, as well as its sudden reappearance on the woodsy trail, baring down on Brady, Melanie and Sandy.

"I do," I said, surprising even myself.

*****

I stood beneath the luxury shower head, practically groaning with relief as the focused spray worked at the knots in my shoulders and back. I had turned the temperature just as high as I could tolerate, and clouds of steam billowed over the top of the glass shower door and out into the bathroom, fogging the mirror above the sink. This was no hotel shower—the pressure was delightfully high, and hot water appeared to be endless. I lost all sense of time as I shampooed and conditioned my hair before lathering up, washing the mildly rotten egg-like smell from my skin. I snapped back to attention as the sudsy water ran down my legs and hit the abrasions on my tender feet. I had really done a number on them. Blisters had formed along the balls of my feet, and dried blood flecked away from where rocks embedded along the path had broken skin. I took special care to wash them thoroughly, despite the discomfort. They would feel a whole lot worse if they became infected.

I dried myself on an oversized, thirsty bath towel that was softer than any I had ever laid hands on. As I slipped into an equally soft matching bathrobe, it occurred to me I should maybe raise my expectations for such things beyond what was cheapest in the home and bath department at the Georgesville Walmart.

I began rehearsing my apology to Melanie as I rummaged through my soft-sided duffel for fresh clothing. I needed to clear the air sooner rather than later. I held out hope I could salvage what was left of our weekend. I chose a pair of faded jeans and a Led Zeppelin t-shirt. I slipped on a pair of cotton socks before realizing my next problem. I had only brought one pair of shoes, and they were currently bloating at the bottom of Lake Erie. I did have a pair of plaid, cushy bedroom slippers. They had a semi-rigid sole dotted with rubbery grippers to prevent me from ass-planting on hard floors. I sighed, sliding them on. With my feet in their current condition, the slippers were better than nothing.

Back to rehearsing my apology.

I'm really sorry, Mel. I shouldn't have been looking at your laptop. I just thought—

Stop. Didn't matter what I thought.

If I could take yesterday back, I would. I had no business reading your work-in-progress, but the title was just so compelling, I couldn't help—

Oh, good Lord. Justification by means of flattery is still justification. Why was this so *hard?* Even Brady seemed to understand what needed to be done. Of course, I imagined Brady had a whole lot more experience apologizing.

I'm an idiot, Melanie. I invaded your privacy, jumped to conclusions, and ran my big, fat mouth. I'm sorry.

Okay, that was better...

If you could just forgive me, I promise I'll never do it again.

Still on solid ground...

But even you have to admit, the title, My Latest Mistake (Lessons in Love), *is a bit—provoking...*

And I'm suddenly in freefall! I used a generous application of imaginary Wite-Out to eradicate that last bit.

I know it might take some time, but I'm going to do whatever it takes to earn back your trust. I want you to trust me as much as I trust you.

Shit.

As good as it sounded and as much as I truly meant it, I couldn't actually say it, at least not until I told Melanie the entire truth about what had happened in West Virginia. She knew I was holding back and had already said as much. While I understood my sister's reasoning for swearing me to silence, I never imagined how quickly it would place an undue burden upon my own relationship. I could either keep my vow to Gina or prove my trust in Melanie, but not both. I was in an impossible position.

There was a light peck on my door.

I crossed the room but hesitated as my hand landed on the doorknob. What were the odds my visitor was waiting with a tarot card heralding my "death?" What were the odds my visitor wore an oversize trench coat and menacing hood? I wasn't good with either option; I couldn't spend the rest of this weekend off premises—or worse while so much with Melanie was left unresolved. My thumb drifted to the lock in the center of knob and was shocked to find I hadn't locked it before hitting the shower. I depressed it with an audible click.

"Did you *really* just lock your door?!"

"Melanie?" I twisted the knob and pulled the door open. She stood in the hallway with hands on hips, her hair piled high into a bath towel.

"Look," she said, refusing to meet my eyes. "This is awkward—"

"I totally agree," I interrupted. "I was just about to—"

She waved my words away. "I need you to call Jasmine."

I motioned her into the room, but she only took a few steps inside. "Well, sure—is something wrong?"

She shook her head and sighed. "No—I mean, not with her. I decided to check in while I was up here. Asked her about her day, and she asked me about mine, and well—kid can read me like a book. Always could. She wanted to talk to you, and when I told her you were in the shower, which *technically* wasn't a lie, she knew something was up."

I groaned, rolling my head backward along my shoulders. "You didn't *tell* her, did you?"

"Of course not!" snapped Melanie. "But if I wanted to, make no mistake about it, I would have. You won't tell me what I can and can't say to my own daughter."

Whoa! Where in the world did *that* come from?

"I wouldn't even begin to—"

"And it's a good thing, too," she said, and I could tell she was on the verge of tears. Angry tears. *Dangerous* tears. "I don't want her worrying about us like she did with me and—"

Ah. Her father.

She shifted course. "I won't have anything spoiling her time at Cedar Point with Billy, Scott and the Caudills."

"Of course not," I said. "What can I do?"

"You need to call her," said Melanie, a tear escaping the corner of her eye, which only seemed to make her angrier. "Tell her we're having a wonderful fucking time. And you'd better be a whole lot more convincing than me." She jabbed me in the chest with her forefinger.

"Fine, I'll call her now. I—well, shit."

"What?"

"I don't have my phone," I said. "I handed it and my keys to Doug while we were out in the boat. I'll bet they're still there."

It was Melanie's turn to groan. She turned and headed for the hallway.

"Hey, listen, it's no big deal," I said, placing a hand on her arm. "Let me use your phone."

She turned slowly, chewing on her bottom lip. "It's in my room. And it's almost completely dead. You could practically get your own in the time it would take me to—"

"You want me to go all the way down to the boathouse and get mine? Are you serious? I could use yours tethered to a charger, if necessary."

She continued to hedge. "I really don't want to stand over you while you're talking to her," she said.

I was thoroughly confused. "Why would you have to do that?"

"Well, you'd need my thumbprint to unlock the phone, and..." Her words trailed off as she shrugged.

"And what?"

"I'm not entirely comfortable with you having my unlocked phone," she finally said. "I mean, look how you were with my laptop."

"For the love of God!" I erupted. "Why would I want to dig through your phone? What could possibly be on there that—"

"*I don't know!*" she returned hotly. "I never would have thought you would go through my laptop either, but—"

A shadow fell across us from the doorway, and we both looked toward its source. Brady stood in the doorway with the goofiest grin on his face.

"What do you want, Brady?" I asked. "As you can see, we're in the middle of something—"

Hysterical laughter climbed the scales before trailing away.

"What's the matter, Brady?" asked Melanie, concern supplanting anger.

"It's Dusty," he said, more laughter spilling forth.

"What, she's joined Sandy on the other side of the island?" I asked. Not gonna lie, I was hopeful.

Just when I thought his laughter couldn't become any more manic, he took it up a notch. "If only," he finally said, and I noticed his duffel bag on the floor beside him. "I just walked in on her and Leroy. In our bed. They were, uh—they were…"

Another round of crazed laughter that died in the back of his throat. He looked at me earnestly.

"Can I crash with you for the rest of the weekend?"

CHAPTER TWELVE

"Why *me?*" I asked. "I mean, aren't there several other rooms still available?"

"What's *wrong* with you?" asked Melanie, smacking my arm. "Can't you see Brady could use a friend?" She turned to Brady. "I am *so* sorry, Brady." He accepted her condolences with puppy dog eyes.

"Thanks, Mel," he said. "I appreciate that. I know you and Dwayne didn't like Dusty very much." He entered the room, duffel in hand, plopping it on the floor just inside the door.

"It isn't that we don't like Dusty," said Melanie, searching for diplomacy. "We just think there's a better fit for you somewhere out there. And look—we were right. Better to find out now, don't you think?"

"It's just so *humiliating*," said Brady, dropping onto the corner of my mattress. "I mean, what in the world can she possibly see in that middle-aged asshole? A receding hairline and a beer gut? How am I going to spend the rest of this weekend looking at either one of them? That's why I can't just take one of the other available rooms. All three border on either Leroy's or Dusty's rooms. I'm not about to listen to what goes on through the walls. I'm going to have to kick his ass."

"Now, just hold up there, Rocky," I said. "Anything and everything we do this weekend will reflect on Boggs Investigations, and that would reflect very poorly. Normally, that wouldn't bother me, but we've already lost what

I assume was an expensive set of binoculars and totaled a golf cart. We're a little top-heavy in the debit column. And Leroy seems to have quite a temper on him. Are you sure you wanna go there?"

"I don't think I can be in the same room when Doug tells Leroy about Sandy," said Brady, running a hand through his dark curly hair. "We were worried about how he would take it, but he's just gonna see it as a free pass to the all-you-can-eat Dusty buffet. And I'm sorry, but I can't promise how I'll react if I see the bastard. One thing's for sure, I'm not scared of him."

I sighed, shaking my head. This was just tremendous! I was in the middle of some high school drama that was unfolding all around me, and I seemingly had no choice but to participate.

Brady looked from me to Melanie, sitting up straighter. "Oh, hey—I interrupted you guys. You were shouting at each other about something."

"I wouldn't exactly call it *shouting*," said Melanie, looking at her feet as she traced an invisible line on the rug. "Jasmine just wanted to speak with Dwayne, that's all. Say, do you think he could borrow your cell, Brady? He gave his to Doug and thinks it's still out on the boat." She locked her eyes defiantly on mine.

"Yeah, sure. No problem. Have her tell Billy I'll call him in a little while."

"That's okay, Brady," I countered, unable to walk away from the challenge. "Melanie was just about to let me use hers."

"Apparently, you didn't hear me when I said my battery was almost dead," she replied, staring me down. "Brady and I will step over to my room to give you a little privacy while you make the call."

Brady looked confused, his cell phone in hand, unlocked and suspended mid-air toward me.

"If I can trust Brady in your room, you can surely trust me with your goddamn phone," I hissed. It was as infantile, involuntary and entirely unstoppable. I regretted it the instant it flew from my lips.

Melanie blinked like she'd been smacked, cool indifference settling over her features in an instant. She plucked the cell phone from Brady's hand and forced it into my own. "Leroy isn't the only asshole here this weekend."

She grabbed Brady's hand and pulled him out into the hall, reaching back in to slam the door behind her.

The wind rushed out of me as I sat down heavily on the side of the bed. I certainly had a hell of a lot to learn about apologizing.

*****

"Hey, kiddo," I said, aiming for upbeat and carefree. "Sorry I missed you earlier. I had an accidental run-in with the lake and had to grab a shower. Do you have any idea what lake water smells like? *Peeee-ewwww!*" A little over-the-top? Maybe.

"What's wrong?" asked Jasmine, instantly suspicious. "You sound funny. And why are you calling from Brady's phone?"

"I sound funny?" My voice hit the level of 'impossibly surprised.' "Can't imagine why. It's probably Brady's cheap phone. It's so old it's almost rotary dial." The *heh-heh-heh* that escaped my lips was painfully fraudulent. "I left my phone out on the boat. I'm lost without it, but I didn't want to keep you waiting."

"Mom didn't sound right, either. Are you two fighting?"

I made a sound like a leaky tire valve. "Fighting? Us? Of course not. Why would we be fighting?"

"That's what I'm asking *you*," she said, direct and to the point, as always. "And remember, you promised you would always tell me the truth."

I was up to my neck in quicksand and about to go under. Note to self: I was done with promises. All they ever seemed to accomplish was to paint me into a corner, and in this case, I was going to have to decide which promise to break, and *quickly*.

"Honestly, it's nothing," I said, sighing. "I mean, you're old enough to know that sometimes adults have a difference of opinion, right? Well, your mother and I are having one of those right now, but it's just a *teensy, tiny* little thing, I promise you." Dammit! Another promise!

"Are you sure? Mom sounded super weird."

"Absolutely," I said, surprised at just how sure I sounded. "We'll work through it at dinner, and by this evening, everything will be just as right as rain. Now, I need you to make *me* a promise."

"What's that?" Jasmine asked warily.

"Please don't waste your weekend worrying about us. This is honestly no big deal. You've heard bigger arguments between us over where to go for dinner or who gets to clean up Dexter's latest hairball."

She snorted. "That's an easy one. *Me.* I *always* get the hairballs."

"I guess you do," I laughed, sensing the opportunity to change the subject. "So, how's the trip going so far?"

"Great! We did a walk-through of the park first just to see what all there is to see. Then Scotty and I rode a couple of roller coasters while Mr. and Mrs. Caudill took Billy through some of the gift shops. We're getting ready to have pizza for dinner."

Relief washed over me. The suspicion had vacated her voice.

"You and Scott are being mindful not to cut Billy out of all your activities, aren't you?"

"*Duh*, Dwayne," she said, and I could easily picture the eyeroll. "Billy wanted to go shopping, and he absolutely insisted that Scott and I hit the rollercoasters. We're going back to the lodge after dinner and will spend the evening in the water park. The entire first half of the day tomorrow is up to Billy, and we'll make sure the things we choose during the last half are things he can do."

"Good girl," I said, realizing yet again what a great kid she was. "Oh, Brady wanted me to ask you to let Billy know he'll call him later this evening."

"Sure," she said.

"All right, then. I'll let you get back to your fun."

"Dwayne?" Shit. She sounded serious again.

"Yeah?"

"I just want you to know how much I appreciate how you don't talk down to me, you know? Like I'm just some dumb kid. Mom wouldn't admit that you had any disagreement at all, even though it was kinda obvious. You're always straight with me. I feel like I can trust you with anything."

My throat tightened as my self-respect plummeted. "I'm glad," I managed. "Tell everyone I said hello, and we'll talk soon. Love you, kiddo."

"Love you, too."

We disconnected, and I lay back, staring at the ceiling. Somewhere between honesty, promises and apologies was a land of purgatory, and I had just pitched a tent.

Oh, stop it! Not *that* kind of tent…

*****

It was nearly seven o'clock by the time I talked myself into joining the others downstairs.

Melanie and Loretta stood side-by-side at the kitchen island, conversing in low tones while Loretta sliced veggies and Melanie beat the hell out of some chicken breasts with a tenderizing mallet. Their backs were facing me as I approached from the hallway, and I kept my head down, making a beeline for the patio door.

Outside, Doug and Brady were gathered around the grill. Doug supervised with a beer in his hand while Brady worked at the grate with a wire brush. I prodded Brady with the edge of his phone and handed it back.

"Thanks," I said. "I passed your message along to Billy."

"I appreciate it," said Brady, pocketing his phone and returning to the task at hand. "Did you work things out with Melanie yet?"

"Not yet," I said. "I keep putting my foot in my mouth."

He nodded. "Yeah, she seemed pretty pissed off."

"So, what was the deal with Loretta and her mysterious noises?" I asked, shifting my attention to Doug. "Anything to it or was it just her stomach grumbling?"

Doug shook his head. "Beats the hell out of me. I didn't hear a thing. I have to wonder if maybe she was hearing—" His eyes slid to Brady as his voice trailed away.

"Oh, yeah," I said, catching his point. "Has either Dusty or Leroy put in an appearance?"

Brady shook his head. "Nah. I guess they're laying low."

"Or they're still going at it." My mouth was on autopilot, and it slipped right out. I didn't think I could feel any lower until I saw the look on Brady's face. "Aw, man, I'm sorry. I'm a dick."

Doug scoffed. "You're both a bunch of pantywaists," he said, polishing off his beer and popping the top off his next. I noticed he had found another cigar and was busily emulsifying it in the corner of his mouth. "If I had any idea whatsoever the sort of hijinks you all fill your days with, I would've never invited you. This is like a goddamn soap opera. How are we ever supposed to get any detective work done?"

"Super easy for you to say when your only long-term relationship has been with your mother," I countered, coaxing a grin from Brady. Score one for the mouth on autopilot!

"I've had lady friends!" Doug said defensively. "I just set my sights a little—higher, that's all."

"Whoa," I said, checking my ears for residual lake water because I couldn't possibly have heard his words correctly. "Exactly what are you saying about Melanie?"

Doug clapped a hand to his forehead just as Brady began to rankle. "Oh, for heaven's sake! That's not what I meant at all. Melanie's a fine woman. Just fine."

"And Dusty?" asked Brady expectantly. Doug's eyes widened, his mouth frozen open while his brain shifted into overdrive, searching for anything positive he could say at all. Brady broke the awkward silence by laughing. "Just busting your chops, Boggs. She's a whore. Clearly, she's anybody's with a pulse. Even *that* loser." He hooked a thumb back toward the house.

"*What* loser? Are you talking about *me?*"

We turned like a well-oiled machine to find Leroy Poole scowling just outside the patio door, his big arms folded across the top of his even bigger belly.

Brady laid the brush aside and clapped his hands together, cracking his knuckles. "If the whore fits—"

I wasn't even sure what that meant, but Brady was already heading toward Leroy, his fingers curling into fists, and Leroy was clearly ready for the confrontation. He stepped down onto the patio, the cords in his arms tightening as his hands tightened into clubs. Once again, I stepped into the line of fire, separating Brady from the man I felt capable of rendering him lifeless.

"*Gentlemen!*" I commanded, proud of the unwavering authority in my voice.

"Fuck off, you faggot," growled Leroy, cocking his arm back before hammering me in the jaw.

I don't exactly remember falling but found myself on my hands and knees on the patio, searching intently for any teeth that might have ejected from my jawbone. A sea of stars played at the edges of my vision, keeping time with my heartbeat as Brady and Doug flailed around with Leroy miles above me. It was almost comical moving my hands just in time to keep them from being stepped on by any one of the guys tussling over top of me.

All the commotion brought Melanie and Loretta at a run, and Melanie still held the tenderizing mallet clenched firmly in her fist. I barely had time to think, *this is how innocent gatherings end up on Investigation Discovery,* before

ISOLATION

Melanie clocked Leroy in the back of the head, dropping him like a stone—well, boulder.

*****

Melanie handed me a damp dishrag to wipe away the blood crusting on my bottom lip. I had managed to hold onto all of my teeth, and I was grateful for that. Dentists were only succeeded by bats on my list of personal phobias. I sat across from Leroy, who was slumped in a chair across from me, his head lolling as his chest heaved with his ragged breathing. We had debated tying him to the chair but decided it would only exacerbate the situation once he regained consciousness. Brady had settled for living vicariously through Melanie's assault on the man and was currently sipping his own beer, coolly regarding Leroy with one leg slung casually over the arm of the chair at the head of the table. We were all relieved Melanie hadn't cracked the man's skull. No one wanted this weekend to end in prosecution—other than the fictional version we had signed up for. We weren't even a whole day into this mystery weekend, and so far, almost every single wheel had come off this bus.

Loretta popped her head out from the kitchen. "Is the grill ready?" she called out to her son. She had returned to the kitchen to marinade the chicken once it was clear Leroy was no longer a threat, although I can't say if anyone actually had any appetite at this point.

"Did you talk to Jasmine?" Melanie asked me, sympathy for my current plight thawing her irritation ever so slightly.

I nodded, wincing. "Do you have any Excedrin? My head's throbbing."

"In my purse," she said. "Were you able to convince her nothing was going on?"

I nodded again. "She's fine."

"And you didn't tell her—"

I shook my head, and my stomach flopped. "No details."

She paused. "So, what *did* you tell her?"

"Melanie," I looked up at her, eyes pleading. "Excedrin—please?"

She nodded curtly and disappeared into the house.

"Maybe some ice water—please?" I called after her, wincing as pain shot through my head. "Hey, Doug, I don't suppose you happened to bring my phone and keys back up here from the boat, did you?"

Doug was carefully laying chicken breasts across the grill, its sweet and sour marinade sizzling upon contact. "Sorry, man. Didn't even give it a second thought. I was focused on getting across the island in that golf cart. I stuck them in the cupholder between the seats."

Melanie appeared beside me, silently passing me three Excedrin and a glass of ice water before heading back into the kitchen to grab the basket of veggies for the grill. I tossed the caplets back and swallowed them all together, hoping for some relief sooner rather than later.

"Still no sign of Rob and Kit?" I asked.

"Nope," said Brady. "I'm starting to wonder if they've met the same fate as Sandy."

Leroy stirred at the sound of his wife's name, mumbling incoherently before settling back into a deep snore. I could sense the collective relief wash across us all. None of us were quite ready to deal with him again just yet.

The sun had nearly disappeared beneath the surface of the lake, and Loretta flipped on the outside lights, chasing away the lengthening shadows creeping in from the woods.

"How long before dinner?" I asked. "Do I have time to go down and get my phone?" I didn't want to admit I'd rather have the task done before daylight surrendered completely to night.

Doug shrugged. "It's not like we wouldn't save you some. Just hurry it up."

I hesitated, hoping Melanie would come back out so I could ask her to join me. I could see her through the window, standing at the sink and working at something while chatting with Loretta. My heart was heavy with the realization she was purposely avoiding me. I really wanted to fix what I'd damaged, and I wasn't above using the smidgen of sympathy I'd detected to my advantage. Unfortunately, she was fully invested in whatever she was doing, and it didn't look like she would be done anytime soon. It was probably just as well. I still needed to fine-tune my apology, and it felt like I was running out of time to get it right. How could I possibly keep my promise to my sister without jeopardizing the most important relationship I had ever known? Surely, Gina wouldn't want that for me. The thought of not having Melanie in my life was unbearable. I stepped off the patio and crossed the lawn, heading for the path that led down to the boathouse. My plaid slippers offered just enough protection to keep my feet from aching with each step, although I was still able to detect the occasional stone embedded in the ground as I stepped on it.

Voices faded away as I continued down the path, replaced by the sounds of water gently lapping at the shoreline, crickets chirping and frogs croaking. Clouds were layered across the darkening sky, reflecting fiery orange from the setting sun and majestic, deep purples from the lake below. It was a gorgeous view, and we were fortunate to have been invited. And what a shitty bunch of ingrates we were! Spatting like schoolchildren, brawling on the patio, damaging property and nauseating sexcapades guaranteed to keep the level of discomfort as high as possible for the remainder of our weekend. We barely had the time or energy to focus on the murder mystery that was unfolding inconveniently around us, and after dinner, I planned to assert a little leadership, especially if Doug wasn't going to. I took a deep, cleansing breath, and before I knew it, I was laughing. It was all so utterly ridiculous. I pictured myself scrambling away from the hooded figure the previous evening and doubled over at the thought, laughing until I wheezed. It *had* to be part of the scripted mystery. I gave Anyssa props for her convincing surprise and subsequent ignorance. I had certainly swallowed it—hook, line and sinker. I wondered if she had secret cameras recording our activity so she might cobble together a promotional video. If so, I had the part of damsel in distress locked *down*.

The gooseneck lantern suspended from a pole at the edge of the dock abruptly flared, triggered either by motion or timer. I stepped out onto the wooden dock and shivered. The breeze drifting in across the lake was decidedly cooler as the sun set, but I'd be lying if I said it was the only thing raising the short hairs along the base of my skull. I couldn't shake the feeling I was being watched. I glanced behind me, scouring the woods and narrow strip of beach, bracing myself for the sudden reappearance of my hooded nemesis. This time, I would stand my ground. I would walk right up and pluck that hood off of its head. If it were my fate to join the "deceased" somewhere off of the island, I would take it like a man and offer no resistance. I was done making trouble, and I meant that all the way around. I was going to be a better friend to Brady in his moment of need. I may not understand what he saw in Dusty, but I could certainly empathize with the embarrassment and betrayal he must be feeling. I planned to stay completely clear of Leroy. It was obvious he was violent and had very little self-control. I told myself I wasn't scared of him, I simply didn't want to besmirch the reputation of Boggs Investigations by means of another physical altercation with him, but the throbbing in my jaw was a steady taunt suggesting I wasn't being entirely forthright.

I grabbed the knob of the door through which Doug and I had previously entered the boathouse and pushed it open, stepping inside. I could see the outline of the boat bobbing gently in the slip and paused to allow my eyes to adapt to the inky darkness within. I probed along the wall just inside the door for a light switch and was pleased when my fingers found a double set of switches almost immediately. The first one activated a lantern mounted outside the open mouth of the boathouse. While it gave visibility to the lake beyond, it only served to drag the inside of the boathouse into deeper shadow. I turned it off and tried the other switch.

Nothing.

ISOLATION

I toggled it back and forth, apparently expecting a different outcome, but was rewarded with only more of the same. I sighed. This was where I would normally pull my phone from my pocket and use its bright white LED flashlight to guide my way, but since retrieving it was the whole point to being here, that simply wasn't an option. I began tentatively feeling my way inside, advancing my slippered feet one half-step at a time toward the boat. I certainly didn't wish to misjudge the dock's edge and lose my only remaining footwear into the lake—or worse yet, break a leg.

I sidled up beside the captain's chair and eased a leg over the boat's edge, dropping into the seat and immediately saturating my slippers.

Awesome!

Standing water had collected in the floorboards, not enough to be worrisome, but enough to give me a sense of the urgency with which Doug had returned the vessel in his haste to come to our rescue. I used my fingertips to explore the area between the seats and was rewarded almost immediately when they encountered my collection of keys resting atop my cell phone. I pocketed my keys and thumbed the switch on the side of my phone, causing its screen to glow dully. It revealed the time as 8:06 PM, the temperature a cool 67°, and the battery with only 3% charge remaining.

Just as its screen began to dim, I caught a reflection out of the corner of my eye from the bench seat behind me. I shifted in the seat to get a better look. A large, black plastic tarp was tucked loosely over something bulky in the seat. I unlocked my phone and activated its flashlight, raising up on one knee and twisting around to face the rear of the boat. I used my free hand to grab the edge of the tarp and lift it away, immediately recoiling as my brain made sense of what I found.

Sandy Poole stared back at me with wide, lifeless eyes, her skin a waxen, ashy gray. Her mouth was forever frozen open in an endless silent scream. I dropped the tarp just in time to catch a flashlight beam weaving its way toward the boathouse through the window on its far side.

I was trapped.

CHAPTER THIRTEEN

I quickly slid my phone into my pocket, hoping my phone's light had gone unnoticed by whoever approached. I lost track of the flashlight beam as it disappeared from view around the windowless rear of the boathouse. My head pounded with renewed intensity as adrenaline coursed through my veins. I scrambled to crawl out of the boat and onto the slip, looking for anywhere I might find cover inside the boathouse. Nothing immediately seemed suitable, and now the boat was knocking against the edge of the slip, shifting side-to-side from my awkward exit, doing its level best to betray my presence.

Sandy wasn't the same sort of dead that Maria had been at the foot of the stairs earlier that morning; Sandy was *dead* dead, and about that, I had no doubt. My crazed flight from the hooded prowler suddenly felt more inspired than foolish, and any reconciliation I had made between our scripted weekend and what I now witnessed went right out the window.

My breath caught as heavy footfalls sounded on the planks outside. With only seconds to make a decision, I tucked myself flat against the wall beside the door's hinges and held my breath, my heartbeat hammering in my temples. The door swung inward, providing me with partial cover as the powerful flashlight beam swept across the front of the boat and settled on the covered body in the back. The tarp hadn't settled completely over Sandy's face, and one eye glistened accusingly, fixed on the hooded figure that stepped through the door. I shrank against the wall, pulling myself as tightly as I could into the wedge of space created by its opening. I could smell perspiration and dank earth emanating from the figure, our proximity so close I could hear its labored breathing. I had been struck by its sheer size the previous evening, but cowering directly behind it, I felt completely dwarfed. I was pretty sure this was not only a man, but a *big* fucking man.

He took a few steps forward, continuing to sweep his flashlight beam to the right, and I realized I only had seconds to retain the element of surprise before I would be revealed through the nine panes of glass in the door I hid behind. I took a deep breath and threw myself into the door with all of my weight, slamming it into his side hard enough to shatter several of the glass panes and elicit a startled, "*Ooooof!*" He staggered toward the boat off-balance, and I seized the opportunity to plow into him again, sending him sprawling headlong into the hull. I teetered on the edge, nearly toppling into the boat behind him but somehow managed to reverse momentum through a wild pinwheeling of my limbs and a healthy stream of pleas to the good Lord above.

The next several minutes were a blur.

The human animal has an innate instinct for survival, a fight-or-flight response that functions on autopilot. My subconscious opted for flight without a hint of hesitation. I had no idea in what ways my opponent might be armed and wasn't about to stick around to find out. I crunched through the broken glass, charging through the door and onto the dock, running like I was on fire toward the path that led to the house. I didn't dare look back for fear he would be *right there*. I could practically feel his hot breath on the back of my neck. I heard a feral grunting uncomfortably close, and it didn't immediately register the sound was coming from me.

I pounded up the path in my soggy padded slippers, sheer panic preventing my feet from feeling any pain. The lighted patio came into view in the distance, and I could see my friends seated around the table, eating and drinking, oblivious to my plight. I tried to call out, but my lungs were already strained beyond their limit. I only managed to gasp and wheeze. It suddenly occurred to me that if my pursuer was armed with a handgun, I was an easy target, charging in a straight line towards the manor. I shifted left, right, and back again at irregular intervals, covering a wide swath of the lawn while continuing forward.

Brady abruptly pushed away from the table, jumping to his feet, and pointing toward me as his mouth worked soundlessly. It was like watching another silent movie as Melanie, Doug and Loretta caught on one-by-one, rising from their chairs to watch my demented approach, which was undoubtedly much like watching a plane attempt an emergency landing.

With only thirty yards to go, my feet got tangled together and went out from under me. I hit the ground face-first, skidding forward a few feet before consciousness took a momentary leave of absence.

*****

I was on my back when I awoke with a start, Brady and Melanie hovering directly above me. It was impossible to focus with their faces so close to mine.

"*Dwayne,*" Melanie said, gently patting my cheek. "Talk to me. What happened?"

I struggled to push them aside and get my bearings, rolling over and rising to my hands and knees. Loretta and Doug observed from a safe distance, standing at the edge of the patio. I must have looked like a wild animal. I scrambled around, frantically looking back toward the lake. I fully expected all hell to break loose when everyone finally caught sight of the behemoth who had prompted my latest mad dash back to the manor.

There was nothing to see.

A full moon had risen high in the night sky, reflecting off the lake and spilling pale illumination onto the lawn and the woods bordering it. A gentle breeze stirred a soft susurration of leaves as gentle background music to what appeared to be a perfectly tranquil evening. It was so far removed from my expectations, it felt like I must be dreaming. I stood and shook my head, rubbing deep into my eye sockets with my knuckles, as if doing so might change what I saw.

I nearly jumped out of my skin when Brady laid a hand on my shoulder. "Buddy, *seriously*. What's going on?" he asked, concern evident in his voice.

A trickle of hysterical laughter escaped my lips. "It was the hooded man," I said, continuing to scour for any sign of his approach. He couldn't have just evaporated into thin air!

I turned back just in time to catch Melanie and Brady exchange a knowing glance.

"I am *not* crazy!" I erupted, instantly furious when I recognized pity in their expressions.

Melanie took my arm. "No one is saying you're crazy, Dwayne."

"Although," added Brady. "Leroy *did* land a pretty solid blow against the ole noggin, there. People with head injuries are known to hallucinate—"

"This wasn't a fucking hallucination!" I roared, pulling my arm away from Melanie. "That *thing*—it was right in front of me! *Bigger* than me! I could smell his breath, his *perspiration!* And Sandy was *dead!*"

Another glance passed between Melanie and Brady.

"Um, yeah," said Melanie. "I was just telling Leroy what happened this afternoon."

"And what a bunch of horseshit *that* is," interjected Leroy from the edge of the patio, where he now stood beside Doug and Loretta. He must have regained consciousness in the time I had been gone. "I don't even want to *be* here, and now my wife is spending the rest of the weekend with her feet up and watching TV somewhere. And you wonder why a guy is open to a little something-something on the side."

Brady's face clouded over, but he kept his mouth shut.

"You don't understand," I said, approaching Leroy. After going toe-to-toe with that hooded monstrosity, I wasn't evenly remotely intimidated by some puffed-up loser like Leroy. "I saw Sandy down in the boathouse. Her eyes were open, and her lips were blue. This wasn't some game. This was the real deal."

Leroy shook his head and scoffed, planting his hands on his hips. "If only that was true—"

I was in his face in an instant, spittle flying on all the hard consonants. "What in the hell is *wrong* with you?! I just told you your wife is dead, and that's all you've got? You're *happy?!*"

Leroy took a step backward. "C'mon, man," he said. "We all know she's not *really* dead. No one's gonna invite us out for a mystery weekend and start killing all the guests."

I wanted to scream. I wasn't getting through to anybody. Even Loretta couldn't look me directly in the eye.

"Okay, *fine*," I said, suddenly calm and rational. "Let's go check it out."

Doug glanced longingly back at his abandoned plate on the table. "Is that really necessary? I mean, we just sat down to—"

"Yes," I said firmly. "And we're going as a team. If the killer is still down there, he can't handle all of us, and if he's not—well, then you can all relax. It's just a matter of me being nuts. Either way, you'll see what I mean about Sandy."

"Yeah—no," said Leroy, turning away and heading back to the table. "Count me out."

"Un-*believable!*" I ranted. "This is your *wife!* If there was even the slightest chance—"

"Not to mention another chance to make a fool out of Dwayne," added Melanie.

My lips snapped together, and I shot her a scathing glare. "Not helping, Mel," I said, and she apologetically shrugged. I shifted my scowl back to Leroy. "Fine, Leroy. I'm a big fan of 'no man left behind,' but no one's going to make you do what you clearly don't want to."

"I'd like to see someone *try*," he said around a mouthful of grilled chicken.

I shook my head, disgusted, and started for the table. Leroy clapped his hands together and pushed his chair back with a loud scrape, assuming I had gone on the offense.

"Relax," I said. "Eat your chicken. I only wanted this."

I grabbed the meat tenderizing mallet from where Melanie had left it lay on a paper plate on top of the table.

"Let's go," I said to the others, marching across the lawn toward the boathouse, the heft of the mallet emboldening my resolve.

*****

"There!" I exclaimed, feeling a rush of vindication as I pointed to the boathouse's side door, still swinging inward on its hinges. I ran ahead with Brady and Melanie on my heels and Doug just behind them. Loretta hesitated underneath the gooseneck lamp mounted on the post at the edge of the dock, straining to catch her breath.

I stopped just short of the door, holding out my arms to keep the others behind me. I tucked low along the wall beside the doorframe and gestured for the others to follow suit. It was pitch black inside, and I had stumbled over a sudden hiccup in my bravado. The killer could still be sprawled out inside the boat, unconscious. Even worse, he could be lurking in the shadows, watching our approach and planning his line of attack. I had shoved and run, never once looking back to see the outcome. I dubiously regarded the weapon in my hand. When I had plucked it off the table, I felt like I was grabbing Thor's Hammer. It seemed to have shrunk en route, and I now felt like I was wielding a toy. Still, I had seen Melanie lay Leroy out with it, so I kept it for good measure. I fished my cell phone from my pocket to turn on its flash and discovered its 3% charge was now fully depleted.

Shit!

"Anybody got their phone with them?" I whispered. "I could use a flashlight."

Melanie and Brady pulled theirs out, activating their apps with a few strategic swipes. Doug stood behind them, staring at his flip phone in utter confusion, turning it over in his hand and looking for a technology it clearly didn't have. I waved him away as Brady handed me his phone.

I took a deep, steadying breath and thrust the phone through the door, peeking around the corner from a vantage point very low to the ground, the mallet in my other hand, cocked and ready.

"Well, huh," I said aloud, standing and stepping into the open doorway. I swung the flashlight from left to right and back again.

"*What is it?!*" Melanie hissed, still pressed against the siding. I motioned for everyone to join me.

There was no one lurking in the shadows of the boathouse.

In fact, even the boat was gone.

*****

We regrouped around one end of the grand dining room table where we had begun our day, bringing the plates of food in from the patio and locking the French doors tight as well as engaging the security foot lock before drawing the twin panels of sheer curtains closed. The plates sat largely untouched as most of us had lost our appetites—well, except for Doug, but by now, is that really such a surprise? Doug had also chosen the seat at the head of the table to assert his authority, which gave us a shockingly intimate view of his less than elegant table manners. All of this, of course, was after Loretta had offered a few concise words of grace.

We had returned to the manor in silence, formulating our own opinions on what was real and what was not, none of us eager to share our thoughts quite yet. The one thing we collectively agreed upon was we no longer wanted to be sitting beneath a spotlight out on the patio, easy targets for anyone in the shadows. Leroy had waited for us to return, helping himself to several pieces of chicken as a trio of empty beer bottles had appeared beside his plate. He was only interested in hearing if we had found Sandy, and once he discovered we hadn't, he headed for his room where I suspected Dusty awaited. I honestly didn't care if I laid eyes on either of them again.

"I told you I wasn't imagining it," I said, breaking the silence while I picked at my plate listlessly.

"Imagining what?" Doug asked with his mouth full. "There wasn't nothing to see."

"But that's my point!" I said. "Where was the boat? Didn't you leave it in the boathouse before you came after us in the golf cart?"

Doug nodded, picking at another piece of chicken. "Well, yeah, but that was hours ago. Anyone could have moved it since then. I mean, did anyone hear the motor? It wasn't exactly quiet."

We looked at each other vacantly before one-by-one our heads began to shake.

"I wasn't really listening for anything after Dwayne came charging up the lawn like he was on fire," said Melanie.

I rankled. I was both shocked and dismayed by her characterization.

She sighed and put a hand on my arm. "You know what I mean. I was worried about you. I wasn't paying attention to anything else."

"Same here," added Brady. "I mean, what in the hell are you wearing on your feet? And what is that—blood?"

Melanie looked down. "Aren't those your bedroom slippers?"

I nodded. "I lost my shoes in the lake when I jumped off the boat, and this is the only other footwear I packed. When I got in the boat, they got soaked. It's just lake water, though."

"I beg to differ," Melanie said, pointing back toward the door where a single reddish footprint could be traced from the hallway directly to where I was seated.

I shook the slipper off, and a small triangle of jagged glass fell to the floor. My foot looked awful, crusted and drying blood speckled across the top with blisters both whole and perforated dotting the bottom. As soon as air hit skin, I gasped and winced, the abrasions making their presence known.

"Can someone please get me a damp kitchen towel?" asked Melanie, sitting on the floor and carefully examining my foot. Doug offered a grease-soaked napkin, while Loretta bustled toward the kitchen. "Where did the glass come from?"

"The boathouse door," I said, feeling further vindicated. "I slammed the door into the asshole so hard it broke several of the panes of glass out of the door. Didn't you all see shards on the ground?"

"I didn't really pay much attention once we saw the boat was gone," said Brady.

Loretta appeared behind Melanie with a dripping kitchen towel. Melanie snagged it, wringing out some of the excess before gently going to work on my foot.

"Well, I certainly didn't break those windows by hitting the door on my *imagination*," I reasoned, inhaling sharply when Melanie hit a particularly tender area.

"I could've sworn I saw a first-aid kit in the kitchen pantry. Loretta, would you mind?" asked Melanie, and Loretta nodded, trotting off again. This was the longest stretch of congeniality Loretta and I had ever shared. It was almost like she—cared. Melanie knelt in, examining my foot more closely. "*Hmm.*"

"Is that a good *hmm* or a bad one?" I asked.

She leaned back and eased off my other slipper. "Your foot's a freaking mess, but as much from the blisters on the bottom as anything else. That glass should have cut you to shreds, but you only have a few lacerations. It looks worse than it is. You should count yourself lucky. Your other foot is wet, but I don't see any blood on it at all."

I pulled it away from her less than delicate probing with a hiss; it still stung, whether it looked as damaged as my other foot or not. She eased my foot back into her grasp and continued cleaning it as Loretta returned with a square white metal box bearing the universal Red Cross symbol.

The room fell back into silence as Melanie dug triple antibiotic cream and gauze bandages from the first aid kit and went to work on my feet. Once she had secured the last strip of gauze, she stood, studying her efforts. "It's not pretty, but it's better than nothing."

I looked like a mummy from the ankles down, but the stinging had subsided, and I looked at my ruined slippers distastefully. "Should I toss these into the washer? I don't have any other shoes to wear."

"What size do you wear?" asked Brady, eyeballing my feet.

"Eleven-and-a-half wide."

"Perfect!" he said. "I'm a size twelve, and I've got an extra pair of loafers you can borrow."

I wrinkled my nose. Borrowing shoes felt like borrowing underwear. I even had my own bowling shoes and no current plans to engage in any other activity where shoe rental was a thing.

Brady laughed. "Fine. You do you. I'm just trying to be helpful."

I grudgingly reconsidered. "Well—I suppose I'd have to double up on socks to keep them from sliding."

"I believe the words you're looking for are 'thank you,'" he said.

I nodded, giving him a tight smile. I don't know why I had such an issue with being gracious to Brady. We hadn't met under the best of circumstances, but I knew he was a pretty good guy overall. Maybe I was just an asshole to everyone. For the sake of self-improvement, I'd take that under advisement.

"Did Rob and Kit ever make it back?" I asked.

"Not that I've seen," said Loretta, reapplying a vivid shade of red to her lips that had largely washed away while she was eating. "And I've been here all day long."

I looked at my phone for the thousandth time. It was still just as dead as ever. "What time is it?"

"It's almost nine-thirty," said Melanie.

Doug cleared his throat as he pushed his plate away, dabbing at the corners of his mouth with a napkin before tossing it on top of the plate. "All right, then," he said. "Let's end this day with a team meeting. Team meeting!"

He clapped his hands and immediately tarnished his own authoritative image by sticking a finger into his mouth to pick at some residual carnage left behind in his teeth. We humored him by pulling our chairs around the table, Brady and me to his right, Loretta and Melanie to his left and pushing our own plates aside. We paid him as much attention as we could; watching him use his fingernail as dental floss was like looking directly into the sun. I had barely eaten anything, but I could still feel something rising in my throat. Mercifully, Loretta had finally completed reapplying her makeup and caught sight of what her son was doing. She smacked his hand away from his mouth.

"Jumpin' Jehoshaphat, son!" admonished Loretta, her penciled-in eyebrows knitting together like chopsticks. "Get your finger out of your mouth! A first grader knows better!"

"*Ma!*" He recoiled, cleared his throat and regained whatever composure he could. "I think it's a good practice to end each day by making sure we're all on the same page."

"There's really only today and tomorrow left," I noted.

"Yes, but still—I think it's something positive we can carry with us back to the office."

I slowly nodded. "Okay. Sounds reasonable."

"I think we should start by identifying exactly who is a member of this 'team,'" said Brady, using air quotes around the last word.

"Well, sure," said Doug, looking around the table. "Clearly all of us are Team Boggs, right?"

I covered my grin as best as possible. *Team Boggs*. I wondered if he would carry *that* back to the office and have it emblazoned on t-shirts as our official work uniform. Nevertheless, I joined everyone else in nodding my agreement.

"What about Rob and Kit?" asked Melanie.

"If they show up, we can invite them to participate, but I'm leaning towards sliding them into the victim category for now," said Doug. Loretta had produced a steno pad and pencil from her bag and was busily taking notes. "Missing, at the very least."

More heads bobbed as Loretta's pen flew across the page.

"Leroy and Dusty?" asked Melanie, looking directly at Brady.

He shook his head. "I say they're on their own. I mean, after what Dusty did—"

"Not to mention Leroy's lack of enthusiasm for anything other than being a violent idiot," I added, unconsciously touching my still-throbbing jaw. "I would agree."

Again, heads nodded unanimously.

"All right, that's settled," said Doug, looking to Loretta to make sure she had it down. He paused for a moment before wading into the next topic. "How many of us believe something truly sinister is going on?"

My hand shot up while everyone else's remained below the tabletop, and eye contact wasn't happening with anyone.

"*Seriously?!*" I challenged. "What's it take to get through to you people? Clearly someone *dying* isn't enough!"

Melanie eyes finally met mine. "That's just it, Dwayne. There's no body. No evidence that anything off script has happened at all."

Brady nodded. "She's right, man. I mean, this is a *mystery weekend*—and it's actually been kind of exciting. What exactly did you expect?"

I was left speechless, shaking my head.

"So, how many believe Dwayne is overreacting?" asked Doug, and I was mortified to watch hand after hand head for the ceiling, but I wasn't ready to surrender entirely, not just yet.

"Okay," I said. "I see how the 'team' feels—" It was my turn for air quotes. "—but I think out of an abundance of caution, we should refuse to be picked off one-by-one. Let's do everything as a group, starting with camping out together tonight. *C'mon!* No man left behind?"

Loretta closed her steno pad and tucked it away. "You can count me out. I have a whole nighttime beauty regimen to follow. I'm not doing it in front of all of you."

"But what about those sounds you heard earlier?" I was not above using fear to my advantage.

"Easy," she said. "Dougie can stay with me. Come on, son." She stood and patted his arm.

"*Ma!*" His protest was cut short by the look she leveled at him. He grumbled something unintelligible before muttering, "We meet back here at ten AM sharp. Meeting adjourned." He followed Loretta out of the room like a puppy with his tail between his legs.

I looked at Melanie and Brady expectantly.

Melanie rolled her eyes, and Brady broke into a toothy, dimpled grin, opening his arms wide. "Roomies!"

Ugh. Maybe I should have given this a little more thought.

ISOLATION

CHAPTER FOURTEEN

Before heading upstairs, we trudged as a team through the kitchen so I could toss my stained and soggy slippers into the washing machine in the laundry room at the far end. I didn't have much confidence I could salvage them, but I thought it was worth a try. Melanie and Brady rummaged around for snacks and drinks, loading up a canvas grocery bag while I treated the stains and set the machine for bulky items—heavily soiled. I pressed the start button, and the machine responded as if a drunken, overweight hamster was galloping for its life in a running wheel.

We stopped by what had originally been mine and Melanie's room, Brady and I waiting just inside the door while Melanie collected some essentials for our impromptu slumber party. We had opted to stay in my current room as Brady's things were already there. She tossed me the pillows from her bed before wrapping the comforter around my neck, then went back for a change of clothes and her toiletry bag. Once inside my room, we dropped it all on the floor and locked ourselves in for the night.

"So, who's sleeping where?" asked Melanie, eyeing the bed.

I had never been less sleepy in my life.

Brady checked his phone. "I don't care. I can sleep anywhere. It's almost ten, though, and I want to catch Billy before it gets any later. I'm going to step into the restroom, and you guys decide." He was already connecting his call as he crossed into the bathroom and closed the door behind himself.

"You can have the bed," I said automatically, sitting on the vintage sofa positioned along the interior wall.

"I don't want to put you out of your bed," said Melanie, perching on the corner of the mattress, nevertheless.

"We could always share it," I said. "I mean, that was the original plan, wasn't it?"

She shot me a wounded look that I couldn't hold. It broke my heart.

"Look, Mel," I began, choosing my words carefully, if not particularly eloquently. "I'm sorry. Really, really sorry. I had no business looking at your laptop, and I completely overreacted. There is no excuse for it. None. But I promise it will never happen again."

Dammit! Out slipped another promise!

Her eyes dropped to her hands, fidgeting in her lap. I wasn't sure she was going to respond when she finally said, "I take promises very seriously, you know. And I don't trust very easily, either. Don't say something like that if you don't mean it."

"I *do* mean it," I assured, moving beside her on the bed and taking her hands into mine. She allowed it but refused to look up.

"What did you say to Jasmine?" she asked, her voice a monotone.

"What?"

She caught me by surprise with the question, and now she turned toward me, her eyes probing my face for my reaction. "I asked you not to let her know we were fighting, not to ruin her weekend. Did you tell her?"

My mouth opened, but I couldn't formulate my response quickly enough. She jerked her hands away from mine.

"*Dammit,* Dwayne! It was just one little thing I asked—"

"And she would have known I was lying," I said, cutting her short. "I made her a promise, too. Remember? When we were at Sarah's, that night she ran away. I wasn't about to break it."

Sarah was Jasmine's grandmother and Melanie's former mother-in-law. Only a couple months had passed since Jasmine had gone through a rather rebellious phase that included a savage attack on her own hair with a pair of kitchen scissors as well as a complete and total rejection of me. We had mended fences by promising to be straight with one another, regardless of how awkward or embarrassing it might be. She had dealt with a lifetime of well-intentioned lies from her late father and wasn't going to put up with it from anyone else, especially me. It was a make-or-break moment in our relationship, and I simply couldn't violate it.

Melanie resumed studying her hands in her lap, reflecting on my words. She knew they were true.

"I told her it was no big deal," I continued. "Everybody has a difference of opinion now and then. I made her promise me that she wouldn't let it spoil her weekend, and she seemed good with that."

"Really?"

"Really. We chatted a little longer about what they'd done today and finished up joking about how many of Dexter's hairballs my mother might leave for her to clean up once we get home. She's fine."

She sighed, visibly relieved. "You're really good with her," she said. "Thank you."

I hooked a finger under her chin and turned her face towards mine. "I need to be better with you," I said. "I'm not going to ask about what you were writing or why or if it has anything whatsoever to do with me or us. I'm not going to try and steal any more glances, and if you ever leave your laptop on with the document wide open, I will promptly leave the room."

"Why should I believe you?"

"Because I believe if you had any real problems with me, you wouldn't hide them in a book. I don't think you *could* hide them in a book. You're not built that way."

She tossed me some side eye. "Are you saying I can't hold my tongue?"

"Well—you're not exactly shy," I said, risking a grin and relieved when she returned it, nodding.

"I *do* want you to read it, but not until it's done. I'm completely out of my comfort zone but have such a good feeling about it," she said. "And you have to know that while I may find inspiration from real life, these are fictional characters in fictional situations. You shouldn't overthink this whole 'who's who' thing. You made yourself crazy for nothing."

"I believe you," I said. "I'm so sorry I reacted the way I did. I don't know if you've noticed this, but I don't have a whole lot of relationship experience. I'm making this shit up as I go along. I ask myself every single day what I've done to deserve you."

"You're not so bad," she conceded, adding, "Sometimes."

"I want you to feel like you can trust me with anything, and I know I'm going to have earn that trust. I promise you, it's my top priority." Yes, it was another promise, but one I was resolved to keep. I was dismayed to see her face cloud over. "What? What's wrong?"

She shrugged. "It's hard to take you completely seriously when—" Her words trailed away, but I knew to what she referred.

West Virginia.

Shit.

I was torn between two conflicting promises, and it was like navigating an impossibly high wire without a safety net.

I sighed. "There will come a time when I can tell you every single thing that happened while I was away, and I will. I just can't right now."

"Because you don't trust me?"

"No! That's not it at all. I trust you with my life. It's just—"

"What, then? What could it possibly be that you can't tell me?" She looked wounded, and I felt like I was rapidly losing what little ground I had gained.

"I made another stupid promise," I said. "That is the *only* reason I can't tell you. And let me tell you, this promise is kicking my ass. I *want* to tell you."

"Then *tell* me," she urged, taking my hands. "I won't tell a soul!"

I felt defeated. "I can't. Not yet."

It was her turn to sigh, but she continued to hold my hands in hers. "This might surprise you, but that actually makes me feel a little better."

I was most *definitely* surprised. "Yeah?"

She nodded. "Between the way you handled Jasmine earlier and this—well, it shows me exactly how rock-solid your word is, even when it's difficult. I take a great deal of comfort in that."

"Are we okay?" I asked.

"We are."

Her eyes locked on mine, and I leaned in, kissing her gently. She let go of my hands and wrapped her arms around my neck, pulling me closer as our kiss intensified, passionate and probing. Tingling heat rushed to my extremities as I slid a hand underneath her t-shirt to cup her breast. She gasped sharply as my thumb found its target.

A knock sounded from inside the bathroom. "Um, guys? I've been done with my call for about ten minutes now. I didn't mind giving you all a few to work your shit out, but I really don't need to hear any of this."

Dammit!

We had forgotten all about Brady.

*****

I tossed and turned for what seemed like hours and now stared at the ceiling high above me. I was both exhausted and elated, and the end result was a rare night of insomnia. Melanie purred rhythmically in the king size bed while Brady lay on a nest of comforters on the floor on the other side of the room. I had decided the couch was the safest option for me. I was afraid I might be unable to keep my hands to myself if I crawled into the bed next to Melanie. We didn't fight often, but there was nothing quite like make-up sex—well, with the possible exception of narrowly-escaped-a-serial-killer sex, but that was hopefully a once in a lifetime event. I didn't want to start something we couldn't finish while Brady sporadically and abruptly spoke in tongues while sleeping at our feet. I couldn't even see what time it was since I wasn't wearing my watch and I had plugged my phone in to recharge at the desk.

Deciding there was no use fighting it, I slid off the couch and fumbled around for my duffel bag on the floor beside me. I thought I might as well use the time to do a little research on Marble Toe Island and the legend of this elusive spectral predator who was making me question my sanity. Thankfully, I had tucked my MacBook Air in my bag at the last moment, almost as an afterthought. Afterthought might not be the right word—despite my burgeoning career as private investigator, at the core I'm still an IT guy. We don't go off the grid easily. And thank goodness for that! I wouldn't have touched Melanie's laptop with a ten-foot pole after finally mending fences.

I sidestepped Brady's outstretched legs and seated myself at the writing desk by the window. Using the information on the welcome note Anyssa had left for all her guests, I was soon logged onto the guest wi-fi, and emails poured in like water. I checked the clock in the title bar and noted it was a little after one in the morning. I muted the sound and dimmed the display so as not to disturb Melanie or Brady and spent the next several minutes catching up. Most of the email was junk, but two of my consultant customers had reached out for quotes on upgrading equipment and software, and Mom had shared several adorable pictures of my new niece, Abbie, doing what newborns do best. Sleeping. Eating. Crying. Although I could see others' fuzzy limbs out-of-focus and at the periphery of the photos, only Jo Morrow was allowed to share the screen with our tiny princess, holding her proudly while rocking, feeding and comforting her. I wondered if she was giving the other grandparents any time at all—much less the parents. The last photo was a closeup of Dexter in the window overlooking my porch, taken from outside. His mouth was open mid-mew, and he looked less than amused. I decided it was time to invest in a cat tree to help him occupy his time indoors. A former classmate built them near Lymont, and I put a reminder on my calendar to get in contact just as soon as I returned. As much as I had been away the past few weeks, I owed it to my little guy. Plus, his backside was getting a little chunky, and a bit of exercise certainly wouldn't hurt.

I pulled up Chrome and cracked my knuckles. It was time to get to work.

A cursory search for Marble Toe Island brought up an extremely brief entry from Wikipedia, identifying it as one of several islands on Lake Erie. This linked back to a full list of the Lake Erie Islands, including to which state or province they belonged, the area in both square miles and kilometers, location by longitude and latitude, as well as whether each was currently inhabited. Finding none of that particularly illuminating, I clicked back into Marble Toe's meager details to peruse more thoroughly.

There wasn't anything very specific about the island's ownership, other than the rather nondescript notation it was private and the standard disclaimer that the page needed additional citations for verification. I would think ownership would be a matter of public record, but who was I to know? There were very few references listed at the bottom of the page, but one article leapt out.

A Great Lakes Haunting by R.J. McBurney. It had been published in the early 2000s by a *Reader's Digest*-like magazine called *Ohio Living* from a small press based in Akron. 'Ohio' in the title borrowed the OSU font and hues and was spelled out like the oh-so-familiar Buckeyes' chant: OH-IO.

I clicked on the link, and a grainy black-and-white photo of the very manor in which we slept appeared on screen. It was taken some time in the 90s and was accompanied by an old school travelogue, the type of thing you might find today in an online travel blog.

> *Before the summer of 1993, it was not for me to say whether ghosts existed—I had no firm opinion on the matter one way or the other. But it was the summer of Alethea Banks, and she was determined to end the season with*

not only proof they existed, but they existed closer to home than one might realize.

We were both students at Ohio University, me in pursuit of an Engineering degree while she was a Liberal Arts major. It was also a summer of love, two young kids falling for each other with everything they had. I would have followed Alethea anywhere that summer, and as a matter of fact, I did.

We lived like hippies out of the back of an old Dodge van, traveling our home state as Leonard Nimoy would say, "In Search Of." I didn't have any expectations about what we may or may not find, only the expectation that I would be sharing the summer with the girl of my dreams. Alethea, on the other hand, had made a list.

Initially, we kept it local, investigating Ohio University's own campus legends. Wilson Hall has quite the reputation as a hotspot for ghostly activity, including disembodied voices, apparitions and objects inexplicably moving. Washington Hall is supposedly haunted by members of a girls' high school basketball team who died in an automobile accident after visiting the campus. And, of course, there's the Athens Lunatic Asylum, also known as the Ridges. I could easily fill entire volumes detailing its sordid history and alleged paranormal events, but I'll leave that for you to investigate. We were sorely disappointed by them all, never experiencing anything more substantial than an occasional case of the willies.

We began to crisscross the state at Alethea's whims, setting up camp for several nights at a time. We visited Pike County and camped out on Big Run Road in Wakefield, hoping to witness the spirits of students who had tragically died during a basketball game when there was an explosion in the boiler room. There are accounts of a phantom cheerleader, visible from behind, standing in the school's ruins, who reveals the extent of her burns only when she turns around.

We found nothing.

We went south to investigate a haunting on Brenner Hollow in Lymont where a two-year-old boy had wandered away from his family in the mid-1920s and had fallen to the bottom of an open well. He hadn't died immediately and was only found several days later, his face frozen in a mask of horror. His cries for help are rumored to be most prevalent in July, around the time the incident occurred.

Again, nothing.

I paused, sucking in my breath as a shiver ran down my spine. Sarah McGregor, Jasmine's grandmother, lived on Brenner Hollow. It was a creepy little dirt road that wound back through the woods where neighbors were few and far between. It could have easily doubled as the setting for Washington Irving's *The Legend of Sleepy Hollow*. I had spent more nights than I could count as a guest of her son—my best friend, Ryan. So many July nights spent camping outdoors, both of us completely oblivious to this tragic occurrence. Our teenaged imaginations would have run *wild*.

Summer was drawing to a close, and classes would soon be starting once more. We had enjoyed our time traversing the state and leaning into the anticipation of what we might find at each of the hauntings we investigated, even though our investigations had yielded nothing. We had saved one of the most interesting places for last, not so much by choice as by necessity. Every place we had visited so far had been accessible by land. Not so for Marble Toe Island, the private residence of the Williams family. Situated on Lake Erie, it was accessible only by boat, and we didn't have access to one. But all that changed after we happened upon an abandoned rowboat while wrapping up another fruitless endeavor in Cuyahoga County.

The story was an enthralling tale of forbidden love between the son of a wealthy Caucasian family from Lexington, Kentucky, and a young slave girl with whom he had become infatuated. The two eventually ran off, but not before the young man had killed his older brother for sexually assaulting his future bride. They lived under aliases for some time in Indiana before eventually fleeing the area entirely by means of the Underground Railroad. They took refuge on

Marble Toe Island during a brutal winter storm on their flight to safety in Canada and wished to make a permanent home there. The only thing they required was the funding to break ground. Once he'd gotten word of his mother's passing, the young man returned to his old Kentucky home with the intention of retrieving a stash of gold that was buried on the family property. With his find, he was able to develop the island as he desired, erecting a sizable manor house where he would go on to live out his days with his slave bride and their children.

It wasn't entirely smooth sailing, however.

They seemed to have brought along the ghost of the murdered brother. He was a hulking man with a face ruined by gunshot. The menacing specter was witnessed by no less than several dozen people throughout the years, its purpose seemingly to shock and disorient. In fact, the lady of the house was once so surprised by its appearance she fell down the manor's grand staircase, breaking her arm in two places. The spirit was rumored to be vengeful towards his brother not only for murdering him, but also for setting in motion the events that would eventually destroy the entire family. Multiple eyewitnesses claimed he also spoke to them, demanding the whereabouts of the Williams family gold.

In early August, Alethea and I set out under the cover of darkness in our boat, powered only by our own four arms and the mismatched sets of oars we had purchased at an estate auction. An enormous storm developed while we were underway, and we barely made it to the island in one piece. We abandoned our boat near the shore, and it was damaged beyond repair when it crashed onto large rocks along the coastline.

Technically, we were trespassing. The island was private, and the manor house was inhabited by the latest generation of the Williams family. As inconvenient and dangerous as our venture had become, the storm had given us a legitimate excuse to be here. We made our way through the woods as lightning flared and thunder crashed, torrential rain obscuring our field of vision.

Suddenly, Alethea grabbed my arm and stopped, staring back from where we had come. An enormous, hooded figure stood on the path, no more than *twenty feet away. His features were hidden under the cover of his cowl as well as by darkness, but a sudden jag of lightning revealed his ruined face. As thunder followed closely behind, we both heard it call for its gold, its otherworldly voice thick and wet.*

We ran like our lives depended on it, following the path, and emerging on the grounds of the manor. We pounded on the front door, undoubtedly startling the occupants out of a sound sleep. Nevertheless, they invited us in and gave us shelter for the night. We tried to explain what we had seen in the woods, but it soon became clear they wanted no part of it. It was equally clear to Alethea and me that they knew more than they were willing to admit.

That August night in 1993, we had borne witness to the ghost of Julian Williams, of that I have no doubt. From that moment on, I was a true believer. I knew ghosts existed because I had seen one with my own two eyes.

Well, how about that? It certainly seemed to validate what we had already learned from Anyssa.

I yawned, rubbing my eyes. It was closing in on two o'clock, and I felt like I might actually be able to get some sleep. I powered down my laptop and took my phone off the charger after confirming it was once again fully charged. I set an alarm for eight-thirty, knowing full well Melanie would already be up to wake me, and crawled beneath the blanket on the couch. Somehow, I felt less intimidated now. Having read the online account from a random third-party corroborating the vision I had seen on two different occasions now gave me relief. I no longer felt as if my sanity was under fire. I closed my eyes and drifted away almost immediately.

*****

Scraping and moaning, the sounds were soft but persistent, and eased me from my slumber. I managed to lift one eyelid only to discover the room still completely enveloped in darkness. I shifted my glance toward the bed and detected motion under the covers, the soft susurration of skin against cotton, shapes shifting into other shapes.

My imagination needed nothing more to shift into overdrive. I slid off the couch so fast I almost landed on my ass. "Brady Garrett, you son of a bitch!" I roared, charging toward the bed. I was certain I would find the bastard doing with Melanie what Leroy had done with his own date only hours before, and I was livid.

"Mmm—*huh?*" Brady's voice, thick with sleep, came from behind me, and I turned toward it just as Melanie flipped on one of the bedside lamps. Brady was still tangled in the comforters on the floor at the far end of the wall, his dark, curly hair leaping from his head in every direction.

"What's wrong, Dwayne?" asked Melanie blearily, yawning. I looked back toward her as she stretched an arm high overhead, twisting sideways. I heard her back ripple and pop before she relaxed, squinting up at me in confusion. She was alone in the bed. She checked the display on her phone which rested on the nightstand. "It's barely five o'clock."

I shook my head, momentarily dazed, but then I heard it again. Scraping and moaning, soft in the distance. "Did you hear that?" I asked.

It was Brady's turn to yawn. "Hear what?"

"*Shhh!*" I insisted, straining my own ears.

Quite a few seconds passed in silence, but then it came again. Brady stood as Melanie kicked her covers aside. We gathered in front of the fireplace near the foot of the bed and continued to listen for another occurrence. We were rewarded more quickly this time.

"What in the hell *is* that?" asked Melanie.

"And where's it coming from?" added Brady.

We listened for the next instance, and when it came, our eyes were drawn to the cold dark mouth of the unlit fireplace.

"I think it came from in there," I said, leaning into the hearth.

CHAPTER FIFTEEN

The sounds died away after that last instance, and no amount of poking or prodding revealed anything hidden within the confines of the fireplace. It seemed to jive with what Loretta had experienced earlier in the day, but we decided there was no need to wake the others. It could keep until morning. To be completely honest, I don't think any of us were in any real hurry to wander out of relative safety and into the shadowy hallways of the mansion. Any way you looked at it, this place was damned creepy in the dark, and it was bad enough the three of us would be running short on sleep, although not for lack of trying.

As we had all struggled unsuccessfully to find a skosh more sleep, tossing and turning in our various spaces, I used the time to try and talk myself down from a couple of ledges. First, what were the odds that Sandy was really dead? I mean, she certainly *looked* dead, but it wasn't like I had checked for a pulse. Once she had been plucked off the hiking trail when Melanie and Brady had gone down to the water's edge to rescue me, we had no real idea of what happened to her. We had simply assumed she was relaxing, feet up and magazine in hand, wherever it is the dead go once they receive their tarot card calling. But what if this were part and parcel of the game, and guests who received their "Death" card may now be willing co-conspirators against the rest of us? It actually made a lot more sense than a ghostly murderer just *happening* to turn up on this particular weekend to seek some bloody vengeance that was actually far more violent and aggressive than any of the legends I had been told or read online.

Second, whatever this hooded figure was, it certainly wasn't ghostly. I had felt the resistance of its weight as I had slammed first the door and then myself into it, knocking it down into the boat. For the first time, I felt a pang of uncertainty and regret. I considered the possibility I might have actually injured someone who had been working for Anyssa, someone who was just trying to do his job only to be rewarded with assault.

It then occurred to me some of our fellow guests might actually be moles, and in on the whole thing from the start. As another flash of Sandy's frozen death mask flashed across the silver screen of my memory, I briefly wondered if she and Leroy might be actors playing parts, but I discounted that thought almost immediately. Sandy, I might be able to buy, but Leroy? No. He was completely off his chain. Not only had Brady caught Leroy in flagrante with his prurient and promiscuous dim bulb of a girlfriend, but Leroy had nearly succeeded in loosening several of my teeth when he had hammered me to the ground the previous evening. None of this was acceptable behavior for an employee to engage in with guests, even if the guests were only here on complimentary passes.

By seven o'clock, Melanie had given up trying to find her way back to Sleepytown. She gathered a change of clothes and her toiletry bag and headed for the bathroom, thus beginning our assembly line march through the shower, one right after the other. By eight, we were in the kitchen, rummaging through the refrigerator and cupboard, deciding what sounded good for breakfast. The sun had crept quietly over the horizon, pale and shrouded in a gray, overcast sky that carried a promise of rain.

Soon, the heady scent of coffee brewing filled the area, complimented by sausage links Brady was browning in a large, electric skillet. Melanie cracked eggs into a glass bowl and beat them into a froth while I chopped onion, mushroom, and a colorful trio of peppers to add to the mix. As I was stirring in a blend of shredded Swiss and Pepper Jack, the olfactory siren song worked its magic on the Boggses, Loretta bustling in while Doug trailed behind, still not entirely awake.

Loretta's mint-green overalls were nearly enough to push back the oppressive gloom of the morning, and as always, I wondered how she managed to apply her makeup with the same garish intensity day after day. Lee Press-On Faces? She skirted the kitchen island while Doug pulled up a stool, practically rubbing the features off his face while his mother poured him a mug of coffee. She then washed her hands thoroughly at the sink, drying them on a dish towel before stepping up beside me.

"What can I do?" she asked.

"I don't know," I replied. "What *can* you do?"

"*Dwayne!*" Melanie admonished, casting me a sour glance as she poured our breakfast casserole mixture into a rectangular glass baking dish.

"I'm used to rudeness from this one," said Loretta, undeterred. She fixed upon Brady, who was in the process of pulling sausage links from the skillet. He had prepared a bowl of pancake batter and set it aside and was preparing to empty the grease from the skillet into a Pyrex measuring cup. "What are you doing, Garrett?"

"I'm making pigs in a blanket," Brady said, carefully pouring off the grease. "It's one of Billy's favorites." He ran a paper towel around the inside of the skillet, reduced the heat and poured the entire bowl of pancake batter into its bottom. He then began haphazardly dropping sausage links into the batter.

Loretta scowled. "Looks more like hogs in a swamp to me," she said dubiously, reaching for the flour and milk.

Brady shrugged. "It may not pretty, but I've never had any complaints."

"Save me that grease and at least a quarter of those sausage links. Where can I find a bowl?" she asked, and Melanie retrieved one from a cabinet in the island.

"Will this do?" she asked.

Loretta nodded. "Now, y'all give Mama some room. I'm gonna do biscuits and gravy like you ain't never put in your mouths before." She cracked her knuckles and began mixing ingredients. Doug brightened visibly at the prospect, and I nabbed a stool beside him at the island.

"I think we heard your phantom noises last night," I said.

"Really?" Loretta didn't sound particularly interested, focused instead on kneading dough out onto the counter, her tongue tucked tightly into the corner of her mouth. I noticed empty wrappers to a whopping four sticks of butter near her workspace and decided that for at least *this* meal, I was going to side with the half of the medical community that had determined saturated fats were healthy, not harmful. "Not me. Slept like a baby. Of course, I'm not sure how much I would have heard anyway over my CPAP."

"Your CPAP?" asked Melanie, apparently forgetting Doug's earlier reference.

Loretta nodded, setting her jowls to jiggling. "I've got the apnea. The CPAP keeps me breathing through the night."

Doug cradled his coffee and cast her a bleary scowl. "And it sounds like a vacuum cleaner. I like to have never got to sleep. Did you figure out what was making the noises?"

I shook my head, taking a sip of my own coffee. "Just some scraping and moaning. It seemed to be coming from inside the walls. It woke us up and repeated a few times before stopping. Couldn't get back to sleep after that."

"You don't suppose it was Leroy and—well, you know who?" Doug asked, eyes shifting towards Brady.

"My guess is that is *exactly* what it was," said Brady, sliding a pile of sausage links over to Loretta. "And good for them! They can keep it up until it's time to go home, for all I care. Speaking of which, I wonder if it's dawned on ole Leroy that he and his wife are gonna have to give that skank a ride home? She sure as hell ain't coming back with us."

"There's always Uber," Melanie said, sliding the baking dish with the breakfast casserole into one side of the stainless-steel industrial oven.

Loretta rounded her dough and patted it lightly with flour. "I don't rightly see how it could be what I heard yesterday. I mean, both Leroy's and Brady's rooms are on the other side of the house from where mine is. No matter which room those two decided to saturate in sin, it would have been too far from my mine." She rummaged through the drawers of the island until she found a rolling pin and began rolling out her dough.

"Not necessarily," said Brady. "Some of these old buildings have crazy acoustics. You know, like the Whispering Gallery in the Capitol Building in Washington. There are some places where you can hear things from yards away just as clearly as if they came from right beside you."

"Or it could be ghosts," said Loretta nonchalantly as she used an inverted coffee mug to cut out biscuit after biscuit from her expanse of dough. "If you believe in that sort of thing."

"Do you?" I asked, watching her transfer her perfectly circular rings of dough to an ungreased cookie sheet.

She placed the cookie sheet into the other side of the oven and turned back to me, surprised. "Well, sure. I mean, there's the Father, the Son and the Holy Spirit, right? I'm sure there are spirits out there that are a whole lot less holy, if you know what I mean. And I wouldn't think I'd have to convince *you* of that. You've been seeing ghosts from almost the minute we got here. Would you hand me that skillet?" She pointed to a cast iron number that was suspended along with several other pieces in a pot rack above the island. I easily snagged what would have taken her three steps up a stepladder to reach.

Normally, I would've rankled at her insinuation, but I was thinking about what I thought I saw when I was first awakened. It certainly *looked* as though something had been underneath the covers with Melanie. I hadn't mentioned it to her or Brady. I mean, what was the point? She certainly hadn't *felt* anything under the covers with her, and after all the ranting, raving and running I had done for the past couple of days, it would have only further strained what little credibility I had left.

"I did find an interesting article on the internet last night," I hedged, keeping my personal opinion to myself. I gave the short version of R.J. McBurney's first-person accounting of his encounter with the hooded ghost of Julian Williams. "It certainly seems to jive with what Anyssa told us about the ghost."

"I'm finding it more and more difficult to believe she only told us the story because Dwayne brought it up," said Melanie, leaning against the counter. "It feels like the ghost of Julian Williams is firmly at the center of whatever this mystery weekend is supposed to be about."

"She's one hell of an actress, then," said Brady. "She certainly looked surprised to me."

Melanie paused as Loretta dropped the sausage links into a food processor and pulsed them into crumbles. She then placed them into the cast iron skillet where she had already deposited the sausage grease and a healthy dollop of butter. It was beginning to smell like a little corner of heaven in here, and my stomach rumbled in anticipation.

"Judging from the goo-goo eyes you were sending her way, I'm pretty sure you would have believed *anything* she had to say," said Melanie. Brady shrugged, trying for righteous indignation, but we all knew he was full of shit. In fact, his brazen display of interest in Anyssa may have been all the incentive needed to push Dusty into Leroy's arms, but I pushed the thought away before it blossomed into an outright mental image. I wasn't about to spoil my appetite by going there. Instead, I watched Loretta pour a combination of milk and cream into her skillet, stirring it into the roux she had made with the sausage, grease, butter and a generous dollop of flour. There was no measurement involved; she eyeballed everything, and for the first time in my life, I trusted her completely. I felt like I was witnessing the creation of a masterpiece.

"What's for breakfast? Smells pretty good."

We all turned to find Leroy stretching in the kitchen doorway. Strained to its limits across his swollen beer belly, he wore a stained A-shirt colloquially and yet fittingly known as a wifebeater. It had once been white in a previous lifetime and was paired with a set of plaid boxer shorts with a peek-a-boo fly that threatened us all with a show that no one wanted to see.

Loretta didn't even look up. "I guess that depends on how much work you're willing to put into it," she said. "And I'm guessing not much. I think you'll find some cereal and granola bars in the pantry. Why don't you grab enough for you and your little jezebel and get on out of here?"

He cocked his head, slowly sauntering toward the stovetop, nabbing a spoon from the counter along the way. "Now, why would I choose cereal when there's plenty to go around right here?"

He started to reach for a spoonful of the thickening gravy, but Loretta pushed his hand away. "This isn't a restaurant, you goon. What? You think you can just show up at the tail end of preparation with a plate, spoon and a big, fat growling belly? Get out."

"Listen, bitch," he said, and Doug eased himself off of the stool. On the other side of Loretta, Brady turned the electric skillet down and set his spatula aside, ready to intercede if necessary; flipping his pancake loaf could wait. Melanie appeared to be mentally counting the number of steps it would take to reunite her with the meat tenderizing mallet that had proven so effective the previous evening. The tension in the kitchen had ratcheted from zero to sixty in the blink of an eye. "I'm going to fix me and my lady friend a plate, and I'll be on my way."

"*Lady friend*?" repeated Melanie. "And just what do you think your wife is going to have to say about your *'lady friend?'*"

Leroy rolled his eyes and laughed. "We have one half of an open relationship. Do you know what that means?"

Melanie shook her head.

"I can fuck whoever I want to, whenever I want to, and she's not gonna do one damn thing about it. She's lucky I let her stay."

Melanie recoiled. "You're *disgusting!*"

"Don't be jealous, sweet thing," he said, making obnoxious kissy faces at her. "There's plenty of ole Leroy to go around." He returned his attention to Loretta while Melanie quite admirably kept the contents of her stomach down. "So, how much longer until it's ready?"

Loretta put a hand on her hip and gave Leroy a withering look. "Do you have a hearing problem, Tubby, or are you just stupider than you look? You can wait until hell freezes over, but you aren't touching one bite of this fine breakfast, you big, dumb gorilla."

"And who's going to stop me?" Leroy sneered uglily, leaning down into Loretta's face.

What happened next was quick.

Doug started around the counter with me right behind him. Melanie went for the mallet as Brady moved toward Loretta's side, but not before Loretta reached out, snagging Brady's hot metal spatula from the counter and backhanding Leroy with it, first across one cheek, then reversing course and tagging the other. Wide-eyed, he staggered backward, hands flying to his face where red marks from the spatula were already taking shape.

"You hit me!" Leroy stated the obvious, completely shocked. Not gonna lie, I was a little stunned myself. "Why, you motherfucking *bitch*—"

He reached out to grab Loretta, but she sidestepped him and grabbed a fistful of his fingers, twisting sideways and using the leverage of her own body to pull his hand into a most unnatural position. Leroy cried out in pain, drawing back his other fist with every intention of laying Loretta out.

"I wouldn't do that if I were you," Doug advised with a confidence I'd never heard before.

Leroy's fist froze in mid-air as he saw that Doug was covering him in a slight crouch, holding a snub-nosed revolver steady with both hands, but he still managed to smirk. "You wouldn't dare."

"You're threatening to assault my mama," Doug returned evenly. "Do you really think I wouldn't?"

Leroy's smirk faltered, then fell away. His fist unfurled and dropped, but not before Loretta gave his other hand another sharp twist, causing him to cry out once more before she finally let go of his fingers.

"I'll give you exactly thirty seconds to grab something out of that pantry and get the hell out of here," said Doug, waggling his gun in that direction.

Palms up, Leroy held his hands in front of himself while backing away from Loretta and crossing to the pantry. Doug covered his every move, laser focused and arms steady. Leroy snagged a box of cereal and sidestepped toward the hall, his cheeks burning crimson while doing his level best to murder us with his eyes. He paused in the doorway. "You've gone too far this time, little man."

"It's hard to take your threats seriously when you're clinging to a box of Captain Crunch," I said, watching the color in his face intensify.

"Yeah, big man over there," Leroy said, pointing at me. "Pretty easy to talk shit when your little buddy's got a gun on me. You just wait." His finger now traveled left to right, covering us all. "When you least expect it—well, you'd be smart to watch your backs."

"You couldn't identify smart if it was the only participant in a lineup," said Melanie. "Watch *this*." She flipped him off with the hand that wasn't holding the mallet.

Just when I thought his head was going to explode, he turned and marched down the hallway, turning left and thundering up the stairs like an angry child who had been sent to his room.

A timer sounded, and without missing a beat, Loretta handed Brady the spatula and peered into her side of the oven. "Biscuits are done!"

*****

Doug and I carried place settings out to the big table in the dining hall while the others finished preparing and plating their dishes.

"You *do* realize we're in a whole heap of trouble here," I said, working on the far side of the table. "Weapons of any sort were strictly prohibited in the agreements we signed. I can't believe you packed a gun!"

Doug looked at me with surprise. "Of course, I packed a gun! It's an essential part of my detective's toolbox! I never leave home without it. And frankly, I'm glad I had it. Leroy Poole is a dangerous idiot. Did you see how he hesitated? He actually debated whether he might be able to outrun a bullet before he finally came to his senses. I've met plenty of guys like him before. Each and every one of them thinks he's the biggest damn dog in the yard. You can't even blink around a guy like that, or he'll be all over you."

"Would you have shot him?"

"Damn straight," said Doug, with a curt nod. "Maybe not to kill, but definitely to put him on the ground. Nobody messes with my mama. And I'm surprised you even have to ask."

He was right. As much as I loved to give Doug shit, had it not been for his snub-nosed constant companion and rather decent marksmanship, I wouldn't have survived my first foray into private investigation.

"Anyssa's not gonna be happy," I noted, nevertheless. "If she can't guarantee the safety of her guests, she'll never be able to find liability insurance for these weekends. And that's if anybody is willing to risk their lives to stay."

Doug shrugged. "Leroy won't say a thing. The only thing worse than a loud-mouthed bully is a whiny little tattletale, and I can't see him going that route. It would be too challenging for his manhood. I think it's best if we just try and stay clear of him for the rest of the time we're here."

Loretta and Brady entered the room followed by Melanie, who guided the serving cart last used by our dearly departed hostess, Maria. They placed the serving plates in the center of our end of the table, and we seated ourselves, Loretta taking the captain's chair while Melanie and I sat to her left, Doug and Brady to her right. The combined aromas from the steaming platters nearly prompted involuntary drooling all around.

Without so much as a prompt, we lowered our heads in unison as Loretta offered thanks for the heavenly grub. The next fifteen minutes were focused entirely on eating, save for the occasional request to pass a particular dish and the polite thanks that always followed. Loretta's biscuits and gravy were indeed incredible, and Brady's dubious looking concoction was far tastier than it looked, especially when covered liberally in maple syrup. Mine and Melanie's breakfast casserole had just enough zip to balance the sweet and savory, and by the end, we had all settled back into our chairs with fresh cups of coffee.

"Thank you, everyone," I said. "Not only was that absolutely delicious, but I think we may have just accidentally worked as a team, so maybe we *are* learning something here, after all. I wonder if we can make it a habit?"

A smattering of agreeable laughter went around the table.

"I wanna know when you became such a badass, Loretta," said Melanie, looking appreciatively at the diminutive, little fire plug. "That was something else."

Loretta shrugged, taking another sip of coffee. "It's just some basic self-defense moves I learned in my ladies' church league down at Valley Methodist. Anyone can do 'em, and it surely makes me feel a whole lot safer. One thing's for sure: you don't mess with a Lady Methodist."

I smiled, amused by the impromptu image of Loretta and her fellow ladies' league members dressed in Pepto Bismol pink leotards with glittery crosses stitched into the sleeves and 'Lady Methodists' emblazoned across the front. Between Bingo nights, bake sales, quilting bees and frying chicken for the county fair, they would fight crime!

I realized the room had gone silent, and Loretta was staring at me. "Do you have something to add, Mr. Man?"

I suppressed my amusement, focusing instead on my coffee. "Not really."

She pushed back from her chair and meandered my way. "Because of all the people sitting at this table, I think that you could benefit the most from a little bit of self-defense training."

"*Pfft!*" I waved her comment away.

"I'm completely serious, you know," said Loretta, inching closer. "I mean, sure, you've got that whole 'Dead-Eye Dwayne' thing down. We've all seen that parlor trick. As long as you've got a target, something to throw at it and enough distance so's you can take your shot, you're golden. But when it comes to hand-to-hand combat, I don't think I've ever seen anyone hit the ground quite so often."

"I don't know what you're talking about," I said, shaking my head indignantly.

"*I do*," said Melanie, wiping her hands on a napkin. "Remember that time you got laid out in Sarah's front yard? Or how about when you ended up in the hospital after getting knocked over the head with a crowbar?"

"Well, *that* doesn't count," I said. "That was assault, and he crept up from behind."

"Well, how about when Leroy nearly knocked you out last night?" Brady was adding his own two cents with a smile.

"I can handle myself perfectly fine," I said. Why was everyone suddenly picking on *me*?

"Really?" challenged Loretta, dropping into an ugly crouch that no one in fluorescent polyester overalls should ever attempt. I stood, backing away from her as she did some sort of bizarre crabwalk toward me. "How are you gonna handle *this*, big fella?"

"What are you doing, Loretta?" I said, taking another step backwards. "I'm not going to spar with you. I'd feel like a real ass if you accidentally got hurt, and besides, your little boy is sitting over there with a gun. I'm not ready to test his threshold."

Doug pulled the gun from his ankle holster and placed it on the table, sliding it away. "What gun?" The little bastard was enjoying himself!

"C'mon, yellow chicken," she taunted, swiveling her hips side to side. "Take your best shot. I ain't worried."

"This is stupid," I said, playfully swatting in her direction. She slapped my hand away effortlessly.

"C'mon, you big wuss," she continued. "You slap like a little girl."

I sighed and put a little more heart into it, lashing out to tag her cheek. Instead, she knocked my hand aside with her left arm while her right hand sailed up and connected with my own cheek, surprising more than hurting me. "What the fuck, Loretta? You know that's where Leroy hit me!"

"*Language,*" she warned, with a cockeyed grin. She was enjoying this a little more than I felt she should. "An attacker's not gonna give two hoots about your tender spots. Now, *c'mon!* Attack me!"

I had had enough. Cursing under my breath in a steady stream that would make Popeye proud, I lunged for her throat. I figured my arms were longer than hers, so as long as I could choke her from a distance, she couldn't get within striking distance. Right?

Wrong.

She ducked, evading my clumsy maneuver entirely and stomped on my already damaged foot. I let out a howl, stooping to grab my foot just as she suddenly came through with an uppercut and connected solidly with the other side of my face.

My head whipped back in a trail of imaginary stardust, and over the chair I went, consciousness barreling towards the nearest exit before I even hit the ground.

CHAPTER SIXTEEN

As much as I adore the sight of my sweet lady's face, I'm growing a tad weary of finding it hovering over me fearfully as I struggle my way up from the murky depths—I've already lost count of how many times we've done this.

"Dwayne? Can you hear me?"

Her voice sounded like it was emerging from a tunnel as she patted my cheeks gently. I nodded, struggling to get up. I could hear Brady and Doug sharing a good laugh at my expense, and just when I thought they were through, the encore came at double the volume. I glanced at Melanie as she helped me to my feet and saw she was having trouble keeping a straight face herself. Loretta, on the other hand, was collecting dirty plates and loading up the serving cart, doing none of the gloating I would have expected.

"C'mon, guys," Melanie said to Doug and Brady. "That's enough."

"Oh my gosh, I'm so sorry, Dwayne," said Brady, shoulders still hitching. "But if you only could have *seen* your face! Oh, wait—you can!" He turned his phone around so I could see the video he had captured of the whole ridiculous thing. Doug only laughed harder, doubling over and practically in tears by this point.

"You're gonna delete that," I warned. I reached for the phone, but Brady snatched it away.

"I most certainly am *not,*" he said. "This is the sort of thing that wins big prize money."

"Or at least a slot on *Ridiculousness,*" Doug managed before collapsing into another fit of hysterics.

"Now, you boys just settle down," ordered Loretta. She shot me a look that was as close to an apology as I might ever see from her. "It wasn't my intention to embarrass the boy—he can do that just fine without my help. My point is that he needs more training. We *all* need more training. We keep finding ourselves in these dangerous situations, it's just foolishness not to be a little better prepared. Now, let's get this mess back to the kitchen. We've got to clean up after ourselves, and then we can start planning our day."

*****

After loading the dishwasher and wiping down surfaces, we decided to take our meeting outdoors. The darkly appointed interior of the manor felt completely oppressive in the cool, gray morning light—or maybe it was just the lingering effect of Leroy Poole, who was likely plotting some sort of revenge for his earlier embarrassment. Either way, we opted for the open space of the patio under a sky that promised eventual rain, donning jackets or sweaters as the temperature was nearly ten degrees colder than the day before. The shoes I had borrowed from Brady were sufficient, although a bit ill-fitting. They were worn in a way that suggested Brady was pigeon-toed, a characteristic I had never really noticed about him, but then again, I didn't exactly spend much time studying his feet. His leather loafers were certainly a better option than my soft-sided slippers, currently air-drying in the laundry room. Miraculously, the blood—if that's what it was—had washed completely out of them.

We carried out fresh cups of coffee and seated ourselves around the patio table. Loretta had her cat-eye, tortoiseshell glasses perched on the tip of her nose, and a pen and steno pad ready to take notes. As our de facto leader, Doug sat at the head of the table with Loretta and Brady on his left, me and Melanie on his right.

"All right, team," said Doug, clapping his hands. "We basically have one more night to solve this mystery. Let's see what we've got so far."

We looked at each other blankly.

"Well," said Melanie, leaning back in her chair. "I guess number one on my list is, what *is* the mystery?"

"I'm not real clear on that one myself," said Brady. "We've mostly just gone from point to point saving Dwayne from himself and his phantom demons."

"You know, Brady, I've had just about enough out of you," I said, pushing back from the table.

Brady grinned, leaning into Loretta. "Careful, Morrow. I've got Killer right here beside me, and she ain't wearing her leash."

"Knock it off!" Loretta barked. "You boys can play all you want when we get home. But for now, it's time to get down to business."

"Fine," I said sullenly, slumping in my chair and folding my arms across my chest.

"Let's start at the beginning," said Loretta, turning to a fresh page in her pad. "The first thing I recall was when we found the maid at the bottom of the stairs." She rolled her eyes. "Dead."

"I beg to differ," I interrupted. "The first thing was when I saw that hooded figure lurking on the beach the night we arrived."

A collective round of disbelieving groans swept the table.

"I'm *serious!*" I insisted. "I didn't have too much to drink, and I wasn't seeing things!"

Loretta's pen hovered over the page.

"Write that down," I said, jabbing at the pad. When she didn't move quickly enough, I was more insistent. "*Write it!*"

She rolled her eyes and added it behind an asterisk along the top margin of her page. I could only imagine the snippy connotation that would eventually accompany said asterisk.

"We can't discount the ghost angle just because Anyssa seemed surprised when I mentioned it," I continued, aiming for a more persuasive tone. "It's one of the more interesting things about this place, and without much prompting, she went into pretty great detail. I think that might have been the plan all along." Their uniformly patronizing gazes only served to piss me off, so I added, "Obviously, I don't think it's a *real* ghost."

"You did," accused Brady.

"I didn't," I said, trying not to sound defensive but failing miserably. "I didn't know *what* it was. It was—unsettling."

"It's been noted," interjected Loretta. "Let's move along. Back to the maid—Maria, wasn't it? The pocket of her apron was torn like something had been taken from her, and there were some kind of marks around her neck, like someone had tried to strangle her. What else do we know? Preferably something that's a little less open to debate."

"We lost track of Sandy yesterday while we were rescuing Dwayne from the lake," Brady contributed brightly before shrugging apologetically at me, his eyes twinkly merrily. "Missing or presumed dead? I'm not sure which way you want to go with that since Dwayne thinks he came across her body last night."

I held my tongue while Loretta deliberated before making another note. "We'll go with, 'Missing/Presumed Dead.' What else?"

"Well," Melanie began, leaning forward to blow on her steaming cup of coffee. "We haven't seen Rob or Kit since they went their own way yesterday afternoon, so we should probably follow up on that. You know, check their room for clues or something?"

Loretta nodded, scribbling on her pad. "We'll put them in the same category as Sandy."

"We haven't actually laid eyes on Dusty either," noted Doug.

"Oh, *I* have," said Brady, with a quick shake of his head, the abomination of the lascivious mental image assaulting him anew. I would have been more sympathetic had he not spent the better part of the morning reveling in my humiliation.

"I mean, we haven't seen her *since* you saw her—well, you know." Doug made a circle with the thumb and forefinger of one hand while playing ring toss with the forefinger of the other. He wasn't particularly known for his subtlety, and Brady looked away quickly.

"Leroy said he was fixing a plate for himself and his lady friend," I said. "It would have to be Dusty, wouldn't it? I mean, there's nobody else left."

"We'll go with that," said Loretta, making another note. "Am I to assume we are going to accept those phantom noises from yesterday and last night as the shameful, lustful groans of fornicating sinners who are clearly on a highway to H-E-double hockey sticks?"

"Very fire and brimstone, Loretta," said Melanie drily. "But yes. I think that's close enough to accurate."

Loretta finished her note and sat back, reading over what she had written. With a sigh, she turned to a fresh page and jotted a title I couldn't read upside down.

"What are you doing?" I asked.

"I'm starting a list of suggestions for Ms. Williams," said Loretta. "She said this was a trial run for her to work out any kinks, and I would think comments from the participants would be welcome. I've got a couple of kinks I'd like to share."

I raised an eyebrow. "Such as?"

"Structure," Loretta replied simply, writing the word on the top line of her page, and underlining it twice.

"Structure? I don't get it."

"Exactly," she said, aiming her ballpoint in my direction. "For an organized game, there is absolutely no structure to what we've been doing here. Other than a dead girl who wasn't really dead and a few others who seem to have gone missing, what's the point of all this? There aren't any clues to tie it all together. We're halfway through the weekend, and I don't have any idea what we're supposed to be doing. And then there's screening."

She paused to make that her second bullet point on the page, underlining it three times.

"I mean, I get why she would invite an up-and-coming team of private investigators who have been in the news lately. She's probably really counting on our feedback to make these mysteries something people will pay big money for. But opening it up to the winners of a radio contest? That's how you end up with people like Leroy and Sandy Poole. Now, don't get me wrong, I've got nothing but sympathy for that poor woman, putting up with the likes of him. But I can't say I'm entirely comfortable around that man. He thinks he's God's gift to women, and he's got a fuse that's about half an inch long. He's made being in that house uncomfortable for all of us."

We couldn't argue her point. And now he had promised retaliation. He seemed like a man who followed through with his threats.

"I don't remember Rob and Kit saying how they came to be here," said Melanie.

"I don't think they did," I replied. "But it's not like we volunteered we were here on a free pass, either."

"No, I suppose not," nodded Melanie. "But I'm still curious. More contest winners? Or maybe—maybe they're working for Anyssa? I mean, she *has* to have feet on the ground here somewhere, doesn't she?"

We deliberated that for a moment, before Doug said, "But why would she plant people in the house only for them to go missing almost immediately? It doesn't make any sense."

Brady sighed. "I've got nothin'."

Loretta flipped her pad back a page and jotted in the margin. "It's still worth keeping on the radar."

"*Oooo!*" Melanie sat up straight. "And don't forget about that Captain Jack guy. Anyssa didn't have any idea what we were talking about. Did you see the look on her face? For sure, he wasn't the one who brought the others, and on a much better boat, too."

"If she was feigning surprise about the ghost, she could have just as easily been doing the same about Captain Jack," I said.

"Slow down! I can't write that fast!" Loretta said, scrawling furiously. We waited what seemed an eternity for her to catch up.

"So, what have we got, Ma?" asked Doug.

"Beats the heck out of me," she answered, tossing her pad and pen onto the table.

"Maybe it's better to ask what we *haven't* got," I said. "Loretta touched on it earlier."

She looked surprised. "I did?"

I nodded. "What we need are clues, and there are a couple of obvious places to start. We've barely explored the mansion. It only makes sense that the majority of clues would be inside, doesn't it? I mean, the island's not exactly huge, but we could run the clock out just wandering around. We should explore any of the rooms we haven't visited, including Rob and Kit's. I think that's where we'll find our clues."

Everyone nodded, agreeing in principle, but nobody seemed ready to move in that direction. Honestly, with Leroy lurking about with a score to settle, I wasn't in any big hurry, either. An alternative occurred to me.

"We should also go back down to the boathouse now that it's daylight. Who knows what might have been left behind? And we might want to do that before the rain starts."

That seemed to do the trick. The nods were more enthusiastic.

Doug stood and clapped his hands together. "All right, then. We've got us a plan. We'll start with the boathouse and then move on to the main house. Let's do this thing."

"It will also keep us out of Leroy's line of fire for a little while, maybe give him a chance to cool down." I tried to be optimistic, but it wasn't selling.

"Do you really think that could happen?" asked Melanie as I took her hand and helped her out of her chair.

I didn't even hesitate. "No."

*****

The boat bobbed lazily in the slip as if it had never been moved.

"You guys *do* see this, right?" I said, feeling a rush of vindication. "There's no chance I'm just imagining this?"

"Of course, we see it," said Melanie. "It must have been returned some time overnight."

The inside of the boathouse was still rather gloomy under the current weather conditions, but we had been able to determine no one else was lurking inside. The others fanned out in different directions, exploring the building's interior while I remained focused on the boat. The tarp was still bunched up in its rear seat, but I held little hope that Sandy was still under it. I used the flashlight on my phone to examine the floorboard in the front, but there was no sign of blood or anything resembling it. In fact, it was spotless, most likely scrubbed clean during its time away. I eased down into the captain's chair and swiveled around to pull the tarp up. There was nothing to see.

"Are you guys finding anything?" I called, carefully inspecting the rest of the boat.

"Nothing out of the ordinary," called Brady from the open end of the boathouse, his features lost in the shadows of the darkening day.

"Me neither," said Melanie. She stood along the starboard side of the boat, peeking into cabinets and underneath a mound of fishing net piled in the corner.

Loretta had found a broom and dustpan, and she was busily sweeping up the shards of glass that littered the ground by the door. Doug squatted at her feet with the dustpan. "Only thing I see is the mess you made," she said. "How about you? Anything on that boat?"

"No," I said. I couldn't hide my disappointment, and I continued to scan the boat with my flashlight. "It looks like it's been cleaned. If there was anything to see, it's gone now—wait a minute." I leaned into the space in front of the passenger seat, practically upside down, and shone my light in the space beneath it.

"What is it?" asked Melanie, standing over me.

"Something sort of shiny," I said, reaching beneath the seat to grab what had caught my eye. I pulled it out and examined it under the light. "Well, huh."

"*What?*" Melanie impatiently peered over my shoulder.

"It looks like a gold coin."

Finally. A clue.

*****

"Maybe we should investigate the other side of the island before it starts raining," I coolly suggested as we let ourselves back into the kitchen from the patio. It had taken a lot less time to investigate the boathouse than I figured, and I was trying to look casual as I scanned the area for any sign of Leroy. It's not that I was exactly afraid, but I certainly wasn't looking forward to whatever retaliation he would eventually serve up. It felt like we were locked in a game of chicken with a suicidal maniac.

"Oh, for heaven's sake, get out of my way!" grumbled Loretta, elbowing past me as she charged down the hallway towards the stairs. "Dougie! Are you coming?"

Doug mumbled something incoherent and hurried along after his mother like a dutiful puppy.

"What was that?" I asked, staring after them.

"Apparently, whatever was ailing Loretta's digestive tract on the way up here has returned with a vengeance," said Melanie.

"And she always takes her son with her to the bathroom?" Brady was amused.

"No, she's just sticking to what we said earlier," said Melanie. "None of us should go anywhere alone."

"With Leroy pissed off and lurking around, it actually seems pretty smart," I noted.

"Wow, he really got to you, didn't he?" said Melanie, and her half-smile felt a bit emasculating.

"I'm only being cautious. Caution is a good thing, right? Being cautious is not a weakness." It came out more defensive than I intended, which only prompted the other half of the smile Melanie had been suppressing.

"It's all right, Dwayne," she said as she ran her palm across my shoulders soothingly. "I won't let that big bad Leroy anywhere near you."

I shot Brady a warning look, and he wisely decided to keep his opinion to himself.

"We should stick with your original thought," she said, patting my shoulders as we headed down the hallway toward the stairs. "Other than the dining room, kitchen and our own rooms, we've barely explored the mansion, and this is where we're bound to find the most clues. We can't let Leroy keep us from doing what we're here to do, right?"

"Of course not," I agreed, sounding much surer than I felt. "While Loretta is, um, occupied, I could see what I can find out about this coin online."

"There's the detective I know and love," she said, slipping her left hand into my right and squeezing before rounding the banister and trotting up the stairs.

Brady and I followed her back to the room where we had camped out the previous evening. I fired up my MacBook, Googling what visual information I could describe from the coin. Fairly quickly, I discovered it was an 1850 Liberty Head $20 gold coin, supposedly worth somewhere between $2,300 and $6,000, depending upon its condition. I was certainly no expert, but it appeared to be in pretty damn good shape.

Brady whistled as he read over my shoulder. "That's certainly a lot of money to just leave lying around."

"You don't think it's real, do you?" asked Melanie. "I mean, that's an awfully expensive clue to leave behind. What if no one ever found it?"

"I don't know," I said, turning it over and examining it closely. "Probably not, but it sure *looks* like the real deal."

A timid knock sounded at the door. I started to answer it, but Melanie was already on her way. "Stay put, dear," she said to me quietly before whispering, "*It might be Leroy!*"

I was never going to hear the end of this.

Melanie opened the door and froze. "Oh. It's you."

I turned to see Dusty standing in the doorway, hands clasped together at her waist as she shifted nervously from foot to foot. Brady's eyes shot toward the ceiling, and he quickly turned his back, excusing himself and heading toward the bathroom.

"Can I come in?" she asked uncertainly.

"I don't think that would be a good idea," said Melanie, her voice suddenly icy cold, completely devoid of the playfulness with which she had just been taunting me.

"Oh, okay, um—" Dusty continued to fidget and stare at her feet. She looked like she was on the verge of tears.

"What is it that you want, Dusty?" asked Melanie, impatient and direct.

"Dwayne?" She craned to look around Melanie and spotted me sitting at the writing desk near the front of the room. "Will you come out here and talk to me for a minute? Please?"

I squeezed my eyes shut and cursed under my breath. *Why me?!?*

When I didn't answer quickly enough, Dusty repeated, "Please?"

Now she was actively crying. *Dammit!*

I pushed myself away from the desk and joined her in the hallway. Melanie sent her one last withering glance before stepping back inside and closing the door.

"I guess she doesn't like me much, huh?" asked Dusty, sniffling.

I sighed. "What do you want, Dusty?"

"I've really messed things up," she said, dabbing at her eyes and nose.

"You think?" I asked incredulously.

And now she was bawling, tears streaming down her face while she hiccupped her way through hysterical sobs. "Everything was g-g-going so g-g-great with my Brady B-b-bear! I-I-I didn't even want us to *do* this stupid weekend!"

"So, this is how you protest? By sleeping with another man? And *Leroy—ugh,*" I shuddered, my imagination supplying more imagery than I ever asked to see.

"No! No! You've got it all wrong!" she said, clasping my arm with both of her hands while her wide eyes fixed on my face. "That man did something to me. I think he drugged me."

I stared at her for a long moment, my mouth hanging open. "What?"

She nodded urgently. "I think he slipped something into my drink."

I shook my head, still not completely comprehending the words coming out of her mouth. "So, what you're telling me is—"

"I think he *forced* me to—," she said, dissolving into tears before crumpling to her knees at my feet.

CHAPTER SEVENTEEN

"We have to call the police," said Melanie.

"*No.*"

It was the surest Dusty had sounded about anything since I had brought her into the room. She hugged herself tightly, perched on the edge of the sofa that had been my bed the previous evening. She wore cuffed blue jean shorts that were too short, and a midriff-baring knit top that was too tight. Her open-toed, high-heeled slingbacks revealed toenails painted bright red. Her cheeks were stained from mascara carried away on a river of tears. Brady paced the opposite side of the room, keeping a considerable distance between them. He was still trying to process whatever it was that was going on.

"You can't just let him get away with this!" urged Melanie, kneeling at the other woman's knees, and looking up into her downturned face. "*Dammit,* Dusty!"

She shook her head firmly. "No."

"Why?" I asked from where I was perched at the foot of the bed. "Why won't you let us call? Help me to understand."

The look Dusty gave me was heartbreakingly forlorn. "Because they'll just see what *he* saw." She indicated Brady without looking directly at him. Whatever thoughts were going through Brady's head were carefully guarded, his face like stone.

Melanie sighed. "Okay. Let's back up. Why don't you tell us exactly what happened? No one's going to judge you." One glance at Brady and I wondered if that was entirely true.

Dusty took a deep, steadying breath. "I'll try," she said before immediately losing her composure again. "I was just so *stupid!* I should've never stayed behind—"

"It's all right," interrupted Melanie, using a soothing tone I'd heard her use when trying to talk Jasmine down from her occasional fits of teenaged hysterics. "You can't change that now, and it doesn't matter. Just start at the beginning."

Dusty took a few more breaths and dabbed at the corners of her eyes. "I was bored," she said meekly.

"I thought you said your stomach hurt," countered Brady. He was clearly still feeling raw and antagonistic.

She sighed, looking at her feet. "*Fine.* I didn't feel like traipsing all around the woods, getting eaten alive by God only knows what kind of insects and ruining a perfectly good pair of sandals for my trouble. I really thought I could talk Brady into staying behind, but—"

Brady whipped around. "Are you saying this is *my* fault?" It was as if he'd physically slapped her.

"*Brady!*" I warned. "Shut up, man. We don't even know what happened yet. Let her speak."

His mouth snapped shut, and he averted his disdainful glare, continuing to wear a rut into the antique rug he was pacing.

After a moment, Dusty continued demurely. "I watched Hallmark for a while, but after the first movie ended, they started playing one I had seen before, and there wasn't anything else on TV. I didn't feel like hanging out all by myself upstairs in our room, so I decided to explore the house. I mean, it's creepy, for sure, but not so bad when it's light outside. I had only been through a couple of rooms when I decided to get some water from the kitchen. That's when I ran into Leroy raiding the liquor in the pantry.

He seemed like he was in a particularly good mood and asked if I wanted him to make me a drink. I thought, 'What the hell?' It's been a minute since I went day-drinking. We sat in the kitchen and started talking. Well, *he* was doing most of the talking. He told me how horrible his marriage was, how self-involved and selfish his wife could be, how completely awful his stepdaughters were, all the while topping off my drink. Of *course*, I knew he was hitting on me. I've seen his type before."

Her eyes flitted to Brady, and the timing couldn't have been worse.

"Are you comparing him to *me?*" he exploded, eyes wide with shock.

She shrank back. "No, baby, not at all. I mean, not *really*. But think about our first date, you know? We went out for dinner, but you weren't quite up to dancing, so you talked me into going back to your place, remember? You were hitting on me *hard*, pouring glass after glass of wine. I don't know that we would have—you know—if I hadn't—"

"Wait a minute," said Brady, massaging his forehead. "Are you trying to say that I made you do something you didn't want to do?"

"*No!* That's not it at all," she said, struggling to find words that wouldn't set Brady off. "Alcohol makes me flirty, but I still know what I'm doing, and *okay*—I was probably a little bit flirty with Leroy. He kept telling me how beautiful I was and how any man would be crazy to just go off and leave me behind. Said he'd stumbled into some money, and he was going to Vegas after this to double or triple it. He said I could go with him if I wanted. He said all the other guys would be jealous with me on his arm. It was nice to hear. But then things started getting weird."

"Weird how?" asked Melanie.

"Time just sort of started dropping away from me," she said. "One minute we were talking in the kitchen and then suddenly, we were up in our room. I don't remember how we got there. My ears were ringing, and everything was out of focus. I think he must have carried me because I can't imagine climbing the stairs like that, but either way, I just don't remember. And I'm not the type to blackout."

Brady snorted.

"*I'm not!*" she insisted. "And you *know* that, Brady Garrett! We've had too much to drink on more than one occasion. When have I *ever* blacked out?"

"You haven't," agreed Brady. "I'm just not sure I'm buying it now."

Melanie slid onto the sofa beside Dusty and put a protective arm around her as the pitiful thing hitched and heaved with renewed fervor. "All right, I've heard about enough out of you, Brady. Frankly, I'm shocked and disappointed. Who are you to question this poor girl's story? It's no wonder she doesn't want to go to the police. She can't even convince *you* she's telling the truth!"

He shrugged, looking away, which only pissed Melanie off even more. She turned towards me.

"Dwayne, would you please take Prince Charming out of here? I'll try and calm Dusty down, see if I can reason with her about calling the police—"

"*No police!*" Dusty practically shrieked, startling Melanie. Brady uttered a mildly derisive chortle, avoiding Melanie's incredulous glare.

Melanie nodded her head toward the door. "Take him next door," she said to me, her eyes locked onto Brady. "I can't believe you're acting like this. After all those times I stood up for you with Dwayne, but I guess he was right all along. You really *are* an asshole."

Brady winced at her words, but his jaw remained firmly set. He wasn't about to back down now. I led the way out into the hall, closing the door behind us as Brady kept his head down, shuffling toward what used to be mine and Melanie's room.

"C'mon, man," I said, reaching out and grabbing his arm, turning him around. "Even *I* know you're not this heartless. What gives?"

Brady's smile was tight and flat before he soon succumbed to a fit of the same hysterical giggles we had heard when he told us of catching Dusty and

Leroy in a clinch. "I don't know, man," he said. "I'm just having a little trouble with the story. That's all." Another short burst of sniggling.

"What in the hell is wrong with you, Brady? If Melanie told me another guy had drugged her, *forced* himself on her, I'd be out for blood."

"Yeah, well, Dusty is no Melanie, that's for sure."

I was at a loss. While I had been slow to come around to Brady's smarmy charm, his utter apathy seemed out-of-character, even for him. "So, you're not going to help us convince her to report this to the police?"

"She's not going to report this to the police," he said firmly, proceeding to the room next door. "Wouldn't matter whether I believed her or not."

"And why is that?" I asked, trailing behind.

He paused in the open doorway, showing me his back. "Because she's not who you think she is. She isn't a nurse's aide, and I didn't meet her in physical therapy. We met on Burblr, and her record isn't exactly spotless."

He went into the room without looking back, leaving me slack-jawed in the hallway with questions piling up inside my head like vehicles careening towards the nearest exit across a freeway of ice.

Maybe this wasn't as out-of-character as I had thought.

*****

"This whole time, you've been *paying* her?" It wasn't my first question, nor would it be my last. I was reeling at the sheer deception of it all.

"*No!*" Brady said hotly. "I've never paid for sex. Not *ever*. Well, at least not what you would think of as *traditionally* paying for sex—"

I held my hand up to stop him while using the other to work at the stabbing pain threatening to blossom in my temple. "I don't want to hear this."

"You asked," Brady shot back.

I alternated between shaking my head and nodding. "Yes. Yes, I guess I did. Okay, let's back this thing up. How did the two of you meet? And let's go with the truth, this time." I dropped into an antique armchair while Brady nervously paced the room. He wouldn't look me in the eye, reminding me of a child who had been caught spinning a web of lies—which was actually pretty accurate.

"I told you," he said. "We met on Burblr."

"What's Burblr?"

"It's a lot like Tinder."

I looked at him vacantly.

"Oh, for heaven's sake, for a computer guy, you are shockingly uninformed," he said, exasperated. "They're dating apps. Burblr is for people with—more specific inclinations."

"So, it's basically an app for hookups?"

"Yes, we can go with that," he replied with more than a hint of evasiveness.

"This doesn't involve, like, genital mutilation or bestiality, does it?" I honestly feared his response.

"*No,*" he said, finally directing some serious side eye at me. "Nothing like that. What is wrong with you? It works a lot like they all do, using your phone's location to let you know when you're near other members with similar profiles. Swipe right if you're interested, otherwise swipe left. I had a lot of free time when I was recovering, so I—well, it had been a while since Nina and I ended things, and well—a man has his needs, right?"

My eyes shot to the heavens as I rotated my hand, urging him on.

"Her profile kept popping up, like every day. I realized she must be visiting someone else in the rehab facility since I sure as hell wasn't going anywhere. Our interests were similar, so—"

"You both swiped right," I finished for him, and he grinned sheepishly.

"It's no big deal, really," he said. "It's not like we're serious or anything. We've been having a good time, enjoying each other's company. Where's the crime in that?"

My snappy retort died in my mouth as I remembered what he had said in the doorway. "What did you mean when you said her record wasn't exactly spotless? Exactly what kind of criminal have you been bringing into our lives?"

Brady sputtered. "It's not like she *killed* someone."

"Tell me exactly what it *is* like."

Brady hedged, walking away from me. "She's sort of into *orfrtz*." He covered his mouth when he said that last bit, and it was lost to me.

"Did you just say she was into *orphans?*"

"Orgies!" he repeated loudly. "She's into group sex, bondage, S&M, things like that."

An unbidden image of Brady and Dusty gyrating within a pulsating din of iniquity leapt to mind, and I forcefully pushed it away before it could etch itself in permanent marker onto the dry erase board of my mind. It was my turn to look away; in fact, I wasn't sure I would ever be able to look at Brady quite the same again.

"All right," I said, trying to sound more worldly than I was or ever would be. "Different strokes for different folks." Another horrible thought sprang to mind. "We *are* talking about consenting adults, aren't we? This isn't some kind of weird sex slave thing with minors, or—"

"God, no!"

I hadn't realized I was holding my breath until it whooshed out of me in a tremendous sigh of relief. "Well, then what's the problem? I mean, sure, it would certainly set some tongues wagging, but it's not exactly illegal, is it?"

"It is when some of the participants are paid for their participation."

"*Oooh,*" I said, slowly getting the picture. My next question just slipped right out. "So, Dusty *was* a whore, just not with you?"

"No," Brady said firmly. "She was picked up along with a whole lot of others who *were* engaged in prostitution, and she was charged along with the rest. It was her first arrest—her *only* arrest—and she got out on probation."

"How can you be so sure she wasn't selling herself?" I couldn't resist playing devil's advocate. Admittedly, I wasn't trying very hard.

"Because she told me so."

"And you *believed* her," I said, rubbing my chin in an exaggerated display of contemplation. "And yet she tells you she thinks Leroy forced himself on her, and you won't even give that a minute of consideration? It seems to me like you're cherry picking the things you want to believe, buddy."

His face clouded over as he glared at me, his mental gears grinding almost audibly to find a reasonable position to take. I held his stare, waiting for any logical response at all, but it looked like I'd be waiting a while. Brady finally broke the stalemate, sitting on the side of the bed and staring at the wall as he absently ran his fingers through his dark, curly hair.

"Why are you so mad at her?" I asked quietly.

He shook his head. "You wouldn't understand."

"Well, for shit's sake, you've told me *this* much," I said. "Try me."

I waited as Brady struggled for words. Finally, he said, "I'm not the sort of guy who handles being alone very well. It's not that I crave constant attention or anything like that, but I've never really had a big circle of friends. Part of it is because of my job. People tend not to trust you when they think you're cataloging everything they say for future use, and in my line of work, I get that—I do. When Terri was still here, I felt like I had everything I needed—Terri, our little boy, Nola and Wendell—"

He referred to his late wife who he had lost in an automobile accident several years ago. This was long before I had known him, but Nola Caudill had told me about the devastating toll it had taken on Brady and his son.

"As much as I try to keep things light for Billy's sake, I miss the companionship of having someone close to me, really close to me, you know? But I'll never find someone who understands me the way Terri did, and I really think I'm okay with that. I could never replace her—I don't *want* to. I'm not looking for anything permanent, just a little company, a little companionship here and there. All my—I don't even know if you can call them relationships—have been completely physical with a loose expiration date set before they even begin. I can't let myself get close to anyone like I was with Terri, I just can't take that sort of risk. I always try and stop things before they go too far, although that doesn't always work out."

Now he referred to Nikki Sanders, the woman he had been seeing when we first met several months ago. She had labored under the mistaken belief they were on the path to matrimony only to be subsequently murdered by a psychopathic lunatic who chose victims based on their proximity to me and those around me. None of this was news, but I waited, sensing there was more.

After a moment of consideration, he continued, keeping his eyes fixed on his flexing hands in his lap. "I feel like you and Melanie are—well, the closest things to friends I've had in forever. I see what you two are building, and it's really good. It's not anything I could ever have or even want with Dusty. Dusty is just—well, she keeps me preoccupied. And I didn't want to tell either of you the real story of our relationship because compared to what you two have, it just seems so seedy and lurid. She and I made up the bit about her being a nurse's aide at the rehab facility because it felt like such a tiny stretch. I mean, we really did meet there. I didn't want either of you to think any less of me than you sometimes already do."

I weighed that last part and suddenly realized that somewhere along the way, Brady and I had engaged in a more meaningful friendship than I had ever given consideration. Sure, we teased and riffed off each other at every possible opportunity, but it had long since progressed beyond my initial distrust and general disdain for the man. It was much more like how I interacted with my brother, Matt, or my high school best friend who also happened to be Melanie's deceased husband, Ryan. Brady actually valued our opinion and reflecting upon the relationship advice he had earlier shared with me, I was startled to discover I valued his opinion, too.

"I would have given me and Dusty one, maybe two more weeks, tops," Brady said. "I thought this weekend was a nice thing for us to do, but she wanted to hit the casinos around Cincinnati. She excels at two things: unbelievable sex and spending money like it's nothing. I really couldn't afford for this to go on much longer. She's helped me run my credit cards into completely uncharted territory. It honestly feels like all of this has been her revenge for us not doing what she wanted to do this weekend, especially all that shit about Leroy taking her to Vegas. She can be a spiteful bitch when she doesn't get her way. It's all just a little too coincidental, you know?"

"So, why would she come back now? Wouldn't she still be with Leroy if that were the case?"

He shrugged his shoulders. "I don't know. Maybe he kicked her out after he got what he wanted. He's not exactly a stand-up guy. Maybe he got sick of her constant yammering. You all might not have noticed, but she talks a *lot,* and some of it's pretty out there."

Oh, yes—we had noticed. I just smiled politely.

"It just feels like she's trying to work her way back into my good graces, and I know how bad it looks when a guy doesn't automatically believe a woman who makes a claim like this, but Dusty isn't just any woman. She loves drama just as much as anything else, so at this point, I honestly don't know *what* to believe. I just know that we're through. I swear, she only had one job to do here—"

"Job?" I asked, thinking she sounded more and more like a prostitute all the while.

He nodded curtly. "To be an attentive girlfriend and not embarrass me in front of my—" His voice trailed away as he rubbed at his face. Try as he might, he couldn't make himself say, 'friends.' "She couldn't even do that right."

I didn't even begin to know what to say. Part of me was furious that Brady had introduced this person into all our lives under false pretenses. I mean, she had been in my house, for God's sake! Did I need to take inventory when I got home to make sure she hadn't fleeced anything valuable? Probably not. I didn't have anything that was valuable enough for that thought to gain any real traction. But the fact the children had been exposed to her bothered me greatly. I might not be able to control who Brady brought around his own son, but I sure as hell expected a little more consideration for Jasmine. Brady needed to get his shit together and start making better choices. It was incredibly selfish for him to involve all of us in this nonsensical charade just because he was horny and desperate for relief.

Still yet, another part of me felt incredibly sorry for him. Had it only been one short year ago when I, too, felt so socially isolated that I had ventured off to my fifteen-year high school reunion with the anxious hope of breaking out of my own rut? And I had been successful, too. It was during that stay when I had met Melanie, the woman I never knew I needed and now couldn't imagine living without. Of course, it wasn't before diving headlong into solving a murder without considering the potential fallout. It wasn't *exactly* apples for apples, but it did involve interacting with a lot of seedy individuals who endangered the safety of my friends and parents before ultimately getting Jasmine kidnapped and almost killed. It was close enough.

"What, no smartass comments?"

Brady's voice pulled me back to the moment, and I noticed he was finally looking at me. I really don't know what apologetic looks like on his face, but I thought this might be it.

I took a deep breath and let it out slowly. "Who am I to judge you for your poor choices."

"And yet, there you go—"

I held up a hand, stopping him. "Calm yourself, Garrett. I'm trying to be magnanimous. This is foreign territory for you and me. I guess I can see how this thing spiraled out of control—would've *never* happened to me—"

"Of course not."

"That's right," I said, nodding. "You know why?"

"Because you are the great Dwayne Morrow," he said, hopping to his feet and resuming his nervous habit of pacing the room. "Always so smug and superior. You never do *anything* that's adventurous or maybe even a little scandalous—"

"No," I interrupted. "That's not it at all."

"Then *what?!?*" Brady demanded, pausing mid-stride to await my response. His face was flushed, and he looked like a child, anxiously awaiting a damning verdict from his parents.

"I would never tell such bald-faced lies to my friends just because the truth was difficult or uncomfortable."

He squirmed as I kept him locked firmly in my sights. And yes, I was fully aware of the hypocrisy of my words while rationalizing with myself at the speed of light. I had no more shared the truth of West Virginia with Brady than I had with Melanie, but I assured myself there were extenuating circumstances justifying my actions, and it would take a lot more than this to convince me otherwise.

Eventually, he offered one short, sharp nod. "So, we're good?"

"As good as we ever were," I said. "But you're going to have to forge some sort of peace with Dusty. If there's any chance at all that she's telling the truth about Leroy, we have to give her the benefit of the doubt."

"Fine." He wasn't happy, only resigned.

"And no more lies!"

"*Fine.*"

"And I'm going to have to tell Melanie," I added.

"Oh, *man!*"

"She needs to know why you're acting like such an asshole, and I'm certainly not going to lie to her. Didn't we just cover this? And you don't want to be on her bad side over this."

"I'm never going to be able to look her in the eye again," he said glumly as we headed for the door.

"Actions have consequences, my friend," I said, clapping him on the shoulder.

"Do we have to tell Doug and Loretta?"

I considered that for maybe half a second. "Nah. They're really more work acquaintances than anything else, don't you think?"

CHAPTER EIGHTEEN

A low rumble of thunder sounded in the distance, perfectly approximating the mood in the room. I had the pleasure of watching pure repugnance blossom across my sweet Melanie's face as I brought her up to speed, while Brady took Dusty back to their room to let her know the jig was up. Melanie felt foolish for believing Dusty was ever a nurse's aide, and I was beginning to realize we might still yet be stuck with her as a passenger on our way back home. After a while, Brady returned to our room alone.

"We decided it would be best for Dusty to spend what's left of the weekend locked in her room," Brady said. "We're pretty much done."

"Is she still insisting that Leroy drugged her drink?" asked Melanie.

"She's kind of backed off that," said Brady. "Especially once she realized she wasn't playing to your sympathetic ears any longer. I guess the money that Leroy stumbled across came in the form of a few gold coins he found in the downstairs hall. From her description, they sound like a match with the one we found. Turns out Leroy was finished with her just as soon as she showed a little too much interest in those coins."

"That's ridiculous," I said. "Surely they both realize these coins are fake, obviously just a part of the game."

"The coins are convincing enough to spark doubt with those two geniuses," said Brady. "She was hoping she could make me angry enough to go over and kick Leroy's ass. She's looking for a little revenge because he bruised her ego. She doesn't take rejection very well."

"Do you actually think she'll stay put?" I asked.

"Probably not. She loves drama. If she can figure another angle to play, I'm sure she'll be back. I don't really care what she does, as long as she does it somewhere else," said Brady. He was trying to avoid eye contact, clearly uncomfortable, but caught Melanie studying him intently. He faced her. "What? Oh, God—just *say* it. I'm a horrible person, I know. Do you want me to go? I can go back to my room and just leave this whole thing to you, Dwayne and—"

"Brady," she interrupted.

"*What?!?*" His eyes finally landed on hers.

She crossed the room and gave him a quick, reassuring hug. "I'm just so sorry. I'm not going to pretend I understand the attraction to that woman, but I do empathize with your loss, even if it's not exactly the same. I lost Ryan long before he was murdered, and I wasn't looking to put myself out there when I met Dwayne, but I'm happier than I've been in a long time—well, at least most of the time." Her eyes shifted to her laptop before landing on me, making the tips of my ears burn. "I know it's scary, but I really hope you get to a place where you can let someone get close to you—you know, without requiring penicillin afterward."

Brady's eyes were beginning to glisten, and he laughed as he tried to subtly dab at the corners. "I didn't realize you were into psychology."

"I didn't realize you were into—well, all *that*," she said, offering just enough of a smile so he'd know she was kidding. He laughed again, and the tension in the room evaporated. "Seriously, though, you're selling yourself short. I know plenty of women who would be perfect for you."

"Plenty, huh?" asked Brady. "You haven't even been in Columbus for a year."

"Well," hedged Melanie. "I know one, for sure."

"Nina Crockett?" Brady asked knowingly. "I don't really think—"

"You two were *so* cute together," she persisted.

"Um, guys?" I interrupted.

They both turned toward me expectantly.

"Can you help Brady make a love connection *after* we get through this weekend?" I asked. "We're running out of time here."

"Sure," said Melanie, directing a forefinger at Brady. "But we *will* revisit this."

"So, what's the plan?" asked Brady, eager for a change of subject.

"We were going to explore the rest of the house," I reminded.

"That's right," said Melanie. "Yesterday kind of fell apart after we had to pull a certain someone out of the lake."

"I thought you were in danger!" I was growing weary of defending myself and was saved by a knock at the door.

"Hey, Doug," I said, opening it wide and looking around expectantly. "Where's Loretta?"

"Breakfast really ain't sittin' well with her," he said. "She's still back in the room, can't stray too far from the john, if you catch my drift. I was thinking you all should just go on without us for a bit. Hopefully, we can join you later."

As another rumble of thunder crept across the lower register, I suspected his motive may not have been entirely altruistic—well, that and the fact I could hear John Williams's robust soundtrack from *Raiders of the Lost Ark* spilling across the cavernous space between where we stood and the open doorway to his and Loretta's room across the way. Indiana Jones was one of Doug's many action hero idols. Relieved at the notion I wouldn't be subjected to Loretta's constant criticism, I didn't pursue the issue. "Sure, if you think we can handle it."

"I've always got my reservations but sometimes we gotta push the chickies out of the nest, don't we?" His laugh was like a chainsaw on my nerves, but I kept my smile steady.

"Well, tell Loretta we hope she feels better," I said. "I'm sure there's a limit for how full of shit even *she* can be, right?"

His nod faltered when the content of my words registered. "Let's meet back here no later than sundown and compare notes. If we hear any more of those strange noises, I'll try and trace the source."

"I thought everyone decided it must be Dusty and Leroy," I reminded him.

"It wouldn't hurt to be sure," he said.

"We'll check out Rob and Kit's room and then head downstairs," I suggested. "There might be something of interest in there."

He nodded. "Good idea. If you come across anything significant or you need my input, don't wait until tonight to let me know."

"Sure," I said. "Same goes for you. And keep an eye out for Leroy. I really don't think he's done causing trouble yet."

Doug waved my concern away. "I ain't scared of that bozo. I've still got my trusty little peacekeeper here." He hiked up the right leg of his jeans to expose the bottom half of his ankle holster.

As he ambled back towards the swelling score accompanying whatever hijinks Indiana Jones was currently navigating, I couldn't shake off the creeping certainty that someone was going to end up shot before this was all over.

*****

"This doesn't make any sense," said Melanie, hands on her hips. "There aren't any guest rooms on the main floor, are there?"

"I don't think so," I replied, sequentially opening dresser drawers top to bottom but finding nothing. "I'm pretty sure Anyssa said they were all up here."

Brady had gone into the bathroom to look for personal effects, but returned in short order, shaking his head.

Since we hadn't all taken our rooms at the same time, a little deductive reasoning was required to figure which of the rooms could be the one used by Rob and Kit. We certainly didn't want to accidentally barge in on Leroy, but his room was easy enough to pinpoint. Pulsating music typically associated with pornography thumped through the door, acting as an early warning system. Of the remaining rooms, we had just finished touring the fourth possibility and come up completely empty.

"They brought luggage, didn't they?" asked Melanie.

I shrugged. "No idea. The first time I laid eyes on them was when we met at the breakfast table. I can understand why none of the beds would look slept in. They were never here overnight, but I can't believe there's no sign of them at all. Nothing in the wastebaskets, no toiletries or bags."

Brady moved to the small writing desk by a window that looked out into the woods surrounding the manor along its eastern exposure. He picked up the welcome packet that had been left as a courtesy in all the rooms. "This one hasn't been opened either," he noted, having checked the packets in the other three rooms as we progressed. "I find that especially odd."

"Yeah? How so?" I asked.

"Without the wi-fi password that's in here, these kids wouldn't be able to use their cell phones. Think about it," he said. "What's the first thing most people do after they settle in from traveling?"

"Check their texts, emails and social media," said Melanie.

Brady smiled. "Exactly. Unless they already *knew* the password."

"You're thinking they work for Anyssa," I said, following his line of reasoning.

"Someone has to be," Brady continued. "Anyssa went back to the mainland with the two maids and the guy who helmed the boat. Someone has to be here to keep things moving along."

"I'm not entirely convinced that everyone went back to the mainland," I said. "We didn't actually *see* them board the boat."

"True, but then where have they been all this time?" asked Melanie.

I took a long moment to consider. "Maybe those noises we were hearing in the walls weren't Dusty and Leroy."

Melanie shuddered. "Now, there's a thought. You're suggesting we have people roaming this house—what, through secret passages? That sounds like the sort of thing Nancy Drew would find."

"Big old places like this have been known to have them," I said. "It even makes a certain sort of sense, considering its origins. Leland and Mary Williams spent much of their time as fugitives. I imagine that would leave a lasting impact on someone. It would be a place to hide when you have no local law enforcement, sort of like a primitive panic room, and with stories of the Williamses' gold making the rounds, I would be surprised if they didn't have the occasional trespasser looking to take what didn't belong to them. I mean, think about that article I found last night online. Technically, that was sort of what that McBurney guy was doing."

"I thought he and his girlfriend were looking for the ghost," said Melanie.

"Well, sure, but they *knew* about the gold, so I'm sure plenty of other less scrupulous people were aware of it, too."

Brady was busily pecking away at walls and peering behind pictures, searching for any sections that sounded hollow or switches that might open hidden panels. He started to the right of the door on the interior wall, moving clockwise around the front of the room and then along the exterior wall, paying special attention to the mantel of the fireplace and all of its ornate mahogany molding before moving along to the wall around the antique wardrobe and finally the wall housing the door to the bathroom.

"If there's anything here, I'm not finding it," he said. "What next?"

I shrugged. "Downstairs."

*****

ISOLATION

We exited the bedroom and followed the hallway as it continued its long run across the front of the house, the resplendent chandelier hanging over the foyer almost within reach on the other side of a sturdy safety rail that prevented anyone from falling to the hard tile floor below. Hand-painted portraits of stern-looking people from another time lined the wall at regular intervals, surrounding the doorway in its center.

It hadn't taken long for me to realize the loafers I borrowed from Brady were more than just a little ill-fitting. The right shoe slipped off and on with almost every step, occasionally dragging my low-rise sock with it. Brady and Melanie pulled ahead while I kept fighting with my sock, unwilling to let my bare feet make contact with the inside of Brady's shoe; I was almost certain he always wore them without socks, and I wanted no part of that.

I don't know if I've mentioned this before, but I have a little issue with feet.

While I absolutely appreciate their design from a practical standpoint, I find them to be the single most unattractive part of human anatomy. I might even go so far as to say repulsive. They should be covered up at all costs, and to me, footwear felt every bit as personal as a toothbrush. For all their undisputedly diligent work, feet are prone to sweat and stink as well as bear the occasional deformity. While the sight of a naked pair won't set me to flight like, say, a bat would, the thought of putting my bare foot inside someone else's shoe raises bile to the back of my throat. I firmly believe that whoever created sandals in those earliest of days simply wasn't trying hard enough. They were guilty of inflicting a crime upon humanity that was still being paid forward to this day.

I paused just outside the door to the master bedroom to adjust my sock once more. As I stood, I shifted my attention to the door. Anyssa had declared the master bedroom off limits, but I didn't think it would hurt to at least take a listen. I pressed my ear against the door, trying to filter out the dueling background soundtracks of Indiana Jones and Leroy's porn. If there was anyone inside, they weren't making a sound. I gingerly placed my hand on the doorknob, debating with myself whether I should check to see if the room was locked. Maybe Anyssa's pronouncement that the room was off-limits wasn't meant literally but instead as reverse psychology?

I had barely begun to turn the knob when Melanie sent a jolt of adrenaline racing through me, calling out, "Dwayne! Are you coming?" She and Brady had already traveled the length of the western corridor and stood at the top of the stairs.

I let go of the doorknob and backed away from the door. "I'm on my way."

As I passed our rooms, I kicked Brady's shoes off beside the door. I couldn't continue to wear them without shuffling in a manner that would keep both feet on the ground at all times but would also likely wrench every muscle I had in my lower back and thighs. More importantly, wearing someone else's shoes was just plain gross.

*****

We made a somewhat perfunctory inspection of the kitchen and the dining room as we had already spent a considerable amount of time in both. We were mostly following Brady's lead, looking for hidden clues behind pictures or hollow spots along the walls. I crawled underneath the massive dining room table to make sure nothing had been affixed to its underside, and Melanie systematically opened every drawer and cabinet in the kitchen to make ensure that one of the pantry doors wasn't actually a secret gateway to Narnia. We found nothing of particular interest.

We moved up to the formal parlor, exploring it more thoroughly. Knick-knacks and bric-a-brac adorned every conceivable surface, and Melanie and I studied each piece carefully as Brady continued knocking on walls and checking behind the wall art. I plinked around on the grand piano enough to tell there was nothing hidden beneath the keys or in the soundboard nestled within its case. Melanie discovered that the window seat at the front of the room was actually on hinges, and opening it revealed an empty collection of antique hard-bodied luggage and an assortment of hat boxes, each of which contained a well-preserved vintage lady's head covering. The whole area reeked of mothballs.

Finding nothing else of interest, we moved back out into the hallway. To the right of the main entrance was a small coat room, accessible from both the entryway and another door out in the foyer. Beyond that and along the eastern interior wall was another closed set of pocket doors. We slid them open to reveal an enormous room running the entire length of that side of the house. It was a combination of library, game room and study, handsomely appointed for masculine appeal. A second set of closed pocket doors opened into the hallway at the midpoint of the interior wall, and a third closed set was near the back, providing the illusion from the hallway that these were all separate rooms. Melanie wandered to the back of the room where built-in bookcases lined the walls along three sides, books of all shapes and sizes filling the shelves. A ladder was affixed to rails to facilitate access to volumes stored on the highest shelves.

Brady was drawn to the burgundy-topped pool table occupying the middle section of the room, a 3-bulb billiard light with Tiffany glass centered above it. A rack was mounted on the exterior wall with pool cues and set of billiard balls in its midsection, and a horsehair dart board was centered on a mat beside it with six darts embedded in its surface. A wet bar was across from the pool table along the interior wall with six stools lined up at its counter. A small, glass-fronted breakfront sat beside it, displaying various mugs, snifters and shot glasses surrounding another plentiful inventory of liquor. Whatever the Williamses had been throughout the years, they certainly weren't Prohibitionists. Heavy ashtrays were scattered throughout the room, although if anyone had ever smoked in here, there was no residual odor. A corkscrew rested in one, and what looked like an ornate drawer pull rested in another. I could almost picture Leland Williams and his friends gathered around, challenging each other with friendly wagers over pool or darts while discussing any number of topics that were of interest to gentlemen of that time.

In the front portion of the room, another elaborate fireplace was positioned between two windows along the eastern exterior wall, and centered in front of it was a cozy grouping of furniture including a stiff-backed sofa in paisley print with matching chairs positioned at both ends of a long, low coffee table squatting between the sofa and the fireplace. Along the interior wall was a magnificent mahogany rolltop desk, stained a rich hue of dark brown they don't seem to make anymore, and polished to a glossy finish. The slats of its tambour were rolled up to reveal ample surface space for writing letters atop a blotter stained from decades' worth of excess ink. A dried-out inkwell sat beside a well-used ancient quill pen. Small drawers and cubbies lined the surface behind the tambour, and many of the cubbies were filled with folded, yellowing pieces of paper as well as envelopes containing correspondence of another era. A heavy wooden chair was positioned at the center of the desk, entirely unlike a modern office chair in both style and comfort, but I took a seat, pulling myself up to the desk's workspace. Starting with the cubby at the top left, I began pulling contents down to where I could sort through them. Brady continued his examination of the walls and fixtures, looking for secret switches and hidden panels, while Melanie scrutinized the shelving in the library. She started on the left, pulling books from the shelf to see if that might trigger a shelving unit to swing open leading into a secret passage. She used the ladder to reach the overhead volumes and continued right, leaving no stone unturned.

A flicker of lightning flared through the windows, chased by a low rumble of thunder, much closer than before. The unmistakable pitter-patter of raindrops sounded tentatively against the windowpanes, and the already meager natural light in the room seemed to diminish even more. A mantelpiece clock ticked away the minutes as we diligently applied ourselves to our individual tasks. I absently reached for the standing lamp beside the desk and switched it on. My eyes were beginning to get heavy.

I jumped at the sudden clatter of pool balls breaking, and I looked over to see Brady watching their progress with a cue in hand. He had a snifter with a liberal splash of amber-colored liquid nearby.

"What are you doing?" I asked. "We're supposed to be working here."

"I'm demanding a break," said Brady, lining up a shot and missing it completely. "We've been at this for almost two hours, and I don't even work for Boggs Investigations."

Melanie wandered up from the back of the room, shaking her head. "I'm not finding anything noteworthy back here." She grabbed a cue from the rack on the wall and began lining up her own shot.

I rubbed my bleary eyes. I'd only made it partway through the contents in the cubbies, enough to learn they were practically a chronological time capsule when searching left to right and top to bottom. I had come across some old bills of lading as well as some personal correspondence to and from one generation of Williams or another. I had set aside an albumen snapshot of Leland and Mary Williams taken in 1861, according to the spidery inscription on its back. They stood ramrod straight on the front steps of this very manor, with five children of varying ages standing nearby. All of them wore impossibly serious expressions, as was customary of the time, save for one little girl with springy dark hair surrounding an elfin face with a mischievous grin. I smiled and touched the picture gently, knowing with certainty that this little one had caused more grief for her parents than all the other children combined. It was fascinating to put faces to the names, and to see how the family had grown after they were settled in.

Another flash of lightning was followed by a more enthusiastic clap of thunder, and the lights flickered. The rain had intensified, making it difficult to see any farther than maybe twenty feet beyond the windows.

I rubbed my eyes again, suppressing a yawn. I was losing focus, so I stood and stretched, my spine popping satisfactorily in response. "I guess we can take a few minutes off."

I joined them at the pool table, but not before pouring myself a glass of whatever Brady was having. The bottles were unlabeled, but their fumes practically singed the hairs inside my nose when I took a sniff. I hoped we wouldn't go blind, but it was a risk I was willing to take.

"Do you want one?" I asked Melanie, holding up my glass, but she shook her head.

"I'm good, thanks." She lined up her next shot and sank two striped balls with one shot. She studied the table while suppressing a smile.

I was impressed. She was running the table while Brady watched helplessly from the side. "Any money riding on this round?"

"Hell, no!" said Brady, laughing. "I never knew your lady was a pool shark."

"We're all learning something new today," I said as Melanie called her pocket and handily sunk the eight-ball.

"There wasn't much to do where I grew up," said Melanie, reloading the rack as Brady fished the balls out of the pockets. "My best friend, Barbie Jane, had a pool table out on her breezeway. We used to play all the time when her dad wasn't using it. Why don't the two of you play? It would probably be more evenly matched."

I tilted my head in her direction. "Are you suggesting I am as pathetic as this guy?" I hooked a thumb in Brady's direction.

"No," said Melanie, lifting the rack and stepping away from the table. "I'm just saying you're nowhere near my level." She grinned, heading toward the desk while I appreciated both her sass and the view of her walking away.

"You know, I'm standing right here," said Brady, offended that our playful banter was centered around his humiliating defeat. He finished his drink and poured himself another shallow round.

"Well, all right, then," I said, choosing my own pool cue. "Let's see what you've got."

*****

We were more evenly matched than I would have guessed. Apparently, my whole 'Dead-Eye Dwayne' skill only comes into play when launching projectiles directly from hand and doesn't extend to sports that require use of another implement. I narrowly took the first game, and by the time Brady had taken the second, he had fully recovered his braggadocio, talking shit in double time. He was also on his fourth drink while I was on my third, and I was beginning to feel the warmth in my cheeks. I mitigated any guilt I felt with the knowledge that Doug was upstairs, stretched out on his fat ass, watching Indiana Jones work his way through a marathon of adventures. There was no doubt Doug excelled at delegation and hands-off supervision.

"We should really get back to it," I said, laying my pool cue across the table.

"Come on," urged Brady. "One more game to break the tie."

"Fine," I said, picking my cue back up.

"Hey, guys," said Melanie. She had been seated at the rolltop desk for some time now, picking up where I had left off. "You need to see this." She held up a haphazardly folded sheet of yellow legal pad.

We carried our drinks over to where she sat, and I leaned in. "What is it?"

"It's a note to Anyssa," said Melanie, handing it to me. "And it's not the only one. They were stashed in the back of the bottom righthand drawer. I liked to have never gotten into these suckers." She indicated the drawer above it which was missing its pull. "These two drawers were missing their handles, but I remembered seeing one in the ashtrays by the bar. Snapped right in. The top drawer had a bunch of birth certificates and other legal papers in it, but I don't know what to make of these." There was a pile of similar yellow notes scattered across the desktop.

"Who are they from?" Brady asked.

"They aren't signed, but whoever it is," said Melanie, "gave her until last weekend to abandon any and all plans for the island—"

Her eyes flicked up to mine.

"Before they take matters into their own hands."

CHAPTER NINETEEN

"I don't like the tone," said Melanie, rereading the notes as I worked my way through them.

"What do you mean?" I asked. To me, they were all just varying versions of the same thing. The sender promised some vague form of menace if Anyssa and her team didn't vacate the premises, and I suspected they related to the rumored gold that was beginning to surface. For the first time, I felt like we were actually onto something.

"I don't know," said Melanie. "They feel threatening. And why are they made out to Anyssa?"

"They seem like perfectly good clues to me," I said. "I mean, why *wouldn't* they be made out to Anyssa? She's the current owner of the property. And look at the timing. If they gave her until *last* weekend to hand the gold over, that would indicate they're probably here right now, the very same time that we are all here. Very convenient. It seems perfectly in line with the backstory we've been given, don't you think?"

She nodded but didn't look completely convinced. Another jag of lightning flickered through the window, causing her to jump.

I continued thinking aloud. "Considering the number of children and grandchildren that must have descended from the original Williams family in Lexington, the potential suspect list could be sizeable. Now, it's up to us to narrow it down. We need to figure out who our 'murderer' is—"

"And find the gold." Brady's comment was punctuated by another slow roll of thunder.

"And since we can't do both, I think it's time we do a little delegating of our own," I said, pointing to the ceiling.

*****

"You smell like hooch!" Loretta exclaimed, wrinkling her nose and sniffing at the air around me. She stepped out into the hallway and pulled the door shut behind her. Indiana Jones had gone quiet, and all we could hear—or maybe I should say feel—was the throbbing bass from whatever perversion Leroy continued to enjoy across the hall.

"Never mind that," I said, trying not to breathe directly into her face. We had stopped by my guest room to collect my MacBook and I had it tucked under my arm, holding the unfolded notes Melanie had found in my hand. Melanie and Brady had drifted into the background, leaving me to fend for myself with Loretta. "I want to bring Doug up to speed and maybe see if you can help us with a little legwork."

"Dougie is not available at the moment," she said briskly, snatching the pages of yellow legal paper from my hands and lifting her horn-rimmed glasses from where they were suspended on a chain around her neck and perched them on the tip of her nose. Her lips began to move silently as she read.

I frowned. "What do you mean, 'Dougie's not available?' How can he not be available?"

She shifted her focus to me. "He fell asleep just as the Ark of the Covenant was scorchin' the living flesh off those Nazi scumbags," she said. "And I'm gonna give him a couple of hours before I wake him up. Poor baby got no more than five minutes' sleep last night what with my CPAP. I'm used to it, but I can see how it might mess with someone else, and it wasn't like he was expecting to be in the same room with me."

"Don't you think he'd rather stay informed of what's going on?"

She scowled at me, frowning. "Don't argue with me, boy. I'm his mama, and I know what's best. Besides, you're reporting this to me, so you've done your part."

I scoffed. "I am *not* reporting to our receptionist."

Her frown deepened. "I'm not your receptionist. I'm the Office Manager. And that means I'm higher up the chain of command than the likes of a part-timer like you."

I ground my teeth behind a firmly clenched jaw and debated snatching the papers out from under her nose. I decided to let it go. We were nearing the end of the weekend and still had much to do. Besides, if she got hold of my arm and sent me sprawling again, I would never hear the end of it.

"I don't care for the tone of these notes," said Loretta, flipping through them. "They seem sort of threatening."

"I thought so, too!" said Melanie, and I couldn't help but glare. Aligning herself with Loretta felt traitorous, a betrayal of an oath we had never taken.

"Well, what would you expect them to say? 'I'd like to take your gold, please. Is that okay with you?' I don't think so. In any event, here." I handed her my MacBook, and she accepted it out of reflex.

"What's this for?" she asked.

"Since you're sitting up here basically doing nothing, you can get on the internet and see if you can learn anything more about the legendary gold of Marble Toe Island. See if you can turn up anyone who might have an interest."

Loretta eyed my laptop with disdain. "I really hate these things."

This was one of my biggest frustrations in working with the Boggses. They had an irrational fear of technology. Our records consisted of paper files stored in ancient metal filing cabinets. Reports were created on an IBM Selectric that weighed about fifty pounds, and after-hours messages were received on a microcassette answering system. These were our sole concessions to modern innovation, never mind the fact I work as an IT consultant. The certainty of being brought down by an internet virus immediately outweighs any consideration that I may know what I'm doing, and it's more than a little insulting.

"I know you know how to use the internet, Loretta," I said. "You've been doing research for Doug at the library since what—his high school days?"

"Are you sayin' that I did my boy's homework?"

"Well, *someone* had to do it. Otherwise, he'd still be squeezed into one of those teeny, tiny little desks—"

"Would you two give it a rest?" asked Melanie, interrupting my fun. She turned to Loretta. "Loretta, it would be very helpful if you could do a little digging, please, while we look around and see if we can discover where this gold is hidden. We've looked everywhere we can think of here, so we might have to go back outside."

As if on cue, another clap of thunder, the closest one yet, shook the walls and windows as rain intensified against the siding.

"We still have the basement to explore," Brady suggested, buying us some more time indoors while Mother Nature continued expressing her rage outside. "We really weren't looking for anything when we were down there before."

"I don't even know the password to this thing," grumbled Loretta, turning my laptop around in her hands. "And Lord only knows what sort of perversion you have stored on here."

"Oh, for heaven's sake!" I said, grabbing for the laptop. "Never mind. I should've never expected you to actually participate. I'll just do it myself."

"No, you won't," insisted Melanie, pushing the laptop back towards Loretta. "This is supposed to be a team building exercise for Boggs Investigations, and you both are acting like children. If you're going to stay up here to watch over Doug, we need you to take on the research while we go rummaging around the dank and musty basement of this godforsaken house. His password is 1-2-1-7 followed by 'W-W'—capitalized—and Dexter with a capital 'D' and all of it followed by an exclamation point."

Slack jawed, I gaped at her. I had given my password to Melanie back when we were working the Eviscerator case in the spring, but I had expected her to keep it to herself. And now, not only had she shared my password with Loretta, but Brady was within earshot as well. This was treasonous!

"What the hell kind of password is that?" asked Loretta, though I had no doubt she had already committed it to her mental filing cabinet.

"Birth date, initials of his favorite superhero—Wonder Woman—and the name of that damned cat of his, all followed by an exclamation point for extra security."

"*Melanie!*" I was shocked. There were no more beans to spill.

"Well, how in the world did you expect her to do the research you asked her for?"

"I would have logged her in before we headed downstairs," I said.

"And if she ever had to pee, it would have gone to screen saver, and she would have needed the password again. This is just easier."

I sputtered, trying to find another way to object when Melanie put a finger to my lips to shush me.

"Teamwork requires trust," she admonished. "Just think of this as the next logical step."

She turned before I could respond and headed toward the stairs with Brady hot on her heels, grinning like an idiot. I made a mental note to change my password just as soon as we were back on the mainland and hustled to catch up.

*****

Once we were back on the main floor, we turned to our right, heading for the door in the wall below the stairs that led to the basement. Just as

Melanie wrapped her hand around the doorknob, we froze in place. A disgusting volley of horking and coughing ricocheted off the walls and was punctuated by a series of rapid-fire sneezes. It all seemed to be coming from the kitchen.

"What the—?" Brady began before I shushed him.

Hugging the interior wall, I crept toward the open entrance to the kitchen with Melanie and Brady sliding right along beside me. I peered around the doorframe to find Leroy clad in his yellowed A-shirt and plaid boxer shorts, his back to us and stooped over, his face hovering mere inches from the surface of the counter beside the stovetop. He used one elbow to keep his balance as he wobbled and wavered, unsteady on his own feet. It didn't take a rocket scientist to figure what was wrong with him; a quick glance to his right confirmed he had taken an exhaustive tour of the liquor cabinet with multiple bottles scattered about. Some were empty and some were not, but all had been sampled, and a few had fallen onto their sides, spilling God only knows how much liquor onto the counter before dribbling down onto the kitchen floor. Leroy remained completely unaware of us, shoveling food into his mouth from the various containers of breakfast leftovers we had put in the refrigerator that morning.

"Didn't Loretta tell him that food was off limits?" whispered Melanie, peering around my shoulder and more than a little perturbed. Brady peeked around her shoulder. I motioned for them both to remain quiet. Having been witness to Leroy's disposition when sober, it didn't take a great leap to imagine how he would be when grossly intoxicated. As far as I was concerned, he could eat as much as he wanted, as long as we didn't have to deal with him again.

Almost as if he heard my thoughts, Leroy abruptly pivoted around, nearly losing his balance. We tucked back into the hallway as he drunkenly bellowed, *"Hull-o-o-o-o-o?"*

It sounded nothing like the Adele song.

This was followed by another explosive round of horking. I feared he was going to aspirate at any moment, forcing me to debate whether I would choose to let him die rather than give him mouth-to-mouth. A third alternative presented itself as he was suddenly convulsively sick, retching from a seemingly bottomless stomach. I instinctively held my nose, highly susceptible to the contagious suggestion of others' vomit. I would most certainly never cut it in healthcare. I had trouble cleaning up Dexter's hairballs. Finally, after a revoltingly wet hiccup, Leroy got control of himself, and the house settled back into the sounds of rain sheeting against its windows.

We stood stock still for what seemed like hours but was probably more like a few minutes. Morbid curiosity nudged me back to the entrance, and I carefully peered around the frame once more.

He had nailed the counters and cabinets, with excess dripping off onto the floor at his feet. He seemed to be oblivious to it all. He had resumed his position hovering over the leftover containers, replenishing his freshly emptied reservoir. I clapped a hand over my mouth and backed away quickly, fighting the bile that raged at the back of my own throat.

I guess I had that one coming.

*****

"Do all basements smell this way?" asked Melanie, scrunching up her nose distastefully at the fetid air surrounding us. The ongoing storm had ratcheted up the level of dankness in the air, and I noticed the cinderblock walls were beginning to show signs of moisture as well. Nobody had miraculously fixed the lights since our last visit, and the space felt more like a dungeon than a basement with what little gloomy light spilled in through the casement windows. We navigated under the guidance of the flashlights on our cell phones.

"Ours always did," I said, reflecting on my parents' house in Lymont. Over the course of my childhood, my father had made no less than three different attempts to dry out our basement but had only succeeded by degrees, and a good, hard rain would make itself known every single time. I'm sure a professional basement doctor could have remedied the situation in short order, but it would have cost more than Todd Morrow would have been willing to pay. He was also a self-professed handyman, and it was more of a concession to the limits of his abilities than he was ever willing to make.

Brady shone his flashlight over a stack of boxes just inside the door. "I wonder whatever happened to that cat that scared the shit out of us."

Good question. I hadn't seen it since our last visit to the basement, which was after Dusty insisted she had seen someone down here watching us on the patio from one of the casement windows.

"I don't know," I said. "It didn't seem to be feral or emaciated. *Hmm—*"

"What?" asked Melanie, looking up from the contents of a box she had pried open, poking through its contents.

"I can't believe I'm about to say this, but what if Dusty wasn't mistaken about what she saw? If the cat can get in and out, maybe something larger can, too."

The suggestion was surprisingly unsettling, and we all swept our flashlight beams around the cavernous space to ensure we were alone. I would have likely shat myself if the cat had chosen that exact moment to make a reappearance, but we seemed to be the basement's only occupants. Overhead, lumbering footsteps moved unsteadily along the hallway as presumably Leroy proceeded to whatever his next destination may be. I caught myself holding my breath as he passed the doorway to the basement and continued to the front of the house. I wasn't sure how he was able to remain upright much less mobile. I hoped the stairs wouldn't prove to be too much of a challenge should that be his intended path, but I certainly wasn't here to babysit.

ISOLATION

"I think I found the circuit breakers," called Brady. He had wandered farther down the exterior wall beyond the double water tanks. After an audible click, he said, "Try the lights now!"

I flipped the switch up and a meager row of low-wattage bare bulbs sprang to life down the center of the space, having the curious side-effect of pushing the periphery into even deeper shadow. Brady stepped out of the shadows at the far end looking quite pleased with himself as he shuttered the light on his phone. Melanie and I followed suit.

"So, what now?" asked Melanie.

I surveyed the dingy space and sighed, overwhelmed by the number of boxes and discarded pieces of furniture that had collected over the years.

"We dig in," I said.

*****

Brady and I wrestled a low sitting sofa he had found near the breaker box to the back wall near the doorway to the stairs so we would have a place to sit other than the filthy floor as we rummaged through the contents of endless boxes. We started with the wall at the rear of the house and began pulling boxes one at a time, beginning with the leftmost stack and working from top to bottom.

Brady quickly found a veritable treasure trove of silver age comic books, which he was sifting through with a sense of reverence and wonder. He mused aloud but to no one in particular whether Anyssa might be willing to part with them if the price was right. Collecting vintage comics was one of the hobbies he shared with his son. Melanie had unearthed several boxes of unopened Butterick, McCall's and Simplicity sewing patterns as well as bolt after bolt of fabric in varying shades and materials. A pile of skeins of brightly colored yarn was steadily growing at her feet.

"I didn't realize you were into sewing," I said, straddling a box of vintage 45 r.p.m records and flipping through the titles. I found hits from virtually every big Motown act of the '60s, including Marvin Gaye, Stevie Wonder, Smokey Robinson and the Miracles, and Diana Ross, with and without the Supremes. There were also a handful of singles from the Beatles, Elvis Presley and a handful of acts with whom I was unfamiliar.

Melanie nodded absently, continued to dig through a collection of buttons and notions she had found. "I used to make my own clothes when I was in school. We couldn't really afford to buy them." She cast me a sidelong glance and grinned. "I'm sure there are plenty of things we don't know about each other, at least not yet."

"It's something you and my mom have in common," I noted. "Maybe it's something you can bond over."

Melanie laughed. "Or something else for us to compete over."

"I don't know why you think my mother doesn't like you," I said for what felt like the thousandth time. "And what do you mean, 'something else?'"

Melanie sighed. "I'm talking about you. You're her youngest—her *baby*. No one's ever going to be good enough for you."

"That's ridiculous," I said. "She doesn't dislike you."

"I didn't say that," she said, tossing a cloth baggie of zippers into a pile at her feet. "And I try not to take it personally. I freely admit I'm a real mama bear when it comes to Jasmine."

"She doesn't dislike Sheila, either," I said, reflecting on my mother's behavior toward my brother's new wife. Melanie was making her sound so much harsher than I ever knew her to be.

"Two key differences there," said Melanie. "Matt is not her youngest, and he and Sheila just gave your mom her first grandchild. Short of walking out on your brother and taking the baby, Sheila can do no wrong at this point. I, on the other hand, come with a ready-made family and my own set of baggage. It's going to be difficult for any woman you date to win your mom over, but for me, it's going to be extra difficult."

"Has she said something I should know about?"

Melanie shook her head. "Not at all. She's never been anything but polite to me, and she's really sweet with Jasmine."

"Then where are you getting all this?"

She smiled, leaning over to drape her arms around my neck. "A woman can tell these things. But don't you worry. I don't scare away easily." She kissed the tip of my nose and returned her attention to the box between her feet.

It didn't take us long to realize we'd never get through the basement at this pace. If we had a week or two? Maybe. But there were simply too many boxes to examine thoroughly, and their contents were already distracting enough to derail any real progress. Once we finished with the boxes we had already opened, we shifted strategy and started moving the stacks around to look for things hidden amongst or behind them. After almost two hours, we had made our way all the way around the outer wall and were on the opposite side of the basement, working our way back along the interior wall. So far, we had found nothing whatsoever pertaining to the gold.

"This is completely futile," Brady said, dusting his hands on his jeans. "There's nothing down here, and if I walk through one more cobweb—"

"I know," agreed Melanie, shaking her head and running fingers through her hair. "I feel like I'm crawling with spiders. And I really have to pee."

I sighed, scanning the meager space we had left to cover and decided they were right. We needed to focus our attention in another direction. We were running out of time.

"All right," I said. "Bathroom break, and then we can discuss the next best steps."

I flicked the lights off as we passed single file through the door to the stairs leading up. Once we were back on the main floor, we were immediately assailed by a rhythmic buzzsaw emanating from the formal parlor. I pressed myself flat along the wall beside the open doors to the parlor and peeked around the doorframe.

"Oh, my God," I said, recoiling and covering my eyes. Leroy had passed out, minus his plaid boxer shorts, on Anyssa's vintage paisley settee, his wee Willy Wonka on display for the whole world to see. It was a sight I would surely never be able to *unsee*. Melanie took a tentative step forward, and I lifted a hand to stop her, shaking my head. "It's just Leroy. In the flesh. And I *do* mean, in the flesh."

She recoiled, stopping in her tracks. "Oh, *eww!*"

I directed us back toward the kitchen where a small lavatory was located on the left side of the room.

The kitchen was exactly as we'd last seen it, although Leroy's earlier explosive expulsion was no longer dribbling into the puddles on the floor. Still, every single container of leftovers remained on the counter, lids tossed aside haphazardly and a spoon resting in the congealing sausage gravy. It was readily apparent Leroy had bypassed the civility of plating up; he had grazed directly from the containers.

"I can't imagine how Sandy puts up with that man," muttered Melanie as she cut a wide path around what I'd come to see as a crime scene, going into the bathroom and closing the door behind her.

"Any idea what we should tackle next?" asked Brady.

"Not really," I said, realizing the sky had lightened by degrees and the rain had stopped. "Maybe we should check more of the grounds? I don't know. Let me give Loretta a quick buzz and see if she's found anything online." I patted my pockets quickly before checking more thoroughly. "Well, shit."

"What?"

"I must have left my phone downstairs," I said, heading back down the hallway.

"Do you want me to go with you?"

"*Nah*," I said, opening the door and pausing to turn around. "I'd rather you stay up here with Melanie, just in case Leroy wakes up. I'll be quick."

I trotted down the stairs and flipped the lights on as I entered the room. As the meager light sprang to life, my eye was immediately drawn to something shiny in the middle of the floor toward the front of the house, almost directly across from where Brady had found the circuit box. I approached the object with caution, sure it hadn't been there just moments before. I was also keeping my eyes open for my phone because I had no real recollection of laying it down anywhere. I knelt and picked the object up.

It was another gold coin.

I stood, slipping it into my pocket and proceeding to my left, going around the underside of the basement stairs. As I continued into the other half of the basement, I again caught sight of something shiny, almost all the way to the rear of the house and partially hidden underneath a section of metal shelving affixed to the exterior wall. My phone sat on one of the shelves, its dark screen glinting in the light from the bare bulb suspended from the ceiling nearby. I might have been able to believe we had missed seeing one coin, but two? It didn't seem likely. I hurried over to the shelving unit and scooped my phone up, slipping it into my pocket. I knelt, reaching for the coin when the shelving unit abruptly swung away from me on hinges, and I found myself staring at the steel-tipped toes of a pair of tan work boots. My eyes drifted upward, following a slender pair of jeans-clad legs before finally focusing on the face above them.

Kit Scarberry stared down at me, her head cocked to the side, her face offering a rueful smile. In her hand, she offered a tarot card.

I couldn't believe my eyes.

I was dead.

CHAPTER TWENTY

Kit leaned forward, her sun-kissed hair cascading around her face and floating above my head. She pressed a finger to pursed lips before offering me her hand and helping me to my feet. She tucked the tarot card into her shirt pocket with an apologetic smile.

"I—" I began, but she shook her head, shushing me again. She turned around, encouraging me to follow her with a quick toss of her head.

For a long second, I couldn't move. I was completely stunned. *I* wasn't supposed to be dead. Not *me*. *Anyone* but me. How could I get to the bottom of this thing if I had crossed the Rainbow Bridge? Wait a minute—I think that's for pets—but you get the idea. It wasn't fair! It was like being ejected from a movie without ever finding out how it ended.

Kit gestured for me to follow with renewed urgency, and it suddenly registered that she stood just inside a doorway leading onto a shallow wooden platform, its safety rails barely visible in the darkness behind her. A gap in the rail suggested the presence of a ladder leading down into unknown depths. I focused on the metal shelving unit which was bolted to a facade of very realistic looking cinder blocks pivoting inward on hidden hinges and providing access to what was an honest-to-God secret passageway! I was thrilled and disappointed in equal measure.

ISOLATION

I stepped through, and Kit eased the door shut, activating a small, handheld flashlight as the panel clicked into place. I couldn't believe this was happening to me. If only I hadn't forgotten my stupid phone!

As if she had read my mind, Kit said, "Your phone." Her voice was barely above a whisper.

I patted my pants pocket absently. "My phone?"

She nodded. "Yes. You'll need to turn it off, please."

I pulled it out, staring at it stupidly.

"It's in the game rules you signed, under the section marked, 'Death and the Afterlife.'"

"There was a section marked, 'Death and the Afterlife?'"

She stared at me, unblinking. "Yes. It's a security risk. Even beyond the temptation to send your teammates a text or maybe even a quick call, we have no way of knowing if you might have one of those tracking apps installed that families use to keep track of each other. You voluntarily agreed to remove that temptation by turning your phone off should you be one of the weekend's casualties."

I was on the losing end of an argument with a pint-sized, freckle-faced Grim Reaper. I made myself a promise then and there to never sign another document without thoroughly reading its contents first. Of course, I had made myself a similar promise after Loretta tricked me into assuming partial responsibility for the lease of the Boggs Investigations office on West Broad. Why was I so much better at keeping promises to others than I was to myself? I powered my phone down.

Kit gestured toward the gap in the wooden rail with the beam of her flashlight. "You first, Mr. Morrow. Those rungs are sturdy. Don't let the looks of them fool you."

As I backed up into the opening, my stockinged feet came into Kit's view.

"You're not wearing any shoes," she noted, a bit startled.

"It's a long story," I said. "But no, I'm not. Is that a problem?"

She grimaced slightly. "It's not exactly a problem, but—oh, well. You'll see soon enough. Too late to worry about it now."

I wasn't sure I cared for the sound of that. My poor feet had been through enough already this weekend, but I began lowering myself, rung by rung into the darkness below. As soon as I had cleared the top few rungs, Kit started down after me, her penlight dancing haphazardly all around us as she carried it between her teeth. The ladder was mounted to thick, wooden support beams, but most of what was directly in front of my face was hard-packed, pungent earth. It felt like I was lowering myself into my own grave. I was beginning to wonder exactly how far down we were going, when my right foot hit the bottom, nearly sliding out from under me in the viscous mud waiting below. In my haste to recover my balance, I sank my left foot even deeper into the mire.

"Sorry about that," called Kit from above me. "But it couldn't be helped. You might be better off without the socks at this point."

I was already peeling them off and tossing them aside when she lowered herself to the ground, stretching her foot as far to the left as possible to avoid the deepest section of the muck, the one I had been drawn to like a magnet.

"I'll try and keep the flashlight beam close to the ground, but you'll want to watch where you step. We have, upon occasion, come across a rat or two down here, as well as some guano you wouldn't want to step in, but that really can't be helped either."

"Did you say, 'guano?' As in *bat* guano?"

"Yes, sir. That's exactly what I meant."

My heart stuttered as the dark space around us suddenly came alive with threatening potential. While I was in no hurry to encounter rats, I couldn't predict what I might do should we encounter bats, although it would undoubtedly involve high-pitched screaming and a wealth of other self-inflicted humiliation. My deeply ingrained phobia with respect to those haphazardly flying creatures of the night, can be traced to early childhood—possibly as early as the birth canal.

I realized Kit was staring at me, a hint of impatience creeping across her features. "Come along, Mr. Morrow," she said. "We need to go."

I cast one last, mournful look above me and nodded, suddenly aware of the uneven and chilly earth beneath my bare feet.

We followed the beam of Kit's flashlight along the earthen corridor and in a mostly straight path. At best guess, the tunnel itself was between four and five feet in width, fluctuating a bit in places and seven or so feet in height, but all of it was unlit, falling into utter darkness before Kit's shadow ever met the ground.

My feet were already complaining to management about their consistently substandard treatment. I think I found every embedded rock or gnarled root along the way, but mercifully no guano. I couldn't keep up with Kit, who proceeded at a good clip with the luxury of familiarity I did not possess. She frequently checked to make sure I hadn't made a break for it. I'd be lying if I said I hadn't considered it, but as another jagged stone bit into the soft underside of my foot, eliciting a startled grunt, I realized I'd never get far. I resigned myself to playing by the rules.

"So, you and Rob work for Anyssa?" I asked as a series of questions floated to the forefront of my consciousness.

"Ms. Williams will debrief you shortly," she said without looking back. The air around us felt supercharged from the storm, and I could detect a faint breeze sporadically kissing my cheeks. I heard water far in the distance, suggesting we were nearing the shore, but it was still pitch black in the corridor, save for the bright beam of Kit's flashlight.

"Is Kit even your real name?"

I didn't think she heard me; her pace accelerated, and I struggled to keep up. My feet were grudgingly acclimating to their current situation, and I gradually quickened my step.

"What about Sandy?" I persisted. "Is she all right? Because she looked pretty dead last time I saw her."

Nothing.

"And what's the deal with that hooded figure? Very intimidating. I'm guessing that was Rob—if that's even *his* real name. Right?"

Now I was just babbling, and I may as well have been by myself.

"So, is this where the gold is?" I continued. "Because we've just about exhausted all the places we could think of, and since nobody knows about this place, I don't know that—"

"*Mr. Morrow!*" Kit turned around abruptly, shining her light in my eyes before taking a deep breath and letting it out slowly. She lowered the flashlight as she exhaled, a smile creeping back onto her face. "I realize you're impatient, I really do. But I'm not at liberty to say anything more than I've already told you. Ms. Williams will meet with you once you arrive at your final destination. She'll explain everything you need to know. But I must remind you that for all intents and purposes, you are among the dead. You need to honor the game rules you agreed to when signing your paperwork yesterday. Short version, we need to keep moving. We need to remove you from the field of play just as quickly as possible, and we could do that so much more expediently if you would just save your questions for Ms. Williams, all right?"

I nodded, only slightly put off by Kit's stern rebuke. Her words showed real diplomacy while her expression suggested I was only one short question away from getting busted in the mouth again.

*****

I quickly lost any sense of how much distance we had traveled. The only thing I knew for certain was we were moving in a nearly straight line away from the manor toward the back half of the island we had only partially explored. My filthy feet were past throbbing, and a suggestion of pale light flickered in the distance. I could hear the lake much more clearly, its surface still agitated from the earlier storm, but it sounded as if the rain had stopped falling, and there were no more sudden cracks of thunder to rent the calm.

The corridor abruptly narrowed in both width and height as daylight strengthened.

"You'll want to watch your head here," advised Kit, stooping herself as she pushed through a small opening. "The support beam is a little low."

I stuck a leg through, landing on—what else?—an uneven pile of large, wet stones. I pulled the rest of myself into daylight and was momentarily blinded, even though the sun still hid behind an unbroken wall of slate gray. Although the storm had passed, another line of ominous clouds was regrouping on the western horizon, promising more of the same. I blinked rapidly, my vision clearing, and I realized we were only a short distance from the secondary dock Anyssa had mentioned in our orientation. It shouldn't have been a surprise. She had told us it was where people went when they died, and look—here I was! This one was almost like an afterthought, freestanding and without a boathouse. Its weathered pilings were driven deep into the lakebed to support the wooden planks that comprised a short and slightly uneven tongue extending over the lake.

The water was still somewhat tumultuous from the storm, and the gleaming white speedboat bobbed in its wake. Jeremy, its captain, stood on the deck clad in a yellow rain slicker. He spotted us as we emerged from the wall of rocks and boulders that flowed down to the water's edge. He motioned us toward him.

I started forward but was stopped by Kit, tugging me to the right. "Not that way," she said. "You'll break your ankle. There's a path over here."

I followed her carefully, quickly discovering exactly how slick the wet rocks were against my bare feet. We stepped off onto a trail barely a foot wide that wound down to meet the dock below. We scurried across the planks to where Jeremy waited above a ladder he had mounted to the side of the boat. He reached down with his right hand, wrapping my left arm in a vice-like grip before practically lifting me off the ground and hoisting me aboard. He didn't even have the courtesy to grunt, as if I were entirely insubstantial. He turned to Kit, but she had already scrambled up and over the edge, nimble as a kitten.

"All right, folks, welcome aboard and let's get this ship underway," he said, stooping to untie the first of two ropes securing the boat to the pilings. "Sorry to be so rushed, but we're fighting daylight and another line of storms moving through. The water's already turbulent enough. We want to get where we're going sooner rather than later." The water beneath the boat abruptly swelled then dipped, and my stomach dropped in response. I staggered over and plopped myself down on the long bench seating that ran the length of the starboard side, clutching its chrome rail in a death grip. Kit seated herself beside Jeremy as he fired up the engine.

Soon we were underway, slicing through choppy water on a circuitous route that would prevent us from being spotted by anyone on the developed portion of the isle. I was certain my absence should have been noticed by now, but I don't know what I expected them to do about it. Initiate a search and rescue mission using the boat that had been returned to the boathouse?

I sighed as I watched the island grow smaller, coming to grips with the fact my services were no longer needed.

*****

I felt curious eyes from all directions as Jeremy expertly navigated through the channel of Portside Marina on Kelleys Island, heading for the slip in which the boat belonged. I suppose I should have considered myself lucky; what would have probably been a rollicking crowd in decent weather had thinned from the previous storm and the promise of more to come. As it was, I stood out like a sore thumb, shoeless in my filthy jeans with drying mud caked halfway to my knees, my grungy cotton t-shirt clinging to my back and saturated by perspiration. I hadn't realized how much exertion was apparently involved in traversing the underground tunnel until the wind stirred, sending a chill through my sweat-stained shirt and raising gooseflesh along my arms.

Once Jeremy had secured the boat, he and Kit escorted me to shore, Jeremy on my right and Kit on my left. I felt like a prisoner being led to his doom as they kept a hand on each of my arms, and I realized Jeremy was keeping his left arm tucked inside his yellow rain slicker.

"Did you hurt yourself?" I asked, nodding my head in his direction.

He chuckled, shaking his head. "Janked up my arm cleaning the boat. Shouldn't have been so careless. No big."

We emerged in a parking area where a nondescript champagne Toyota Camry and its tall and gangly Samoan Uber driver waited for us. He looked disdainfully at the muck clinging to my bare feet, and I could only shrug my apologies. Hopefully, Kit would tip him well. Jeremy waved us off and turned back toward the boat as Kit held the rear door open for me before sliding into the front passenger seat herself. She gave the driver instructions too quickly for me to catch and then buckled herself in.

"Give me your sizes," she called to me over her shoulder.

"Excuse me?"

"Your sizes," she repeated before listing, "Shoes, pants, shirts, underwear. You can't go around looking like that. Ms. Williams is going to have some items sent to your hotel room while you clean up."

"Oh," I said, unaccustomed to and a little uneasy about such service. I listed my sizes as she captured them in real-time in a text and forwarded them to whoever would be serving as my personal shopper. My own phone felt heavy as the brick that it currently was, nestled in my pocket and without power. I wondered how many times Melanie had tried to call or text me. If our roles were reversed, I would have likely been frantic by now. I wondered if she felt as disjointed as I did. Being separated from my pack wasn't a consideration I had entertained while preparing for this weekend, and I was finding it surprisingly difficult to be a good sport about it.

I barely had time to get comfortable when we reached our destination, less than a mile down West Lakeshore Drive at the picturesque Kelleys Island Venture Resort—I only knew this because it was inscribed in a fancy font on a placard mounted in the center of a low brick wall surrounding an assortment of flowering groundcover and small thatches of well-tended shrubbery. The lodging itself was a stately, two-story structure shaped in an 'L,' its crisp pale-yellow walls warm and inviting beneath a roof of pine-green shingles. I caught the suggestion of a pool behind the flowerbed as we passed, turning right and then right again, and parking in a lot that was less than half full.

Kit turned in her seat and handed me a key card. "This is your stop," she said. "You'll be in Room 120, which is on the first floor. Your suite has both poolside and streetside entrances, and once you've been debriefed, you're welcome to use any of the facility's amenities. Your clothes should be delivered to your room shortly, and Ms. Williams will call you on the bedside phone to give you further direction."

I took the key card, and she clamped down on my hand.

"If I can remind you one last time," she said, boring holes into my eyes. "Please do not be tempted to contact your friends in any way. There is very little we can do to enforce this request, other than to appeal to your sense of fair play."

I nodded, attempting to pull my hand away, but she held tight.

"You should also know if we discover that you *have* contacted your friends, Boggs Investigations will no longer be eligible for the grand prize, should they solve the mystery," she added emphatically.

"Sure, fine, whatever. I don't have any intention of—wait a minute." My comprehension finally caught up with the entirety of her warning. "What do you mean, 'grand prize?'"

She looked at me curiously. "It was mentioned in the promotional literature. If the mystery is successfully solved before noon on Monday—tomorrow afternoon—the winner will receive a $1,000 cash prize. *Provided*, of course, that the winner plays by the rules. I figured since you all were working as a team, you planned to split the proceeds somehow. I guess that would be at the discretion of whoever's in charge of your team—is it, Dirk? Dirk Boggs?"

"Close enough," I muttered. She finally released my hand, and I scowled, my understanding suddenly complete with this new information. That little shit! Doug hadn't mentioned the reward because he never had any intention of sharing it with anybody—well, other than maybe with his mother.

"All right, then," she said. "I have to get back to the island. Things are really heating up, and the next several hours should be very exciting!" The shift in her expression was almost comical as it went from elated to disappointed in an instant, all for my benefit. "I'm so sorry you won't be able to witness things firsthand."

"I'm sure you are," I said wearily, getting out of the car and shutting the door behind me. She waggled her fingertips at me as the driver backed out of the parking space and retraced his own route, taking them back toward the marina.

For the moment, I was on my own.

*****

I located my room and had barely let myself in before a series of sharp raps sounded against the door, startling me. Glancing through the peephole, I saw a short, brown-skinned man with a close-fitting cap of jet-black hair. He shifted on his feet outside the door in jean shorts and a sleeveless printed tank top. Dangling from the fingers of one hand was a red plastic shopping bag.

I opened the door, smiling as he handed me the bag. It had 'Unc'l Dik's' printed on it. "Thank you," I said, reaching for my wallet. "How much do I owe you?"

He shook his head, "It's already been taken care of."

"Well, let me give you a tip for your trouble—"

He waved my money away, again shaking his head. "It's already been taken care of. Enjoy your stay, Mr. Morrow." He handed me the bag with a nod and a smile, turning back toward the parking lot.

"Thanks, again!" I called after him, tucking my wallet away and closing the door. Surely, there would be an itemized invoice coming from Anyssa before all of this was over.

I carried the bag back to the bedroom at the rear of the suite and dumped its contents onto the bed. A pack of tighty-whities, a pair of khaki shorts with a built-in stretchy cloth belt, and a psychedelic tie-dyed shirt with 'Kelleys Island' emblazoned across the front all tumbled out, followed by a rugged-looking pair of cushioned flip-flops with a leather toe thong. I groaned inwardly. The entire outfit screamed tourist, but the footwear? *Ugh.* I hadn't thought to mention my aversion to sandals and the feet they put on prominent display, and whoever invented the toe thong was nothing short of a masochist. It was the foot version of having an enormous popcorn kernel wedged firmly between your teeth.

Oh, well. Beggars could not be choosers.

I went into the bathroom and started the shower, adjusting the water just as warm as it would go. I stepped back into the bedroom and began peeling off my filthy clothes, pausing when my hand brushed against the cell phone in my pocket. I fished it out, staring at its oblong, black shiny screen. My finger slid across the side, tracing lightly over the volume and power buttons. What would it *really* hurt if I checked to see if anyone had sent me a text? I was aware of apps like Find My Kids that utilized GPS to help parents pinpoint the locations of their children in case they got separated. These same apps were also frequently used to help spouses keep track of their wandering partners, which I believed spoke to a much greater problem in their relationship, but in any event, I didn't have anything like that installed on my phone.

I had almost talked myself into powering on my phone when the landline beside the bed suddenly chirped, startling me and causing me to drop my cell on the mattress. I scooped up the receiver. "Hello?"

"Mr. Morrow! Hello, this is Anyssa Williams!" Her voice was warm and just happier than shit. "I hope you are finding your accommodations satisfactory?"

"Very nice," I said, looking around the room for any hidden cameras that might be telecasting my activity. My eyes flicked to my cell on the bed guiltily, and I couldn't help but feel the timing of Anyssa's call had been remarkable. "Thank you for the clothes," I added. "I'm afraid I wasn't very presentable."

"No problem at all," she said warmly. "Just think of them as your consolation prize."

Hmm. Maybe an invoice wasn't forthcoming, after all.

"Kit mentioned something about a debriefing—?" I ventured.

"Yes. Now that you have reached this stage of the game, there are a few things I would like to go over with you sooner rather than later, if that's all right with you."

"Certainly."

"I'm guessing you must be famished," she said. "There's this great little place close to the marina called Captain's Corner. Dinner and drinks are on me. How about I send a car for you around seven? Will that give you enough time to get ready?"

I caught sight of my reflection in the mirror across the room and flinched. I looked like I had come straight from a pig pen.

"Sounds wonderful," I said sincerely, and my enthusiastic stomach grumbled agreeably. I had pictured us in a small interrogation room, facing off across a cold metal table under the harsh glare of a bare bulb burning overhead. This sounded so much better.

"I look forward to seeing you then," she said warmly. "Goodbye."

"Good—" The phone clicked in my ear. "—bye."

I cradled the receiver and scooped my own phone off the bed, carrying it to the dresser on the other side of the room and slipping it into the top drawer. If I could quit smoking, I could surely manage to keep my hands off my phone for a single day.

As I shed the rest of my clothes, stepping through steam and into the shower, it occurred to me, and not for the first time, how very apt the comparison between these two addictions actually was.

CHAPTER TWENTY-ONE

Anyssa stood, waving from a table by a window in the front corner of the restaurant as I entered the bustling establishment. It would appear the streets were less traveled because everyone had taken shelter in here. There wasn't a free seat to be had, not even at the bar. Boisterous conversation was punctuated by laughter and the clinking and clattering of assorted dinnerware. Servers wove expertly through the din, carrying trays at angles that defied gravity. With far less grace and a whole lot of apologies, I worked my way through the compact space.

"Mr. Morrow!" she exclaimed with a warm and winning smile. She took my hand into both of her own, and I felt myself flush a little around the edges. She had a way of making you feel as if you were the only person in a crowded room, and it was a little like looking directly into the sun. She wore an off-the-shoulder emerald blouse with an obsidian brooch pinned where the sweetheart neckline dipped at her cleavage; crisp, white pleated slacks completed the outfit. She sported just a dab of eyeliner around her eyes, as her radiant, light-brown complexion was already flawless and needed no cosmetic assistance.

"So nice to see you again, Ms. Williams—"

"*Please,*" she interrupted. "It's just Anyssa."

"And enough with the 'Mr. Morrow' stuff. As the old saying goes, Mr. Morrow is my dad," I said, pulling her chair out for her before taking my own seat across the table. "And might I say, you look lovely this evening."

Dimples blossomed in her cheeks as her already radiant smile intensified. "Thank you, Mr.—Dwayne. You're too kind. And you look—" Words failed her as she struggled to find something somewhat gracious to say.

"Like a tourist," I finished for her, and we both laughed.

"I was going to say 'clean,' but yes, your description is more apt," she said, taking a sip of translucent burgundy liquid from a tall-stemmed flute. She motioned for her server, a plain-featured pencil of a girl with mouse-brown hair pulled to a knot at the nape of her neck, and she hurried over without hesitation. "I'll have another of these, Paula, and please bring the gentleman whatever he would like."

Paula turned toward me expectantly.

"Um, sure," I said. "Can you make a whiskey sour?"

She nodded. "You got it," she said, melting back through the crowd behind her.

"So, tell me," said Anyssa, leaning forward and clasping her fingers together. "Have you enjoyed the weekend so far?"

I laughed again. "Well, *hmm*. Let's see. I'm dead, so I guess there's that."

She covered her face with both hands, grinning. "Other than that! Other than that!"

"Well, sure. You've got a lovely piece of property, and the house is really something else. I was just beginning to feel like we were getting somewhere when—well, you know." I indicated myself sitting across from her. "Death."

She took another sip from her wine, emptying her glass just as Paula brought her refill along with my whiskey sour. The cocktail was my attempt to be sociable; I usually took my whiskey straight, but never in public. I had exactly zero desire to make a spectacle out of myself in front of others, and whiskey straight can sometimes be unpredictable.

Paula traded glasses with Anyssa, and asked, "Did you know what you wanted? Any appetizers?"

"Why don't you bring a hummus plate for now?" Anyssa requested. "It will give my guest a chance to look at the menu."

"Sure, no rush," said Paula, slipping away again with Anyssa's empty glass.

"As I explained to everyone when we met yesterday, this whole weekend is a giant trial run of what we hope to offer as a premium experience for guests who are willing to pay. We've already identified a number of things we would have done differently, but that's what trial runs are all about, right? They help illuminate that which isn't immediately obvious. Take for instance, the resistance to the releases. I never in a million years would have guessed that would become such a sticking point," Anyssa said.

"I would also guess you never in a million years thought you'd have a guest quite like Leroy Poole, either," I said, rolling my eyes before sipping at my drink.

She chuckled. "No, certainly not. He's been rather volatile, I understand. Maybe even violent? I want you to know how very sorry I am, Mr.—Dwayne. I had no idea whatsoever that he might be capable of anything of the sort, and we are already discussing prescreens we must have in place before we ever take this endeavor live. I'm hoping you weren't hurt too badly."

Pride swelled like a balloon in my chest. "Not at all," I said quickly, adding, "Barely felt a thing."

"Oh, good," she said, and as I recognized the relief evident in her voice, I also realized she must have eyes on the ground at the manor. How else would she have known about the altercation between me and Leroy the previous evening? This was followed by another disheartening thought, and I sat back in my chair, shaking my head in disbelief.

"Is that what all this is about?" I asked, watching the smile drop from Anyssa's face. "Buttering me up and playing on my ego so I'll be too embarrassed to say that bastard practically knocked teeth out of my mouth? Do you have something there for me to sign? Something that releases you from any liability for what happened?"

I was getting louder, and she was flustered as folks nearby began to take notice. "No—not at all! The release that you signed earlier would cover all of that—"

I pushed back from the table. "Son of a bitch," I grumbled to myself, feeling massively foolish.

"Please, Mr. Morrow! *Dwayne,*" she urged, reaching out and taking my hand again. She looked like she was on the verge of tears. "I promise you, that is *not* the case. First and foremost, I am concerned about your well-being. I've barely slept knowing Mr. Poole is still roaming about up there, and it has nothing at all to do with whether I get sued or not."

"Then why am I here, and he's not?" I demanded.

"Because with his assault on you, he made it plain he wasn't adhering to any laws, much less playing by any silly game rules. Can you imagine his reaction if Kit showed up with a tarot card in his face? I have been *this close* to sending the authorities." She held her thumb and forefinger a hair's width apart.

"What stopped you?"

"The way your team responded," she said. "You circled the wagons, so to speak, telling Leroy under no uncertain terms he was on his own. And that Boggs woman is surprisingly formidable."

"He promised revenge."

"And then he found the liquor cabinet," said Anyssa. "He was passed out before the afternoon was even underway."

"You have no way of knowing how long he'll be out or what he'll be like when he wakes up," I said.

She ran nervous fingers through her close-cropped hair, shaking her head. "Listen, I'm *sorry,* all right? I might have made a bad call, but who can say? I've got so much riding on this weekend and to interrupt it prematurely would be devastating. It felt like your team had things under control. It seemed like the right choice at the time."

I shook my head in disbelief, easing my chair back up to the table. Out of the corner of my eye, I spotted Paula hovering nervously in the background with the hummus plate stacked high with carrot sticks, red peppers and wedges of pita bread. I motioned her over and took the plate from her.

"I think we're gonna need another minute, Paula," I said, and the patrons nearby attempted to return to their own conversations, pretending they hadn't been hanging on our every word.

"Of course," said Paula, smiling nervously while backing up, and she was practically across the room already.

"I promise you, we're monitoring things very closely," Anyssa said earnestly. "At the very first suggestion of trouble, I will send reinforcements and pull the plug on the whole thing, I assure you. Now, please. Can we just talk?"

I was disgruntled, but I nodded my head. "What's left to talk about?"

"Well, first, let's try and get through what will be our standard exit interview for anyone who becomes deceased during the course of our game. It's very short, I promise," she said, retrieving an iPad from the messenger bag she had carried into our group meeting. I picked up the menu, eyeing it casually as my impatient stomach grumbled audibly. The various heavenly aromas surrounding us were nearly overwhelming.

"Fire away," I said, nabbing a carrot and tracing a line through the hummus before popping it into my mouth.

Anyssa consulted her tablet. "Have you been in contact with anyone else from the island since your demise."

"Only Kit and Jeremy, the skipper from the boat. Do you have to keep doing that?"

"Doing what?"

"Referring to it as my death or my demise—it's really morbid."

She shifted her eyes up from her tablet, grinning slightly. "Sorry." She looked relieved as the tension between us had cooled considerably.

Paula was back, and this time we gave her our orders. Anyssa opted for the cranberry pecan chicken salad while I went with the Lake Erie perch with extra tartar sauce and a wedge of lemon. I also requested another whiskey sour and this time, asked for a double. I figured I was in for the evening.

"Describe the progress you or your team made when searching for the gold," she said, sampling the hummus.

I blinked. "Didn't you say you were monitoring things closely? Can't you just rewind the video and watch for yourself?"

She looked at me curiously. "I think you're overestimating my capabilities. Other than a couple of security cameras near the entrances, there isn't any ongoing surveillance. Did you think I had secret cameras stashed throughout the house spying on your every word and every activity?"

"It doesn't seem so far-fetched," I said. "You seemed to know an awful lot about what happened with Leroy."

"You were out on the patio when he hit you. And Kit was on site when Mrs. Boggs set him straight. You may not have seen her, but she was watching. When I refer to us monitoring *anything* on the island, I mean through my *team*, my eyes and ears on the ground. I would never install video or listening devices in areas that should rightfully be considered private. That would be a gross invasion of my guests' personal space, and quite frankly, there are some things I can go my whole lifetime without actually seeing. However, understanding your thought process is of great interest to me. So, if you wouldn't mind, can you describe your team's progress?"

I emptied my drink and considered my response. I didn't want to be *too* forthcoming and decided to dance around our various mishaps as best as I could. After all, Doug should be accountable for his own actions and could explain the condition of the golf cart in his own exit interview.

"I'd say we were a little slow out of the gate," I said. "We weren't really sure what to make of that business on the stairs with Maria—"

"Oh my God," laughed Anyssa, rolling her eyes and burying her face in her hands. "*First* thing that went wrong, and it was just *awful*. I felt so badly for Maria, God bless her heart. She was trying so hard to stay in character, but she's not a trained actress, and that Rhodes woman wouldn't stop picking at her."

"Yeah, that Rhodes woman is something else, all right," I agreed drily.

"It wasn't just her, though," said Anyssa. "That whole business with the ripped apron pocket? That wasn't a clue. Maria actually caught her pocket on the newel post as she was coming down the stairs and ripped it open. She had a few of our gold coins in her pocket as well as a drawer pull, clues you were supposed to find but instead, they went bouncing down the stairs and scattering to who knows where. If I hadn't mentioned this was a quest for gold during our orientation, you wouldn't have had any idea what you were even looking for. We'll certainly do *that* better next time."

Paula brought my drink, and Anyssa signaled for another glass of wine.

"We decided to explore the island, see what we might find outside," I said.

"Yes," said Anyssa, and I was reminded again I wasn't telling her something she didn't already know. Even if her cameras were limited to covering the entrances to the manor, she would have been completely aware of our comings and goings. "I noticed your team split up. Was that your initial strategy?"

"More or less," I hedged. No need to explain that Melanie wasn't speaking to me at the time or that Loretta was plagued with diarrhea and shoes unsuitable for hiking.

"Even after I advised against it, you took the boat out," she said, and it wasn't a question.

I was automatically defensive. "*I* didn't want to take it out. As a matter of fact, if it had been just me, it would have never happened. I know nothing about driving a boat—"

"Piloting a boat," corrected Anyssa.

"—yeah, that either. But Doug insisted on it. My choice was to tag along or get left behind."

"No, that was good," she said, making a note on her tablet. "Sometimes, we employ a little reverse psychology as motivation."

I looked at her incredulously. "So, you *wanted* us to take the boat out?"

"It was a resource at your disposal," she said noncommittally.

"So, when you said the master bedroom was off-limits—"

She shrugged. "Exactly how could I have enforced *anything* as being off-limits?"

As I processed that notion, Paula brought our plates and placed them before us. "Everything look good?" she asked. "Can I bring you anything else?"

"Everything looks wonderful," said Anyssa, smiling brightly, her composure once again intact.

We took a break to savor our food. The perch was delicious and Anyssa's salad was almost too pretty to eat, not that it prevented her from digging in. We allowed the conversation from the other diners to fill the space between us. As I stole an occasional glance at Anyssa, I found myself admiring the way she carried and conducted herself, despite her misstep with Leroy. At least she was capable of *making* a decision, something a shocking number of us cannot do without arduous deliberation and consultation with others, as if our own opinion can never be fully trusted.

"Do you approve?" she finally asked.

"I do," I said, and I wasn't just referring to the food. "Did you have any more questions?"

"Just a few," she said, sipping her wine and blotting the corners of her mouth with a napkin. She cast a sidelong glance at her tablet, which she had propped up against the window. Outside, daylight had already begun to fade into night, and another line of ominous black clouds was congregating along the western horizon. "So, you and Mr. Boggs went out onto the lake in the boat, while Ms. McGregor, Mrs. Poole and Mr. Garrett explored the grounds."

"That's right," I said. "Although they didn't really find anything. Doug and I spotted them on the trail from out in the lake, and that's when I saw that hooded figure again, and I know I didn't imagine it. Are you allowed to tell me about that? You know—now that I'm deceased or whatever?"

"Why don't you tell me what *you* think it is?" Her eyes were playful, and at least she wasn't telling me it was all in my head.

I took a sip of my drink as I collected my thoughts, surprised to see I was nearing the bottom of the glass. My hesitation was strictly for show as I signaled to Paula for another. "At first I thought it must be Kit's boyfriend, Rob," I began, watching Anyssa's eyes twinkle. "I mean, what are the odds that she would be working for you, but he wouldn't?"

"But you didn't actually know that Kit was working for me at the time," said Anyssa, watching me closely. This felt more like a final exam than an exit interview.

"No," I agreed. "And I didn't think that then. At that point, Rob and Kit had gone off, exploring on their own. We've all been young, dumb and in love once. We know how that goes. We just wanted to give them their space."

"You might be surprised to learn that Rob and Kit only met a few short months ago, each of them answering an ad I placed in the *Plain Dealer* looking for college age kids to help administer a test of sorts," she said.

"They're both certainly better actors than Maria."

"They both had backgrounds in theater. That was part of their appeal," she acknowledged. "Maria worked for my Uncle Simon and Aunt Mavis, and I'm doing what I can to keep her employed now that they're gone. She's such a sweetheart, and while she may not win any Oscars, she's up for anything. As you may have noticed, she's one hell of a good cook, too. But we're getting off track. At some point you thought the hooded figure must be Rob, but not now?"

"No," I said, finishing my drink and setting the glass aside.

"And why not?"

"He wasn't big enough," I said, shrugging as Paula unobtrusively swapped my empty glass for a fresh one. "This hooded guy was a beast. I'm not exactly small myself, but I felt lost in his shadow. It seems so obvious now." I chuckled.

Anyssa looked surprised. "It does?"

I sipped my drink and nodded. "It was your skipper, Jeremy."

She smiled crookedly. "And why would you think that?"

"When he boosted me onto the boat back at the island, he practically lifted me off the ground with just one arm. Dude's a behemoth. I noticed he was keeping his left arm tucked inside his rain slicker. I hope I didn't hurt him too badly."

She grimaced. "Hairline fracture of the ulna," she said. "I guess you nailed him pretty good with the door to the boathouse, but he caught the worst of it when you knocked him into the boat. He hit his arm on something trying to protect his face as he lost his balance."

"He scared the shit out of me."

"He was supposed to."

"I guess I owe him an apology."

She shrugged. "If it will make you feel better. I've already apologized, and truthfully, it's a bit of an occupational hazard. I mean, who can foresee every little thing that might happen when you've whipped someone into a panic?"

"I wouldn't say I was *panicked*—" I was finding it very difficult to take my foot off the gas when it came to defending myself.

"Whatever you say, Dwayne," said Anyssa, her eyes still twinkling mischievously. "But you didn't figure any of this out until after Kit had collected you, so your teammates still have no idea about the identity of our ghost figure?"

"That's right. Am I allowed to ask a question?"

"Sure," she said, pushing her salad aside. "Whether I can answer it or not is a different matter."

"Is Sandy Poole—you know, alive? 'Cause she looked mighty dead the last time I saw her."

"I can confirm that Mrs. Poole is alive and well," she said. "As a matter of fact, I wouldn't be surprised if you ran into her back at the resort. I believe she's your next-door neighbor."

It was nearly a draw whether I was more relieved that Sandy was alive or mortified by my gullibility. "Wow," I finally said. "I'm certainly glad to hear that. That was some makeup job you did on her. I could've sworn she was dead."

"So, I've heard. But that was no makeup," said Anyssa, finishing her wine and setting her empty glass beside her salad plate. "It must have been the lighting, or lack thereof in the boathouse. You scared her as badly as she scared you. She was waiting for Jeremy to transport her away from the island when she saw you approaching. She hid underneath a tarp in the back and held her breath, hoping you wouldn't notice."

"Why didn't he just take her on the boat he had docked at the back of the island?" I asked.

"The three of you were so close when he presented Mrs. Poole with her tarot card. He couldn't risk alerting the three of you by starting its motor. He had her leave a shoe behind along a different path and took her through the tunnels leading back towards the house. There's an offshoot that goes right down to the boathouse."

I nodded, feeling like I was getting a tiny peek behind the Wizard's curtain. "How does she feel about her current status? You know, as a fatality of the game?"

"Oh, she's having a ball!" Anyssa said. "She's been exploring the island and hanging out by the pool. I get the feeling Leroy doesn't take her out very often."

I nodded. "I get the feeling you're right."

She steepled her forefingers beneath her nose. "Share with me your strategy for today," she said.

I brought her current starting with breakfast before taking her through our day of exploration and finishing with my poorly planned solo trip to the basement to retrieve my cell phone. "I'm guessing I would still be there had we gone downstairs as a group," I said.

"That is correct," she confirmed, nodding her head. She reviewed the notes she had made on her iPad. "I guess that's all I need for now."

"Can you tell me about the sounds we heard that seemed to be coming from inside the walls?" I asked.

Anyssa slid her iPad into her messenger bag and signaled Paula for the check. "I'm not at liberty to discuss that at the present time."

I sat up straighter in my chair. "But there *is* something to discuss, isn't there?"

She tilted her head to the side, her face devoid of expression.

"And what about those notes from the rolltop desk?" I asked. "Melanie and Loretta both thought they seemed particularly threatening."

Something flickered in her eyes as she reached for her messenger bag, absently rummaging through it. After a moment, she sighed and set the bag aside.

"Clues," she said. "Hopefully, they will help point your team in the right direction. They're running out of time to find the gold."

"So, there *is* gold to find?" I asked.

She nodded. "Yes."

"But it's not real gold, right?"

"If I had a stash of real gold, I would hardly need to put myself through all of this, would I?" She slid her credit card forward as Paula brought the check. "Be patient, Dwayne. By this time tomorrow, you'll have answers to all of your questions. We just need to let the game play out for now. I need to visit the ladies' room before we go. I'll send for a car to take us back to the resort, all right?"

"Sure," I said, finishing my drink and nudging my glass away. I was a little warmer around the edges than I had intended, but again, what was the harm? My evening was free. I watched Anyssa weave her way through the crowd toward the facilities.

I realized the sun had completely set in the time it took us to finish our dinner, and I caught the vague flicker of lightning far in the distance. I wondered what progress Melanie and Brady may have made in my absence and whether Loretta had been successful in discovering anything useful online. I wondered if Doug was still sawing logs, dreaming he was in an adventure worthy of Indiana Jones. I sincerely hoped that Leroy was still out of commission.

It didn't seem possible, but the cozy restaurant seemed even more packed than it was when we had first arrived. People stood in clusters near the bar, chatting animatedly with sporadic laughter making it impossible to tell what was playing on the sound system. As I waited for Anyssa to return, I absently scanned the room, deciding this would be a nice place to bring Melanie under different circumstances. As I narrowed the focus of my people-watching to the folks at the bar, I did a double-take as my brain suddenly recognized a familiar face among them.

It was Captain Jack, the cantankerous old coot who had brought us to the island on a trash-covered pontoon. I had nearly forgotten about him, and for the briefest of seconds, our eyes locked.

CHAPTER TWENTY-TWO

A shadow fell over me, and my line of sight was abruptly interrupted. I leaned sideways, trying not to lose sight of the man. Frustrated, I looked up to see who was blocking my view and found Anyssa watching me intently.

She took her seat as Paula returned with a black plastic check tray containing the receipt, her credit card and a pen. "No rush," she said, smiling as she set the tray by my hand. Anyssa looked vaguely annoyed as she placed a perfectly manicured forefinger on the tray and slid it towards herself, causing Paula's smile to falter slightly. "Thank you, ma'am. I hope you enjoy your evening. Please come back and see us again."

I craned to look past Paula as she retreated toward the kitchen, but Captain Jack was gone. I sat back in my chair and sighed.

"You look like you've seen a ghost," Anyssa said with a wry grin, adding a generous tip to the receipt despite her earlier annoyance before signing with a flourish.

"No ghost—at least not this time," I said. "I just saw that other guy you have working transportation to and from the island."

Her expression was blank. "I don't have anyone else working transportation, just Jeremy. Oh, that's right! During orientation, you mentioned something about a man who, frankly, sounded like a pirate and his—pontoon, did you say? I thought you were kidding, although I have to admit, I didn't really get the joke."

"It was no joke," I said, standing and scanning the patrons, as well as the pedestrians strolling along the street outside the window, but it was like he had vanished into thin air.

Anyssa was confused. "So, your team *wasn't* on the boat Friday night with Jeremy, Rob and Kit? Jeremy called to tell me you hadn't arrived at the expected time and wondered how long he should wait. He had other responsibilities that evening, too, so I told him to wait as long as he could. Later, when I saw your team on the surveillance cameras, I just assumed you had shown up before Jeremy departed."

"No," I said. "We thought Rob and Kit came over with you on Saturday morning."

"Huh-unh. I needed them here to begin some preliminary setup. So, there really *was* another boat?"

I studied her expression carefully, but she seemed completely sincere and more than a little baffled. "Yes, there sure was."

"I honestly don't know what to tell you," she said, looking around the room. "I don't know anyone who even remotely fits the description, and certainly no one who is working for me. I guess I have some digging of my own to do, too. The car should be here, if you're ready."

We stood, and I followed her to the door, pausing once we stepped out onto the sidewalk. A different Uber driver waited at the curb in a maroon Nissan sedan. "You know, I think I'm going to walk back, if that's all right with you," I said. "It's not very far."

"Are you sure?" she asked, acknowledging the driver with a forefinger and a smile.

"Yeah," I said, nodding. "I've never been here before, and I wouldn't mind taking a look around."

She looked up at the starless sky. "You're liable to get rained on," she warned. "There's a storm moving in."

I shrugged and walked her to the car. "It's only water. I'll be fine. Thank you so much for dinner. It was delicious."

"You're very welcome," she said. "We'll be bringing the others back tomorrow afternoon around two. I'll send a car to the resort for you and Mrs. Poole around one-thirty to take you to the marina. We'll swing by to pick you up before heading back to the mainland, and then we can have a postmortem of sorts on the ride back to answer any questions and tie up any loose ends. Sound good?"

"Works for me," I said, trying to mask my impatience. I held the door for her as she lowered herself into the rear seat, and I waggled my fingers as the Uber driver eased away from the curb.

I scanned the street earnestly as another flicker of lightning skipped silently across the western sky only to be followed seconds later by a low, ominous rumble. It was my intention to find Captain Jack and figure out exactly what in the hell he was up to.

*****

I spent the next hour or so scouring the blocks around the restaurant, looking for any sign of the crusty old man but coming up empty. I passed darkened windows of gift shops that had already closed for the evening, and I had to remind myself it was Sunday. Everyone's hours were likely to be shorter. I wandered through the Casino Bar and Restaurant and by the time I crossed over to Dockers Waterfront Bar, my feet were beginning to complain. It felt like those damn toe thongs were sawing through the flesh of my toes. Discouraged, I stepped up to the bar and ordered another whiskey sour.

"Woo-hoo! Oh, *woo-hoo!*"

The high-pitched call wafted in from the dockside seating area, accompanied by a familiar metallic jangling. I turned to find Sandy Poole waving at me from one of the tables, her collection of bracelets dancing on her arm. She held up what appeared to be a high-capacity margarita glass, its contents diminished by half, and judging from the flush in her cheeks, it wasn't anywhere near her first. She gestured for me to join her, and I figured what the hell? I was ready to call it quits for the night anyway. I paid for my drink, adding a generous tip, and thanked the bartender before carrying my glass outside.

Sandy clumsily tried to stand, and I motioned for her to remain seated. The last thing I needed was for her to stumble over the edge and into the lake. Personally, I had already spent more time than I liked bobbing around in the lake's churning water.

"It's Mr. Morrow, isn't it?" she said, offering me her hand.

"Dwayne," I said, smiling and taking her hand delicately. "And you're Sandy, right?"

She nodded, positively aglow, and fruity fermentation adhered to her like perfume. I worried for her physical safety if she wandered too close to a tiki torch. "I guess we're the big, ole losers, huh?"

"Guess so," I said, sitting across from her. "Were you as disappointed as I was?"

"Oh, heaven's no," she said, sipping her drink. "I'm having the best time."

"Really?"

"Abso-fucking-lutely!" she exclaimed, holding her glass in the air, whooping her way into a heartfelt giggle that was weirdly contagious. My grin broadened as I raised my glass, and we clinked them together. "I haven't been *anywhere* in the longest fucking time. Who in the hell knew we had someplace like this right here in Ohio? I mean, *seriously*, right? Don't get me wrong, the mystery weekend sounded amazing, too, but Leroy was bound and determined to spoil it all, and you can bet your ass that he would have, wouldn't he? Fucking asshole."

She dipped into a giant beach bag resting against her chair and retrieved a cigarette case, pulling out a smoke and lighting it. She offered me one, and I'd really like to tell you I politely refused being the righteously reformed smoker I claim to be, but I was on my third whiskey sour—or was it my fourth?—and my hand was on autopilot, helping itself to one of her smokes. Whatever the brand, it was mentholated, and I didn't give a shit. I lit the tip and took a deep drag. Despite the fact it felt like I was inhaling warm Vick's VapoRub, it was ridiculously satisfying.

"So, tell me," she said, blowing out a plume of smoke and suddenly serious. "Exactly how much of an asshole *has* he been?"

Well, shit. I didn't want to get into *this*. I had no intention of discussing Leroy's excursion with Dusty, much less the humiliation of being nearly knocked out by the guy. What was left?

"He found the liquor in the pantry," I said, feeling like a tattletale, and she threw her hands into the air.

"*Of course!*" she barked, and what few patrons remained snapped to attention. "I swear, that man has a sixth sense if there's liquor nearby. I hope he kept his pants on."

Lightning rippled over Sandy's shoulder, and I had a sudden flash of Leroy sprawled out in the formal living room, Little Leroy on full display, and a tiny part of me died. This was not a line of inquiry I wanted to pursue.

"I have to tell you that you scared the shit out of me," I said, raising my glass and nodding appreciatively.

"Yeah? How so?" she asked, sloshing a bit of her drink onto the table as she clinked hers with mine, once again.

"You looked dead!"

She squealed and covered her face. "I scared *you?* You scared *me!* Here I was, waiting for Jeremy to take me away when you suddenly appeared outside the window. I about wet my pants!"

She doubled over, her bawdy laughter once again attracting attention from our fellow patrons, and at this point, I didn't really care. I liked this woman. I admit, it might have been as much because I disliked her husband so very intently, but other than being a wee bit over the top in both volume and presentation, what harm was she causing anyone?

"And criminy, did you ever do a number on poor Jeremy," she continued after she caught her breath.

I winced. "I feel bad about that."

"Me, too, the poor thing. He cursed you up one side and down the other, and don't you dare tell him I said this, but it was almost worth it because I got to steer the boat!" she clapped gleefully, her bracelets jangling like a noisy windchime. As abruptly as before, her earnestness returned, and she grabbed one of my hands in both of hers. "Please tell me you worked things out with that pretty little blond girl."

I took another hit from the cigarette and smiled. "Melanie? Yeah, we're fine. How did you know—?"

"I'd like to say a woman can tell," she said, patting my hand before releasing it. "But it didn't take a crystal ball to know what was on *that* girl's mind. She was madder than a wet hen and needed an ear to chew. She was pumping your reporter buddy hard for information, thinking he might be able to provide some magical insight into the inner workings of the male brain and why you all are so goddamned insecure and pigheaded, but that's a lot like asking one idiot to explain another."

"Wow," I said with a surprised laugh. "Let's not hold back or anything, Sandy."

"Sorry," she said sheepishly, sipping her margarita and signaling for another. "Swear to God, I didn't mean that personally, but I've never really been known for having any filters, so there you go. It's just men, in general. Y'all don't know when you've got something good until you've gone and ruined it. You should appreciate your lady for exactly who she is, because that's exactly why it was good in the first place. Do you hear me?"

"Loud and clear," I said, nodding slowly and realizing sound advice sometimes comes from the most unlikely of sources. "I guess I'll probably always be a work-in-progress."

Sandy harrumphed. "We all are, and that's just fine. You've just gotta keep those lines of communication open, 'cause there's nothing worse than feeling like you're never heard."

"Why do I feel like we're talking about you and Leroy, now?"

Her face clouded over. "I know you'll never see it, but Leroy was all right in the beginning. He used to do all the right things and say all the right things. He understood that flowers should be sent to me at work because it made all those other girls jealous. He took me to fancy restaurants almost every week, and he kept his hands off my daughter, something my second husband never seemed to be able to do. I mean, *okay*, Amber performs in a gentlemen's club. It's not like she's selling herself on the street. She's doing what she has to do to survive and keep food in her babies' mouths. And Leroy never had a thing to say about it until after I let him move in. That's when the dinners and the flowers stopped, but his opinions got louder, and his belly just keeps right on getting bigger."

She was getting misty-eyed and melancholy, and I wished I hadn't ventured down this path.

"He's my third husband," she said matter-of-factly. "I just seem to keep skimming the turds out of the bowl. Maybe I'll do better with number four." She clumsily batted her eyelashes at me. "Are you *sure* you and that pretty little girl are gonna be okay?"

"Yes, absolutely!" I quickly said. I felt heat rising into my cheeks as my eyes avoided hers. She was at least twenty years my senior, and I feared she was mistaking my friendliness for something entirely different. I nearly jumped out of my skin as her foot found my ankle, and she burst out laughing, once again drawing attention to us.

"That's awesome, and I'm very happy for you both. I really mean that. Your babies will be beautiful, just you wait and see," she said, her s's a little low on air. She pulled back into her own space, and I felt a wave of relief wash over me. The wind gusted suddenly, threatening to topple her margarita, but her reflexes weren't *that* far off; she plucked it up by its stem and finished it in one long swallow. Lightning flared again, and the rumble of thunder chasing it was closer.

"Looks like a storm's brewing," I commented as more of the bar's clientele drifted toward the exit. "We should probably get back to the hotel. Would you like for me to send for an Uber?"

She shook her head. "Nah. I've got my tablet here. I can send for one when I'm ready." She reached into her beach bag and extracted a Galaxy tablet. "I think I'm gonna sit here for just a bit longer unless they decide to kick me out. You know, these islands are really interesting. I can't believe I've lived my whole life right here in Ohio and didn't know a thing about them. It's almost like having our own little piece of the ocean in our backyard."

"I guess it is," I agreed.

"I'd love to come back when I've got more time to explore. I had some friends once who vacationed in Put-in-Bay over on South Bass Island, and they just had a ball. Maybe I can get my fourth husband to take me on our honeymoon there, huh?"

"Maybe," I said, looking for an opportunity to escape without being rude. It was far easier said than done as Sandy never seemed to run out of words.

"And there's all these interesting facts, too!" she marveled. "I spent the better part of my afternoon going down a rabbit hole on Google. For instance, did you know that the number of islands in the lake depends on how deep the water is, and that changes throughout the year? Sounds nuts, but I guess it's true. And Lake Erie doesn't just touch Ohio. It also touches Pennsylvania, New York and our mortal enemy, Michigan. Go Bucks!"

I jumped as she shouted that last bit, but it was reliably answered with a return cry from what stragglers remained outdoors. If there had been more of an audience, we would have undoubtedly degenerated into a chorus of "O-H!" followed by cries of "I-O!" Beats the hell out of me, but it's an Ohio thing, and if you know, I shouldn't have to explain anything to you.

"Don't forget Canada," I added, and everyone stared at me like I was an idiot.

Sandy picked up where she had left off. "I had the TV on when I was getting ready this morning, and I came across this program on the Travel Channel all about haunted Ohio, and after all that talk about the ghost of Julian Williams on the island, it just drew me right in! One section was about Great Lakes hauntings, and part of me would just love to come back and explore some of those sites. But I ain't gonna lie, part of me is scared to death to bear witness. If I saw a real, live ghost, I'd pass right out."

I don't think she understood the incongruity of her statement.

"This one really stuck with me," she said, shivering slightly while pulling up an article she had bookmarked on her tablet. "There was this orphanage up in Vermilion, which I guess is right down the road a ways from where we caught the ferry to Marble Toe. It was founded by this nutty religious guy named Johann Springer—no—Sprunger. Him and his wife, Katharina ran the place, although there was lots of folks who claimed she wasn't just his wife but his sister, too. Her father also had the last name of Sprunger, and that's just a little too all in the family, if you're picking up what I'm putting down. They both came from Indiana where they ran another orphanage called Light of Hope, and Johann had a couple of unrelated businesses on the side. They did have one thing in common, though."

"Yeah? What's that?" I asked, stubbing out my cigarette.

"They all burned to the ground. Seemed like fire followed those folks wherever they went, and so did death."

I had to admit I was a little intrigued. "How so?"

"Three innocent little girls lost their lives in the fire at that orphanage," she said, her finger trailing down her screen. "And before the Sprungers even moved to Ohio, they lost their own little girl and a baby boy who either died at birth or was stillborn—I'm not really sure which. After that, they got obsessed with religion and decided to leave Indiana to pursue the Lord's work by helping orphaned children, or at least that's how they

ISOLATION

thought of it. They caught wind of an abandoned property near Vermilion that was over 500 acres and already had a number of farm buildings standing. There was also a rundown mansion that could be used as housing for the workers the Sprungers would hire to help run the new Light of Hope orphanage they had built on the grounds. They only hired folks who shared their same extreme beliefs."

"You keep saying things like 'nutty' and 'extreme' when you talk about them. Exactly how off the wall were they?" I asked.

Her eyes floated up from her tablet to fix on my face from beneath penciled-in eyebrows. "Well, for one, they dug up their dead daughter and took her with them to the new property to rebury her there. Is that extreme enough for you?"

I blinked. "Guess so. The place almost sounds like a commune."

Sandy nodded, skimming her tablet. "It sort of does. But they couldn't have found a place with a more tragic history itself. The original owner, this guy named Swift, lost two of his own children on the property, ten years apart. And then he went broke over a bunch of bad investments he made in the railroads. When he couldn't afford the upkeep any longer, he sold it to some famous psychic guy, last name Wilber, and there's rumors of seances and rituals that were held on the property all the freaking time. *Supposably*, Wilber's children were able to talk to the ghosts of the dead children who appeared during these events. But then, Wilber lost four of his own grandchildren to diphtheria, and while official records claim this happened *after* they moved away from the property, residents claimed that was all horseshit. They believed those grandkids not only died on the property but are still buried there *to this day!*" Her jaw was set as she nodded knowingly, staring a little too long for my comfort.

"That's some story," I said, looking up to the sky and hoping for a little rain or anything else to give me an excuse to break away. It was abundantly clear that extricating myself from Sandy wasn't going to be easy.

"As Christly and noble as the Sprungers plan may have sounded, the reality was more like a nightmare. They housed over a hundred orphans there and treated them like animals. They were barely fed and barely washed, and their rooms were overrun with rats. Sprunger allowed neighbor farmers to rent the children, more or less as slave labor, and these poor children were subjected to horrible beatings. The orphanage's reputation got so bad that the State of Ohio eventually investigated, but there weren't laws on the books to cover these types of institutions. Worst yet, old man Sprunger freely confessed to nearly everything he was accused of and was *still* allowed to continue to run the place until he died a couple of years later. I mean, *seriously?!?* By then, the orphanage was completely broke, and Katharina had to sell the place. What children were left were sent to other orphanages or placed with family, if any other family could be found. A few of these children went back to Indiana with Katharina—along with the dead daughter she once again had plucked out of the ground to be reburied once she settled." Again, she shuddered visibly. "I could barely sleep last night thinking about it."

"Funny you say that, but I was having a little trouble getting to sleep myself last night, and I stumbled onto an article from the 90s that was actually about Marble Toe Island and the legend of the Williams ghost," I said. "A couple of college kids in love, spending the better part of their summer looking for some kind of proof that ghosts are real and finally finding what they were looking for on Marble Toe Island."

"I'm pretty sure I read about them, too," she said. "Wasn't that just awful?"

I reflected upon what I had read, and with the possible exception of the young couple losing their boat in the storm, I wouldn't have classified any of what I had read as awful. "Why do you say that?" I asked.

Sandy lifted her tablet closer to her face and began pecking at the screen. "It became a real obsession for those two, didn't it? And my goodness, that poor woman! Olivia, wasn't it?" She continued to search for the articles on her tablet.

"Alethea," I corrected, the unusual name sticking with me for some reason.

"That's right! Here we go," she said, poking at her tablet some more. "These folks just wouldn't leave the Williamses alone, would they? And after how nice Ms. Williams's aunt and uncle treated them that first time they turned up uninvited, and in the middle of a storm, no less."

I was more than a little confused. "Either we're not talking about the same people, or I must have missed that part. The article I read was a short essay on ghost hunting in Ohio that ended with this R.J. guy and his girlfriend finally seeing a ghost on Marble Toe Island."

"That's right," nodded Sandy. "He published that article without asking permission from the Williamses, and all it did was bring a bunch of unwanted attention to the legend of the Williams' gold, as well as its ghostly guardian. Damn near every weekend brought trespassers of some sort, all of them thinking they would either find a ghost or go home with a fortune. Some of those folks were downright threatening. But none were as persistent as those original two. The Williamses eventually took out a restraining order barring them from the island, but that didn't even slow them down. If it hadn't been for the accident, they would probably still be hassling Ms. Williams to this day."

"What accident?" I asked as lightning was reflected on the lake's surface, and thunder, more ominous than before, rumbled across the starless night sky.

"That last time R.J. and Alethea went, it was raining every bit as hard as it was the first time. The lake was choppy, and before they reached the island, Alethea went overboard. Her body wasn't recovered for weeks."

"Oh, my God!"

"By then, they were married with a little boy of their own, and now this poor little guy was going to grow up without his mother. It was all too much for R.J., and I guess he just snapped," she said. "Swore there was a curse on the island and that it was all because of the gold that should have never been there in the first place. He vowed to drive the Williamses away in order to break the curse and free the spirit of the ghost that he believed was trapped there. He was a raving lunatic by then. He was eventually committed by the State as a danger to himself and to others. Here's a picture of him being taken into custody."

She swiveled the tablet in my direction, and I quickly read the first paragraph of the news article.

NELSONVILLE MAN VIOLATES RESTRAINING ORDER AGAIN

MARBLE TOE ISLAND—Police were dispatched to the private residence of Simon and Mavis Williams to arrest Richard Jackson McBurney for once again violating a long-standing restraining order the couple was forced to seek out after McBurney made a regular habit of trespassing on their property. He was placed under psychiatric observation following his claims of ghostly activity on the island as well as expressing his beliefs that the island must be destroyed in order to free the spirits trapped there, including the spirit of his recently deceased wife, Alethea. Mrs. McBurney drowned in the lake on the couple's previous attempt to breach the island's perimeter.

The article was over twenty years old, and my eyes shifted to the black-and-white picture under the headline. Four officers struggled to restrain the man who was being led away, his eyes bulging in their sockets and spittle frozen in flight as he was photographed mid-arrest. My breath caught in my throat as recognition dawned.

Richard Jackson McBurney was none other than our mysterious Captain Jack.

CHAPTER TWENTY-THREE

A fat droplet of rain landed on the screen, distorting McBurney's anguished features.

"You've never seen this man before? I mean, like—in person?" I asked, a little more urgently than intended.

"Well, no. Should I have?" Sandy used her napkin to wipe the moisture from the screen before tucking her tablet back into the safety of her beach bag. "Frankly, I think I'd be a little scared if I did. Lord only knows what he'd be up to this time."

Her observation sent my imagination into overdrive, flashing through a series of frightening possibilities.

She looked up as another volley of lightning forked across the sky. "I guess that's God's way of calling it a night," she said, pushing away from the table. The last few stragglers who had remained by the lakeside were already heading for cover indoors. "I'm goin' in and send for an Uber. You're welcome to ride back with me if you want."

My mind continued to race, the wild-eyed image of McBurney burned into my mind. I nodded absently as a few more heavy drops of rain struck the top of my head. "No, you go on."

"Are you sure? You're gonna get soaked out here."

"A little water never hurt anyone," I said distractedly, getting out of my chair. I was already scanning faces, hoping for a little dumb luck—okay, a whole *lot* of dumb luck. I had seen McBurney no more than half an hour ago. Where could he be?

"Well, all right, then," said Sandy. "I sure did enjoy talking with you tonight, and I'm sorry for anything Leroy might have put you folks through. I don't know why I ever thought he'd enjoy this. Best part of my whole damned weekend was getting killed, and I kid you not."

Dammit, it was hard to remain courteous when I wanted nothing more than to get the hell out of there, but Jo Morrow had raised her boys right. I smiled and took Sandy's hand, tipping my head slightly. "The pleasure was all mine, I promise you. We'll talk again, tomorrow, all right?"

Her cheeks dimpled as she smiled and waved at me before turning to dart inside the bar, where she immediately set about summoning transportation on her tablet. I passed through the dimly lit interior, probing every corner as I proceeded through the front entrance and out onto the sidewalk.

The raindrops were more frequent now, and one landed on the back of my neck before slipping beneath my collar and running down my back. I hung back as a minor exodus of patrons followed me outside, merging into the light pedestrian traffic traveling in both directions. Some hopped into golf carts or waiting Ubers, while others chose bicycles that were secured to racks near the various business entrances. A handful opted to dart away on foot. I tried to catch every face as it passed, hoping against hope I would once again spot McBurney, but the streets were draining like a leaky bathtub and with surprising speed, and the craggy old man was simply nowhere to be found.

I turned and nearly walked right into one of Kelleys Island's finest. He was broad-shouldered, square-jawed and chiseled in a way that scoffed at my ridiculous, three-mile-a-day jogging routine that, admittedly, hadn't been routine for well over a month. His face was at least sixty percent scowl as he placed a hand on my shoulder.

"Now, whoa, there big fella," he said. "Are we lost?"

There wasn't even a hint of a smile on his face, but I tried to find one of my own that would hide the escalating panic I was beginning to feel. "No, sir. I was just getting ready to head back to the resort."

Impossibly, his scowl deepened. "Had a little bit to drink, have we?"

His line of questioning caught me off guard. It wasn't like I was staggering around on the sidewalk or out into the street, and what was with all this royal 'we' shit?

"Well, yeah," I said. "I had a couple of drinks in the Casino. Just like all these other folks—" I swept my hand around to implicate my fellow patrons only to discover they had mostly dispersed. My hand fell to my side. "I'm not breaking any laws, am I?"

He studied me long enough to make me wonder. "No, sir. But there's a bad storm headed this way, and I would strongly advise you to get to wherever you are staying just as soon as possible."

"I will," I said with a tight smile. "Thank you, officer."

He turned and crossed the empty street, climbing into a patrol SUV I hadn't noticed was parked along the opposite curb. He started it with unnecessary aggression, making the engine roar repeatedly. Its bright headlights sprang to life, but he just sat there, continuing to monitor me, his expression unreadable. I turned and began walking slowly west, headed in the direction of the resort, but stubbornly refusing to hurry. I didn't much like being told to clear out; this was a public place, it was still America, and I wasn't committing any crimes.

As I passed the nearly empty Casino Bar and Restaurant, Portside Marina was visible on my left, and I could see the lake was growing more agitated as boats bobbed and shifted in their slips. I didn't realize how tightly I was wound until the police officer slowly cruised past on my right and relief washed over me. I wasn't quite ready to go back to the resort just yet. Something felt off, but I couldn't put my finger on it.

I feared I was becoming an alarmist, and I wondered exactly when *that* had happened. Since we had arrived on the island, I was the first to feel threatened, the first to believe someone had *actually* been killed—even in my own head, I seemed uncharacteristically prone to panic. I couldn't afford another public misstep. I'd never hear the end of it. Maybe I had been too ambitious throwing myself into this excursion so quickly after all that had happened in West Virginia. I pictured my sister's face and my parents' anguish, and I started to get angry all over again. I looked up at a night sky that was now drizzling and pushed those thoughts away. I didn't have time to wade through all of this again right now.

I looked back toward the marina and was surprised to see our spiffy white speedboat off in the distance, still occupying the slip where Jeremy had parked it. I figured he and Kit would have headed back to the island long ago. Two figures stood on the boat's deck, engaged in spirited conversation. I decided to wander down and ask if either of them had seen the elusive Mr. McBurney or his unmistakable pontoon when I heard footsteps rapidly approaching from behind across the wet pavement.

"Mr. Morrow?"

I was as startled by the familiar voice as it sounded like it was to see me. I turned to find Kit, her head cocked curiously to the side underneath the cover of a bright red umbrella.

"What are you doing out here?" she asked. "You're getting soaked. Is everything all right?"

I did a quick double take. If Kit was here, then who was on the boat? "I'm fine," I said guardedly. "I was just taking in what I could of the island after I had dinner with Ms. Williams, but I guess I misjudged the timing as far as the weather goes. Is that Rob out there on the boat with Jeremy?" I pointed as the drizzle intensified into steady rain, making it difficult to see anything clearly at such a distance.

"No," Kit answered, following my gaze and squinting. "Rob hasn't left the island since we first arrived. It's up to him to keep the game moving along. It's probably one of the other boaters who's anchored nearby. Jeremy's friendly with just about everybody he meets, especially the ones who have boats docked here. It's not a bad network of friends to have if you run into trouble out on the lake. Listen, I've really gotta get down there. We're late getting back, and if we don't hurry, we're not going to beat the worst of this storm. You should get yourself back to the hotel. This is mild compared to what's in the forecast."

I didn't even have a chance to ask about McBurney or the pontoon as she hurried past me and down the path leading to a network of walkways servicing the slips. Whoever had been engaged in conversation with Jeremy had disappeared while my attention was on Kit, and I watched as she handed Jeremy her umbrella before allowing him to effortlessly hoist her up onto the boat with his good arm. I lingered long enough to watch him untether the boat and ease his way back onto the lake, accelerating once he had cleared the marina. Beacons mounted across the stern rhythmically winked, fading into a darkening curtain of rainfall.

A staccato ripple of lightning illuminated the marina in rapid-fire succession. I was reminded of an angry schoolteacher, angrily flicking overhead lights on and off to quiet rowdy students whose only response was more rumbling thunder, resonating through the ground beneath my drenched feet. I wiped rain from my eyes, ready to begin the long journey back to the resort when I caught a hint of motion out of the corner of my eye. Someone was approaching quickly from the far end of the sidewalk, head lowered, and hands buried in the pockets of a dark, water-resistant parka I desperately wished was my own. I eased into the shadows of the Casino Bar and Restaurant, keeping my head down but eyes fixed on the figure as it moved purposefully closer and closer still. It crossed within feet of me without ever looking up, and I was surprised to find I was holding my breath. I caught a hint of disgruntled mutterings from a one-sided conversation, and based on the vocal inflection and gait, I was pretty sure this was a man. I watched as he crossed Lakeshore Drive and climbed into a golf cart parked across the street and facing west. He performed an awkward U-turn near the intersection of Division Street and Lakeshore and continued east, but not before another round of lightning briefly illuminated the area.

I was almost certain it was McBurney, and he was getting away.

I needed transportation, and I needed it quickly. Golf carts weren't exactly race cars, but I could never keep up with him on foot. Just down the street from where I stood, I saw a prominent sign advertising Kelley Island's very best rate for golf cart and bicycle rentals, but the business was obviously closed, its windows dark. The taillights of the golf cart were dwindling quickly when I spotted an old ten-speed bicycle leaning against the wall along the side of the Casino Bar. I took a quick glance around, and with nobody nearby to witness, I pulled the bike toward me and hiked my leg over its crossbar, settling onto the narrow seat. Technically, it was stealing, but I had every intention of returning it—eventually. I hoped its owner would understand the urgency and be forgiving.

After a bit of a wobbly start, my balance kicked in, and I pumped my legs just as hard as I could, rapidly picking up speed as I set out in pursuit of the golf cart whose taillights had only just disappeared.

*****

As if those damned sandals weren't already incredibly uncomfortable dry, you can imagine how awful they felt fully waterlogged, my toes struggling to keep them on my feet as I pedaled as hard as I could through the driving rain. My shirt was plastered to my back, and I had lost sight of my quarry. More accurately, I had never regained sight of my quarry after its taillights had disappeared into the night. Although I wasn't exactly sure what the top speed of a golf cart was, I knew it was considerably slower than an automobile, so I was a little surprised when after almost ten minutes of steadily slogging along, I seemed to be the only one on the road, and I was beginning to feel conspicuous. I had left the business district behind some time ago, and darkened neighborhoods stretched off to my left while a narrow ribbon of sand abutted the increasingly turbulent surface of the lake to my right. I fully expected Kelleys Island's finest to pull up behind me at any moment, investigating a report about a stolen bicycle. I paid closer attention to my surroundings and was just about to turn around, sure I'd missed him when I spotted a cart-like silhouette in another burst of lightning, pulled into a thicket of bushes just off the road to my right. The cart was clearly empty, and I tucked in behind it, dismounting the bike before leaning it into the bushes where it wouldn't be easily spotted from the road. A narrow trail cut back through the brush, and I followed it cautiously, keeping an eye out for McBurney. I paused as I reached the narrow strip of sand, a feeling of victory washing over me.

Directly ahead and tossing about in the tumultuous tide was the pontoon, moored to what appeared to be an abandoned dock based on its state of disrepair. I didn't see McBurney anywhere on its deck, but he had to be nearby. I recognized that once I left the cover provided by dense foliage, I would be completely vulnerable, visible to anyone even remotely paying attention, and I took a moment to ask myself if it even mattered. I had no idea what this man was up to, or whether he was up to anything at all, but his presence alone raised questions, and I wouldn't be able to rest until I had some answers. It had been over twenty years since McBurney was arrested for repeatedly violating a restraining order for trespassing on the Williamses' property and was subsequently placed under psychiatric care. I couldn't imagine an innocent reason for his return to a place so synonymous with tragedy. Would the restraining order even still be in effect after all this time? And what possible reason could there have been for him to transport us to the island when we arrived?

I strode purposefully across the sand, approaching the pontoon as a low rumble of thunder vibrated through my bones. I took a tentative step out onto the low dock, realizing how significant the level of its disrepair was. Entire planks were missing and what I stepped on felt spongy. The pontoon was tied to a couple of mooring buoys anchored in the rotting wood of the dock, rollicking up and down with the agitated tide. I could feel each time the boat struck the eroding bumpers along the edge of the dock and stepped back onto the decidedly more stable hard-packed sand behind me.

I shielded my eyes against the rain and studied the boat's deck. McBurney's collection of empty beer cans had grown since he had deposited us onto the island, and they clattered around noisily as the boat churned with the water. The long tarp covering the rear portion of the pontoon's deck remained in place, although the height of it had diminished considerably. I was summoning the courage to go back out onto the dock and board the ship when a brilliant burst of lightning momentarily turned night into day, and I sensed rather than heard something behind me. I turned and barely had time to register the determined scowl McBurney wore as he lashed out, catching me full in the face with something blunt.

My head snapped back, and I was falling.

Dammit, why was *I* the one who was always getting knocked out?

*****

I woke up choking as water sloshed over the edge of the boat and into my face. My head was splitting as I struggled to orient myself, my dinner attempting to reemerge with nauseous vengeance. I tried to sit up and quickly discovered my arms had been bound at the wrists, my legs by the ankles, and the boat was no longer moored to the dock, its motion complicating any maneuver I attempted to right myself. I could hear McBurney cursing and muttering to himself from the helm, and realized I was in the stern, beside the area covered by plastic tarp. It took several attempts, but eventually, I managed to shift into an upright position, completely winded with my back resting against the gunwale. McBurney's back was to me, fully focused on keeping the boat on course, and I had no doubt whatsoever where we were heading. Another flash of lightning illuminated the long barrel of a rifle he carried in a sling over his shoulder.

Darin Miller

I was pretty sure my face was already well acquainted with its stock, and I ran my tongue over my teeth to make sure they were all still accounted for. Thankfully, they were. I had no interest in becoming acquainted with its business end, so I kept still, concentrating on keeping my dinner down as the boat skipped and lurched across the treacherous water.

I had no sense of direction, and the flickering lightning only caused my head to spin, so I closed my eyes and rested my head against the rail, testing the strength of the ropes that bound me. They weren't cutting off my circulation, but there was very little give, either. They were the same sort of heavy rope McBurney had used to tether his boat to the dock, and it was highly unlikely I would be breaking through them anytime soon.

Panic was beginning to nibble around my edges.

I took a deep breath and opened my eyes, keeping my focus strictly inside the boat, as water splashed up and over the side, empty beer cans drifting from one end of the boat to the other and back again. I spotted the handle of something, possibly some sort of tool, sticking out from underneath the tarp at my feet, and I stretched my legs out in an attempt to trap it between my heels and pull it towards me. After four or five awkward tries, I finally succeeded in bringing it out into the open only to discover it was a hammer. Short of beating my own foot to a pulp so I might be able to extract it from the rope's coils, I wasn't sure what good it could do. I almost kicked it back out of sight in frustration but reconsidered as lightning reflected off the barrel of McBurney's rifle. The hammer might come in handy in ways I had yet to conceive. I was able to coax it close enough to reach down and grab with my hands, tucking it back under the tarp but beside me where I could easily reach it. It was better than nothing at all.

McBurney's cursing and raving reached a whole new level, and I realized he was barking at me. It was difficult to tell because he still showed me his back, his hands locked onto the wheel while he focused on the turbulent surface of the lake ahead. I strained to pick out words from what was largely unintelligible. With the storm raging and sheets of rain bouncing off the pontoon's deck, it was how I imagined acoustics might be inside a running dishwasher.

"—stop playing fucking dead back there, do you hear me? *Say* something you son of a bitch!" His groan was pure frustration as it carried back to me on a wave of rumbling thunder. He was wound so tightly he couldn't stand still, shifting from one foot to the other and intermittently smacking his own head while calling himself a battery of disparaging names. I started to worry he was going to knock himself out, and then we would truly be fucked.

"Captain Jack," I called, but my voice was barely a squeak. I cleared my throat and tried again. *"Captain Jack!"* He had no way of knowing I'd discovered his actual identity, and I thought it might make me seem less of a threat if we kept it that way.

He dared to glance over his shoulder at the sound of my voice, and he erupted into hysterical laughter when he saw me wincing up at him from where I lay. "Oh, thank you, God—thank you, God—thank you, God—" he rambled over and over. If I wasn't mistaken, what I heard in his voice was pure relief.

We hit another rough patch as a strong gust of wind landed like a physical blow, and water surged up and over the side, racing in a foamy trail straight underneath me and up the legs of my saturated khaki shorts. The temperature was beginning to drop, and my teeth had begun to chatter. McBurney was saying something else, but I couldn't pick it out of the commotion.

"What?!" I bellowed, wondering if he was any more successful hearing me than I was hearing him.

"—sorry!" It was all I could pick out.

"I can't hear you!" I screamed.

He let loose with another disjointed laugh and lifted an open hand, shaking it as if to say never mind. The fact he didn't appear to be in any hurry to shoot me felt like a good sign, and I allowed myself to relax, if only a little. I stopped trying to communicate, figuring it behooved us both to let McBurney keep his focus on getting us to our destination in one piece. He seemed considerably less agitated, and I hoped it wasn't just a calm before another terrifying storm.

When lightning flared again, I finally caught sight of a land mass off in the distance, dead ahead. McBurney spotted it as well and throttled his laboring engine even harder. I had no way of knowing which side of the island we were approaching, and there were no lights to serve as a guide. It occurred to me that in a storm such as this one, the power may have been knocked out entirely, leaving Melanie and the others to grapple about in the dark. As if that thought wasn't unpleasant enough, it also occurred to me that with the power down, there would be no wi-fi service. Whatever we were up against, we wouldn't be able to call for help. We were completely on our own.

We abruptly struck something solid on the port side of the boat, and I was startled to realize the darkened entrance to the boathouse was looming dead ahead. We had entered the slip and bumped against the deck on the left, and how we kept from running into the small motorboat inside was beyond me. McBurney cut the engine and hurried about the business of securing it to the dock as quickly as he could while the pontoon shifted and bucked like wild cattle. I watched his progress, and out of the corner of my eye, I noticed the handle of the hammer had shifted with the torrent of water that had soaked my undies and was once again peeking out from underneath the heavy plastic tarp. I used my fingertips to scoot it back under cover as McBurney suddenly loomed large above me.

"I'm going to have to beg your apologies, and I'm thanking the good Lord above that I didn't split your skull open earlier, but I panicked," he said, his voice just as gravelly as I remembered. "I don't know why in the world you'd be messing in my business, but I just can't have it—not now."

"What are you doing?"

"I don't have time to explain myself, either. I'm going to have to leave you here for a bit. I'm sorry I can't make you any more comfortable, but you shouldn't even be here in the first place. I've got a promise to keep, and I can't let you or anyone else stop me. I hope to be back soon, but if not, you should be as safe here as anywhere else."

I didn't care for the sound of that.

"What about my friends?" I asked as he turned to collect a small rucksack I hadn't seen earlier, one that likely carried one or more implements that could easily free me from my current predicament.

"What about your friends?" he replied, sliding the rifle from his shoulder, and checking to make sure it was loaded. He seemed satisfied with his findings and slung it back into position.

"If you lay so much as one finger on—"

His deranged laughter quickly silenced any foolish bravado I was trying to assert. He turned his attention back to me and leaned in uncomfortably close. "I admire your gumption, boy, trussed up like a damned hog but still acting like you have any say at all in how things are going to go from here." He patted my cheek firmly. "You just relax. I'm here to put a stop to things. This land is tainted—*evil*. I don't know if it was the Williamses that caused it or something even older. I've really got no interest in seeing anyone else get hurt, but it ends here—tonight."

He stood and turned, checking himself once more before climbing out onto the dock, the sound of his heavy work boots fading as he hustled along the wooden planks and beyond my view.

Lightning raced across the sky, and I used the illumination to search my surroundings, hoping against hope I had overlooked something that might help me free myself from the ropes, but all I saw was the very end of the hammer, still stubbornly sticking out from beneath the tarp. I wondered what was keeping it from sliding all the way underneath, and I leaned forward, grabbing the tarp with both of my hands and tugging it to the side.

Darin Miller

I stared uncomprehendingly as water ran from my forehead down into my eyes. Underneath the plastic was a smattering of empty wooden crates with their lids pried loose and cast aside, as well as one that had been knocked over, its contents spilling out onto the rain-slicked deck. I'd seen something similar way back when I was in my high school ceramics class. Bricks of modeling clay wrapped in brown wax paper to keep the material pliable—but I had seen enough Bruce Willis movies to know this handful of bricks wasn't modeling clay.

And even if I hadn't, the "C-4 EXPLOSIVE" printed on the outer wrap was a pretty big fucking clue.

CHAPTER TWENTY-FOUR

For a long moment, I was afraid to move, fearful that any sudden motion might cause the explosives to spontaneously combust, taking me, the boathouse and who knows what else with it. I was certainly no munitions expert, but I suspected the few bricks I found could do more than enough damage. The lake suddenly swelled beneath the boat, causing it to bump roughly against the pilings, and it served as a slap to the back of the head from Mother Nature. If these explosives had any real sensitivity to motion, we would have blown sky high several times over as tumultuous as our journey across the lake had been. I almost let myself breathe a little easier before wondering if a direct lightning strike might do the trick, and I renewed my efforts to find something suitable for getting myself untethered and away from the source of my anxiety.

After scanning the deck for what seemed like the millionth time, I realized the storm had calmed into a steady rain. The starless sky was brightened less frequently by nature's fireworks than before, and the echoes of thunder were distant enough to suggest they had crossed the border into Canada. The overall reduction of volume in the nighttime soundtrack had a surprisingly calming effect on me, and I began to examine my surroundings with a fresh perspective, broadening my scope to include the entire area around the boat, not just the garbage that was floating or rolling about on the deck. My eyes settled on the heavy rope securing the pontoon to the slip, and I traced it from the dock back to the boat. The rope was wrapped several times around a heavy-duty horn cleat mounted to the edge of the boat and tied off in a bulky knot. The cleat's metallic ends protruded from both sides of the coil, and I had my first glimmer of hope.

I pushed away from the stern, flopping awkwardly onto my side. I wriggled forward inch by inch, learning to use the boat's ebb and flow in the rocky water to maximize my momentum, squirming with more fervor when the boat leaned in the appropriate direction. I couldn't get the taste of dirty lake water out of my mouth as, by necessity, my face remained inches from the filthy deck and the act of breathing necessitated the occasional accidental sip. After what seemed an eternity, I finally reached the starboard side and worked myself into a seated position in front of my target. I was thoroughly winded and had lost all sense of time. It felt like McBurney had been gone for hours and at any moment, the diminishing fury of the passing storm would be dwarfed by a monstrous explosion.

I've really got no interest in seeing anyone else get hurt—

McBurney's words drifted into my mind unbidden as I inhaled deeply and let the rainwater wash over my face. What happened while I was away? Who had gotten hurt and how badly? If anything had happened to Melanie, I would never forgive myself. The time I had wasted earlier in the weekend being invasive and insecure seemed especially petty now. Time was a precious commodity, not a promise, and if I could just get us out of this mess, I vowed not to waste another second. I leaned backward against my shoulders and used muscles I didn't know I had in my legs to inch my way up along the gunwale. For a scary second, I thought I was going to tumble backwards over the edge and get squashed between the pontoon and the slip, but I regained my balance and rested my backside along the edge. Thankfully, McBurney had tied my hands in front of rather than behind me. This was going to be awkward enough without having to attempt the maneuver behind my back. I wedged the exposed end of the metal horn cleat into the knot and began diligently pulling, prying and twisting at it until

ISOLATION

I finally felt a little give in the line. My first instinct was to try and wrench free, but I forced myself to patiently work at it a little longer, afraid I might accidentally tighten rather than loosen the knot. Eventually, I had enough slack that I could extract first one hand, and then the other. I rubbed circulation back into my hands and wrists before setting to work on the ropes binding my ankles.

Finally free, I hoisted myself over the edge of the boat and onto the dock and hauled ass to the manor house, praying I wasn't too late.

*****

The sky lit up in a staccato burst of eerily silent pyrotechnics, illuminating the home from behind. I slowed as I approached, marveling at how completely the sprawling manor had transformed into everything a haunted house could ever be in a matter of a few short hours. All the windows were dark, and I assumed the power must have gone out sometime during the storm. It didn't really surprise me after the blustery wind we had encountered on the way back. The front door stood open, swaying inward on its hinges, offering a cryptic invitation and beckoning me forward. I resisted the urge to rush in, instead pausing to consider my options.

There was no sign of McBurney, nor anyone else for that matter. For all I knew, he could be just inside the door, watching my approach with his rifle trained on me. Where in the hell *was* everyone else? It was like everybody had disappeared off the face of the earth. I cast my eyes left and noticed that someone had the foresight to lower the umbrella over the patio table and tie it off before the storm hit. Otherwise, it would likely be pinwheeling its way across Canada. The paned doors leading to the kitchen were closed and dark, as uninviting as the rest of the whole damn place. Still, I elected to skirt the front of the house and move towards the patio, considering it the lesser of two evils. Something about the open front door just felt like a trap.

I crossed the patio and pressed myself flat against the siding, listening to water raging through the gutters above and gushing out from downspouts at the various drops around me. The rain had slowed to a drizzle, but I was soaked completely through, the gusts of wind penetrating my clothing as if it weren't there. I couldn't keep myself from shivering as I inched my way toward the French doors, frequently peering over my shoulder to make sure no one was sneaking in from behind. I leaned in and wrapped my hand around the knob closest to me, sure it would be locked and forcing me to face whatever waited in the shadows of the main entrance.

To my surprise, the latch clicked, and the door opened.

I kept hold of the knob, afraid a sudden gust of wind might tear it out of my hand and send it smashing into the kitchen wall, alerting anyone inside to my presence. I stepped inside and closed the door carefully, latching it. I wasn't really keen on the idea of anyone sneaking up on me, either.

The house was preternaturally quiet, devoid of any of the white noise we grow accustomed to from electrical appliances going about their business in the background. My eyes were slow to adjust to the sudden darkness as the only light spilling in came from the occasional flashes of lightning through the double French doors, and those were becoming increasingly less frequent. We had opened the sheer curtains this morning, and they remained as we had left them. I kicked myself for tossing my cell phone into a drawer back at the hotel on Kelleys Island. I thought the best way to avoid temptation was to completely remove it, but I really could have used its flashlight right about now. I could barely see more than a couple feet in front of me, and the interior only got darker the farther I ventured in. I tried to picture the layout of the kitchen from the few times I had been in here.

ISOLATION

I reached out, feeling for the island I knew should be to my left and almost immediately planted my hand in something wet and viscous. I closed my eyes and shuddered, recalling the disaster Leroy had made of the kitchen, including a particularly nauseating round of projectile regurgitation, and I would have bet money I had just stuck my hand directly into it. I couldn't contain the high-pitched screech that escaped my mouth when I felt something lick my goo-covered fingers.

Lightning flickered, illuminating the cat who had previously scared the shit out of us in the basement. He had jumped onto the island and was diligently cleaning the mess from my hand, which I was relieved to recognize as nothing more than sausage gravy. The rest of the kitchen remained a disaster, just as Leroy had left it—maybe a little worse. I reached out with my clean hand and scritched the little fella between his shoulder blades, eliciting a peep followed by a low and satisfying rumble that modulated with each lap of congealed gravy from my fingers.

"Sorry, little guy," I whispered, pulling my hand back and wiping the remnants against my soggy shorts. "I've got things to do. Help yourself to whatever you find. There's plenty here to choose from."

I waited for the next flash of lightning to work my way quickly around the island, avoiding any of the mess in between. Once on the other side, I was dismayed to see a field of broken glass between me and the laundry room. Shattered liquor bottles littered the area, their contents combining into a puddle of mixed cocktail in which the shards floated like ice. Who could say if this was the result of Leroy's drunken clumsiness or because of some other altercation? For the first time, I had a true appreciation for the uncomfortable and waterlogged sandals on my feet. Their thick, crepe soles would take the brunt of any broken glass I might encounter, and quite frankly, my feet had been through enough.

My goal was the laundry room. I was pretty sure I had seen a heavy-duty Maglite on a shelf with the laundry supplies when I had laundered my slippers earlier. This house was too large to investigate in utter darkness with any sort of efficiency, and I couldn't help but feel time was running out.

Where in the hell *was* everybody?

It took everything I had not to call out, but I was still unsure of the lengths to which McBurney might go to stop me. My jaw still throbbed from where he'd clocked me with the butt of his rifle.

I fumbled my way past the island and used my outstretched arms to keep from running into any obstacles as I headed toward where I knew the laundry door was located. I found the doorframe and discovered the door was already pushed inward, the room beyond a black hole. After bumping into the front-loading washer, I reached up and found the wire rack mounted on the wall above it. I discovered the Maglite almost immediately and switched it on. Its illumination was startlingly brilliant, and I automatically shielded it with one hand. I may as well have sent a flare up if anyone was paying attention. I paused for a second, but all I heard was rain against the siding and my own ragged breath. Keeping the flashlight partially shielded and aimed at the ground, I stepped back out into the kitchen which I could now safely navigate using its peripheral luminescence.

The gray tabby peeped from the corner of the kitchen island, curiosity about the moving beam of light I carried more powerful than his desire to clean up Leroy's mess. I rubbed a knuckle under his jawline in passing, and he rumbled in gratitude, reaching out to bat playfully at the flashlight. I missed my cantankerous old Dexter.

Moving out into the hallway, I immediately noticed the door to the basement stood wide open, blocking my view of the left half of the corridor beyond it, and anyone or anything could be hiding there. I sighed. It was one thing to be cautious, but I was teetering on being paralyzed by fear, and that wouldn't do. I needed to find my people and make sure they were safe from whatever lunacy McBurney had planned for this evening. As far as I knew, they still thought they were playing a game and had no idea whatsoever about the very real threat McBurney presented. I needed to sweep this place as quickly as possible.

I proceeded down the hall under cover of the open basement door, and as I drew even with the open pocket doors to the formal dining room on my right, I covered the flashlight beam and darted sideways, stepping into the room. Once inside, I shone the light in all directions, and quickly determined the room was empty. I peered around the door into the hallway just as another volley of lightning flared through the large window framing the chandelier at the front of the house. I was relieved to find the rest of the corridor just as empty as the section in which I stood.

I paused at the open doorway to the basement, listening for any sign of activity below, but all I heard was another rumble of thunder, even more distant than before. At least Mother Nature was finally giving me a break, and I would take whatever I could get. I closed the basement door carefully and proceeded down the hall to the parlor.

Aware I was still dripping wet and leaving a trail wherever I went, I paused at the parlor door to keep from dribbling onto the expensive floor coverings in the room. Bringing the flashlight around, I was relieved to see Leroy was no longer playing nudist on the settee. However, an empty liquor bottle rested on its side on the rug in front of the sofa, some of its spilled contents soaking into an antique Persian rug, and a stain of questionable origin sullied the middle seat cushion.

I turned and crossed the foyer, glancing up the grand staircase as I passed. No one was visible on the stairs or through the rails bordering the wraparound hallway. With the next faint pulse of lightning, I confirmed there was no one lurking in the entryway or behind the massive front door, which still stood wide open. I decided it would be best to close it so no one could sneak up on me from behind. From there, I poked my head into the combination library/game room/study and scanned from one end of the long room to the other with the Maglite. It was exactly as we had left it, balls scattered across the surface of the pool table with cues deposited haphazardly across its felt surface. Three empty lowballs were lined up along the minibar, getting stickier by the minute because we hadn't thought to rinse them out, but there wasn't time for good housekeeping now. After confirming no one else was in the room, I headed for the stairs.

Keeping the bright beam of the Maglite against my leg, I darted up to the landing before veering left to ascend the remaining stairs to the hall. I risked uncovering the light so I could scan the wraparound corridor and verified at a glance I was the only one there. I hurried toward the front of the house, starting with what had originally been mine and Melanie's room. I opened the door while barely poking my head inside, casting the flashlight beam from one end to the other and coming up empty. I continued left to right, checking each room and finding no signs of life in any of them. I shuddered at the poor choice of phrases my mind had landed on.

At the end of the hall, I turned right and paused for a moment outside the door to the first guest room on my left. It had been Leroy's and Sandy's room. The last time I was here, a steady stream of animalistic grunting against the soundtrack of every porno movie ever made had poured through the door. With no source of power, it simply wasn't a possibility now, but I was still reluctant to open the door. The only thing I dreaded as much as running into McBurney and his rifle was another altercation—or agonizing game of peek-a-boo—with Leroy. If I had drank as much as he did, I'd be down for the count, but who knew what state he would be in? He was unpleasant on a good day and downright combative when drunk. I would prefer to simply avoid him altogether. I might be the only person I'd convinced that I wasn't scared of him, but I wasn't looking for trouble, either. In good conscience, I couldn't leave him behind and potentially in danger.

Dammit!

I opened the door and pushed it in, softly calling, "Leroy?"

The room looked like it had been hit by a cyclone. Clothes were strewn all over the floor, and the bed sheets and comforter were wadded together

ISOLATION

in a clump at the foot of the bed. The contents of Sandy's makeup bag were spread across the small desk and surrounded a portable magnifying mirror, which stood on a shiny, aluminum stand. It reflected the flashlight's beam back at me as I scanned the area. Crumpled towels lay on the floor beside the bed, trailing back toward the darkened bathroom, and they looked like they were damp. I suspected the room might look a whole lot different if Sandy's stay hadn't been cut short so abruptly, but left to his own devices, Leroy Poole was an inconsiderate pig. I could only imagine the amount of damage to Anyssa's property he had already caused. I backed out of the room, pulling the door shut behind me.

I was surprised to discover I had once again been holding my breath. It came out in a whoosh, and I'd be lying if I didn't admit I was more than a little relieved I hadn't run into the asshole.

There was one more guest room along this short corridor, and I checked it before hanging a right and checking the next three. There were signs in the last of these that Doug had once occupied its space. The bed was unmade, and an empty paper plate rested on the bedside table, but he must have moved his belongings in with Loretta when we had decided it was better to travel as a pack.

Only Loretta's room and the master bedroom were left to explore.

As I opened the door to Loretta's room, the flashlight was immediately knocked from my hand.

I hadn't even realized I had let my guard down until it was too late. I barely perceived the upward motion as what felt like a sledgehammer connected solidly with my groin, and I was down, profanities flowing from my mouth as I cracked my knees against the hardwood floor. My lower bits had instinctively drawn up into my body, finding places to hide I didn't even know existed. A hard wave of nausea rolled over me, and hot tears obscured what little I could see. I was suddenly sent sprawling onto my side as my attacker leapt onto me, and I swear to God, I heard growling before teeth met the flesh of my shoulder.

I knew that growl.

"*Loretta?!?*" It didn't stop her teeth from sinking in. "*Dammit*, Loretta! Get off of me!"

I rolled over, squashing her beneath me and felt the wind rush out of her. She let go, and I rolled away, fighting the urge to vomit while curling into a fetal position and praying for a quick and merciful death. My insides were roiling, and now my nose was running, too.

"Dwayne?" She got to her knees and crawled across to me. "Oh, thank the good Lord above, it's you!"

I wasn't sure how a shot to the crotch could have affected my hearing, but it must have. Loretta was *never* happy to see me. I kept trying to coax the boys back into place by pushing down on my lower abdomen, and eventually, the world stopped spinning.

Once I was able to speak without fear of spontaneously retching, I asked, "Where is everybody?"

"I don't know," she said, leaning forward to retrieve the Maglite from where she had knocked it from my hands. She remained on the floor beside me. "Dougie went down to the kitchen to make us a plate for dinner a little over an hour ago, and he hasn't been back since."

"How about everyone else?"

"Melanie and Brady came up here looking for you, but good Lord. That was hours ago. We figured you had been—well, you know, that you were—"

"Dead," I finished for her.

"Well—yeah," she said. "So where *were* you?"

I gave her the shortest possible version of my evening, beginning with my premature demise in the basement and ending with my discovery aboard the pontoon.

"Do you really think Captain Jack plans to blow this place up?" The gravity of our situation was slowly working its way through Loretta's thick skull.

"His name is Richard McBurney, and I'm pretty sure of it," I said, getting to my feet and helping Loretta to hers. There wasn't a single part of me that didn't hurt at this point. "He thinks the island is the cause of all of his problems, and I get the feeling he's not too concerned with his own personal safety."

"And how about the rest of us?"

"He said he didn't really *want* to hurt anyone, but it didn't exactly feel like a promise. How long have the lights been out?" I asked.

"They blinked out sometime after Dougie went down to get our dinner," she said. "Sounded like that storm was right on top of us, and I wasn't really surprised when they blew."

"And it didn't seem strange when Doug didn't come back?"

"Well, of course, it seemed strange! It's just that—" She was ruffled, and her voice trailed off.

"It's just what?"

"I might have nodded off for a bit," she said.

"Oh, for the love of God—"

She pointed a talon in my direction. "You just watch where you're takin' the Lord's name, young mister."

I was dumbfounded. "Did you and Doug do *anything* today? I mean, other than lay around, stuff your faces and watch the *Indiana Jones* marathon?"

She was quick to flare. "I did plenty! I spent a couple of hours playing around with that stupid computer of yours trying to find anything new that we didn't already know about the Williamses' gold."

"And did you find anything?"

"Well, not really—but I found more than a couple of stories about the property itself, and I can see where this guy McBurney would think it was cursed. His wife wasn't the only one who met her end on or around this island. Over the years, no less than a dozen ships have gone down and there have been at least as many deaths. Wouldn't surprise me at all if they turned it into one of them episodes of *Haunted* on Netflix. What seems to link it all together is they were all after the Williamses' gold."

I shook my head. "That's nuts. I mean, I know Anyssa is leaning into the legend, too, but every single piece of 'gold' we've found is fake. Why would people think there is still something to be found here?"

"I don't know why people believe half of the nonsense that they do, but they do."

"And it never occurred to you to look for Doug when he didn't come back with your dinner?" I asked. "You didn't maybe think to find Brady and Melanie and make sure they were okay?"

"I decided to shelter in place," she said, still defensive. "We said we were going to stick together, and I figured someone would eventually come to me."

"Were you scared of the dark?" I couldn't contain my sarcasm. I wasn't ready to let her off the hook quite yet.

"*No!*" she bristled. "But I don't have one of those fancy smartphones like y'all do, and my flip phone doesn't have a flashlight. I don't see too good in the dark with my cataracts and all. I didn't want to trip over something and break a hip. My friend, Irma Jean, broke her hip last winter. She stepped on some black ice and went down hard. She's never been the same."

"I would've thought your need to feed would have overcome that."

She scowled, placing her fists on her hips. "Keep it up if you want me to kick you again, 'cause I'm warning you, I'm about ready to permanently adjust your octave."

I shielded myself and held a hand up in surrender. "No, no, no. I'm done. You just stay over there."

She deliberated compliance long enough to make me nervous. Finally, her fists relaxed and dropped to her sides. "So, what should we do now?"

"We need to find everyone and try to get off this island."

"You don't think they were—you know, 'killed' like you were?" she asked, using air quotes where appropriate.

"I don't see how," I said. "I was taken back to Kelleys Island by Jeremy and Kit, and they were still there until shortly before I headed back as a hostage on McBurney's pontoon. They wouldn't have had time to come back here and round anyone else up, and besides, I don't think they would have risked taking anyone else back out onto the lake with the storm moving in."

"Well, can't we just call for help? Didn't Ms. Williams leave an emergency number in our welcome packets?"

I shook my head. "There's no cellular service out here, and with the power down, wi-fi calling doesn't work, either. Even if the power came back on, your flip phone is too old and doesn't support that kind of connectivity."

"What about your phone?" she asked.

I chewed on my bottom lip, reluctant to answer. I had been kicking myself ever since I had needed its flashlight and realized it wasn't with me.

"It's not with me," I finally said, keeping it short and simple. "And like I said, without power, it doesn't really matter. We need to find everyone and—"

There was a sudden flash of orange-tinged light just beyond the heavily curtained window on the front-facing wall of the room, brighter and more sustained than any mere flash of lightning, and the subsequent boom that rapidly followed shook the entire house. Stunned, Loretta and I gaped at each other.

Somewhere on the island, something had just ferociously detonated, lighting up the entire night sky.

CHAPTER TWENTY-FIVE

"Holy shit!" I exclaimed from the covered porch. I had left Loretta trailing along behind me on the stairs as I raced to assess the situation. The entire western hemisphere was aglow with a flickering orange light and thick black smoke poured into the night sky, drifting toward the manor house as the winds once again began to gust.

"What happened?" gasped Loretta, grasping my arm to steady herself. She was winded from running down the stairs.

"I think it's the boathouse," I said. "I'm going to check it out. You can either wait here, or—"

"Oh, no," she interrupted. "I'm not letting you out of my sight."

I really couldn't blame her at this point, but as she placed her hands on her knees and stooped to steady her breathing, I couldn't help but see her as a liability, slowing my progress and quite possibly getting all of us killed in the process. I ran to the far side of the porch and was overjoyed to discover the other golf cart still parked underneath its metal awning, its electrical cord uselessly connected to a heavy-duty outlet mounted to the side of the house. While it wasn't currently charging, it had been until the electricity went out, and I imagined if it wasn't fully charged, it had to be nearly so. I swung my legs over the porch rail and hopped down to the path below, hurrying over to the waiting cart.

ISOLATION

I zipped around to the front of the house and stopped the cart at the foot of the stairs.

"C'mon," I urged Loretta as she ran a finger over the plastic passenger seat, frowning.

"It's wet," she groused.

I sighed, still very much aware of the soggy clothes that clung to my own skin. "Either get in or stay here, but I'm going."

"All right, all right," she said, hoisting a stubby leg into the car and scooting onto the seat with a look of utter dismay plastered across her face as her pedal pushers absorbed moisture like a sponge. I barely waited for her to bring her other leg aboard before I whipped the cart around and onto the path headed for the boathouse.

The wind shifted toward us, and thick black smoke enveloped the cart, momentarily blinding me. An occasional flicker of flame lapped at the dark night from behind the woods obscuring our view of that portion of the lake. The top speed of the golf cart wasn't nearly fast enough for me, although Loretta was clinging to the roof support for dear life as I bounced us down the trail. My thoughts were wandering into dark territory, and I couldn't seem to stop them. What if Melanie, Brady and Doug had been in the boathouse, ready to go for help when Richard McBurney had come across them? What if he had detonated those last blocks of explosive to keep them from escaping, and I was too late to save them? Acid roiled through my gut as dread enveloped me as completely as the noxious smoke polluting our airways.

I rounded the final bend to the boathouse and skidded to a halt.

The boathouse and its slip were completely obliterated, and planks blown loose from the dock were burning brightly up and down the sandy shore. Scattered amongst them and burning every bit as brightly were remnants of the boathouse, its skeletal frame engulfed in hot, angry flames. I got out of the cart and picked my way through the fiery wreckage, tucking my nose and mouth into an elbow while squinting against the waves of smoke and heat that worked against me. The pontoon had disintegrated beyond recognition, although the burning carcass of the speedboat was discernible, bobbing helplessly in the debris-riddled water.

"*Melanie!*" I screamed, scanning the site for anything remotely resembling a human being. I was beyond caring if McBurney heard me. "*Brady!*" Downright desperate, I even tried, "*Dusty!*"

Loretta joined in behind me, unleashing a bellow that utilized every single bit of her diaphragm, "*Doug-ieeeeeee!!!!*" She sounded as hysterical as I felt. "*Doug-ieeeeeee!!!!*"

I choked on a noxious plume of smoke that crept beneath my elbow. Loretta took hold of my arm, a steady stream of prayers flowing from her lips as tears streamed down her cheeks.

"Do you see anybody?" she asked fearfully.

I cleared my throat and wiped moisture from my own eyes. "I don't."

I tried to sound hopeful, but judging from the destruction around us, I could only imagine what a blast of C-4 could do to a human body.

"What should we do?" she asked.

For a moment, all I could do was shake my head, dazed. "We keep looking for them," I finally said, and we helped each other back to the golf cart.

*****

My mind raced as the golf cart labored back towards the house, my foot pinning the accelerator to the floor. I had pretty thoroughly inspected the house, and although I hadn't actually gone down into the basement, I had listened at the top of the stairs and had gotten no indication that anyone was down there. It was impossible to imagine Dusty maintaining that level of silence for even the shortest length of time.

Unless she was already dead. Maybe they were all already dead.

My thoughts kept leaning towards the sinister, and I had to force them away. McBurney had said that he didn't want anyone else to get hurt, and when I thought back, he really sounded sincere. Tortured, but sincere. It was all the hope I had, and I was going to cling to it until I was proven wrong.

"Look out!" shrieked Loretta, reaching over to grab the steering wheel before pulling it hard to the right.

I slammed on the brakes instinctively as Leroy staggered in front of the golf cart, shielding his eyes against its halogen headlights.

"*Hullo?*" he slurred. "Sandy? Is that you?"

Thankfully, he had at least recovered his boxer shorts, although he wore them backwards, again paired with his now-familiar stained A-shirt stretched across his ample belly. His brassy, unkempt and thinning tendrils of hair stood wildly on end, and his eyes were bloodshot, wild and confused.

"Shit," I muttered to myself. His timing couldn't have been worse. I cleared my throat. "Nope, not Sandy. It's just us."

His squint tightened as he tried to focus on us. A few long seconds passed before recognition dawned. "Oh! It's the peacekeeper and the kitchen troll. Have you seen my li'l Sandy?"

How he remained upright was a true mystery. His consonants were as soft as rotted fruit, and once he stopped leaning against the front of the golf cart, he staggered about like the ground was moving beneath his feet.

"Your little Sandy is safe on Kelleys Island," I supplied. "Where did you come from?"

He pointed toward the lake, and I knew that was wrong. He had just approached from the direction of the house.

"Have you seen any of the others?" I asked, trying a different approach.

His face squirreled up as he thought long and hard. "No," he finally said. He staggered sideways, almost losing his balance and pointed toward the dark house. "Do you know why the lights are off up there? I keep flippin' the switch, but nothin' happens."

"There was a storm, you big drunken fool," said Loretta impatiently. "It knocked the power out."

He seemed even more confused. "That doesn't make any fuckin' sense."

"I'm guessin' not a lot does in your current state of mind," she continued crossly, and I grabbed her arm.

"Let's not get him going again," I quietly urged.

She pulled her arm away and looked at me with disdain. "You really *are* afraid of this guy—"

"Will you lower your voice, please?"

Her laugh was little more than a bark. "I will not. First thing we're doing when we get off this island is to take you shopping for a whole drawerful of big boy pants, you big cream puff."

The urge to strangle her was sudden and powerful, but I was determined to keep my priorities in order. "Let's focus on getting off the island first, okay?"

"And just what do you propose we do next?"

I thought about that for a moment. "We should go around to the other side of the island. There's a smaller dock over there. That's where Kit and Rob have been taking people once they were—you know, murdered or whatever."

"Why would they be over there?"

I was running out of patience. "What's with the fifty fucking questions, Loretta? I don't know where they are, but they have to be somewhere, and I'm running out of ideas. Do you have any thoughts? *Anything?*"

Loretta's eyes locked on me, and she froze, her expression cool and indignant. I've learned to recognize when Loretta is debating slapping the foul language right out of my mouth, and this was definitely one of those moments. I decided to defuse with reason.

"And besides, at this point, Jeremy's boat is the only way off the island."

Her frown lines deepened, but the cold fury dissipated from her eyes. "And what do we do with *this* one?" She pointed to where Leroy had decided to take a seat in the middle of the dusty path before us. "We can't in good conscience leave him here."

And why not? My inner voice was surprisingly amoral and very loud.

Loretta scowled at my hesitation. *"Dwayne."*

"Fine," I grumbled, getting out of the cart and meeting her on the other side of Leroy.

"Hey, what do you think you're doin'?" He clumsily swatted us away as we each tried to take an arm.

"We're taking you to your little Sandy," cooed Loretta. "Come on, big fella. Upsy daisy."

We got him to his feet and awkwardly walked him around to the rear of the golf cart where he more or less tumbled into the backseat.

Loretta wiped her hands on the sides of her pale pink petal pushers and stared down at the sad lump that was Leroy. He was already snoring. "I'm seein' that wife of his in a whole new light," she said, shaking her head. "That poor, poor woman."

*****

"What's that over there?" Loretta pointed off to our right as we continued along the path into the woods.

"It's where your son wrecked the other golf cart," I said. The headlights washed over the cart's back end, still tilted drunkenly into the ditch on the right, its rear left tire a good two feet off the ground. "And this is about as far as we can go in the cart. The terrain gets a little too uneven from here."

I stopped the cart and turned its engine off.

Loretta looked over her shoulder at Leroy, sprawled across the rear seats, eyes closed and smacking his lips while digging for China in the crack of his ass. "What are we gonna do with him?" she asked. "It's one thing to get him up off the ground and into the cart, but I'm barely gonna be able to manage myself without propping that goon up."

"We'll have to leave him here, and don't go laying another guilt trip on me," I warned her. "It's his own damn fault that he's in this condition. If we find the others, I'll get Doug and Brady to come back and help me bring him down to the dock. It shouldn't be too far from here, so let's not waste any more time."

"Do you really think we'll find the others?"

"I'm sure of it," I said, avoiding her eyes while climbing out of the cart. The only thing I was sure of was that we were running out of time. I didn't believe for one second that McBurney's master plan was to blow up the boathouse, and I expected another explosion at any moment. I wondered if the first had been visible from any of the nearby islands. I reckoned it was too much to hope that help was already on its way.

I couldn't stop thinking of all the stupid bickering I had done with Melanie over the weekend and how lucky I was to have her and Jasmine in my life. In times of crisis, bargains flow like water. I promised to be more respectful, less insecure and nothing short of forthright if I could just find my girl safe and sound. Don't get me wrong, I wanted to find the others, too, but these promises were for Melanie alone. McBurney may be crazy as a loon, but he had lost his Alethea, and with that I could most certainly empathize. The very thought of losing Melanie affected me in ways I would have never thought possible.

I waited for Loretta to join me before turning on the Maglite and focusing it on the path ahead. One last parting glance at Sleeping Beauty in the back of the cart, and we soldiered on.

*****

The rain had stopped entirely, and a full moon peeked through the diminishing cloud cover, barely visible through a tangle of upstretched tree branches. We had just passed the 'No Trespassing' sign Anyssa had mentioned during our orientation, hanging on a rope strung between two posts on either side of the narrow path we traveled. We realized the other dock must be near.

We emerged from the woods just as we approached the summit of a gentle slope, and the unmistakable sound of voices drifted up from below. I left both caution and Loretta behind as I charged forward, hoping against hope they belonged to the folks we had been seeking.

I crested the ridge but stopped so abruptly Loretta ran into me.

"Is—it—them?" Loretta managed, grabbing my shirttail to prevent me from plunging headlong into the field of boulders that littered the hillside below us.

"Yeah, but—" I steadied myself and squinted, focusing on the bustling activity below.

Something was wrong.

Dusty led the charge, zigging and zagging toward the ramshackle dock where the transport boat was tethered, bobbing up and down in the churning water. She was completely hysterical, wringing her hands while her sobs carried up the hill. Rob trailed close behind, and it looked like he was carrying Kit in his arms. Melanie and Brady followed while Doug struggled to keep up.

"What's going on?" asked Loretta, peering around me.

I could only shrug. "I'm not sure."

"Doug-*ieeeeee!*" she shrieked, practically deafening me in one ear while waving her arms above her head like she was bringing a plane in for a landing.

Everyone except Dusty pivoted to find the source of Loretta's dulcet siren song. Dusty stayed on course; she was clumsily navigating the rickety dock, heading toward the boat.

"*Ma!*" Doug called back, returning her wave.

Using the flashlight for guidance, we picked our way down the narrow path, keeping each other steady until we reached the narrow strip of sand that bordered the shore along this end of the island.

"What happened?" I asked, pulling up between Melanie and Brady so I could get a better look at Kit. Her eyes were closed, and her skin was alarmingly pale, save for a gnarly gash that stretched from her temple to her forehead. Dark blood trickled up into her fine blonde hair, where it had begun to clump and mat.

"*C'mon,* people! We need to get out of here!" Dusty wailed from the deck of the ship. Her thick mascara drained in thin rivulets from her eyes to her chin. All she got from us was a series of annoyed glares.

"She fell down the stairs going down into the basement," said Rob. "She must have gotten tangled up in her feet—I really don't know, but she hit her head pretty good, and I can't get her to respond."

"But she *is* breathing, right?" I started to reach for her as if there was something I could do, but I had no more medical training than I did investigative training. I wasn't even sure I could find a pulse with directions.

Rob nodded, swallowing hard. "We got word from Ms. Williams that rotation had been detected in the clouds from the storm that just blew through here. We had to abort the game and initiate our tornado protocol. We were lucky that nearly everyone was in the kitchen. We headed for the basement, and she just went *down*."

"It was awful," said Melanie, tucking her arms around me. "I was right behind her, and the sound of her head hitting the wall—" She shuddered.

"But then the power went out and we lost our wi-fi calling, so I can't even send for help. We need to get her to a hospital," Rob said, concern evident on his face.

"Isn't there a radio on the boat you can use?" I asked. Between *The Poseidon Adventure* and *Friday the 13th Part VIII: Jason Takes Manhattan*, I'd seen enough maritime disaster movies to expect *some* way of sending out a 'Mayday!'

Rob's humorless laugh didn't bode well. "We *had* one," he said. "It got boosted at the dock when Jeremy and Kit took you over to Kelleys Island. They've had a rash of equipment thefts lately. I swear, it's almost like we've been—" He stopped just short of saying 'cursed,' but we all knew where he was headed. "Help me get her onboard, will you?"

Brady and I followed him onto the dock to the edge of the watercraft while the others gave us ample room to maneuver. We climbed aboard, continuing to ignore Dusty's ongoing meltdown while Rob passed Kit across to me and Brady. We eased her gently to the deck while Rob climbed aboard and scrambled to nab a seat cushion to place under her head. The ship abruptly lurched as the lake shifted around us, and Dusty sat down hard, a fresh wave of anguish washing over her. Melanie and Doug climbed aboard next, and they were working to boost Loretta up from the dock.

"Can someone please sit with Kit and keep her steady? I guess I'm going to drive this damn thing," grumbled Rob impatiently. His nerves were steadily fraying. He flailed in our general direction, and Loretta scurried over to relieve him, taking Kit's head into her lap once she had squatted lotus-style onto the wet deck.

I scanned the coastal area. "Where's Jeremy?"

"I have no fucking idea," said Rob, hurrying to the first of three cleats where the boat was tethered to the dock. "When we heard about the tornado warning, he went to find Mrs. Boggs and that Poole guy. I haven't seen him since."

"*Shit!*" I exclaimed, looking back toward the narrow trail Loretta and I had only recently descended.

"What?" asked Melanie, following my gaze.

"Leroy Poole," I said, shaking my head. "He's passed out in a golf cart up there."

"So, we leave him!" said Rob, unfurling the first thick line of rope. "It's no big deal. The worst of the storm has passed. Jeremy can just bring him back to the mainland in the other boat."

"No, he really can't," I said, and Rob froze, his head pivoting in my direction as he detected the certainty in my tone.

"And just why is that?" He struggled to keep his composure, but it seemed to be a losing battle. The cords along the sides of his neck stood out, and he had developed a nervous tic in his left eye. The knuckles on his hands clutching the rope were practically white.

"It isn't there anymore," I said. "Didn't you all hear the explosion?"

Rob dropped the rope and stood up straight. *"Explosion?"*

"Yeah, sure, we all heard it," said Brady. "I just thought there must have been a lightning strike that was particularly close."

"Why are you using the word explosion?" asked Rob, moving towards the second cleat, his eye ticking in time with his accelerated heartbeat. "I don't care for the sound of that. I don't care for that at all."

I sucked in a deep breath. "Then you're really not going to like the rest of what I have to tell you. The boathouse and the boat? Gone. Most of the dock is burning in little pieces scattered up and down the coastline. And you've got a crazy man running loose on the island with a bunch of explosives."

Rob recoiled like I had physically assaulted him, and then he unleashed a jaw-dropping torrent of obscenities that caused Loretta's complexion to burn bright red all the way to the tips of her ears. She held onto Kit protectively as he kicked and thrashed about, propelling Dusty to new heights of hysteria. She scooted away from him on her backside and pulled her knees up to her face, hugging her legs tightly.

"Can't we just go?" she pleaded in a voice ragged from sobbing.

This was getting nuts. Someone was going to have to take charge and with no one volunteering, I waded right in. "Go," I said to Rob. "Get Kit back to the mainland. Take everybody else with you. I'll stay behind and find Jeremy and Leroy. Send someone back for us as soon as you can."

Make no mistake about it, my motivation had very little to do with Leroy Poole. That stupid asshole pretty much deserved whatever he got. But I was feeling more than a little guilty about breaking Jeremy's arm, and he had no idea of what he was wandering into back at the house. I had to try to avert yet another tragedy from happening on this godforsaken island.

I wasn't fully prepared to be met with such resistance.

Melanie was the first to cry foul. "No way," she said, shaking her head vigorously. "There is no way I'm letting you out of my sight again. It was bad enough when I thought I had lost you in a stupid game, but this is entirely different. I'm staying."

I tried to reason with her. "You need to stay safe for Jasmine. There's no reason—"

"Don't you *dare* use my daughter like that!" She was instantly furious, and I was suddenly stammering like a fool. "You're not going to shame me into playing it safe every time things get a little dicey, and I can't *believe* you don't know that by now!"

Brady was right behind her. "And you're out of your flipping mind if you think *I'm* going anywhere. I am literally right in the middle of breaking news! I'm not gonna walk away from a story like this. I plan to return to work with the latest headline already in my back pocket!"

Okay, no real surprise there, but then Doug stepped forward.

"I'm in, too," he said. He looked back toward Loretta who was still cradling Kit's head in her lap. "Ma, Rob's gonna need you to keep doin' what you're doin'. I'll catch up to you as quick as I can."

Loretta simply nodded and returned her attention to Kit. It was a little like *Invasion of the Body Snatchers;* I had never seen her so nurturing.

"You really don't have to do this," I protested. "There's no reason we all—"

"The hell you say!" Doug snapped. "It was Boggs Investigations that was invited on this little shindig, and I *am* Boggs Investigations. You really need to get that through your thick head. We have a credible threat on the island, and I guarantee you there is no one more qualified with respect to munitions than me. I'm staying."

I stared, my mouth hanging open. I wanted to argue with him—hell, I *always* wanted to argue with him, but he made a good point. The teetering stacks of *Guns & Ammo* covering every available surface back in the office attested to that.

"Well, then great, it's been decided," said Rob, preparing to loosen the last of the ropes securing the boat to the dock. "Now, if you could all please just *get the fuck off of the boat!*"

CHAPTER TWENTY-SIX

"Tell me what you know," said Doug as the sound of the boat's engine faded into the night. We had barely made it onto the dock before Rob opened up the throttle, lurching out into water still frothy from the storm.

I filled them in as concisely as possible. I couldn't shake the feeling we were running out of time. It seemed like an eternity since the boathouse had exploded, and the subsequent calm was shredding my nerves.

"I think McBurney plans to blow up the house," I said. "He wants to make this island uninhabitable because he thinks it's cursed. He's armed, but he claims he doesn't want to hurt anyone else."

"Do you believe him?" asked Melanie.

I was surprised by how quickly I nodded. "Yeah, I guess I do. He could've killed me if he wanted to, but instead, he tied me up and brought me back to the island. My guess is it was because he didn't want me to sound the alarm before he had a chance to execute his plan. But I don't know what might happen if Jeremy confronts him. He might not *want* to hurt any of us, but I think he could if we got in his way. He's determined to have this over and done with tonight."

"This is bad," Doug said. "Are you sure it was C-4 you saw?"

"I *can* read," I said irritably. "It was printed on the outer wrap."

"Any idea how much of this stuff McBurney has?"

"There were a few bricks on the boat, but there could have been more underneath the tarp, I don't know. There were a lot of empty wooden crates. What are we doing here, Doug?" My impatience was making me antsy. If Doug insisted on taking the lead, I could force myself to fall in line for only so long. We needed less talking and more action.

"Let's collect Mr. Poole and the golf cart," said Doug, plodding through the dense, wet sand toward the trail Loretta and I had followed. "Jeremy went back through the tunnel when he was looking for Ma and Mr. Poole. He would have to be at the house by now. I'm surprised you didn't run into him."

"We didn't see anyone other than Leroy," I said, pulling ahead of Doug so I could illuminate our path with the Maglite. Melanie and Brady stayed close behind.

"Should we break into groups?" asked Melanie, eyeing the entrance to the tunnel as we passed it. "What if Jeremy is somewhere in the tunnel?"

"Absolutely not," said Doug. "That tunnel is pretty much an extension of the house. I got no idea how many bricks of that stuff McBurney has planted or where, but I wouldn't want to be down there when the next one blows. The tunnel could collapse, or the blast from the explosion could be sucked right through there, killing anyone in its path. That's not a risk we need to be taking, especially when we've got a golf cart up here and it's our fastest way back to the house."

"As long as *you're* not driving." It was a petty observation, but I couldn't help myself.

We crested the slope and stepped around the rope barrier that was intended to keep us away from the secondary dock. I suspected it would have done very little to dissuade me had I stumbled upon it earlier—forbidden fruit and all, but that was neither here nor there, at this point. I led us back toward the clearing where we had left Leroy and the cart. I was beginning to think I had somehow made a wrong turn when the Maglite caught a hint of metal, reflecting off the framework of a golf cart ahead. I could immediately see something was amiss. The driver's side rear tire was suspended in the air, and the cart's undercarriage was far more visible than it should have been. I was looking at the cart that Doug had wrecked.

"What the hell—?" I mumbled, more to myself than anyone else, before sweeping the Maglite in a complete circle around the clearing.

The other golf cart was gone, and so was Leroy Poole.

*****

I was getting winded, and the hard leather thongs of my sandals had thoroughly abraded the skin between my toes, but I did my level best to keep up with the others as we hurried back along the path. We kept on the lookout for Leroy and the other golf cart, which I fully expected to find wrapped around a tree at any moment.

"Why do you suppose McBurney's holding off?" asked Melanie. "Wouldn't you think it's possible that someone on one of the islands nearby might have seen the fireworks when the boathouse blew up?"

"I'm not sure," I said. "Maybe we'll luck out and Jeremy will have disarmed him."

"Do we ever have that kind of luck?" asked Brady.

"No," I admitted. "But we've got to try and give Jeremy a heads-up. It's the least I owe him after breaking his arm."

"You did *what?*" asked Melanie incredulously.

"He was playing the part of our resident ghost that you all thought I was imagining," I said, feeling somewhat vindicated and maybe just a touch salty. "When he came in behind me at the boathouse the night I saw Sandy, I knocked him into the boat and—well, I'm probably not his favorite person right now."

Brady laughed. "I guess I'm a little relieved to know it wasn't all in your mind. You've been acting less than normal lately—"

"*Brady,*" warned Melanie, smacking his arm.

"What?" he said, flinching and rubbing his bicep. "I'm just saying that he—"

"I know what you're saying," she said. "You can just keep it to yourself."

He held his hands up in surrender, and we continued along in silence. I knew what he was saying, too, and I wasn't really offended. In fact, I was more than a little relieved myself, but it was nice to hear Melanie leap to my defense. The events I had experienced in West Virginia related to my sister's current circumstance were murky at best. I had been drugged and would always wonder how much of what I remembered was real or merely a byproduct of hope. Being unable to rely on my own senses was new to me, and it had practically debilitated me for weeks. Participating in this weekend event had been a conscious choice intended to force myself back into something resembling normalcy. The last thing I needed was to have my sanity challenged yet again by witnessing imaginary ghosts and goblins.

A chorus of bullfrogs serenaded us from our periphery as nocturnal sounds began to creep back in now that the storm had passed. I stifled a cry as a rabbit burst from the underbrush to our right, crossing through the flashlight's beam and diving into the cover of thick growth on our left. Droplets of water from saturated treetops continued to sprinkle down when provoked by the occasional gust of wind stirring their branches, showering both us and the forest floor, as we followed the trail toward the house.

"So, why *do* you think he's waiting?" asked Melanie, breaking the relative silence. "I would think he would want to be finished with all this."

"I don't know," I said. "He might not have had all of his explosives in place yet. Who knows?"

"But why would he have blown up the boathouse so far ahead of everything else?" she continued. "It kind of seems like an unnecessary risk, doesn't it? I mean, what if it *was* seen from one of the other islands?"

"I wondered that myself," I said. "But if the police, Coast Guard, or *whoever* monitors things on the lake are coming to our rescue, they're sure taking their sweet time."

"That would be your Coast Guard District 9," said Doug authoritatively. "They are responsible for search and rescue, maritime safety and security, environmental issues, icebreaking and overall law enforcement." He sounded like a tour guide.

"You said you saw some of that shit on the boat," said Brady. "Do you think maybe it was hit by lightning?"

"Not a chance," said Doug. We were in his wheelhouse now, and he had taken the reins. "C-4 is an extremely stable compound. It can only be detonated with a blasting cap or something like it. You can lob a brick of C-4 onto a campfire and all you'll get is some poison fumes for your trouble."

"So, you *don't* think the boathouse was an accident?" asked Brady.

"I'd be hard pressed to see how," said Doug. "And there's something else that bothers me."

"Yeah?" I asked. "What's that?"

"How could the storm knock out the power like that?"

I scoffed. "Are you kidding me? This was one hell of a storm! It happens all the time back in Lymont. All of those overhead power lines strung from pole to pole. We don't have nearly so much trouble in Grove City where most of our power lines are buried underground."

Doug was already shaking his head. "But that's just it. There *aren't* a bunch of overhead power lines here. The only ones I saw were the ones running from the main house down to the boathouse and between the lampposts along the lakeshore."

"He's right," said Melanie, nodding. "Ms. Williams told us this place is more or less self-sufficient. There's an electric generator behind the shed out beyond the patio, and it's powered by a natural gas well on the island."

I looked across to them vacantly. "Okay—what am I missing here?"

Doug sighed impatiently. "What are *most* electric generators used for?"

My expression shifted not one single iota. I was hyperaware of the pain in my feet; it was a race to see which of my two big toes would be sawed off first.

"Do you even know what an electric generator *is?*" he persisted, and I had had about enough.

"Of course, I know what one is!" I barked irritably. "I've got one back at my own damn house. You switch your house over to it when you've lost power in a storm—*oh*. Okay. I think I get where you're going with this. The island uses the generator all the time, but the principle is still the same. It shouldn't be as vulnerable to weather."

"Exactly!" said Doug, snapping his stubby fingers. "I seriously doubt if the power outage was accidental."

"And without power, no one can use their cell phones to call or text for help, giving McBurney all the time he needs to get his explosives in place, even if someone stumbled upon him in the process," I finished the train of thought.

"But that brings us right back to where we started," said Melanie. "Why would he blow up the boathouse first? What possible reason could he have had?"

We trudged along in silence for several moments, deliberating Melanie's question. The answer came to me in a flash. "He must have known I wasn't on the boat anymore," I said. "I honestly don't think he would have blown it up if he thought I was still aboard."

"You're putting an awful lot of trust in a lunatic," said Brady. "How can you be so sure?"

"Doesn't really matter what Dwayne believed," interjected Doug. "But I think he's right."

"Yeah?" I was surprised.

"From what you described, the C-4 was still in its outer wrap, correct?" asked Doug.

I nodded.

"You didn't see anything stuck into any of those bricks anywhere? A metal rod? Any sort of wires?"

"Nothing like that, no."

"Those charges weren't armed yet," said Doug. "McBurney would have had to come back to attach some sort of blasting cap before he could detonate any of 'em. He would have had to have known you had gotten away. He would have figured you would make a beeline for the house. Maybe it was his way of drawing you back out?"

"But what about the rest of us?" asked Brady. "I don't get it. Are we just some sort of collateral damage? If this McBurney guy is really trying not to hurt anyone else, wouldn't he want to make sure that *all* of us were out of the house?"

None of us had a ready answer for that. We lapsed back into silence as we continued along a trail that seemed never-ending. The woods were less dense at this point, and I expected us to emerge near the manor at any moment.

"Do you think Anyssa had cameras hidden throughout the house?" Brady offered. "Maybe McBurney found a way to tap into them."

I shook my head. "Only at the entrances to the house, or at least that's what she told me. She said she didn't have any desire to invade anyone's privacy. That's why she had Rob and Kit embedded with us. They were her eyes on the ground."

We reached the edge of the woods and followed the trail out into the open where it would soon wrap to the right around a grassy knoll, and the manor house would once again be visible. Although any ambient light from the explosion had greatly diminished, dark plumes of smoke continued to rise in the distance, carried toward us on an easterly wind, and the first waves of charred ruin arrived as an assault on our olfactory senses. There was still no sign of Leroy Poole or the golf cart, and I would've lost money on that one. I was certain he would have wrecked the damned thing by now.

As we continued along the path, the house slowly came into view—big, dark and ominous. Anyone could be standing watch behind its many darkened windows, and we would have never been the wiser. With no power to assist, nothing burbled from the cherubic centerpiece of the fountain on the front lawn, and it seemed to be staring, as if anticipating our arrival. No one stood on the veranda to greet us, and the front door was closed, although I could have sworn Loretta and I had left it open in our haste to see what had caused the great, big boom earlier—but who could be certain? It was all just a blur now.

I couldn't speak for anyone else, but the extreme sense of vulnerability was making my skin crawl. As storm clouds continued to dissipate, the full moon had emerged and was visible through the lofty pines behind the tallest spire of the roof. Its luminescence was bright enough that I felt comfortable turning off the Maglite. Besides, the flashlight was a beacon drawing attention to our exact location, and I already felt overly exposed as it was.

"Maybe he has an accomplice," said Melanie, and I nearly jumped out of my skin as she unexpectedly broke our pensive silence.

"What are you thinking?" I asked.

"Maybe McBurney knew when we were out of the house because, like with Anyssa, he has someone working with him on the inside—wait, what's that?" She pointed to the edge of the path ahead to our right.

I reluctantly switched the Maglite back on and followed her finger with its beam. A parallel set of ruts tore through the turf bordering the lawn before leaving a twin trail of trampled grass leading back and around the fountain, continuing on toward the side of the house where the patio was.

"I think we've just picked up the trail of Leroy Poole," I said.

We hurried across the front lawn, following the tracks around the side of the house, and just as soon as the patio came into view, I couldn't contain a short, derisive laugh. As the others pulled alongside me, I shone the light on the full spectacle before us.

The passenger front bumper of the golf cart was interlocked with a broken piece of siding near the kitchen entrance from where the cart had been steered directly into the house. The patio table and several of its chairs had been bulldozed and were pushed out into the side yard, along with the porch umbrella that had sprung back open and now looked like it belonged in an oversized Mai Tai. One of the double doors to the kitchen stood open, and if I wasn't mistaken, the engine to the golf cart was still running. Leroy was nowhere to be seen.

I looked to the heavens, closed my eyes, and sighed. "Any suggestions, O Great Leader?" I directed this at Doug.

When he didn't immediately respond, I cast an eye in his direction. He was either lost in deep cogitation or was working his way through a subdural hematoma—I couldn't be sure of which. His thick brows were furrowed tightly together as he massaged his stubble-covered chin between thumb and forefinger and rocked slightly back and forth on his heels. I looked to Melanie and Brady, but only received a pair of shrugs in return.

"There's a couple of things I'm trying to puzzle through," Doug finally said. He turned to Melanie. "I'm inclined to agree with you that McBurney has an accomplice. It's the only way I can figure he could keep tabs on when the house is empty, and knowing the house is empty is critical to McBurney's final plan. That is, if he actually gives two shits about hurting anyone else, as Dwayne seems to believe."

He paused, looking at me quizzically, but I only nodded my affirmation. I didn't have the luxury of indecision, and my gut instincts had rarely failed me before.

"Rob sure was in hurry to get out here," I suggested. "Maybe he knew what was going on."

"His girlfriend was unconscious after suffering a major head trauma," Brady interjected. "Don't you think you'd be just as eager if the same thing had happened to Mel?"

"But she's *not* his girlfriend," I said. "Anyssa told me they were both college students hired because of their background in drama."

"Hey, co-workers fall in love all the time," countered Brady. "As a matter of fact, I—"

"*Hey!*" snapped Doug, drawing our attention. "Would you two Marjories stop playing spin the bottle and focus, please? Whoever it may or may not be ain't the most important thing here."

"Yeah? So, what is?" I asked.

"I'm guessing those bricks of C-4 you found on McBurney's boat were the first ones you'd seen, right? I mean, when y'all were galivanting all over this house today like the Scooby gang in search of clues, you didn't spot any others, did you?"

"If we had come across anything like that, I'm sure we would have noticed," I said, bristling at the suggestion of incompetence.

Doug nodded and went right back into his deep meditation.

"Oh, for heaven's sake, *what?!?*" I demanded.

"If you didn't see anything earlier, then I'm going to have to assume McBurney's been using this time to get his charges in place. If it were me, I would be planting them in the basement to bring everything down from below, but I guess there's no real way to—"

I motioned him on with the roll of a hand.

"Anyways, I'm also going to assume, based on the size of this place, that McBurney is using several bricks of explosive."

"Okay, that tracks," I said.

"The boathouse blew after all of the lights went out, right?"

"Yes," I confirmed.

"So, he couldn't have really automated the process," he continued. "He would have had to set a timer by hand that would give him enough time to get out before the boathouse blew. But when you've got multiple bombs you want to go off in a short period of time, you can't just be runnin' around setting timers by hand. You'll blow your own fool head off before you get 'em all set."

"Where are you going with this?" Patience was never going to be my strong suit.

Doug scowled. "Cell phones, are you gettin' me? Burner phones, in particular. Terrorists use 'em all the time to trigger detonators. The bomber can go right down the list of cell phone numbers, and all from a safe distance."

"I'm not so sure McBurney is all that invested in his own safety," I said.

"Doesn't matter," said Doug. "He's invested enough to make sure the job gets done, and for that, he has to stick around at least until the last one is triggered. Does anyone see what the problem with that is?"

Melanie began to slowly nod. "With the power out, no one can make a phone call. He may have knocked it out to keep us from calling for help, but until he turns it back on, he can't blow the place up."

Doug touched the tip of his nose and pointed to Melanie. "Exactly."

"Okay, so we're safe as long as the lights are out," said Brady.

I was beginning to get the picture. "I think that just might be a safe bet. So now, the question is, *where* did the lights go out?"

Doug looked at me like I had lost my mind. "In the house, Dwayne. The lights went out in the house," he said slowly, motioning toward the darkened building.

"I know *that*," I grumbled. "What I mean is, was the power cut at the generator or downstairs at the circuit box?"

We all looked back toward the shed that was a miniature version of the manor house. The generator was inside.

"It doesn't really matter, does it?" asked Melanie, taking a few steps toward the shed. "Either way, we should be able to control the situation without going back into the house."

"How do you figure?" I asked.

"If the generator's not running, we just have to stand guard and keep anyone from starting it back up," she said. "And if it is running, we simply turn it off. McBurney can flip the main all he wants, but if the generator isn't running…"

Her words trailed off, and she shrugged.

I laughed, scooping her into my arms and kissing her forehead. "You are *brilliant!*"

"Hang on," interjected Brady, disrupting my euphoria. "Didn't you say McBurney had a gun?"

The smile slipped from my face as I set Melanie back on the ground. He might not *want* to hurt anyone, but if anything constituted backing him into a corner, this was it. "Shit. Yeah—yes, he does."

Doug stepped forward and hiked up his right pant leg. "Well, so do I."

The snub-nosed pistol secured to his ankle looked like a toy, but it was better than nothing. I said a silent prayer that this whole mess wouldn't degenerate into some sort of lopsided gun battle.

We picked our way through the wreckage into which Leroy had rendered the tasteful patio arrangement and paused long enough for Brady to reach inside the golf cart and switch off the ignition. We continued to the shed, where Brady and Doug each opened one of its wide double doors so I could direct the Maglite's beam inside.

The generator chugged along at the rear of the tiny space, and I was torn between relief and panic. I was only a few short steps away from halting its operation, thereby removing McBurney's ability to restore power to the house.

"I can't believe I'm saying this," I said, hurrying forward. "But I think your idea for signing us up for this weekend may actually be working, Doug. Anyssa's game may have gone out the window, but what we've done right here shows some incredible teamwork!"

I located a knob labeled 'Main Switch' and leaned in to reach for it.

"I'm going to need you to stop what you're doing."

I froze, my fingers inches away from the switch, and turned around slowly.

Jeremy's formidable frame blocked our exit, his expression unreadable. Nestled in the crook of his arm but completely unmistakable was a double-barreled shotgun, its business end pointed our way.

CHAPTER TWENTY-SEVEN

We picked our way back to the house like a chain gang minus the chain; following orders is a no-brainer when the man bringing up the rear is holding a gun. It might have been helpful had Doug actually taken his pistol from its holster when he had been satisfying Brady's concerns, but frankly, I was torn, currently leaning toward the belief it was probably better left strapped to his ankle. While I might be willing to believe McBurney didn't want to hurt anyone else, I held no such convictions about Jeremy. His hardened expression made my blood run cold. I didn't care for the odds should he and Doug find themselves squaring off in a duel.

Because I carried a Maglite, Jeremy ordered me to take the lead and light the way. Melanie, Brady and Doug followed, and we all kept our free hands where Jeremy could see them.

A short burst of static came from behind us, and Jeremy said, "You can go ahead and power up, but don't do anything yet. I'm bringing everyone inside." Another squelch of static.

The house remained dark as I worked my way around the left front bumper of the golf cart and stepped through the open door to the kitchen, shining my light straight ahead and down the darkened hallway. I briefly considered going for some of the cutlery scattered along the counter or maybe even the meat tenderizing mallet that had proved so effective earlier, but any move I made would only jeopardize those who were behind me.

While Jeremy appeared to be far calmer and more collected than the live wire that was McBurney, I wasn't ready to challenge his resolve when it came to using his weapon. None of us could outrun buckshot.

"*Hullo-o-o?*" drifted piteously down the hall from the front of the house. I groaned as Leroy stepped into the Maglite's beam at its furthest reaches, shielding his eyes against its bright glare. His hair seemed determined to escape his head, and he must have busted his nose somewhere along the way. Dried blood crusted his upper lip and chin, and his already stained A-shirt had absorbed most of the overflow. "Is that you, Sandy? I've been looking for you everywhere. Why won't any of the lights work?"

"Stay right there, Mr. Poole," said Jeremy from behind me. "Let us come to you." His voice was rock steady, and I found that more unnerving than anything.

Leroy teetered on his tiptoes, as if leaning in helped his comprehension. "Okay," he finally replied, sidling over to the wall beneath the staircase and leaning into it for support. I couldn't imagine how he was able to remain upright. He worked at his face with trembling hands, and when he reached his nose he cried, "*Ow! Ow! Ow!* What the fuck?!? Did somebody *hit* me?"

"Just take it easy, Mr. Poole," said Jeremy. "Everything is going to be just fine. Mr. Morrow? Will you lead us to the foyer?" His voice was smooth like butter. I thought he might have had a fine career ahead of himself as a hostage negotiator if he hadn't already committed himself to a life of crime.

Just as we reached the end of the hall where Leroy struggled to stay on his feet, the enormous chandelier centered high above the foyer suddenly burst to life, causing all of us to recoil and shield our eyes as they adjusted to the sudden onslaught. A thrum of white noise followed, indicating the kitchen appliances had resumed their normal functions. Any hope I had for controlling the situation completely evaporated.

"I need everyone to remain calm and keep your hands where I can see them. Mr. Morrow, please toss the Maglite into the parlor. I don't think you'll be needing it any longer," said Jeremy, eliminating any possibility of me using the flashlight as a bludgeon or projectile. He used the sling on his wounded arm to support the butt of the rifle, his finger resting on the trigger while his other hand kept both barrels trained firmly on us. He carried the weapon so easily, as if it were an extension of his own arm. "If you could all gather at the foot of the stairs, please?"

We followed his directions with the exception of Leroy, whose reliance on the support of the wall had only grown. He stared stupidly in Jeremy's general direction.

"You too, Mr. Poole," he said, urging with his rifle. "C'mon."

"Oh, for heaven's sake, leave him alone," said Melanie. "Can't you see he's barely able to stand? He's no threat to you."

Leroy's head swiveled in Melanie's direction, and he smacked his lips together. "Who're we talkin' about here? *Sa-a-a-y*—has anyone seen my little Sandy? I been lookin' for her ever'where." His consonants were as soft as soup, and the tremors in his hands were constant. I suspected this man's liver was approximately the same size and texture as a walnut.

Jeremy observed Leroy while considering Melanie's request. "Fine," he finally said, casually strolling in Leroy's direction. He kicked Leroy's feet out from under him, and Leroy abruptly dropped to his bottom, completely startled into childlike submission. "But I'm going to need him to take a seat."

"*Hey!*" protested Melanie, taking a tentative step forward before Jeremy urged her to reconsider, shifting the shotgun in her direction. She wisely backed off. She grumbled, "You didn't need to do that. You could have just *asked* the man."

Jeremy's smile was little more than a leer. "Pardon my manners, ma'am. I've just about run through all the patience I've got. Now, I need everyone to carefully place their cellphones on the floor and kick them over to me—slowly, slowly—"

Melanie, Brady and Doug began to comply cautiously, but I could only stare at him. "I can't," I said. "My phone's back in my room at the resort on Kelleys Island. You can search me if you want."

I took a step forward and he took a step back, the shotgun unwavering. He was less than amused. "Just stay where you are and turn your pockets out."

I reached into my soggy pockets and pulled out the linings as Melanie and Brady kicked their phones toward Jeremy. Out of the corner of my eye, I spied Doug taking his time easing his ancient flip phone to the tile. My breath caught, and I knew immediately what he was going to attempt. I couldn't help but imagine every single way this was likely to go left of center. Douglas Boggs was never going to be known for his subtlety and grace.

"Now, lift your shirt and turn around slowly," said Jeremy, still focused on me. "Let me see your waistband."

I did as he asked, but even more slowly. I made as much a spectacle of myself as I could to keep Jeremy's eyes on me and away from Doug. "See?" I said. "I've got nothing."

Doug's phone went skittering toward Jeremy's feet, and when he saw it, he laughed out loud. "What in the hell is this thing? A toy? I haven't seen one of these in years—"

In a cringeworthy slow-motion moment, Doug grabbed for his pistol, intending to rise fluidly from his crouch and take a shot at Jeremy, but the pistol got hung up somewhere between its holster and his pants leg—possibly both—and abruptly discharged.

Jeremy's eyes widened while Doug screamed out in pain.

"I'm hit! I'm hit!" he wailed, falling to the ground, and cradling his foot. The gun slipped from his grasp, sliding a few feet towards Jeremy.

Jeremy's calm facade shattered like glass as perspiration sprang out across his forehead. *"Everyone get back! Get back!"* he screamed, lifting the shotgun's sight to his eye. He eased forward and stretched out a foot to pull the gun back towards himself, stooping to pick it up and pocket it when he felt he had put enough distance between himself and the rest of us.

Behind him, the door leading to the basement suddenly flew open, and R.J. McBurney burst through, his hair every bit as wild as Leroy's. He still carried the backpack I had seen him take from the boat, but he carried it snug to his chest, clenched tightly in both white-knuckled hands. He no longer had a shotgun strapped over his shoulder, and I guessed it might be the one Jeremy was currently wielding.

"What in the hell was *that?*" he asked loudly. "I thought I heard gunfire!"

Doug continued to roll about on the ground, cupping his right foot into both hands. I could see a trickle of blood seeping through his fingers, so I was pretty sure this wasn't just for show. I hate to say I told you so, but from the moment I first saw that little gun, I *knew* someone was going to get shot before the weekend was over.

"It's just the Boggs guy," said Jeremy, but his voice had lost all trace of its soothing timbre. It was now tinged with hysteria, and I found that particularly worrisome for someone still brandishing a weapon aimed in our direction. "Everything's under control."

"I don't like this. These people shouldn't even *be* here!"

"I know, I know," said Jeremy, anxiously dabbing at the perspiration on his forehead with the back of his hand before returning it to steady the shotgun. "I'll get them out of the way."

"How much longer do you think we have?" he mumbled to Jeremy as he passed between us, heading for the foot of the stairs and protecting his backpack with his body.

"You'll need to give it a few minutes for all of the equipment to initialize," said Jeremy. "We may need to restart the wi-fi router. Sometimes it tries to come online before the satellite link is ready."

"Son of a *bitch!*" McBurney spat as he sprinted up the stairs.

"Where are you going?" asked Jeremy with more than a trace of panic in his voice.

"Not very far, my boy," he said, stopping at the landing where the stairs branched east and west. He turned to face us all. "Only far enough to be out of reach. I am not going to let one more thing get in my way tonight. It's the twentieth anniversary of my sweet Alethea's death. Oh, sweet Jesus in Heaven above, help me to see this thing through." He dropped to his knees and began rummaging through his backpack.

A tumbler suddenly fell into place inside my mind.

My boy.

"You're the McBurney boy," I said, staring at Jeremy. "You're the little kid who—"

"Lost his mama," he said, nodding jerkily. "And before too long, they carted my Pops off, too. Yep, that's me, all right. Pushed into the foster care system at an age where nobody wants you. And if they do, it's only for the government paycheck, not because they have any real interest in you. But most of them were scared of me just based on my size alone, so, you know—" He shrugged, and his voice trailed away.

"You don't really want to do this," I said, and my mouth was off and running, simply trying to buy us a little time. "I mean, what do you expect will come out of this? If you and your father don't get yourselves killed setting off these bombs, you're gonna get hauled into custody just as soon as the police arrive. You'll spend years behind bars and for what? To get revenge against Anyssa Williams? She was barely any older than you when your mother drowned."

"This isn't about revenge!" roared McBurney from where he now stood at the top of the landing. His backpack lay open at his feet, and he held a smartphone in his hand. I could see its screen flickering as it powered up. "It has *never* been about revenge! It's about this *place!* It's just—it's just—can't you feel th-th-the—*wrongness* of it all? It's like this island doesn't even *belong* here! When Leland Williams settled on this island after stealing his family's gold and murdering his own brother, he brought a curse here with him! People have been paying the price for Leland's selfishness for generations, but it will end here tonight, one way or the other, I promise you!"

McBurney was far too consumed with his own obsession to reach, so I directed my attention back to Jeremy. "It's not too late to stop this," I said. "You can get your father the help he needs. You haven't done any *real* damage—well, okay, I don't know how much responsibility for blowing up the boathouse belongs to you, but Anyssa seems like a reasonable woman. We can talk this through."

Jeremy shook his head vigorously. "No, we've come too far for that. I can't send Pops back to one of those facilities. They didn't want to help him at all. They just wanted to keep him sedated. Half the time, he didn't even know who I was, and you know what? I've really come to believe that he's right. Have you *heard* about all of the tragedies that have happened around here? Far too many for it to be coincidental. It *has* to be this place."

"Surely you've got somebody out there who cares about you, someone who doesn't want to see you waste a bunch of years behind bars," I ventured, growing desperate. My hopes of appealing to Jeremy's senses were quickly fading. He seemed already resigned to the outcome his father had planned, and if he was buying into the idea of this ridiculous curse, I wasn't sure how else I might reach him.

"No," he said, his voice expressionless. "I've never had anyone. Not after Mom died and Pops went away. I'm not the kind of guy people like to be around."

I glanced at Melanie and Brady, hoping they might have another avenue to explore, but their faces were unreadable.

"I don't think we'll have to restart anything," called McBurney from the top of the stairs. "The phone seems to be connected to wi-fi."

"Good," said Jeremy, keeping the shotgun trained on us.

Doug had worked his way across the hall toward the parlor where he remained seated on the ground, resting his back against the wall beside its door. He had stopped groaning, but he continued to clutch his wounded foot with both hands as pain clearly registered across his face. Leroy remained sprawled against the wall across from him, his head lolling to the side. It sounded like he had begun to snore.

"All right," said McBurney. "It's time for you to get these folks out of here. Take them down to the dock—I mean, where the dock used to be. I've got the phone numbers programmed into my speed dial. Once I start, I'm going in rapid sequence. I'll start with the charges in the tunnel, follow with the ones in the basement and finish with the one in the shed by the generator."

"But what about you, Pops? Aren't you coming with us?" asked Jeremy, uncertainty creeping into his voice.

"Don't you worry about me, son. I'll be right behind you. Now, get these people out of here."

"But Pops—"

"*Do as I say!*" he barked, and Jeremy's mouth snapped shut. McBurney could only hold his son's gaze for so long before looking away, and in an instant, I think we all understood he never expected to make it out of this alive.

"You two," said Jeremy, indicating Melanie and Brady with the muzzle of his shotgun. "Help Mr. Boggs to his feet, please, but slowly. I honestly don't want to hurt anyone else but don't test me with any more of your amateur heroics." He looked back toward his father, his lower jaw trembling.

Melanie and Brady each took a side and helped Doug to his feet—well, foot. He kept the wounded one suspended off the ground, droplets of startlingly crimson blood falling upon the white ceramic tile. They gently guided him around Jeremy and toward the front door.

"Wait right there by the door," directed Jeremy as he shifted his attention to Leroy who was still completely oblivious and sawing logs. He gently kicked the bottom of Leroy's foot. "Mr. Poole? *Mr. Poole.* I'm going to need you to cooperate with me here."

Leroy's eyes fluttered as his head rolled from one side to the other, and he smacked his lips together thickly. *"Mmmph?"*

"Mr. Poole!" repeated Jeremy loudly. He nudged his bare foot more insistently. "I need you to get up now. Wakey, wakey, you stupid son of a bitch!"

With Jeremy's last kick, Leroy's eyes snapped open. "I'm here," he slurred.

"Come on, you sorry piece of shit," said Jeremy, nudging Leroy with the muzzle of the shotgun. "Come on. On your feet, buddy."

Leroy shifted blearily from one ass cheek to the other, and as he tried to push himself up from his seated position, a perversely lengthy burst of flatulence squeaked out. "Pardon me," he hiccupped. "Li'l gassy there—"

And just like that, another tumbler suddenly fell into place.

Gas.

"Oh, shit," I muttered, the ramifications suddenly crystal clear in my mind. I turned to McBurney who was watching our progress from above. "Mr. McBurney—R.J. You need to stop this right now. You're going to kill us all."

His expression contorted with confusion. "What in the hell are you talking about, boy? Haven't I been telling you all along that I've got no interest in hurting anyone else? Do you think I'm lying to you?"

"Listen to me," I said, and the urgency of my tone caught Melanie and Brady's attention. They stopped to listen, keeping Doug upright between them. Leroy had finally found his feet and leaned against the wall, awaiting further instruction. Jeremy kept the gun trained on Leroy, but his focus was on me and his father. "It might not be your intention to hurt anybody, but that is exactly what's going to happen once you start detonating those charges."

"That's a bunch of shit!" countered McBurney. "Why would I bother with having Jeremy take you all down to the dock?"

I shook my head. "You don't understand. How much do you know about the power generator?"

McBurney's eyes were wild with impatience, his cell phone at the ready, clasped in his hands. "It provides the island's power. What's the big deal? We've been over that."

"But where does it get *its* fuel?" I asked, and while McBurney looked at me like I was insane, I could almost see the lightbulb over Jeremy's head as realization sank in.

"Oh, Pops," he said woefully. "We need to rethink this. That generator runs on natural gas."

I shook my head. "It's not just natural gas, it's a natural gas *well* that's native to this island. It's a self-perpetuating system. Any one of those charges could cause the well to detonate, blowing this entire island right out of the water and taking every one of us with it."

The only sound came from the steady tick of the grandfather clock in the hallway. I watched McBurney's expression shift from confusion to realization before finally landing on outrage. The anguished cry he suddenly emitted sent a shudder all the way down my spine. He lifted his fists into the air, barking obscenities like machine gun fire, but he continued to hold the cell phone clutched in his right palm. For a brief moment, I thought he was going to throw it to the ground, but he took a deep, steadying breath, and his rage morphed into maniacal laughter. It raised the hairs on the back of my neck.

"Well, then," he finally said, turning around to face us. "I guess that's it, isn't it?"

I breathed a sigh of relief and sent a quick smile to Melanie, Brady and Doug. I thought I had finally gotten through to McBurney, but when I saw their expressions shift to terror, I realized I must have misread him. I looked back to find McBurney tapping away on his cell phone's screen. Judging from the look on his face, I knew it was too much to hope he was calling the authorities.

"What are you doing, Pops?" asked Jeremy nervously. "You heard what Mr. Morrow said. We can't do this as planned. We—"

"*Shhh,*" he instructed, his voice soothing in the most frightening way imaginable. "I can't go back now. I've promised your mother I would see this through." He looked towards the heavens. "Alethea, my sweet darling—this isn't exactly how I planned it, but we'll all be reunited soon. You, me, and our sweet, baby boy."

He turned his attention to the cell phone in his hand as all hell broke loose in the foyer. We all came to the same resolution simultaneously, our voices colliding as we frantically begged Jeremy to do the unthinkable and shoot his own father. It was all too much for Jeremy to process, and I could see our pleas were bouncing away unheard.

What transpired next happened so quickly I'm not sure I can adequately describe it. The chandelier began to flicker rapidly, plunging us into and out of darkness. I glanced up at McBurney just in time to catch the suggestion of a hulking, hooded figure standing directly behind him. As I struggled to process what I was seeing, the chandelier suddenly flared brighter than ever, and its many tiny bulbs began to burst, one by one, showering glass down onto the ceramic tile below. McBurney cried out and I heard a rapid series of thuds as he toppled down the stairwell. Something struck my foot, and when I looked down, I saw the face of McBurney's cell phone staring back at me. The first call had been placed and 'Calling' flashed at the top of the screen. I hurriedly scooped the phone into my hand, bracing for an explosion while jabbing at the disconnect button repeatedly, realizing our lives depended on it.

The message flashing on the screen abruptly changed from 'Calling' to 'No Signal,' and I dropped to my knees in a fit of hysterical giggles. I looked over to where McBurney lay at the foot of the stairs, his arm twisted behind him at an unnatural angle. I was relieved to see him blink back tears at the realization that his plan had failed. I really had no desire to see the body count for this particular legend grow, and the McBurneys had been through enough. Jeremy had already tossed the shotgun aside and sat beside his father on the floor, comforting him in hushed tones.

Brady opened the front doors to allow a little moonlight in, and we could hear the sounds of helicopters approaching from across the lake. I looked back toward the landing in wonder, trying to find any possible logical explanation for what I had seen, but there was nothing more to see. Everything was as it had always been, save for the faint scent of ozone in the air.

I was surprisingly calm for someone who had little choice but to believe his life and the lives of his friends had just been saved by the ghost of Julian Williams.

Who was I to question such things?

EPILOGUE

The next few hours were a blur. Helicopters landed, rescue boats arrived, and the questions were never-ending. We huddled together under blankets on the sandy beach as the island was virtually stormed by various branches of law enforcement. We watched as R.J. McBurney and his son were led away, Jeremy in cuffs, but R.J.'s injuries sparing him that indignity. It was difficult to remain angry with either of them. As I watched the dawn break across Melanie's beautiful face, my heart ached for them. I could barely remember a time before Melanie was in my life, and the thought of losing her was unfathomable.

A little further down the beach, Leroy Poole sawed logs, belly-up with his exposed limbs splayed out as if he had drifted off while making snow angels. He was in for one hell of a sunburn.

Doug had merely grazed his foot when he had accidentally discharged his firearm. Medics cleaned and dressed the wound, and now Doug was hobbling along, trailing after the Cleveland Police Bomb Squad, riddling them with questions and making a general nuisance of himself while they dismantled the undetonated charges scattered throughout the tunnel and inside the basement. They located the last one underneath the generator that still purred reliably along, providing power to the main house.

Anyssa Williams arrived shortly after dawn, and we learned that everyone on the transport boat had arrived safely on the mainland. Kit had awakened along the way, and she was being held for overnight observation at Firelands Hospital in Sandusky. We also learned we were nowhere near solving the scripted mystery. Apparently, the tunnel leading to the island's secondary dock wasn't the only secret passage on premises. The house itself contained a network of narrow corridors between the walls, accessible through secret panels in the fireplaces, and that's where the phantom noises we had heard were emanating from. The noise was meant to lure us to investigate, but we found other reasonable explanations and had moved on.

These secret panels could only be opened by special keys, the first of which had been in Maria's pocket when it had torn. While Leroy had recovered the planted gold, we never did find the key. Another was hidden in plain sight in the library, and while we had found that one, we had only guessed one of its possible uses as a drawer pull. Anyssa was still puzzling over how McBurney's threatening notes had ended up back in the desk drawer; she specifically remembered putting them into her messenger bag, and I couldn't help but wonder if we might have gotten some otherworldly assistance at that point, but I was keeping that to myself. I had already been subjected to more worry and speculation about my mental health than I cared for. In any event, the misdirection had prevented us from discovering the passageways, which would have led us into the master bedroom, where the heavy wooden base of the four-poster bed was home to a veritable fortune of gold coins—had they been real.

Ultimately, the mystery weekend was deemed a total failure, and Anyssa was currently leaning toward the idea of converting the place into a bed and breakfast. As for Doug's intended goal, which was for us to learn how to work better as a team, I think we fared significantly better. Time will tell once we get back to the office.

Brady accompanied Anyssa as she wandered about the property in a daze, taking in the destruction of the boathouse while Brady brought her up to speed on the evening's events. You would've had to have been blind to miss the sparks flying between the two as Brady patiently answered her questions, giving her his undivided attention. She was quite a step up from Dusty; I was cautiously optimistic Brady might not screw this one up.

Melanie leaned against me as I kept my arm wrapped around her protectively. The storm from the previous evening had given way to a cloudless sky of brilliant blue, and we stared out in comfortable silence over the open water as officers worked around us, efficiently executing the duties they had been trained to perform. Once we had completed our exhaustive questioning, it was as though we were invisible.

"What are you thinking about?" she asked, looking up at me with hazel eyes flecked with gold.

I smiled and kissed her forehead. "Would you think I was crazy if I told you I thought I saw a ghost?"

She smiled and snuggled more tightly against me. "*Another* ghost?"

"I'm serious," I said.

"I thought Jeremy was your ghost."

"Not then," I said. "Back in the house. You know—when the lights went crazy."

For a moment, I didn't think she was going to answer. Then she sighed. "No, I wouldn't think you were crazy."

I closed my eyes and for just a split second, I was back in West Virginia, sedated and riding in the back of an ambulance. I could see my sister's face hovering in front of me, concern for my well-being apparent in her expression. I remembered everything Gina told me, and the promise I made to keep it all to myself, but I couldn't shake the uncertainty I'd carried once I had awakened in a hospital bed with Melanie waiting anxiously by my side. Had any of it been real?

My throat was thick, and I swallowed hard. "What would you do if I—um—" I looked at my feet.

"If you what?" she asked, giving me her undivided attention. She brushed aside an errant strand of golden hair from her forehead, and I had never seen anyone so lovely.

I stumbled through a laugh and cleared my throat. "You know—if I, like, lost my shit or something?" I stuck my tongue out, crossed my eyes and spun a forefinger in a circle at my temple.

She laughed and settled back against my chest. "Well, that's an easy one. I'd be outta there so fast you wouldn't even have time to kiss my ass goodbye."

I pulled away, looking at her with mock outrage. She smiled sweetly and placed a hand against my cheek.

"You big dummy," she said. "I'd just lose my shit right alongside you. We'd get ourselves a room for two in the loony bin."

"Really?"

She nodded. "And besides. I saw it, too."

I searched her face to see if she was pulling my leg, but there was no sign of mischievous deception.

"*Really?*"

She shrugged. "Whatever it was, I think you saw it that first night, too. It couldn't have been Jeremy. He was back on the mainland waiting to bring Anyssa and the Pooles over in the morning."

Well, how about that? Maybe I wasn't losing my shit after all.

"So, are you saying you believe in—" I began.

She tutted, bringing up a forefinger and cutting me off. "I'm not saying anything of the kind. Especially around—" Her voice trailed off as her eyes shifted to Brady, who was positively fawning over Anyssa amidst the rubble of the boathouse. "It would just make his day, and we don't need that sort of thing showing up in print, now, do we? I'm just saying we saw *something* and leaving it right there."

I smiled, and we fell back into comfortable silence for a few moments more.

"I'm really sorry about earlier," I finally said.

"About what?"

"You know. Your book—or whatever it is you're working on. I shouldn't have invaded your privacy, and I was an idiot to jump to conclusions."

She nodded slowly. "Yes, yes you were. But I believe you've learned your lesson. We're past that, and you should let it go. I have. I trust you."

I felt a tightness in my chest and recognized the guilt for what it was. I didn't deserve this woman. Here I sat, keeping a secret from her I had promised to my sister, and it was tearing me apart. I felt an overwhelming urge to unburden myself, and before I knew it, words were spilling from my lips.

"There's something I've been meaning to tell you," I said, my pulse racing. She looked at me expectantly, but I was having trouble meeting her eyes.

"Yeah?"

"Well—you know, I've been thinking a lot about everything that—um, you know—"

She waited patiently, a hint of a smile playing at the corners of her mouth.

My own mouth had turned to sand, and I was stammering like a fool. "—um, since you brought me back from West Virginia, I haven't really talked about—um—" I sighed and stared into my lap.

She took my hands into hers. "Take your time. I'm not going anywhere."

I was humbled by the simplicity and sincerity of her statement. She had barely left my side since retrieving me from that hospital in Morgantown and had refused to press for details I wasn't ready to divulge. I knew I could trust her with anything.

"I think you and Jasmine should move in with me," I said, startled by what fell out of my mouth.

She looked at me uncertainly. "You realize I still have, like, nine months on my lease, right?"

"So what? We'll see if we can find someone else to buy out the lease, but even if we can't, you were already prepared to pay rent anyway. You're practically living at my house already."

She pursed her lips, considering my offer. "I can't do anything without discussing it with Jasmine," she said. "I mean, she's just now getting used to her new school. It would mean another big change, and I—"

"Not necessarily," I interrupted. "If she wants to stay in the school she's in, she can. I don't exactly have set hours. I can provide transportation."

"But what if she—" Melanie's voice trailed off.

"What?"

"What if she doesn't want us to move in with you? After all the change I've put her through this past year, I don't know if I—"

I placed a fingertip against her lips. "*Shhh.*"

She looked up at me expectantly.

"If she doesn't want to, then we won't. I'm as invested in her happiness as you are, and I'm not going to pressure anyone to make a decision before she's ready."

She smiled, leaning back into me, and nothing felt more natural. I hadn't said what I set out to say, but in time, I would. This was the woman I wanted to share everything with, and it didn't need to happen all at once.

We were in it for the long haul.

THE END

COMING SOON

ABDUCTION
Dwayne Morrow Mystery #6

PROLOGUE

"Stop the car! Stop the car!"

My eyes flickered sideways toward the passenger seat where I found Melanie doubled over in the eerie luminescence of my Hyundai's dashboard lights. She looked awful.

I cut to my right with little regard for the traffic around me. I was greeted by a chorus of angry horns as I awkwardly bumped my front passenger tire up onto the curb and slammed on my brakes. Rain fell in sheets across the pavement, illuminated by headlights as cars swept by on this dark, dismal evening I desperately wished belonged to anybody else.

"I'm going to be sick," she mumbled, covering her mouth with one hand while fighting the seatbelt with the other.

I unlatched my own and threw my door open into oncoming traffic. More angry honking, and as I stepped down to the glistening pavement, I alternated between flipping a pair of angry birds and apologetic, palms-forward hand waving. I scurried around the back of the car to where Melanie knelt by the curb, retching herself into dry heaves. I helped to steady her against the car as she gulped for air between expulsions.

I've never felt so helpless in all my life.

Cars continued to whiz by in both directions along the four-lane city street, and I hated everyone inside of them. They were bound for destinations made by choice, and absolutely no one would choose to go where Melanie and I were heading.

Woefully inept at saying the right things at times like these, I stuck with the simple and inane, soothingly repeating things like, "I'm right here, sweetheart," and "Just breathe…breathe…"

Eventually, her hiccupping breath slowed and settled into a pattern approximating normal. I held her steady with my right hand as I rubbed her back with the palm of my left. "Do you think you can stand?" I asked.

She nodded, wiping the corners of her mouth with the back of her hand. I helped her to her feet, and once she was upright, she leaned against the SUV, a fresh wave of anguish sweeping over her. "Oh, God—I don't think I can *do* this," she cried.

"*Shhh, shhh,*" I soothed, folding her into my arms and tucking her head beneath my chin. I could feel rather than hear the sobs that caused her body to quake against mine. I was afraid to say anything more as we clung to each other in the pouring rain.

For everything I had been through, I'd never been called to identify the body of a loved one, much less someone so young.

ABDUCTION
Dwayne Morrow Mystery #6

COMING SOON

acknowledgements

Wow, gang!

I can't believe we've made it to *Dwayne Morrow Mystery* #5! And I feel like we're only just getting started…

Before I say anything more, I should warn you these acknowledgements contain the mildest of spoilers, so if you haven't read the book yet, you might want to go back and do so first.

I have to admit, our last outing, *Diversion*, was a lot more intense than anything I had put to paper before. I was poking and prodding at some very dark personal history, and while I couldn't be happier with the outcome, it took a little bit of a toll. I really needed this next one to be lighter; it's kind of ironic considering how dark the cover photo, featuring a full moon nightscape, is. But as soon as I saw the photo, I had the first piece of inspiration for my story. I could picture that island just as clearly as if I were standing right there…even if I had to make the entire thing up. You certainly won't find Marble Toe Island on any Great Lakes map.

The next inspiration came late one Saturday night while watching an old movie on TV.

Growing up in the 80s, I was always a fan of popular horror movies. I'm not just referring to the classics that have stood the test of time, like John Carpenter's *Halloween*, Brian De Palma's *Carrie*, or William Friedkin's *The Exorcist*, but also all of the slasher films they helped to inspire. This book owes a huge debt of gratitude to a 1986 curiosity written by Danilo Bach and directed by Fred Walton. Still enjoyable to this day, it's called *April Fool's Day*, and if you're a fan, you might recognize a couple of character names I borrowed with a loving wink.

I set out to write this story with just one "simple" rule I was determined to follow: Nobody dies in this one. There may be a character or two who bit the dust before the story ever began, but that's all backstory…

Do you know how hard it is to write in a genre casually referred to as 'Murder Mystery' when there are no murders?

Challenge *accepted!*

I sincerely hope you enjoyed reading it as much as I enjoyed writing it. I just love Dwayne and his crew of misfits.

I am delighted Lynne Hobstetter, Teri Lott and Traci Steele agreed to once again suffer through the roughest draft of this story. Their feedback and comments are invaluable, and this book would have suffered greatly without their talents. Thank you, thank you, *thank you!* And as always, any mistakes, factual or otherwise, are completely my own.

Special thanks to Diane Kinser for offering her historical expertise with respect to the Underground Railroad and how it figures into the Williamses' backstory. Every attempt was made to respectfully reflect that tumultuous period of American history, and if I got it wrong, that's on me, not Ms. Kinser. Thank you, Diane! You always inspire me.

What started out as a wink turned into a full-on nod. Thank you, Ryan and Joy McBurney. Nothing but love for you both.

To the people of Kelleys Island…I am apologizing right up front for all the things I probably got wrong about your beautiful island. I have not yet visited, although I plan to this summer. I relied on Google Maps, internet images, and any number of articles I found online to help construct the portions of the book that occurred there. In my head, it was gorgeous, even on a dark and stormy night. I promise to spend a great deal of tourist dollars by way of apology, and I beg your forgiveness…

Finally, and most importantly, thank *you* for continuing on this journey with me, Dwayne and all the rest. I am so grateful to everyone who has given these books a chance. There's so much more to come!

Until next time,
Darin Miller
Grove City, Ohio – March 2023

ALSO AVAILABLE

REUNION
Dwayne Morrow Mystery #1

CIRCUMVENTION
Dwayne Morrow Mystery #2

RETRIBUTION
Dwayne Morrow Mystery #3

DIVERSION
Dwayne Morrow Mystery #4

about the author

Darin Miller grew up in Rosemount, a suburb of Portsmouth, Ohio. He currently resides in Grove City, Ohio. While he has worked in Information Technology for three decades, he has *not* solved a single, solitary crime to date. He is the author of the Ohio-based *Dwayne Morrow Mystery* series. With equal parts action, humor, suspense and mystery, the series features characters you're sure to love—and in some cases, loathe.

Stay current with updates, free downloadable short stories and other special promotions at www.darin-miller.com.

Made in the USA
Middletown, DE
30 January 2024

48347403R00205